NAPOLEON'S LOVES

DÉSIRÉE—Ardent and uncomplicated, she was Napoleon's first real love.

JOSEPHINE—Sophisticated and of noble birth, with a pride to match her master's, she charmed and schemed her way to Empress.

GEORGINA—Precocious, adventurous, beautiful —and Napoleon's mistress.

MARIE WALEWSKA—She sold her body to the foreign conqueror in exchange for Poland's freedom.

MARIE-LUISA—The pretty, nubile daughter of the Austrian Emperor, she became Napoleon's second Empress—and gave him the son and heir he craved.

NAPOLEON AND LOVE
was originally published by Quartet Books Limited.

Napoleon

and

Love

Philip Mackie

A POCKET BOOK EDITION published by
Simon & Schuster of Canada, Ltd. · Markham, Ontario, Canada
Registered User of the Trademark

NAPOLEON AND LOVE

Quartet Books edition published 1974

POCKET BOOK edition published March, 1976
2nd printing .... January, 1976

This POCKET BOOK edition is printed from brand-new
plates made from completely reset, clear, easy-to-read type.
POCKET BOOK editions are published by POCKET BOOKS,
a division of Simon & Schuster of Canada, Ltd.,
330 Steelcase Road, Markham, Ontario L3R 2M1.
Trademarks registered in Canada and other countries.

Standard Book Number: 671-80306-9.
Printed in Canada.

CONTENTS

Part Three:

THE LAST LOVE

I don't believe in the sort of love that exists in novels. It is nothing like human nature. In novels, love lasts for years; it is unchanged by absence; is so strong that if one loves one no longer wants to sleep with other women. None of this is true to life. Novels give rise to false ideas.

NAPOLEON,
St. Helena, 13 October 1817

PART ONE

BONAPARTE
IN LOVE

1. EUGENIE

A quarter of a century later, at St Helena, fat, impotent, old before his time, dying by degrees of a cancerous stomach ulcer, he talked to General Bertrand about Désirée, and Bertrand wrote it down that night in his secret journal, covering the big exercise-book pages with his cramped and microscopic shorthand. Désirée Clary had been the first girl the Emperor was fond of. He was going to marry her when he was at Marseille, when she was already his sister-in-law. She was very young then. She came to his room in Joseph's house one day and hid under his bed. He had her maidenhead. It was because he had had her maidenhead that afterwards, when she was married to Bernadotte, he made Bernadotte a marshal, a prince, and finally a king.

None of this was news to Bertrand. During his years with Napoleon he had heard it a dozen times, as he had heard the story of every one of Napoleon's victories, on the battlefield and in the bedchamber. But he wrote it all down, uncritically, without comment, because the Emperor was his god, and the god's words were to be recorded and preserved, not for others to read but simply because they were the words of a god.

A few days later, the Emperor spoke of Désirée again —he was reading Bernadotte's memoirs, which brought her back to his mind—and Bertrand wrote the words down again, though most of them were the same as before. True, he saved himself some late-night labour by abbreviating each word to the fewest possible letters. Th. E. sd. th. at Mar. D. ws. th. 1st g. h. ws. fnd. of. Désirée was extremely surprised and upset when she learnt of his marriage to Josephine. H. hd. bn. th. 1st m. to hve. her.

Whatever Napoleon said and Bertrand wrote, there, on

a pestiferous rock in the South Atlantic, in 1821, so long after the event, it didn't matter much to Désirée. In 1821 she was Queen of Sweden and Norway, on a private visit to Paris, seeing her old friends who lived there still, having her hair done as only the French coiffeurs could do it, being measured for new dresses by the great couturiers of the rue de Richelieu.

In any case, had it been an event of any great importance, the loss of her maidenhead on a warm April morning in 1795? Such a hurried, scrambled, confused affair, did it even deserve to count as an event?

They were in his room, and he had locked the door, but her sister Julie was somewhere about the house, and so was his brother Joseph, and so were the servants, and someone might come looking for them at any moment, knocking at the door and expecting an answer. They were on his bed, but it was hard and narrow, made for a single soldier, not for a pair of lovers. They were in each other's arms, but they had not dared to undress any more than was absolutely necessary, and the buttons and the braid of his uniform were pressing into her soft flesh and hurting her. They were feverishly excited, longing for each other, mad for each other, but she was virginally ignorant and he was inexperienced and inexpert.

Something was achieved by the act, but what she felt was not at all what she had supposed she would feel. She had imagined an ecstasy: what happened was hardly even a pleasure.

It didn't much matter. What did matter, what was important, was that she and Napoleon loved each other, and would love each other always, and would be married just as soon as Napoleon made a formal request for her hand, and her mother and her brother gave their consent and their blessing. And then the war would come to an end very quickly, before Napoleon had to do any more fighting, and he would leave the army and join the Clary family business, and because he was so clever he would be very successful as a businessman and would become

3

very rich. And they would live happily ever after and have lots of beautiful children.

She sighed with pure happiness, at the thought of the greater happiness that was to come. Despite the buttons and the braid, she hugged her husband-to-be.

'Napoleon . . .'

He sighed too, and murmured her name as she had murmured his.

'Eugénie . . .'

It was his name for her, his secret and special name, one of her baptismal names but no one else ever called her by it. It symbolized the fact that she was his alone: Désirée to everyone else, but Eugénie was his possession.

In the Clary drawing-room, Napoleon was stiff and ill-at-ease, conscious that the Clarys were rich and he was not, conscious that even in revolutionary times it was remarkable to rise to the rank of brigadier-general by the age of twenty-five, but above all conscious that his uniform was patched and shabby and he couldn't afford to buy a new one.

'Madame Clary . . .' A stiff bow to Eugénie's mother.

'Monsieur Clary . . .' A stiff bow to Eugénie's brother, twice her age and already made pompous by his wealth.

At least, thank heavens, the father was dead. The old man had made it clear that Napoleon was welcome as a friend but not as a suitor. Eugénie had heard from her sister that their mother had heard their father say, 'One Bonaparte in the family is enough.'

Napoleon coughed behind his hand and began the speech he had rehearsed in front of his mirror.

'Madame—Monsieur—I believe that my brother Joseph has already spoken to you on my behalf, and that I have your permission to approach you more directly in this matter. I therefore have the honour, formally, to ask for your consent . . .'

It was more difficult to say the words than he had thought it would be.

4

'. . . consent for me to marry your daughter, Madame . . . your sister, Monsieur . . . Eugénie—'

He had not meant to say 'Eugénie'. The name had come out of his mouth of its own accord. Madame Clary was puzzled.

'Eugénie?'

'I beg your pardon—Désirée. I myself call her Eugénie. Sometimes. It is one of her names. As, of course, you know.'

Madame Clary was looking at him strangely. His manner must seem awkward and his words must seem stupid. He plunged onwards.

'Since you have already given Désirée's eldest sister to my own elder brother, I trust that I may hope for an equally favourable answer . . .'

Madame Clary's expression was polite but not favourable.

'Désirée is very young.'

'Seventeen.'

'Seventeen is very young.'

He brushed aside the poor excuse—'If I may say so, Madame, my own mother was married at the age of fifteen.'

'In Corsica.'

'Yes.'

'We are not Corsicans.'

'No.'

'Here in France . . .' Her vague gesture implied a world of difference.

'Corsica is part of France.'

'But Corsicans are hardly . . .'

She didn't finish the sentence. Hardly what? Hardly French? Or hardly civilized? He mastered the impulse to ask her. He must try his best to be patient with his future mother-in-law.

'Madame, many French girls marry at seventeen.'

'Désirée is a very young seventeen.'

'Madame Clary, your daughter is certainly old enough to . . .'

He thought better of it. It would not be a good idea to tell her that particular piece of information.

'. . . is certainly old enough to marry. Whether she is Corsican French or Provençal French. And I must suppose that you have nothing against Corsicans, as such. Since you permitted your elder daughter to marry a Corsican.'

He had broken down her feeble defences. It only remained for her to admit defeat. But pompous Nicolas stepped into the breach.

'With your brother Joseph, it was different.'

'Oh? How different?'

'Joseph is not in the army.'

'Is that in his favour, or in mine?'

'We must consider the question of property. And prospects.'

So that was it. Mother and brother had worked out their tactics beforehand. Mother would be prudently protective and say that the girl was too young. Brother would be businesslike and say that the suitor was too poor.

'We could hardly give our permission for Désirée to marry anyone who does not possess property, or at least have very good prospects of coming into property.'

Napoleon was very stiff and contained and correct: 'As you are aware, my family has estates in Corsica.'

'Corsica is occupied by the English.'

'For the moment.'

'And in any case, Joseph is the eldest son.'

'Yes.'

'Who will inherit the estates.'

'Yes.' It was not worth mentioning that the estates were not worth inheriting.

Nicolas pressed on, in his heavy lumbering way. 'You yourself have no prospects for yourself, as we understand these things.'

'I am a brigadier-general.'

'Forgive me. On the unemployed list.'

'For the moment.'

'Forgive me. Unpaid.'

6

'For the moment.'

'Forgive me, but . . .'

What was the pompous fool going to say next? Napoleon decided to say it for him.

'You mean, a brigadier-general at the age of twenty-five is dead or dismissed by the age of twenty-six?'

Nicolas flushed. That was exactly what he meant. He would have been polite enough to phrase it more politely.

'In the present unsettled state of affairs . . .'

He was on the defensive now. Napoleon mounted a counter-attack.

'The present unsettled state of affairs is exactly the right one for me. I am going to Paris very soon, to report to the Ministry of War. They are bound to re-employ me: I am the only officer in the French Army who understands the correct use of artillery in modern warfare. The rest are still living in the days of Condé and Turenne. But as I proved last year at the siege of Toulon—'

He stopped. There was no point in going on. What did a woman and a civilian understand about the great generals of the seventeenth century, or about what happened at the siege of Toulon? He had to find a simpler way of explaining the important facts of life.

'Whatever the state of affairs here or in Paris, France is still at war. War means rapid promotion. I am not the type that gets killed. I am much too good a soldier to be dismissed. I shall rise in my profession. A major-general —paid—is very well-paid.'

Madame Clary and Nicolas looked at each other and silently agreed, she to speak first.

'General Bonaparte—Désirée is only just seventeen.'

'So I must wait?' He rapped it out.

'Napoleon, we like you. We have a high regard for you. We have nothing against your marrying Désirée—in time —that is, if—'

'If I rise?' Again, rapping the words out, like the beat of a drum.

'If you rise.'

'How high? Major-general? Full general? What?'

Nicolas came to his mother's aid.

'My dear Napoleon, we are simply being practical. As you would be for your own family. One wants to see the members of one's family comfortably settled. Reasonably well-off. With a position in life. I'm sure you agree with me.'

Napoleon particularly disliked Nicolas when Nicolas was sure that Napoleon agreed with him. But he needed his consent to the marriage. He did his best to make his voice agreeable.

'May I assume that when Désirée is a little older—'

'Is older,' Madame Clary said quickly.

'—and when I have persuaded the War Office to employ me again and pay me again—that you will give your consent to the marriage, and that, in the meantime, Désirée and I may consider ourselves as being engaged?'

Madame Clary said, 'I think we should wait and see. Until we are all quite sure.'

Napoleon was firmly in control of his anger and his disappointment. But he couldn't let placid Madame and pompous Nicolas get away with it quite so easily.

'In that case, Madame, perhaps you would speak to your daughter about her behaviour?'

He was pleased to see that he had shaken her out of her smugness.

'Her behaviour? What? Why?'

'I must tell you, only yesterday I found her hiding in my room.'

'In your room?' Madame was shaken to her foundations.

'Under my bed.'

Madame and Nicolas stared at him, startled. What would be the next thing he said?

Napoleon, formal and courteous: 'As you know, Madame, I love your daughter, I wish to marry her, I respect and honour her. But I am sometimes taken aback by French ways, French manners. They are hardly the same as Corsican. Good-day, Madame. Monsieur . . .'

He turned stiffly and marched out. It had been a defeat, but he had made it seem almost like a victory.

But it had been a defeat, and he knew it. Joseph and Julie could not persuade him otherwise. He was a realist.

'They have refused me.'

'No . . .'

'In so many words. They made it perfectly clear.'

'They want to be sure that you're a good match, that's all.'

'Were you a good match, Joseph?' He turned abruptly to face his sister-in-law. 'Was he a good match for you, Julie?'

'I wanted him.'

'Your sister wants me.'

'But, of course, it was easier for us, because Joseph was—'

'The eldest son?'

'Yes.'

Joseph said pacifically, 'Don't blame me, it's not my fault.' But his over-charming smile showed how pleased he was at being the eldest son, and also how pleased he was at its not being his fault.

Napoleon said sharply, 'With a title you can't use. And an estate you can't touch.'

'The Revolution won't last for ever. Nor will the war.'

'The war will last long enough.'

'For what? For you?'

'To prove that a soldier is as good a match as a civil servant.'

Joseph seemed amused. 'I agree with you, of course.' (Of course he didn't agree. The way he said it showed that he didn't mean it.) 'The problem is to prove it.'

'I shall prove it.'

Sensible Julie could see that Napoleon was close to losing his temper, and probably had been wanting to lose his temper ever since his interview with her family. Napoleon did not enjoy asking for anything: still less did he enjoy being refused.

'Napoleon, my family do like you. They like you very much.'

'So they told me, while rejecting my proposal.'

'They haven't rejected it. You must understand that. They haven't said "No". They've simply said—'

'That I must wait.'

'Perhaps not for long.'

She tried to put it as hopefully as possible. Napoleon did not enjoy waiting, not even for a moment.

Walking in the garden with Joseph, while Julie went to see to their dinner, Napoleon was silent for a time, so Joseph was silent too, out of sympathy and out of discretion: anything he said, however meaningless, might easily be the wrong thing to say.

At last Napoleon spoke, broodingly: 'I'm not sure I can wait.'

'I'm afraid you'll have to.'

'I need Eugénie—Désirée—whatever her name is—now.'

'Not a chance.'

'At least, I need her dowry.'

'Be patient. Wait.'

The calm sensible elder brother, married and dowered and settled, with nothing to wait for. Napoleon looked at him with a sudden flash of anger in his eye.

'Because that damned family think that Corsicans are inferior? Or is it just that Corsican second sons are inferior?'

Joseph put on his charming it's-not-my-fault smile again. 'Whatever they think, you still have to wait.'

'How much dowry did you get with Julie? A hundred thousand francs?'

'Yes. Why?'

'Désirée would have the same?'

'I imagine.'

'I need it.'

Joseph laughed. 'Mercenary?'

'I must go to Paris. If I stay here, the Ministry of War

will continue to forget that I exist. All employment is in Paris, all promotion is in Paris. They're bound to give me something.'

'So you'll be paid again. You won't need the dowry.'

'What I need is a chance. But it has to be the right chance. I shall refuse whatever they give me, if it isn't the right chance for me.'

'Can you refuse? As a soldier?'

'There are ways of doing it. You ask for sick leave, so they have to appoint someone else. Or one department issues an order, you persuade another department to countermand it. But it may take time. I may have to buy time. Which means food.' He looked at his frayed sleeve-ends. 'And a new uniform, to show myself in public.'

'So that's why you want to marry Désirée?'

'Do you disapprove?'

'No.'

Napoleon had recovered his good humour. They grinned at each other. They knew each other far too well to have secrets, and far too well ever to disapprove.

'Apart from needing money, I need a wife. Désirée is pretty. She pleases me. She loves me. Docile. Adoring.'

'I thought you were wedded to the science of ballistics?'

'I have the same recurring sexual desires as any man. I don't care for whores: the expensive ones are too expensive for me, the cheap ones are too dangerous. When I finally die, I want it to be a cannon-ball, not syphilis. And I don't care for mistresses, *affaires, amours*—another man's woman, another man's wife. It takes up too much time: being a lover is a career in itself. I have my career, which is something quite different. The sexual question is not important. It exists. One has to settle it. I want to settle it once and for all.'

'And what you really want is to be a major-general.'

'I want to command more than I do now.' He punched his fist into his other hand. 'If that damned family would let me marry her tomorrow, next week, would give me her and her dowry—'

'They won't.'

'Can you lend me money?'

Joseph clucked his tongue. 'Difficult.'

'Julie's hundred thousand francs?'

'Tied up in investments.'

'I would be an investment.'

Joseph said mildly, 'I am supporting the rest of our family. One mother, three young brothers, three sisters. At the moment, none of them earning a single sou.'

'Yes. I beg your pardon. I'll do without money.'

'A few hundred francs, if you like—'

Napoleon almost shouted, 'I said I'll do without! I'll do without! Somehow!'

Désirée came running into the garden, breathless but bursting with something to say which couldn't be said while Joseph was there. Joseph smiled and found a reason for going into the house. The moment he was out of sight, Désirée threw herself into Napoleon's arms.

'Napoleon . . .'

'Eugénie . . .'

She would not be kissed, not until she had asked him and been answered—

'Why did you tell my mother about my hiding under your bed?'

'Ah . . .' He needed a moment to think of a good reply.

'You told her you found me hiding in your room. Under your bed.'

'As I did.'

'It was a secret.'

'I only told her that I found you *under* my bed.'

'But why did you tell her?'

'I was trying to convince her that you were old enough to be married.'

'She was furious with me.'

'I was, at that moment, rather furious with her. For not letting me marry you tomorrow, next week, as soon as humanly possible.'

She forgave him, and put up her mouth to be kissed, and kissed him almost before he kissed her.

'She says I'm not to see you—at least, not to see you alone. I'm not supposed to be here now. I can only stay for a moment.'

'I shan't tell her.'

'I'll come to your room again. When I can.'

'I shan't tell your mother anything ever again.'

'I love you, Napoleon.'

'I love you.'

'Call me by my name. Your name for me.'

'I love you, Eugénie.'

They kissed again, a long kiss, then walked through the garden arm-in-arm, like husband and wife.

She said, 'We will be married.'

'Yes. Of course.'

'Whatever they say.'

'Yes.'

'Shall we run away?'

'Your mother would be even more furious.'

'Let her be.'

'Your family would cut you off, with no dowry—'

'I don't care.'

Napoleon did care, but could hardly say so.

'Running away is a beautiful idea . . .' He pretended to consider it. 'No. We'll wait.'

'Oh, I don't mind waiting. So long as I can see you every day.'

'And come to my room when you can.'

'Yes.' She offered her mouth again, as a sign that she was all his.

'Our secret.'

'If you keep it.'

'I will.'

He kissed her, but briefly. It was time to be serious and to give her his instructions.

'Your mother and your brother are practical people. We must be practical too. You must please your mother. You must pretend to obey her in everything.'

'Yes.'

'But keep asking her permission to marry me.'

13

'Yes, I shall.'

'Every day. Ask her.'

'I shall.'

'Make it clear to her that you will marry no one but me.'

'I'll swear it.'

'Tell her you're pregnant—' He stopped himself. The idea might work but it might be disastrous. 'No. Don't. We'll have secrets but no lies. Simply tell her that you'll never look at another man, that we must be married very quickly, very soon . . .'

Joseph came from the house, whistling a tune, tactfully noisy.

'I apologize. Dinner is ready rather sooner than expected.'

When she had gone, Joseph raised an eyebrow.

'Well?'

Napoleon said, 'Paris. As soon as possible.'

'Have you told her you're going?'

'I'll tell her before I go.'

Perhaps he was sensible, as he told himself he was, or perhaps a coward, as he felt himself to be. He did not care for emotional scenes. On the morning of his departure he sent her the briefest possible note, asking her to come to him quickly. She came expecting love, and found him in a most unlover-like mood. She sat, disconsolate, on the uncomfortable edge of his bed, while he paced up and down his room at a military pace and hardly looked at her.

'I don't want you to go.' She was being very brave and not crying. She thought he might at least look at her and see how brave she was being.

'You must understand the situation.'

Her heart sank. She didn't want to understand the situation. She loved Napoleon, but not as a lecturer. He was going to lecture her.

'There, in Paris, the War Office, the army, the whole thing is in a state of disorganization. Of chaos. The government is bankrupt. It doesn't know where to turn for money. And because it's bankrupt, it'll have a rebellion on its hands very soon. This state of affairs—'

'—is dangerous,' she said.

'—is the right one for me. Those fools are bankrupt because they can't win a battle, they can't win a war. Winning a battle means loot. Winning a war means big loot.'

'And you can win a war for them?'

'At least I can win a battle. Who won the siege of Toulon?'

'You did.'

'Yes. By my siting of my guns. And I can do it again. Whenever they want me to.'

With luck the lecture was over. He stood silent. She said, in a small voice, 'Kiss me.'

He came and sat by her, on the hard bed-edge, and when she turned her face he kissed her, but as if it were a duty. His mind was not in the kiss.

She tried again. 'I love you, Napoleon.'

'I love you.' His mind was not in the words.

'Eugénie?'

'Eugénie.'

If his mind was elsewhere, perhaps she should try to follow it. She said tentatively, 'I'm sure you'll cover yourself with glory.'

'Glory comes from common sense and a mathematical education.'

She had to make some sort of reply.

'Does it?'

'Which is why I chose to be in the artillery.'

'For the glory?' She hoped she'd got it right.

'For the winning. In order to win.'

'Oh.'

'The key to every victory lies in the proper handling of the artillery.'

She was wandering, lost. She could think of nothing to say.

'I am the only general in the whole of the French Army who understands this.'

'I'm sure.'

'All their commanders are out of date—infantrymen, cavalrymen. Any fool can be a cavalryman. Not even a fool would join the infantry. Cannon-fodder. I prefer to be the cannon.' He was on his feet again and pacing the room again. 'I must find my chance. Wish me luck.'

'I do.'

'I'm told that Paris, now, is the city of luxury, dancing, pretty women—for those who have money and power—and starvation, for those who have not.'

She said what came into her head. 'I'm afraid of those pretty women.'

He stopped pacing, and smiled, and held out his arms, not to embrace her but to show her his shabbiness.

'D'you think they'll look at me? Dressed like this?'

She went into his arms to tell him that his uniform didn't matter, he was beautiful, she loved him.

At the garden gate his aides were waiting: Captain Junot and Lieutenant Marmont, and a carriage in the road beyond, to take the three of them away. Désirée held Napoleon's arm, to keep him with her for one moment longer.

'Will you write to me every day?'

'Will you?'

'Every day.' She said it. But he hadn't said it.

'Give your letters to Joseph. He'll know where I am, he'll send them to Paris with his own. And I'll write to you through Joseph.'

'What will you say in your letters?'

'You'll see.'

'I want to know now. I want to hear your first letter now.'

'I shall say, "My beloved—"'

'You must go on calling me Eugénie.'

'I shall say, "Eugénie, my beloved—my whole life belongs to you."'

He stopped, and hoped that he had said enough. He

had no experience of writing love-letters, and no great powers of improvisation.

She said, almost in a whisper, so that no one else could possibly hear—Joseph and Julie ten yards away, Junot and Marmont at twenty yards . . . 'I shall say, "I am very bad at putting my feelings into words. I shall never be able to tell you how much I feel for you. But wherever you are, however far away—my whole life belongs to you." I shall write that every day, in different ways, in better words if I can find them . . . Will you write to me every day?'

'I shall be very busy in Paris. I'll write as often as I can.'

'Please, every day?'

'Every other day.'

He kissed her hand, then went quickly to Julie, then to Joseph to embrace him.

He said in Joseph's ear, 'Persuade that damned family that I'll make an excellent husband. As soon as you can.'

'I'll try.'

'At least, before I die of starvation.'

He turned quickly away and marched to the gate, to his aides, to his carriage. Désirée stood with her eyes fixed on him, waiting for him to turn back for one last look at her, one smile, one wave. He did not turn back. He was gone.

As soon as she got home, she started to draft her first letter to him.

> Every moment is a sword plunged into my heart, because every moment is taking you further away from me. I know you had to go, but how much I regret that I let you go! It is only half an hour since I last saw you, but to me it seems a hundred years. The one thing that can keep me alive in your absence is the knowledge that you love me and will always love me . . .

She stopped, and put aside the page, and started on a new version.

It is only an hour since you left me. To me it seems a century . . .

Napoleon wrote to her the next day, from Avignon, and enclosed it in his letter to Joseph.

To Citizeness Eugénie Clary, Marseille.

I am at Avignon, very unhappy at the thought of being so far away from you. The journey has been dull and disagreeable. We were held up for several hours by the flooding of the river Durance. I shall not be able to receive any more of your letters until I arrive in Paris. Make sure that there are some waiting for me the moment I get there.

Tomorrow night I shall be in Lyon.

Good-bye, my sweet one. All my love, from him whose life belongs to you.

N. Bp.

She to him:

I write without knowing where or how this letter will reach you. You say that Joseph will know your address in Paris. Why didn't you tell it to me? Then at least I could have imagined you arriving there in your carriage, as I have imagined you driving every mile of the road, and every yard of every mile.

A friend of Joseph's has arrived here from Paris, a member of the Convention. He says that Paris is very gay and amusing—the Parisians are really enjoying themselves now that the Reign of Terror is all over. I do hope that the pleasures of life in Paris will not make you forget your loving friend. Keep your oath, you swore to love me for ever, as I swore to love you. I will do everything here, as you must do everything there, to make sure that we shall be married as soon as ever it is possible, and then we will never be parted again, never, never, as long as life shall last . . .

Napoleon, in Paris, replied to her letters every other day, or every few days, or at least reasonably often, whenever he could, from time to time.

2. PARIS

In Paris, the great Terror was over at last. The Jacobin extremists—Marat, Robespierre, Saint-Just—were safely dead. On the day of Napoleon's leaving Marseille, the Public Prosecutor himself, Fouquier-Tinville, after a trial lasting forty-one days, went to the guillotine for having sent so many others there.

It was a time for the ladies of the aristocracy and the high bourgeoisie to come out of hiding or out of the prisons where they had waited to die; a time for them to reopen their salons, and to dance. Dancing was all the rage. Greek dresses were all the rage: diaphanous, transparent, cut low to show the breasts, slit high to show the legs. Pleasure was all the rage, and voluptuousness, and sensuality.

Three women were the new queens of Paris, the rulers of the rulers of France. Thérèse Tallien, daughter of a banker, with two husbands already discarded at the age of twenty-one, and so deliciously pretty that every man longed to eat her all up, from top to toe. Juliette Récamier, wife of a banker, but with his agreement still a virgin at eighteen, and so angelically beautiful that every man wanted to kneel down and worship her. And Rose Beauharnais, not as young as the others, not as faultlessly handsome, but with a grace and a charm, so soft, so pliant, so totally feminine, that she was almost as greatly admired and as greatly desired.

In a corner of Barras's salon, Brigadier-General Bonaparte, newly from Marseille, looked at the women as they danced past, enchantingly graceful, smiling enchantingly at their partners and at the whole world. He, by himself, awkward, glowering, wished he were anywhere else, any place where he would not be disturbed by the perfumed eroticism of the atmosphere, by the marvellous women he could see but could not touch. The marvellous women glanced at him as they passed—out of curiosity, perhaps; it could hardly be out of interest. He did not dare return the glances. Their eyes were an embarrassment to him. They could see what was plain to see: his aloneness, his awkwardness, his shabbiness, his provincialness, and his unimportance.

Paul Barras, aristocrat turned revolutionary, terrorist turned moderate man, constant only in his pursuit of money and pleasure and power, requested Brigadier-General Bonaparte to be so good as to call at his office the next morning. Napoleon found him in the Luxembourg, lolling in a big chair behind a big desk.

'Monsieur Barras.'

Barras smiled smoothly. 'For no good reason, we still retain the Revolutionary forms of address.'

Napoleon corrected himself. 'Citizen Barras.'

'As one ex-nobleman to another. Do please take a chair.'

'Thank you.' Napoleon sat and was silent. He had yet to make out what lay behind the affectation of indolent politeness.

'I'm so glad you could come to my reception last night. Did you enjoy yourself?'

'Unfortunately I have never learnt to dance.'

'Oh, but you must. This year, everyone dances.'

'So I saw.'

'It's very natural. We dance to celebrate our miraculous survival.' Barras skilfully acted a hesitation and a charming apology. 'I do beg your pardon.'

'Why?'

'I think you yourself were in some way connected with Robespierre—?'

'I was on his brother's staff for a time.'

Barras nodded sympathetically. 'A pity, for your career.'

'I was posted to his staff. By the Ministry of War.'

'Still, a pity. Oh, I know, you're a soldier, not a politician.'

Napoleon said, 'I am becoming a politician.'

Barras's indolent eyes opened a little wider, as if to see him better.

'How sensible. In whose interest?'

'My own.'

'How very sensible. The only possible party. Forgive me if I say, what a pleasure to talk to a general who isn't a fool . . . So, from now on, you'll be more prudent in your choice of jobs.'

'Yes.'

'Since everything is self-interest these days. Which is why I make it my business to meet unemployed generals. There may be a day when our interests coincide.'

Napoleon said, 'The Ministry of War has posted me again.'

'Oh? Where to?'

'To Brittany. To command a brigade. A brigade of infantry.'

Barras first chose his words carefully and then said them carelessly. 'If I were you, I'd ask for sick leave.'

'I have. Two months' sick leave.'

'Are you getting it?'

'Yes.'

Barras laughed. 'General, you are a man after my own—no, not heart. After my own mind.'

Barras's secretary opened the door, and two of last night's marvellous women came into the room, smiling enchantingly, moving towards Barras as if they were still dancing to last night's music.

'Paul!'

'Paul darling!'

'We've decided what you shall do today.'

'We've come to take you to the country.'

'A picnic. A feast.'

'Which you are providing.'

'At Rose's house at Croissy.'

'We've decided.'

Barras had risen and gone forward to meet them, kissing their hands.

'My dear Rose—my dear Thérèse—'

'It's such heavenly weather, you can't possibly want to work.'

'I never want to work.'

'France can govern itself for a day.'

'It can do it as well as I can.'

'So it's all arranged,' said the one called Rose. 'I've sent your servants on ahead, to get everything ready—'

'How thoughtful of you, Rose.'

'And we've brought your big carriage, to be comfortable in—'

'How even more thoughtful.'

'Yes! All we have to do is go. As soon as—'

Napoleon was steadfastly looking at the wall, but he knew that they were looking at him.

Barras, raising his voice a little, said, 'May I present General Bonaparte?'

Napoleon bowed stiffly in their direction, from a distance.

'Citizeness Beauharnais—Citizeness Tallien—who make a habit of interrupting me—'

They smiled briefly and vaguely in Napoleon's direction, from a distance.

Barras said to them, 'Rose—Thérèse—my angels, my loves—one minute and I shall be with you.'

'Not more than one minute.'

'I swear it.'

He escorted them to the door, and came back to Napoleon, acting a charming apology again.

'I'm so sorry. They are my dearest friends, and two very important people . . . I was about to say, when they burst in on us—you, of course, are an artillery expert.'

'Yes.'

'Yes, I remember your brilliant gunnery at the siege of Toulon.'

'Were you there?'

Barras smiled. 'In charge.'

Napoleon had been a major then. He remembered his incompetent commanders. He didn't remember Barras. 'Forgive me—?'

'In political charge.' Barras smiled again, perhaps to show that he took ultimate responsibility for the victory, but none for the previous military mistakes. 'My dear general, spend your sick leave in Paris. Keep in touch with me. Call on me here or at my house whenever you please. Our day will come. In the meantime, enjoy the new Reign of Pleasure. Move in society, practise dancing, make love to pretty women. I take it that you like pretty women?'

'Yes.'

'Our Parisian women are the prettiest in the world. I advise you not merely sexually but politically. All decisions now are political decisions. All political decisions are made, not in the council chamber, nor in the committee room, but in the salon and the boudoir, under cover of a flirtation, or in the middle of a dance. Here, in Paris, women are politics.'

From his dilapidated lodging-house bedroom in the rue du Mail, Napoleon wrote to his brother in Marseille.

Dear Joseph,

I urge you to speak to Désirée's family again, and persuade them to agree to the marriage. If they ask what my position is now, and what my prospects are, tell them that I have been offered command of a brigade, but that I am in expectation of something better, as I have yesterday and today had long discussions with Paul Barras, who has promised me his aid and support. You may remember that Barras was in political charge at Toulon. He is now the most important man in the Convention. He can do a great deal to advance my career.

I must get this marriage settled. Quite apart from

the question of my needing the dowry, the thought
of women is too much in my mind . . .

Désirée said to Joseph, 'Why doesn't he write to me more
often?'

'He has so much to do.'

'But you said he wasn't doing anything.'

'He has been working very hard at finding something
to do—'

'But you said he turned down the command of a brigade.'

'Yes, but—'

'Why didn't he take it? Then my family might have
agreed!'

Joseph wished to high heaven that Napoleon would
come back to Marseille and make his own excuses.

'It was an infantry brigade, which is not what he wants.
He is in fact about to start work, temporarily at least—'

'Doing what?'

'At the Topographical Bureau of the Committee of
Public Safety.' Joseph said it lamely. It was a lame thing
to say. He tried his best to make it sound more impressive. 'Helping to make plans for the invasion of Italy.'
It did not sound impressive.

After a time Désirée said, not looking at Joseph, 'He
does still want to marry me?'

'More than anything else in the world.'

Two big warm tears came out of her eyes, out of her
loving heart. 'Oh, I know he does, I don't doubt it. He
promised to love me always.'

'He wants to get the marriage settled.'

'So do I.'

'I'll speak to your mother again. And your brother.
And you must speak to them.'

'I do. Every day. They tell me to wait.'

'Yes, well . . .'

'I don't mind waiting,' she said. 'If only he'd write to
me more often.'

Joseph thought of his brother, who had no liking for writing love letters, who took no pleasure in repeating words he had said before, who detested waiting for anything or anyone, and who had no regard for any man who spent his time dreaming of a loved one when he could have been taking the path to fame and fortune.

Joseph said, 'He does, in every letter he writes to me, send you his very warmest regards.'

Napoleon stamped up and down his shabby room in the rue du Mail, a letter from Joseph in one hand, an enclosure from Désirée in the other. Reading them had done nothing to cure his savage discontent.

'Well?' he cried to the wall. 'Will she or won't she? Will they or won't they? That's all!'

Captain Junot came bounding up the stairs and into the room, a big grin on his face and a bottle of wine in each hand.

'Will they let her or won't they let her!' Napoleon shouted. 'Either! Or! That's all! One word! Yes or no!'

'Women are problems, not solutions. My father sent some wine. Where's the corkscrew?'

Napoleon threw it at him.

'The problem is simple. Either we marry—or we break it off.'

'Ah. It's Désirée.'

'There is never a decision.'

'We arrive at a certain point. We should, in all logic, move forward from that point. We do not move forward. We do not move! Nothing happens! Something should happen, but nothing happens!'

Junot said cheerfully, pouring two big glasses of wine, 'And if there is one thing you really can't stand, it's nothing happening.' He gave one glass to Napoleon. 'Drink to something happening soon? Anything happening?'

Napoleon said, 'Shall we solve the problem for ourselves?'

'Only thing to do.'

'Shall we go to Turkey?'

'Turkey?'

'Yes.'

'Why not? You say so, and Turkey it is.'

Napoleon threw two official documents at him. 'The War Office issued two orders today. Both on the same day. One striking me off the list of employable generals. The other putting me in charge of the military mission to Turkey, with the special task of reorganizing the Turkish artillery.'

Junot said, 'Turkey. Ah. Good. Big fat beautiful girls.'

'Meanwhile, the Committee of Public Safety has decided that I am not to be allowed to leave France, because of my indispensability at the Topographical Bureau.'

Junot said, 'No Turkey. Oh, well. French girls. I prefer French girls.'

Napoleon said, 'We'll stay here. At least the Committee, and Paul Barras, and the Convention, know that I'm loyal to the Republic. And they're going to need every loyal general they can find.'

'Trouble brewing?' Junot asked hopefully.

'Yes.'

'Yes, every second man I meet seems to be a Royalist and a rebel and any day now he's going to take over the government.'

'Every second man? I'd say two out of every three.'

Napoleon was cheerful again, at the cheering prospect. They clinked glasses.

Junot said, 'Good. I like trouble. Same as you. Even better than girls.'

Napoleon said, 'Trouble could be my chance.'

On that day in October, Barras's temporary headquarters at the Carrousel was crowded out with a great moving, swaying, bustling throng, some of them soldiers trying to argue like politicians, some of them politicians trying

27

to act like soldiers, all of them full of words but all of them finally uncertain and indecisive, unwilling to take the final responsibility for any act for which they might finally be held responsible. Oh yes, something had to be done quickly, the rebels had to be defeated, the Republic had to be preserved, the government of the moderate man had to be saved—but it seemed extremely likely that the rebels were strong enough to destroy that moderate government, so, of course, it was necessary to hedge one's bets, the art of politics being quintessentially the art of survival. It would not do to be the man who led the forces of the Convention against the rebels, and lost.

At the centre of the turmoil, Barras wore for the occasion the uniform of a full general. He was one who could not hope to hedge his bets. The Ultras of the Right, and the Royalists, would hardly wish to spare an aristocrat-regicide: a man who had not merely betrayed his own class but had done his best to exterminate it.

Junot, big and strong, came pushing through the crowd, using the voice he had used as a sergeant in the artillery to shout commands above the sound of the guns.

'Right, get out of the way then! Clear the way for General Bonaparte! Out of the way!' A salute for Barras. 'General Bonaparte reporting, sir! And Captain Junot!'

He saluted again and stepped smartly aside for General Bonaparte to step forward.

Barras said, with nothing of his usual indolence, 'General Bonaparte, a state of emergency has been declared. The Committee of Public Safety has placed me in command of the army. The Royalists and the Extremists in Paris have risen against the Convention.'

Napoleon said—rapping out the words, the fewest possible words, like the quick-march beat of a drum— 'How many men have they got?'

'Twenty thousand? Perhaps more?'

'How armed?'

'Swords. Muskets. Anything. Everything.'

'How many men have you got?'

'Five thousand regulars. Plus three thousand militia—if we can find them, and if we can manage to make them fight.'

Napoleon said, 'Then it depends on your artillery.'

Barras said, 'I appoint you to command the artillery.'

'How many guns?'

'Forty. Mostly eight-pounders.'

'Where are they?'

'Sablons.'

'What cavalry have we got? Here?'

Now that he was appointed to command, he no longer said 'you,' he said 'we'.

Barras shouted, 'Captain Murat!'

A big handsome Gascon swashbuckler came shoving forward through the crowd, and gave a magnificent salute.

'Captain Murat, cavalry—sir!'

Napoleon turned his eyes on him. 'How many men?'

'Two hundred. Well-horsed.'

'Take them to Sablons. Now. Fetch the guns. Here. And ammunition. As much as you can carry. As fast as you can. Is that clear?'

'Sir!'

Captain Murat saluted again, even more magnificently, and was gone.

Barras said, 'General Bonaparte. I foresaw a day when our interests might coincide. I think the day has come.'

'Yes.'

'Oh, one thing I am instructed to tell you. The rebels are, of course, Frenchmen. The Committee of Public Safety, and the Convention, are most anxious that we, as Frenchmen, should not kill Frenchmen.'

'I understand. We are still the Revolution.'

'You will therefore show great discretion in your choice of the ammunition you use, and in the number of rounds you fire. In the exact pointing of your guns—at the rebels, or over their heads. Etcetera. Etcetera.'

'I understand.'

29

Barras said, very much more clearly and decisively, 'But the task is to save the Republic.'

Napoleon said, 'I understand.'

Outside the Tuileries, Napoleon sited the guns brought by Murat. The day wore on, and the great mob of rebels came nearer.

Junot said, 'Give orders to load?'

'Yes.'

'What with? Blank?'

Napoleon said, 'Grape-shot.'

Junot grinned. 'The Committee? And the Convention?'

Napoleon said, 'I am commanding the artillery.'

One of Barras's aides struggled through the crowd to him.

'Message from the Convention. We are not to open fire on the rebels unless the rebels fire first.'

Barras said: 'Message to the Convention . . . No. Why bother? The Convention has ceased to exist.'

The rebels broke through all the government barricades, all the infantry defences. With muskets and bayonets, pikes, anything, everything, they swarmed onwards, victorious, towards the Tuileries, to seize the centre of power. Napoleon's guns fired grape-shot into them, round after round. In less than an hour the rebellion was over. The Republic was saved.

3. ROSE

When Madame Beauharnais arrived, she found Barras studying himself in a long mirror, with his tailor and hosier and hatter in anxious attendance. He was wearing an embroidered coat in the style of Henri IV, a sash fringed with gold and silk stockings; and it was difficult to tell whether he found the sight of himself more pleasing than amusing, or more amusing than pleasing.

'Good morning, Rose. Do you like it?'

'I love it. But what is it?'

'Guess.'

He made a sign to the hatter, who came forward and reverently presented him with a splendid three-plumed hat. Barras bowed low to Madame Beauharnais, and put it on.

'To help you guess.'

'For a fancy-dress ball?'

'My uniform as a member of the Directory.'

'In that case, it's superb.'

'The rulers of France must show themselves to be the rulers of France.'

'In the fashion of two hundred years ago?'

'We are doing our best to put the clock back.'

When the tradesmen were dismissed, she said to him, 'The uniform is very beautiful. And so are you.'

She offered him her mouth. He looked at it with interest and admiration, but politely refused the offer. 'My dear Rose, much as I adore your mouth—'

'No—?' The offer was still there.

'*Because* I adore your mouth—'

'So—?'

'Let me not spoil it. It has taken two hours to put it on.'

'Is that a compliment?'

'Of course. You're an artist. A great painter.'

'I would gladly have ruined my work of art. To thank you.'

'For what?'

'My house in rue Chantereine.'

'It's finished?'

'Finished, furnished, perfect.'

Barras said, 'Rose, you have thanked me often enough, with something more substantial than a kiss.'

'Often. But enough?'

'I shall come to supper with you soon.'

She smiled sweetly. 'I shall make you welcome.'

'In the meantime, will you do something quite different for me?'

'Anything. What?'

'I've invited the hero of Paris. I'm putting you next to him at lunch.'

'Paul, I thought you were the hero of Paris?'

'No. I am merely the King of the French Republic.'

'Ah. General Bonaparte?'

'You met him once. Briefly. With me.'

'Did I?' She tried to recall. 'Oh yes. I think I remember. A pale-faced little Corsican?'

Barras said, in the voice he used when he wanted something understood very clearly, 'I should like you to be nice to him.'

She raised her eyebrows. 'Am I not always nice?'

'I should like you to be as charming as only you can be.'

Her smile lost none of its sweetness. 'I'm not sure I want to be charming to pale-faced little Corsicans.'

Barras said, with an edge on his voice, 'Rose, I assume the house is not, in fact, finished? There are bills still unpaid?'

'Yes, of course, bills. There are always bills.'

'Deserve well of me by being agreeable to my collaborator. My right hand. The man who made me one of the Directors.'

'Yes, so I've heard.'

'The man whom I have made Commander-in-Chief of the Army of the Interior. Have you heard that, too?'

'No.'

'The announcement was last night. I'm not the only one who has been trying on a new uniform.' He looked at her sideways. 'Is he less pale-faced now?'

'Much less pale-faced.'

'Good—so let me tell you quickly—he's a soldier, he'll be ludicrously punctual, before all the others. Compliment him on his triumphs.'

'Do I know them?'

'Last month, at the Tuileries—'

'Oh, of course I know that.'

'Remember the phrases. Brilliant handling of the artillery. Put down the rebellion. Saved the Convention, saved the new Constitution, saved the Republic. Can you remember that?'

'Yes, I think so. Is that all?'

'The siege of Toulon, last year.'

'He was there?'

'Major then, promoted brigadier-general for gallantry.'

'I shan't remember that.'

'Brilliant handling of the artillery—keep saying that, you won't go far wrong.' He saw Napoleon coming in. 'Sit where you'll look most elegant.'

He went quickly forward. 'My dear general—'

'My dear Barras.'

'I thought of inviting thousands, to celebrate your appointment. But I decided to limit it to a handful of friends, all of them your ardent admirers. May I bring you together with one of them, who is burning to talk to you?'

Rose had arranged herself on a sofa: she had long learnt the art of arranging herself, as one arranges flowers to look their best.

'Rose, of course you know General Bonaparte—you met him some months ago, at my office—'

'I remember very well.' She held out her hand to him. 'General . . .'

33

He bent stiffly and kissed her hand.

'Madame . . .'

She smiled enchantingly and patted the sofa. 'Come and sit here by me.'

Barras said, 'Rose—General—would you excuse me for a moment? I must divest myself of this quite absurd costume.'

He bowed and went away. Napoleon was alone with the marvellous woman. Once, in her presence, he had felt violently self-conscious because his shabby old uniform was so old. Now he felt equally self-conscious because his splendid new uniform was so new.

She said, 'What did Paul say to you, when you came in? About me?'

'Nothing.'

'Didn't he tell you I came here specially early, in the hope of a moment alone with you?'

'No.'

'I'm so glad he didn't. I asked him not to. I wanted to tell you myself.'

'I am flattered.'

'No, not at all. I was simply longing to say what I've been saying to everyone else. How wonderful it was'— she found the right phrase '—the way you saved the Republic.'

'Ah.' He knew that his responses were stupidly inadequate. She might think him a great general, she must find him a fool.

She said, 'By putting down the rebellion.'

'I did what had to be done.'

'What I so much admired was your . . . your brilliant handling of the artillery.'

'At the Tuileries.'

'Yes.'

'I simply put the guns in the right places.'

'Ah, but who else would have put them in the right places?'

'No one.'

34

'No one at all,' she agreed.

'At least, no one in the French Army.' He began to feel a greater ease. She was not only charming but sensible. And she was interested in his subject.

She said, 'Tell me.'

'About—?'

'The siting of the guns.'

'I sited them to cover the main approaches to the Tuileries and the Louvre.'

'How well you did it.'

'In accordance with my knowledge of the capabilities of the eight-pounder—'

'Ah yes, your knowledge.'

'After that, the only crucial decision I had to make . . .' He stopped. 'Forgive me. It's not a matter to be discussed with a woman.'

'No, go on . . . Please go on. I'm fascinated.'

Napoleon said, choosing his words carefully so that she should not be disturbed by the sound of blood, 'The Convention wanted me to put down the rebellion without killing anyone. Victory without killing. It's not possible.'

'Quite impossible.'

'To them, the French people was the sacred Ark of the Covenant. Firing on the French people would be a violation of all the principles of the Revolution. They failed to understand that rebellion is war. And they failed to understand the principles of war.'

'Yes . . .' The word was said with such depth of sincerity. She was the most encouraging listener in the world. And it was possible to tell her anything.

Napoleon said, 'I made my troops fire live ammunition, straight into the crowd, for a very good reason. When a mob knows little or nothing about firearms, it's the worst policy to start by firing blanks. They hear a great noise, they're frightened, perhaps they fall back for a moment. But then they look round, they see there's no one killed or wounded, they pluck up their spirits, they come at you ten times as hard as before—and to beat them you

finally have to kill ten times the number you'd have killed
if you'd used live ammunition in the first place.'

She had not taken her admiring eyes off him for a
moment. 'You put things so clearly.'

'Thank you.'

'Because you understand them so clearly.'

There were other people coming into the room: Barras's notion of a handful of friends seemed to be thirty
or forty. Madame Tallien ran up to the sofa where they
sat, and cried, 'Rose, dear!'

Napoleon jumped to his feet.

'Thérèse dear! Do you know the famous General Bonaparte?'

Thérèse turned her marvellous dark eyes to meet his.
'Oh yes, of course we've met. More than once. Haven't
we? I know we have.'

'Madame . . .' He bowed.

Madame Beauharnais said to him, 'Thérèse is my very
best friend.'

'If you would care to . . .' He offered her his place on
the sofa.

'No, no, I must find Paul, I have something I absolutely must ask him before we have lunch. Where is Paul?
Rose, what have you done with him?'

'He went to make himself less absurd.'

'What do you mean?' Thérèse looked across the room
and saw Barras coming in, his normal elegant self. 'Oh,
there he is. Not absurd at all.'

'Not now.'

Thérèse flashed a smile at them. 'Forgive me, Rose—
General—I simply must . . .'

Madame Beauharnais said, 'Dear Thérèse. Isn't she
delicious?'

'Yes.'

'But now she's left us, you can sit down again and look
at me again.'

'I would in any case wish to . . .'

He had got half-way through a compliment without

knowing how to finish it gracefully but respectfully. Her
smile understood the compliment and forgave him the
clumsiness. Since she had bidden him look at her, he
looked at her. She said, 'Tell me about the siege of Toulon.'

At the other side of the room, Thérèse Tallien said to
Barras, 'I must know. Have you told her?'

'Told whom what?'

'Told Rose.'

'About—?'

'About us.'

'Ah. No. Not yet.'

'Paul darling, if I'm going to be your mistress—'

'Thérèse, darling, you are my mistress.'

'You must tell her. It's so awkward. I can't have secrets
from my best friend.'

'Your best friend, and mine. I shall break it to her
very gently.'

Napoleon, gazing into Madame Beauharnais's eyes,
said, 'I saw immediately that the key to the capture of
Toulon was a fort which commanded . . .'

He stopped. She gently prompted him. 'Which commanded . . . ?'

'I beg your pardon, my mind was wandering.'

'Where was it wandering to?'

'To your name.'

'Oh?'

'Is your name really Rose?'

'Marie-Josèphe-Rose. Really.'

'Marie-Josèphe-Rose.'

'All my friends call me Rose . . . Shall we be friends?
Will you?'

He said slowly, 'I should like to think of a name for
you.'

Her eyes were wonderfully soft and kind, and wonderfully private, as if there were no one else within a hundred miles. But then her eyes warned him that the room
was in fact full of people. And her mouth said, '. . . was
a fort which commanded . . . ?'

He brought his mind back to Toulon.

'. . . was a fort which commanded the harbour.'

Barras stretched himself out in an armchair and said, 'He is, of course, incredibly busy. With Paris still half-rebellious and still half-starving. Which reminds me to say, what a perfectly delicious supper that was.'

Rose said, 'You supplied it.'

'Only the raw materials.' His eyes travelled around the room. 'In much the same way as I supplied the raw materials for your boudoir. The fact that the room is a miracle of intimacy and charm—ah, that's not my doing, but yours.'

'You are being particularly nice to me tonight—why?'

'Aren't I always nice?'

'Yes, of course, Paul. And what do you particularly want me to do?'

Barras gazed at the ceiling. 'As I was saying, he's incredibly busy and he's a demon for work. But he does have to eat from time to time. I beg of you, ask him to lunch, ask him to dinner here, whenever you can.'

'I already sit next to him at dinner three times a week, at your dinner parties.'

'Yes. I do the placing.'

'All he does is gaze in my eyes and tell me about tactics.'

'Gaze in his eyes and listen.'

'But he's a bore. The worst kind of bore. A military bore.'

'Yes, indeed. I entirely agree. But I do advise you to cultivate his acquaintance. I have a feeling that he may become the second most important man in France.'

'Second to you.'

'Of course. Which is why it suits me to be friends with him, and to have you friends with him.'

Rose said almost petulantly, 'I am not sure that it suits me.'

'Then for my sake.'

'But I do so hate being bored.'

'But you are quite miraculously good at not showing it.'

'You want me to listen to him.'

'It is one of your great skills.'

'Anything else? Am I to throw myself into his arms?'

He looked at her in mild astonishment. 'Good heavens, no. That is, not unless you want to. Unless you think it might be amusing for you.'

'Does he know that I'm your mistress?'

'Rose dear, what an extraordinary question to ask.'

'Is it?'

'You're behaving very strangely tonight.'

'Does he know I'm your mistress?'

Barras raised his shoulders. 'He and I talk of nothing but politics and war. We don't talk about you.'

'Do you suppose he knows?'

'I was never any good at supposing.'

'Do you suppose?'

He sighed, to show her how patient he was being. 'Paris knows. Our Paris. I doubt if he knows. He is inexperienced in these matters. And his mind is on other things.'

She said, 'Am I your mistress?'

So that was the real question, the one she had been moving towards.

'Rose, you could have asked me that so much more straightforwardly, and so much sooner.'

'Well. Am I?'

He rose from his chair and went to sit by her, taking her hands in his.

'I shall be deeply disappointed if I don't go to bed with you tonight.'

'That is not quite an answer.'

'I shall always be delighted to go to bed with you whenever possible. Is that?'

She smiled. 'It will do.' She offered him her mouth, as a peace token.

'At this time of night—with the greatest of pleasure.' He kissed her.

Held in his arms, she murmured, 'I'd only wondered whether you were throwing me out of your arms and into Bonaparte's.'

'Rose, you know very well, you will always do as you please.'

'Sometimes as you please.'

'Shall I give you my sage advice? Bonaparte is an important man—'

'Not as important as you.'

'No. And not yet rich—but he will be.'

'Not as rich as you.'

'No.'

'No one is as rich as you.'

'Oh yes. Two or three bankers. Speculators. Swindlers . . . But the choice is yours. You know me. When did I ever throw a mistress out of my arms? I'm far too lazy. I never do. Not even when I take a new one.'

She looked steadfastly into his eyes for a time. There was nothing to be seen in them, except that he had been amused by their conversation.

'Yes, Paul,' she said. 'I know you.'

He said softly, 'Is it time for bed?'

In her bed, after Rose and Barras had enjoyed each other, he said, 'Write Bonaparte one of your tiny reproachful notes. Of course, you know how impossibly busy he is, but why doesn't he come to call on you? You're good at writing tiny reproachful notes.'

To please him she got out of bed and went to her writing-desk and wrote just such a note: to please Barras, because it was still the best policy to please Barras, when she could do so at no great inconvenience to herself; and also because Barras was not to be trusted, and if he cast her off she would need a new protector, and if Bonaparte did in fact become rich then he might be a useful person to fall back on.

When she had written the note she read it out to Barras, who lay in bed listening with a fine critical ear.

You no longer come to see a friend who is fond of you. You have completely abandoned me. Why? Come to my house on Thursday for lunch. I must see you and talk to you about your affairs. Good night, my friend. Till Thursday.

Barras thought for a time, and then said, ' "Till Thursday. I embrace you".'
She added the three words, then rose and went to him. She said, 'I have added the words, "I embrace you".' She embraced him.

Napoleon replied with a note saying:

I cannot imagine what has made you reproach me. I beg you to believe that no one desires your friendship more than I do, and no one is as ready as I am to prove it . . .

Rose, in her boudoir, after lunch, said, 'And you really do forgive me for not having invited any one else?'
Napoleon said, 'I should not have forgiven you if you had.'
She made a little curtsey to him before she came to sit down. 'Thank you.'
'I do not shine in public.'
Her mouth protested prettily. 'Now you've spoilt the compliment.'
'No. I was simply dispraising myself.'
'But you weren't speaking the truth. General Bonaparte, for the first time, I have caught you out in a lie.'
'I was very honestly trying—'
'Honestly?'
'Yes.' He felt hurt. Did she question his honesty? Or could it be that she was making fun of him?
Rose said, 'Then you chose the wrong word for yourself. Oh, you don't twinkle in public, like so many of my friends. You don't sparkle, like some of them. But you do shine.'

He was wrong. She had not been making fun of him. She was, as always, completely frank and sincere.

He said, 'I feel that I hide my light.'

'How could you? Unless you close your eyes.'

'Are they so.. . . ?' He hesitated to choose an adjective himself. She would do it better.

'I must find the word for you again. The light in your eyes is . . . brilliant, perhaps? No, that's not right. Dazzling? No. I've go it. Blinding.'

In the search for the right word, it was necessary for her to look deeply into what she was describing, and therefore for him to return the look. He said, 'The light in your eyes is . . . soft. Warm. Tender.'

She said tenderly, 'Shall we agree that we admire each other's eyes? I invited you here to talk about your career.'

'Ah. Well . . .' But he couldn't take his eyes away from hers.

'What are you going to do next? What do you want to do?' She turned her head and released his eyes, as a kindness.

'It depends on the Directory. You know them as well as I do.'

'I think it depends on you.'

There was no possible harm in confiding in her. There might even be some good in it. In any case, she was worthy of his confidence. He said, 'We're bound to attack in Italy soon.'

'Are we?'

'In the spring—if the Directors have any sense. I've made plans for an invasion of Italy, they've seen my plans. We can knock the Austrians out of the war. We can march through the whole of Italy. If the Directors use my plans. And if they put me in command.'

'Then they must.'

'Also, we can come back from Italy with enough loot to make this country rich again.'

'Then they certainly must.'

'That is what I want to do next.'

42

She said very seriously, 'We must all do our best to make sure that you are put in command.'

He felt that she was making him a promise, a solemn promise. He felt a strong obscure desire to promise her something in return.

He asked abruptly, 'And you? Next?'

'We're not talking about me.'

'Yes. Please. I want to know what you want to do.'

She spread her hands, in a charmingly simple gesture. 'I am a woman—what does a woman want? To go on living. To have a little happiness. To find happiness in her children, if nowhere else. As I do. You know my children. I adore them.'

'Yes.' He had met them: a handsome boy and a pretty little girl.

'Poor things, with no father. You know my husband was killed in the Reign of Terror.'

'Yes.'

'Simply because he was an aristocrat. Though he had commanded an army for them. He was their best general. But they killed him.'

'Yes.' General Bonaparte did not have such a high opinion of General Beauharnais's talents, but this was hardly the moment to say so.

'You know I was arrested too? And condemned to death too? For being an aristocrat? And for being Alexander's wife?'

'Yes, I know.' She was speaking the truth. Barras had told him her history.

She sighed. 'Poor Alexander. Oh, it was an arranged match, I was much too young, straight from Martinique and straight from school. And Alexander was . . .'—she hesitated delicately—'. . . not perfect. But I loved him. I suppose I'm a loving woman.' Tears were standing in her soft warm tender eyes. 'Since his death, I have simply gone on living. For the sake of the children. Oh, I don't mean to be tragic, I don't want to be sad, it's silly to cry . . .'

Napoleon said involuntarily, 'No . . .'

She said, not looking at him, obviously trying to hold back her tears, 'My life is full of amusements. I have friends, I go to dinners, I go to dances. But the friends are only friends, and the amusements are not happiness. Since Alexander, there's been no one, no one at all, who has been more than a friend. It's very lonely, for a woman who has so much love still to offer, and who wants to be loved.'

She turned towards him and looked up at him with beautiful wet eyes. Napoleon was disturbed deeply, profoundly, to the depths of his being.

She said, in a small voice, 'Help me to find a little happiness.'

Her eyes were raised to him. Her mouth was raised to him. He took her in his arms and kissed her, with a wild passionate protectiveness.

That night in her bed, in her arms, he murmured, 'My darling Josephine . . .'

She murmured, 'Darling, my name is Rose . . .'

He murmured, 'My name for you is Josephine.'

She murmured, 'Mmm . . . Happiness . . .'

For him, it was a happiness incredibly far beyond anything he had ever experienced, far far beyond anything he had ever even imagined. Her body was a revelation to him, a miracle of nature. Her love-making was a miracle of art. He had not known that his own body, his own love-making, could be miraculous too, with a miraculous partner.

Afterwards, in his own apartment, he wrote to her:

Seven in the morning. I awake full of you. The memory of yesterday's enchanting evening will not let me rest. Dearest, incomparable Josephine, what power you have over my innermost self!—You will wake at noon and read this letter. Three hours later I shall be with you. Till then, *mio dolce amor,* I send you a thousand kisses, but send me none, for your kisses are still with me, your kisses are burning my heart!

4. JOSEPHINE

She went to Paul Barras's office, to talk to him. Barras decided to be particularly difficult and obtuse. He seemed to take a pleasure in deliberately annoying her. For the first time for a long time, she found herself almost on the point of losing her temper. She simply could not manage to make Barras understand what the situation really and actually and truthfully was.

She said, yet again, in a voice that was starting to get out of control, 'Yes, Bonaparte comes to my house. Yes, he admires me, he pays court to me. Yes, he says he's in love with me. But I do not go to bed with him. And I shall not. I don't want to. However much you want me to.'

Barras, infuriatingly at his ease, said, 'Rose darling, I'm not accusing you of anything, except of being a liar.'

She cried in a passion of indignation, 'I am telling the truth!'

'I do admire you for the way you say that. It would convince anyone, except me.'

'I do not want your General Bonaparte!'

'Oh, really? Whom do you want?—What a stupid thing to ask. I take it back, I didn't say it.'

She pronounced, with tremendous emphasis, 'I . . . want . . .'

'Oh God, don't say it's me.'

She threw away her big voice and used her small one. 'You used to love me.'

'Rose, if you're going to use words like "love" I shall have to ask you to leave.'

She started to cry. She was good at crying. At the moment it seemed to be the only thing left to do. But Barras continued to be heartless.

'Darling, I have seen you cry far too often—'

A secretary came quickly in at the door.

'Get out!'

The secretary went out again, even faster. Barras smiled.

'There. Wasn't that thoughtful of me? You must never be seen with your make-up streaky.'

She said, 'You are a swine.'

'Yes.'

'You want to get rid of me.'

'No.'

'You do. Don't you?'

'I have no wish to get rid of you. I should rather like to get rid of the cost of you.'

'It's the same thing.'

'I do hope not. Rose, you're being mercenary. I am being practical.'

'You are being a swine.'

'Rose, you and Thérèse are the two most expensive women in the world. I know Thérèse's father is a banker, but he's doing rather badly at the moment. And I know I'm rich: but not even Croesus could support the pair of you.'

She said, in a hard voice, 'Give up Thérèse.'

'I told you, I never give up a mistress. Especially a young one.'

She couldn't stop herself. Her hand flew out and slapped his face.

Barras said imperturbably, 'And she's your best friend. Extraordinary. You're so different. You go to bed with men because you enjoy it. She goes to bed with men because they enjoy it.'

'My men enjoy it more than hers.'

He considered the statement for a moment. He was fair-minded in these matters.

'Yes, that's true. She has great generosity but no great skill as yet. She is young.'

'And I am not young?'

He smiled politely. 'Darling, you are thirty-two.'

'Twenty-eight.'

'Of course, twenty-eight. Actually thirty-two. Time you had a settled position in life. Do you know what you should do with General Bonaparte?'

'I've told you, I don't want him!'

He said quietly—the good friend, the sensible adviser —'Rose dear, you are almost penniless, and a terrible spendthrift. You don't have to want him. But marry him.'

When she got back to her house, later than she had intended, Bonaparte was there already, pacing up and down her boudoir in that maddeningly military way of his: impatient to see her, nervous, anxious. The moment she came into the room he ran to her and clasped her in his arms.

'My darling, my heart, my angel, my treasure. I was dying of impatience. But now you've come . . .' He gazed into her face. 'You've been crying!'

'No . . .' But she knew that she couldn't deny it. Tears were the best of all weapons; but after crying she needed half an hour alone with her make-up box.

'You've been crying! Why? Tell me! Please! If anything has caused you pain—if anyone has caused you pain—you must tell me!'

He tried to hold her, but she escaped from his arms. She needed to be at a little distance from him, under not too close a scrutiny, while she decided what had happened to make her cry. It was not just a question of inventing a good story which he would believe. The story had to be made to serve several of her purposes, all at the same time.

She said, 'I went to see Paul Barras. He'd asked me to come. I didn't know why. But I thought I might be able to talk to him about . . . about you.'

'About me?'

'About your being given command in Italy. Paul's a very old friend. And you said yourself, the question of the command would be decided by the Directory, and he is the most influential of the directors. But . . .' She decided to risk it. 'Napoleon. Forgive me. There's something I've never told you. I've never dared to tell you.'

'What?'

She said, with heroic candour, 'For some months now, Paul Barras has been paying court to me. Trying to make love to me. Trying to persuade me to become his mistress.'

A sound came from Bonaparte's mouth, like a long-drawn sigh, but its meaning was surprise and horror.

'Of course, I wouldn't dream of it. I told him so a hundred times. But he refused to give up hope, whatever I said. And now—you know he's been pretending to be mad about Thérèse Tallien, he goes everywhere with her—'

'Yes . . . ?'

'It was simply to try to make me jealous. He told me that today. He offered to give up Thérèse, completely, if only I would . . . you know . . . do what he wanted . . .'

The long-drawn sigh again.

'And when I rejected him again, I wouldn't even listen to him, he—oh, darling, I don't want to tell you this, but he got hold of me, and tried to . . . tried to *make* me . . .'

'What?'

'I screamed. Someone rushed in. And then I think I must have fainted.'

Bonaparte, eyes blazing, beside himself with fury, said, 'I shall kill him!'

She had gone too far. 'No! No, darling.'

'I shall challenge him to a duel. And kill him.'

'No. No, you mustn't. He's a friend.'

'He's a swine!'

'Yes, but . . . Darling . . .'

She went to Bonaparte, and put her soft arms round his neck, and made him look into her soft eyes, and kissed him with her flower-soft mouth.

'Darling, yes, he was wrong to want me like that. But he's a good friend. A useful friend. He's very important, he can be very useful. Darling, think what he can do for your career. Think of Italy.' She saw that she was winning. 'Darling, we must both think of your career. And Barras knows now that he must never say such things to me again. Darling, forgive him. And kiss me.'

She saw that she had won. He kissed her.

Barras said, 'I think the Italian command will almost certainly go to you. I say "almost", because . . . well, Carnot doesn't like you, but he's in favour of your appointment, and he is, of course, our great military expert. I need hardly tell you that I myself am devoted to your interests. However, the other three directors are still wavering, and might go one way or might go another.'

Napoleon said, 'Who are my rivals for the job?'

'There would be no question of rivals, if only . . .'

'If only what?'

Barras took him into his confidence. 'You know how dreadfully conservative all revolutionaries are. You are young.'

'In war, youth is an advantage.'

'Yes, but not in old men's eyes. And you are Corsican.'

'I am French.'

'Yes, but not French French. We are so insular.'

Napoleon said, 'I am twenty-six until next August. I can't change the date of my birth—nor the place of it.'

'You could do something to help.'

'What?'

'Have you thought of getting married?'

'I have thought of it.'

'A Frenchwoman, of course. It would give you more Frenchness. And more—forgive the word—more substance. More solidity.'

'I have thought of that too.'

Barras said judicially, 'If you married a suitable person, the Italian appointment would be—what shall I say?—in the bag.'

'You believe?'

'I guarantee it.'

Napoleon brooded. Barras glanced at him. The moment had come for the brilliant suggestion.

Barras, obviously running through in his mind a hundred first-class possibilities, said, 'Why don't you marry someone like—let's think—Rose Beauharnais? Old French family—noble, which is not at all a bad thing these days. Husband commanded the Army of the Rhine at one point —an idiot as a soldier, he was guillotined for inefficiency, but we've forgotten that by now. Yes, she'd do quite well. And, of course, she's rich.'

Napoleon raised his head sharply. 'Is she?'

'My dear fellow, didn't you know? All those plantations in Martinique? She's rich as Croesus.'

Barras could see that he had said enough. A suggestion, however brilliant, must never seem to be more than a suggestion. It was time to turn the conversation to other things. But he had to take one precaution first.

'If you're interested in the idea, you could talk to Jerome Calmelet, who handles her business affairs. Do you know Calmelet?'

'No, I don't.'

Now the precaution. 'Say so, and I'll have a word with him first.'

Josephine said, 'No! I won't marry you!'

'Josephine—'

'You just want my money!'

'Josephine, I love you for yourself alone—'

'Then why did you go to see Calmelet?'

'Ah. I—'

'Behind my back?'

'I went to see Calmelet—'

'To find out if I was rich!'

'No!'

'And what did he tell you?'

'That you were rich—'

'Exactly! So then you asked me to marry you!'

He stood silent, because there was nothing he could say, and anything he could say would be misinterpreted and turned against him. But silence might lose everything, and he could not afford to lose.

'Josephine . . . my darling . . . if you can think that, then you are unfair to me, and I am the unhappiest man in the world. How can you possibly believe that I don't love you for your own sake? For whose sake, then?'

Josephine, wounded, unhappy, on the brink of tears, said, 'My money.'

'No! Never! I want you with nothing! With nothing at all!'

'I don't believe you.'

'I'll prove it to you!'

'You say that. But you can't prove it. You know you can't.'

He felt strangely exalted, as if this were his moment of decision, his moment of destiny, the moment that would decide his future life. The words sprang into his mouth.

'I'll prove it! I'll behave as if you came to me with nothing! I'll ask for nothing from you! Everything you own now will continue to be yours as it is now! Everything I give you will be yours and yours alone! I'll make you an allowance from my pay as a general! To continue for life! Because I want to be your husband for life!' He could feel that she was softening, she was weakening, she was giving way. 'Josephine, I adore you. I want you by my side every day of my life. I want you in my arms every night of my life. I want to be a father to your children. I want you to give me more children, my children. But, most of all, I want *you!* I want you to be my wife, my partner, my helper . . .'

She said, in the tiniest possible voice, 'And you don't want my money?'

'No, no, no!'

'But I've discovered what you do want. You want me to help you get the Italian command. As I can help you.'

'I want you whether you can help me or not.'

She said, with that extraordinary simplicity of hers, 'But if I'm your wife, of course I will help you. I think a wife must always help her husband as much as she can. It's very important to help one's husband. Really help him.'

She was his. He threw himself at her feet.
'I worship you.'

Josephine's friends swarmed to her house in the rue Chantereine, to congratulate her doubly, on her forthcoming marriage and on General Bonaparte's appointment as Commander-in-Chief of the Army of Italy. Paul Barras came with Thérèse: smiling benevolently, implying without quite saying it that he had played more than a small part in bringing about both these happy events.

Her lawyer Raguideau arrived at the house as the last few guests were leaving. Madame Beauharnais received him with perfect courtesy, as always; with great charm, as always. Raguideau was ugly and dwarfish, almost a dwarf, but she made him feel well-made and handsome. Yet, behind the courtesy and the charm, there was that morning something else which was not at all usual. Some secret thought was amusing her. She was trying very hard not to laugh. Raguideau could not imagine why. What he had come to see her about was hardly a laughing matter. But, certainly, a laugh was bubbling inside her, doing its best to find its way out. Her eyes were laughing, and most of all when they glanced towards the window recess. Why the window recess? Raguideau could see nothing there but the curtain. Well, laughter or no laughter, he had to proceed to business. He took his draft of the marriage contract from his bag.

'Would you care to read it, Madame? Or would you prefer me to read it out to you, together with my comments and explanations?'

'Read it out to me, please.'

'Certainly, Madame.'

'Read it loudly. And clearly.'

'Loudly?'

'And clearly. Please.'

She was glancing towards the window recess again. Why?

He cleared his throat. 'May I have your permission to begin with a general comment which applies to the whole contract, and indeed to the whole question of the marriage?'

'Please do.'

'As your legal adviser, I feel that I should be failing in my duty if I did not give you my most careful opinion, without any concealment or reservation—'

'Raguideau, I am longing to hear it.'

'Madame Beauharnais,' he said, in a suitably solemn voice—he prided himself that it was quietly impressive—'I advise you against this marriage.'

'Could you say that again? Louder?'

'I beg your pardon, Madame?'

'I'm not quite certain I heard you properly. And I do want to be quite sure. Louder? Dear Raguideau? Please?'

He said it again, louder, since she wished it. 'Madame, I advise you against this marriage.'

'Do you? Why?'

'I entreat you, Madame, break it off before it's too late. This man is an adventurer, a Corsican adventurer. He has nothing—absolutely nothing—but his uniform and his sword.'

'Raguideau, I'm sure you're right, and that's very good advice, and I'm grateful. But I don't think I can break it off now.'

'You are not yet married, Madame.'

'But I have to marry him next week, before he leaves for Italy. It's all arranged, Raguideau. Really, honestly, I can't change it.'

'If it is your considered decision—'

'I'm afraid it is.'

'—then at the very least I must insist on giving you the fullest protection in this contract.' He opened out the document and adjusted his spectacles importantly. 'I have, for example, inserted a clause here, in which General Bonaparte specifically declares that he owns neither land nor goods of any kind apart from his personal wardrobe and his military accountrements—'

General Bonaparte strode from behind the curtain and said, 'Strike out that clause.'

Raguideau stared at him. 'I beg your—?'

'Strike it out!'

Josephine said sweetly, 'Raguideau, I don't think you've met General Bonaparte?'

General Bonaparte said, 'I am the Commander-in-Chief of the Army of Italy. This is my uniform. This is my sword. I am going to be richer than any man you have ever known.'

The municipality had taken over the once-splendid house of the noble Mondragons as the Town Hall of the Second Arrondissement. The marble, the gilt, the panelling—whatever was immovable—had survived the Revolution, drably and dingily. The furniture had not survived.

At eight o'clock in the evening Citizeness Beauharnais arrived at the mayor's office with her three witnesses: Paul Barras, Jean Tallien, Jerome Calmelet. It had seemed to her appropriate to invite Thérèse's husband.

At nine o'clock the mayor grew tired of waiting, even for a general, and went off home to his supper.

At ten o'clock there was the clattering and clanking of two soldiers hurrying along the corridor, and Napoleon came in at a quick march, with an out-of-breath lieutenant at his heels.

He marched to Josephine and kissed her hand. 'A thousand apologies. Work. Where's the mayor?'

Barras said, 'The mayor's gone. That thing there is the acting registrar.'

Napoleon looked and saw a scarecrow asleep on a chair by the miserable fire.

'That?'

'That.'

He marched to the scarecrow and shook it. 'Come on, marry us as fast as you can!'

'What?'

'Come on! I've only got forty-eight hours!'

The scarecrow staggered to its feet, or rather to its foot, and hobbled—it had a wooden leg—to the desk.

'Birth certificates?'

Barras quickly produced and presented a document, and said, with a perfectly straight face, 'Sworn statement that Citizeness Beauharnais was born in Martinique, at present occupied by the English, and that it is therefore impossible for her to produce a birth certificate.'

'Age, then?'

With an even straighter face, Josephine said, 'Twenty-eight.'

Napoleon thrust forward a similar piece of paper. 'Sworn statement that I was born in Corsica, at present occupied by the English, and therefore cannot produce a birth certificate.'

'Age?'

With a face as straight as anyone, Napoleon said, 'Twenty-eight.'

Barras allowed himself to smile, at last. He had enjoyed helping Josephine to subtract four years; he had not known that Napoleon would add two. The equalization of their ages would make a splendidly repeatable joke.

The one-legged scarecrow said, 'General Bonaparte, citizen, do you consent to take as your lawful wife Madame Beauharnais, here present, to keep faith with her, and to observe conjugal fidelity?'

General Bonaparte said, 'Citizen, I do.'

'Madame Beauharnais, citizeness, do you consent to take as your lawful husband General Bonaparte, here present, to keep faith with him, and to observe conjugal fidelity?'

Madame Beauharnais said, 'Citizen, I do.'

The scarecrow seemed to be considering what to say next. Napoleon said, 'For God's sake get on with it! I leave for Italy the day after tomorrow!'

The scarecrow, galvanized, said, 'General Bonaparte and Madame Beauharnais, the law unites you.'

Désirée, in her room in Marseille, not crying, but trembling a little, wrote:

So you are married! Your poor Eugénie must no longer love you or think of you. Married! I cannot face the thought! I cannot survive it! But I know that I must try to be brave, and must wish you all happiness in your marriage. I pray that the wife you have chosen instead of me will make you as happy as I had hoped to make you, and as you deserve to be. All I ask of you is that in the midst of your happiness you spare a moment to pity the fate of Eugénie, and that you do not quite forget her . . .

Napoleon wrote to the Directory:

I have requested Citizen Barras to inform the Executive Directors of my marriage with Citizeness Beauharnais. The trust in me which the Directory has shown makes it my duty to inform the Directory of all my actions. My marriage is a new bond to unite me to my country. It is one more pledge of my firm resolve to entrust all my fortunes to the Republic.

While Junot waited by the door, Napoleon said to Josephine, 'I'll send for you as soon as I can. As soon as it's safe for you to come and join me. In the meantime, I'll write to you every day.'

'I shall live for your letters.'

'And you must write to me every day.'

She said, 'Darling, I'm so bad at writing letters.'

'Every day. Promise me.'

'I'll try.'

They embraced. She clung to him as if she would never let him go.

The next day, Barras, giving a reception, greeted Madame Bonaparte as she arrived.

'So he's gone.'

'Yes.'

'We must have supper one evening soon.'

She smiled. 'If you are free?'

'I can be free.'

'I shall invite you. Quite soon.'

They exchanged beautiful smiles.

He said, 'I did promise your husband to look after you.'

Napoleon, in the big carriage that was bowling bumpily along the long road to Italy, took from the pocket nearest his heart a miniature of Josephine, and gazed at it in adoration and pride.

Junot and Marmont caught each other's eye. Their Commander-in-Chief was becoming as regular in his habits as clockwork. They waited for the next thing he would do.

He did it, as he had done it every hour before. He handed the miniature to Junot, carefully, reverently.

'Look at her.'

Junot looked, and said, 'Beautiful.'

After a suitable period of looking he handed the miniature to Marmont. Marmont said, 'Really beautiful,' and handed it back to Napoleon.

Napoleon said, 'I am married to the most wonderful woman in the world.'

5. GENERAL BONAPARTE'S WIFE

Junot gave his last-moment advice in an undertone. 'Look him straight in the eye.'

Murat, never less than superb, said, 'Where else?'

Junot marched into General Bonaparte's office, saluted, and said, 'Colonel Murat requests an interview, sir.'

The idea had been for Murat to stay outside till General Bonaparte gave permission for his entrance, but the big stupid Gascon marched in behind Junot.

'Colonel Murat reporting, sir!'

Murat and the general looked each other straight in the eye. Murat made it quite clear that he was willing to go on not blinking for ever.

'Colonel?'

'Substantive major, acting colonel, sir. Promotion because I got those guns for you in Paris. You remember the guns, sir.'

'What are you doing here in Nice, Colonel Murat?'

'Come to join you, sir.'

'Have you been posted to the Army of Italy?'

'Look to you to arrange the posting, sir.'

'Posting as what?'

'You have no colonel aide-de-camp, sir. A Commander-in-Chief must have a colonel aide-de-camp, sir.'

The general turned a keen eye on Junot, his newly promoted major aide-de-camp. Junot did his best to blush and decided to grin instead.

'Colonel Murat's a friend of mine, sir. I told him.'

Murat generously decided to add a word or two of explanation. 'Decided to transfer from my own regiment, sir. My regiment's not fighting. You're going to fight.'

The general said, 'You like fighting?'

'Yes, sir.'

'Why?'

'From Gascony, sir. Gascons like it.'

The general said, 'You did well, bringing those guns from Sablons.'

'Thank you, sir.' Murat made it clear that the compliment was deserved.

'But what do you know about war?'

Murat considered for a moment. Then a brightness came into his eye. He had thought of the answer.

'Good for quick promotion, sir.'

'Anything else?'

'Good for loot.'

'Anything else?'

Murat considered deeply. Was there anything else? Thank God, the answer flashed into his mind: at least, a perfectly good answer.

'Women?'

Napoleon, late that night, alone at last in his office, by the light of a single candle, wrote:

I have not spent one day without adoring you; I have not spent one night without imagining you in my arms; I have not passed one hour without cursing the ambition and the desire for glory which have torn me away from you. Tomorrow we march into Italy. But what are the tortures of hell, to one who suffers as I am suffering? You do not love me as much as you did, you perhaps have already consoled yourself, you have not written to me for four days! Josephine! Josephine! Tell me! Have you ceased loving me?

When she entered Barras's salon there was a great excited murmur from those present, a buzz of words which was, in effect, a round of applause. Her host came to greet her more quickly than he had ever done before. He kissed her hand with positively unprecedented admiration.

'My dear Rose. Or shall I say Josephine?'

'Whichever you wish.'

The others could see them but not hear.

'Rose last night, Josephine now.'

She smiled. 'Ah, last night was a whim.'

'Of yours, and of mine.'

'It was nostalgic.'

'I was grateful. But how much more grateful I would have been—let me lower my voice, though I'm sure they can't hear us—if I had known that I was making love to the wife of our most successful general.'

'Oh, were you? Is he?'

'Does no one tell you the news?'

'Yes, sometimes. What news?'

'Darling, doesn't your husband write to you?'

'Incessantly.'

'Did you receive a letter today?'

'Every day.'

'Then you must know.'

Josephine said, 'His handwriting is almost illegible. I save them up for when I'm feeling particularly strong.'

Barras looked over Josephine's shoulder and said quickly, 'Carnot's on his way towards us. Listen. Bonaparte has won three battles in five days, the Austrians have lost four thousand men, the Piedmontese are already asking for an armistice—'

He broke off as Carnot came up to them: the organizer of the victories of 1793, now the strategist of the Directory.

Carnot said, 'Madame Bonaparte, your husband is the most brilliant soldier—'

'Since you, general.'

'Since better men than me, a hundred years ago or more. D'you know what he's done?'

Josephine said, hoping she'd got it right, 'Won three battles in five days—'

'With unpaid, unclothed underfed troops. By sheer military genius.'

'I'm so glad.'

'There's just one thing which I'm afraid will make you not so glad.'

'Oh?'

'We can't let you go there and join him. At least not yet.'

Josephine looked at Barras with a mute request for help. What on earth was Carnot talking about?

Barras said, 'We received a letter from your husband today, asking for our permission, as members of the Directory—but I'm so sorry, we can't possibly allow you yet . . .'

'Allow me to join him?'

Carnot said, 'Our apologies, Madame. For the best of all reasons—for the success of the campaign—we must refuse our permission. I've seen generals with a wife by their side. It takes their mind off the business in hand. We must ask you to be patient.'

He bowed stiffly and moved away. Barras allowed himself the discreetest possible smile.

'Carnot is, of course, our greatest expert on these matters.'

Thérèse Tallien came up, radiant, embracing Josephine. 'My angel, my darling, I missed your entrance—was it superb?'

Barras said it for her. 'Superb.'

'Of course. You're the heroine of the hour. Well, Bonaparte is the hero of the hour, so you must be the heroine, mustn't you? Mustn't she, Paul?'

'Indeed she must.'

Josephine said, rather faintly, 'Thérèse, dear, shall we sit down for a moment?'

'Yes, of course. Why?'

'I have to recover. I think I've just had a narrow escape.'

At two in the morning, Napoleon sat at a rustic table, in a farmhouse in the hills above Lodi, and wrote:

I have received the letter which you were obliged to send unfinished because you were going to the country. In the spring it is much more pleasant in the country, and no doubt you have a nineteen-year-old lover with you. I am in despair: your letter is as cold as friendship. But how strange of me to complain! Your first letters were too warm, they excited my senses, I longed for something cooler; but now what you send me has the icy coldness of death . . .

Josephine read, out loud but haltingly, because the handwriting was so appalling:

' "My dearest, I am not jealous, only troubed. The fear of not being loved by you—ah, if you are ever untrue, beware the vengeance of Othello!" '

She looked up from the letter and smiled at Arnault and Hamelin and Louise.

'He really is a strange man, Bonaparte.'

Then she was reading the letter again:

' "But I create these tortures for myself. Farewell until tomorrow, *mio dolce amor*. The thought of my wife and the thought of my victory over fate: these are all I have in my mind, these are my only desires . . ." Don't you think that's strange?'

Arnault said, 'To love you so much?'

'To be jealous and not jealous, to want me warmer and colder . . .'

'I think he's a better poet than I am.'

'This is poetry?'

'Raw poetry. Naked poetry.'

'Dear Arnault, you wrote me such a pretty poem.'

'Dear Madame, I am your worshipper. But if I had felt as strongly as your husband feels, then my poem would have been less pretty, but more beautiful.'

Josephine said, 'I think I like poems to be . . .'

'Pretty?'

'I was going to say, civilized. Hamelin, don't you agree?'

Hamelin said, 'I am equally your worshipper. But alas, no judge of verses.'

'And I like letters to be witty, and full of gossip—'

'Ah yes, there I'm with you.'

'—and scandalous stories about people I know, and jokes that I can tell to my friends before they tell them to me.'

Arnault smiled. 'Yes, I do see that Bonaparte is sadly lacking.'

'So there! You both agree with me.'

Louise Compoint said, 'And reports on the latest fashions—'

'Exactly!' Josephine was triumphant. 'When has he written me a single word about the fashions in Italy?'

'Not once,' Louise said.

'Never! You see?'

Hamelin said, 'I'm sure he could tell you the fashion in greatcoats.'

'No, he has no feeling even for uniform. So long as it keeps the cold out. As if one wore clothes to do that!'

Arnault looked at the gossamer muslin that showed rather than covered her breasts.

'Josephine, what do you really think of your husband?'

She said, after a moment, 'I think he is a very brave man.'

'But . . . ?'

'I wish he could learn to be amusing.'

Thérèse Tallien sailed in, escorted by a splendid Hussar, all silver braid and gold lace.

'Darling, I brought Captain Charles, because he simply must be here when I show you.'

'Show me what?'

'This!'

Thérèse threw off the cashmere shawl that covered her head.

'Oh!' cried Josephine and Louise.

'Isn't it marvellous?'

Over her short dark curls she wore an even curlier blonde wig.

'Thérèse! You've done it!'

'Charles made me. He insisted.'

Captain Charles said, 'Don't you think it's the most heavenly thing?'

'It's incredible.'

'I assure you, blonde wigs are going to be all the rage.'

Thérèse said to Josephine, 'You must get one too. Straight away.'

Charles said, 'A month from now, any woman with dark hair will be painfully conspicuous in good society.'

Josephine looked at him, amused. His hair was positively black. 'And any man?'

'Thank heavens, dark-haired men will still be *à la mode*.'

Arnault said to her, 'You must write and tell your husband.'

'Oh yes, he's dark, isn't he?' said Charles.

'More dark than fair.'

'Then he will pass.'

Arnault said, 'I think he will.'

Thérèse Tallien clapped her hands at the thought of a pleasure. 'Oh, Charles has the most marvellous new joke about Bonaparte. Charles, do tell it.'

'If you're sure they haven't heard it?'

'Quite, quite sure.'

Charles looked questioningly at Josephine. 'May I—?'

'Please—I adore new jokes.'

He glanced round to make sure that they were all ready for it.

'It's a riddle. Why is the Austrian Emperor feeling so constipated? Because Bonaparte is on the Po!'

He laughed, and they laughed, Josephine as much as anyone.

She really did adore new jokes.

Napoleon wrote:

Murat will be with you by the time you receive this. By now he will have explained to you, my adorable darling, what I have done so far, what I am going to do, and what I am longing for. I sent Junot to Paris, with my brother Joseph, three days before Murat started, and gave Junot orders to bring you back here. But Junot had to go by the coast road, which takes a week longer; so Murat will be in Paris first, and you must come to Italy with him. If by any chance you cannot come immediately, I shall be inconsolable. But surely you will come, you will be here, at my side, at my heart, at my lips, in my arms. Take wings, come, come! . . .

Barras, in his office at the Luxembourg, smiled agreeably at Murat and said, 'On the question of his wife, General Bonaparte has already written to us more than once.'

Murat, equally agreeable, said, 'So I imagine.'

'Until now, the view of the Directory has been against allowing the general's request.'

'I imagine that, too.'

'For obvious reasons.'

'Yes, I'm sure.'

'What makes a man fight? What makes a man fight at his best?'

Murat said, 'Look, I agree with you. I'm just telling you what Bonaparte wants.'

'You've made it very clear. But we must consider the success of the whole campaign.'

Murat said, 'I have orders to fetch her. Whatever you say.'

Josephine came in, at her prettiest.

Barras said, though his smile was wearing thin, 'And, of course, we must consider Madame Bonaparte herself.' He bowed and kissed Josephine's hand. 'Dear Madame, how kind of you to come here so very promptly.'

She was being her most charming. 'When I heard that Colonel Murat had arrived—'

Barras said, quickly but gently, to help her—'General Murat.'

'General?' Her most enchanting smile. 'Congratulations.'

Murat said, 'Brigadier-general. I was lucky, some people got killed.'

Barras said, 'General Murat has brought us the terms of the armistice which your husband has made with the King of Piedmont—'

'Oh, yes?'

'—and also a reaffirmation of your husband's desire to have you with him in Italy.'

'Oh.'

'Which, of course, I must discuss with the other members of the Directory.'

Murat said to her affably, 'I have orders from Bonaparte to take you back with me.'

Josephine's most enchanting smile was fixed on her face.

'General, I'm sure you have a thousand things to do in Paris. But you must come to lunch with me very soon, and tell me all your news.'

'Delighted.'

'I do so want to talk to you, and hear all about Italy, and all about the campaign.'

'Whenever you wish, Madame.'

'Tomorrow? Lunch tomorrow?'

'Delighted.'

'Tomorrow, then.'

Murat said, 'I have orders from Bonaparte to write to him telling him the situation here, as soon as we've talked.'

Josephine said, 'Yes, of course you must write to him. After we've talked tomorrow.—I've a better idea, not lunch, there'll be dozens of people at lunch, it'll be difficult to have more than a few moments together. Supper. Come to supper. And we can really talk, for as long as we like.'

Murat's eye gleamed. 'Delighted.'

'Supper, then. Tomorrow.'

Murat bowed, and kissed her hand, and went. Barras

said, 'How enjoyable to see you practise your wiles on someone else.'

Josephine, smiling no longer, said sharply, 'I will not go to Italy.'

Barras continued to find the subject enjoyable. 'My dear, you must grasp the fact that any decisions about you, from now on, are entirely political.'

'I will not follow an army, and live in ditches.'

'I don't think Bonaparte does that.'

She was starting to be petulant and plaintive. 'Italy is a stupid boring country. And all my friends are here.'

'And your husband is there.'

'If he wants to see me, he can come back to Paris.'

'No. I'm afraid we won't allow that.'

'On leave. Soldiers get leave.'

Barras said—though he never had any great hope of getting her to understand a political necessity—'Bonaparte, in less than two months, has smashed half the Austrian Army.'

'Well? Give him a week's leave. He's earned it.'

'If he is to carry on at the same rate—'

'You mean you don't want to give him leave.'

He sighed. She really was much too concerned with her own personal wishes and whims. 'I mean we want him to carry on at the same rate. Not so much in order to smash the other half of the Austrians. But because this country is bankrupt, and we can get fifty or a hundred million francs out of Italy. Indemnities from all those little kingdoms and dukedoms. Penalties. Protection money. Blackmail. Quite apart from the loot which is more straightforwardly stolen. I'm sending your husband a dozen art experts, to pick out the most valuable paintings from all those Italian galleries, to wrap them up and to send them back here . . . There is a great marvellous mass of money there for the taking. That money can save France, and the government.'

'And you,' she challenged him.

'And me. I am a part of the government.'

'I am not.'

He raised his eyebrows. 'You are the wife of the liberator of Italy. Of our potential saviour. You can't imagine how proud I am these days—those nights—when you invite me to your bed.'

He was being impossible. She decided to make things clear to him, once and for all.

'Barras. I will not go.'

'Shall I tempt you with a thought?'

'I can tempt you. I don't really think you can tempt me.'

But, he thought to himself, one can always appeal to your desire for money.

'We have already written to Bonaparte—'

'We?'

'We, the Directory. We've decided to split the Italian command into two parts. We shall send General Kellermann to take over the war in the north, against the Austrians; it's bound to be rather dreary from now on. Kellermann can do it as well as anyone else. And that will leave Bonaparte free to march south, through the Papal States, down to Rome, down to Naples. Liberating. And plundering.'

She said, stony-faced, 'I am not tempted.'

'I need hardly tell you, there has never yet been a general who didn't keep a percentage of the plunder for himself. Good heavens, we don't mind, it's normal. But it's bound to make Bonaparte one of the richest men in Europe.'

Her voice was diamond-hard, with a cutting edge. 'Then he'll be able to afford an expensive wife in Paris.'

'Ah. I must explain. He's the perfect person for the job, he moves so fast, quite incredibly fast. But do you see our problem?'

'No.'

'Will he move faster if he has you there, in his arms, in his bed; or if we keep you here, and he has to finish the job before he can have you in his arms again?'

'Obviously, if you keep me here.'

'But—will he grow discontented and rebellious; will

68

he cease doing what we want him to do; if we continue to refuse him the pleasure of his wife's company?'

Josephine—bad-tempered, mutinous—said, 'I can be ill. Not well enough to travel.'

'Yes. But for how many months?'

She suddenly smiled.

'Thank you, Paul.'

'Oh, why?'

'You have given me an idea.'

In Milan, Napoleon dictated letters to Marmont, who had invented a serviceable form of shorthand to keep pace with the fast staccato utterance.

'. . . "No doubt General Kellermann would fight the campaign as well as I have done; but to divide the command in Italy would in my opinion ruin everything. Kellermann believes himself to be a good general—"'

Marmont gave a little whistle, between his teeth, as a warning signal. Napoleon paid no attention.

'"—but I cannot agree to serve with him; and in any case I am convinced that one bad general is worth more than two good ones. War, like government, is a question of tact."'

Marmont murmured, 'Right.'

'"In the present situation in Italy . . ."—which they know nothing about, except what I tell them—'

'Put that in the letter?'

'No . . . "—it is essential that you have a single commander-in-chief, in whom you place your complete confidence. If it is not myself; if Kellermann arrives on this side of the Alps; then I shall not complain; but I shall resign my command and return to Paris forthwith."'

'End of letter?'

'Yes . . . And I am worth more than a government which can give an order like that.'

'Paul Barras, I should think. The style is his.'

'They are all incapable of governing. They have no judgement in large matters.' Napoleon suddenly laughed. 'Well, that tells them what to do.'

'Yes, it does.'

'Oh, add another paragraph, while I'm in the mood for giving them orders. "On the question of my wife, I must once again insist—" '

Almost automatically he had taken the miniature of Josephine from his breast pocket, to gaze at her while he spoke of her. He looked at the miniature, and the colour vanished from his cheeks.

' "—once again insist—"?' said Marmont.

He turned his eyes to Napoleon. Napoleon was white-faced, ghastly, trembling, staring at the miniature.

'Marmont. The glass is broken.'

Marmont deliberately kept his voice level and matter-of-fact. 'Give it to me, sir. I'll have a new glass put in.'

'Marmont. My wife is ill.'

'No. Why? Why should you think that?'

'I am Corsican. We have second sight.' He grasped Marmont's arm tightly, painfully. His whole body was trembling uncontrollably. 'My wife is ill, or unfaithful.'

After supper, in the house in rue Chantereine, Josephine arranged herself on the chaise-longue to make the prettiest possible picture, and seated Murat where he would have the best possible view of the picture.

Her eyes spoke sincere admiration, almost to the point of hero-worship.

'It must have been terribly difficult for you, fighting in those mountains.'

'Yes. It was rough work, I suppose.'

'It was marvellous, how you fought your way across the Alps so quickly.'

'Well, the troops hadn't eaten for weeks and hadn't been paid for months. You've no idea what an incentive that gave them, to get through to those cities in the plain.'

Josephine felt rather annoyed. Murat was dismissing her compliments too airily, as if they weren't really compliments. She decided to make them more obvious: he was stupid enough not to mind.

'You must be very brave.'

'I'm from Gascony.'

'Of course. I should have guessed.'

'We're natural soldiers.'

She saw it all now: he had such a good conceit of himself, it was quite impossible to flatter him. It also was quite impossible to tempt him, since he already believed himself to be totally irresistible. Obviously one could go to bed with him, but that would achieve nothing: he would simply take it as a matter of course. She wondered if the best technique might be almost to go to bed with him, but not quite.

She said, 'I adore very brave men.'

He gave her his most irresistible leer. 'As we adore very beautiful women.'

'Who are "we"? Gascons?'

'And cavalrymen. And Gascon cavalrymen twice as much as anyone else.'

'War and women.'

'That's what we live for.'

'And now you're the idol of Paris. Ah, Murat, what a time you're going to have.'

'You think?' He was positively twirling his moustache.

'We're wild about you already. All those victories. Every woman in Paris will be at your feet.'

'Well, yes, I imagine.' His conceit was quite unbelievable.

'The hero's reward,' she said.

'Well, yes, that's the way we look at it.'

It was becoming a game. She was starting to enjoy it. But it was time to turn the conversation to her own purposes.

'Murat, I'm afraid you'll be spoilt if you stay in Paris long enough. How long can you stay?'

'Well, there's this problem.'

Innocently she asked, 'What problem?'

'Bonaparte wants me back in Italy as soon as possible.'

'Of course he does.'

'With you.'

'Of course he wants me there.'

'Yes.'

'He wants. But you must also think of what I want.'

Murat said, 'Madame, I am your very humble servant.'

'Thank you.'

'But he happens to be my Commander-in-Chief.'

She said, 'And I am his Commander-in-Chief.'

'I'm sure you are.'

'So what matters is what I want. And I want . . .' She made a beautifully deliberate pause, and turned her eyes on him.

'What do you want?'

'I want you to stay in Paris as long as you can.'

He was smirking. 'Do you? Why?'

She kept her voice very simple and very sincere. 'Because after all that fighting you've earned a holiday. Because you deserve to be flattered and pampered and spoilt by beautiful women. Because I adore brave men, and Gascon cavalrymen twice as much as anyone else.'

Murat might be slow in apprehension, but he was not backward when a clear opportunity was offered. In the twinkling of an eye he was out of his chair on his knees by her side, seizing her hand and kissing it passionately.

'Dear Madame . . .'

'Josephine.' She corrected him softly.

'Dear Josephine . . .'

She spoke tenderly, but quickly, before the situation could get quite out of control. 'Dear Murat. How strong you are.'

'Yes.'

'Murat, you must be very gentle with me. I must tell you something.'.

'Ah?'

'I would adore to have you make love to me, but . . .' A pause, meaning, do I dare tell him? '. . . but at this moment it's not possible. Shall I let you into a secret?'

'What?'

'No one knows yet, not even Napoleon. You must write to him and break the news to him. I am not very well. It's a difficult time for me, physically, because . . . because I am pregnant.'

Napoleon suddenly appeared in the doorway of his office, shouting for his aides.

'Marmont! Marmont!'

They were so close at hand they didn't need to be shouted for. They followed him quickly into the room.

'Shut the door.'

Muiron shut it. The general had a letter in his hand. He was in a state of high excitement.

'Marmont.'

'Yes, sir?'

'Marmont, I was right.'

'Yes, sir.'

'I told you, I'm Corsican, I see these things, I feel these things. I knew she was unwell. A letter from Murat. She's pregnant.'

'Congratulations, sir.'

'Muiron—'

'Yes, sir?'

'Get me the best decorator in Milan. The best furniture-maker. The best upholsterer. Today.'

'Yes, sir.'

'I must have a suite of rooms made ready for her here. A salon. A boudoir. A bedroom. Whatever she can possibly need. Furnished . . . as for a queen.'

'Yes, sir. I understand, sir.'

'Ready for her quickly. Within a week. I have a presentiment that she has started her journey by now, that she's on her way. She could be here in seven days, if she hurries. But she mustn't hurry. Marmont, I'll write letters to Paris. Now. Or, if she's started, to wherever she is on the road.'

'Yes, sir.'

'She must, above all things, be careful. She is bearing my child.'

Napoleon wrote to her:

> So it is true that you are pregnant! I have Murat's letter. He says that this has made you ill, and that he does not think it advisable for you to undertake such a long journey yet. But I have a presentiment that you are feeling recovered already, and are already on your way, and this thought fills me with the most passionate joy. Of course you must travel by way of Piedmont, the road is much better and shorter, I shall be able to take you in my arms all the sooner. I burn with the desire to see you, and to see how your adorable little belly carries our child. Oh, my darling, you must travel gently, you must travel quietly. You must not be ill. What do a few days matter, so long as you keep our child?—I am Corsican again, I can see the future. I know that you will give me a son. And he will be as beautiful as his mother, and he will love her as much as his father does; and when we are both old—very old— a hundred years old—he will be our comfort and our happiness . . .

Josephine, all suppleness and all grace, was certainly the best dancer in the room, even without being the great General Bonaparte's wife. And her partner, Captain Charles, was equally certainly the best partner. As the dance ended, Barras came up to her to congratulate her, in his invariably charming way.

'For a pregnant woman, you dance incredibly well.'

'I am not very pregnant.'

'No, I didn't think you were.'

'Just a little bit pregnant.'

'But is it wise?'

She opened her wide innocent eyes. 'To dance so well?'

He had led her a few steps apart. 'So well? So much? With Captain Charles?'

'Captain Charles is a marvellous partner.'

'Indeed, he is.'

'The most marvellous dancer.' She smiled at Charles as he joined them.

Charles bowed. 'The first requirement for an officer.'

Barras said coolly, 'In Paris, yes.—Dear Madame, I simply mention the thought that you are not the only person who writes letters to Italy.'

'Do you mean Murat? I've dealt with him.'

'I mean your brother-in-law, Joseph.'

'Is he here?'

'For your own sake, I am taking you to talk to him.'

Junot looked from afar at Josephine as she crossed the room on Barras's arm. Without taking his eyes off her, he said to Murat, 'D'you think Bonaparte knows she used to be his mistress?'

'His? Whose?' Murat deigned to look. 'Oh, Barras!'

Barras brought Josephine to her brother-in-law Joseph. 'Monsieur Bonaparte arrived only yesterday from Italy. I'm sure you're longing to talk.—Monsieur Bonaparte, may I ask you to look after your sister-in-law? She feels a little faint.'

Josephine did her best to seem a little faint. 'It's nothing, really.'

'Nevertheless, you must be careful.'

'Yes, you're right.' She looked appealingly at Joseph. 'If we could sit down?'

Junot and Murat, surveying the field, looked across at delicious Madame Tallien, who was talking to someone of no military importance.

Junot said, 'Who's that with her?'

'Captain Charles.'

'He looks like a hairdresser.'

'Adjutant-General's Department. They all look like hairdressers.'

'She's too good for him.'

'Yes, so I've told her.'

Junot looked sideways at Murat. 'Good enough for you?'

Murat said with superb casualness, 'I must keep up my average. A different woman a night.'

Josephine, not at all strong, charmingly fragile, said to Joseph, 'If you could help explain to him when you write . . .'

'I'll do my best.'

'Thank you, Joseph.'

'Though my brother is not very good at listening to explanations.'

'Tell him I long to be with him. Of course, I do. But more than that: more important than that: I long to give him a child.'

'I'm sure he also thinks that more important.'

'And when one is only two months gone . . .'

'Yes, of course.'

'And such a long journey, on those dreadful bumpy roads . . .'

Two days later, Barras came to call on General Bonaparte's wife.

'To make sure that you are the first to hear the good news, and that I am the first to tell you.'

'What good news?'

'The Directory met this afternoon, and arranged your journey to Italy.'

'What?'

'The thing is decided.'

'But in my present condition——'

'Yes, how are you going to get out of that?'

She was furious with him because of the decision, and even more furious because he was mocking her.

'Why have you changed your minds?'

'Because the situation has changed.'

'How has it changed?'

'New letters from Italy. Your husband has grown, not exactly rebellious, but decidedly discontented.'

'I thought you were going to make him rich.'

'Oh, I imagine that's happening anyway.'

'In Rome, and Naples, and so on——'

'Bonaparte says he can plunder the South with one

hand and conquer the North with the other. And if he says he can, I'm afraid he can.'

'Aren't you the government? Aren't you supposed to decide what he can do and what he can't do?'

Barras spread his hands out wide. 'We're politicians. When a general becomes a great hero, politicians run for shelter.'

'Like cowards.'

'My dear girl, there's no point in quarrelling with Bonaparte over trifles.'

'Am I a trifle?'

'A charming trifle. Yes.'

She started to cry. He watched her politely, but not sympathetically.

He said, 'We have written to your husband, saying that we yield with great reluctance to your strong desire to join him.'

She cried.

He said, 'Look on the bright side. What do you enjoy in life? Dancing, and spending money, and making love. You can do these things in Italy, too.'

She said, 'I hate you.'

'My dear, your husband has a palace waiting for you.'

'I don't want a palace! I want to stay here, in Paris! My house is here! All my friends are here! I like it here!'

'Darling Josephine, in Italy you will reign like a queen.'

Sobbing her heart out, she said, 'I don't want to reign like a queen!'

6. THE QUEEN OF ITALY

She was to travel to Italy with Murat and Junot and
Joseph Bonaparte, and, of course, with Louise Compoint
to be her part-companion and part lady's maid. And
Hamelin was to travel with them, because he was an
old friend and he hoped to do business in Italy. And
Captain Charles was to travel with them because he was
posted to the Adjutant-General's Department in Milan,
and he had become a friend, and it would be so much
pleasanter for him not to have to travel by himself.

Barras had made all the arrangements, and was greatly
concerned for their comfort, and was anxious that nothing should happen to mar their departure or to delay it
for a single moment.

'I've ordered three berlines. They're not quite as comfortable as your chaise-longue, but almost. If you travel
fairly slowly.'

'Towards an impatient husband?'

'Once he knows that you have left Paris he will be a
happier man. And you'll hardly travel fast, with those
mountainous wagonloads of luggage.'

'And in my condition.'

He bowed to her. 'Of course. I had forgotten your
condition.'

'I have not.'

'Dear Josephine, in your berline there will be room
for you to lie down. Ample room. Room for two people
to lie down.'

'No, no, we shall all be busy admiring the countryside. Now, whom shall I choose as my travelling companion? I think Joseph, because he's the handsomest.'

'You flatter me.'

'And because he will flirt with me in a safe brother-in-law-like way.'

Joseph said gallantly, 'Beware.'

She rewarded him with a ravishing smile. 'But no, of course you'll want to travel with Hamelin, you're both businessmen now, you'll want to talk business.' She moved quickly to Hamelin.

'Hamelin, could I ask you one thing . . . ?' She took his arm gaily and led him aside. 'Would you do one thing for me, before we go?'

'Anything, very gladly.'

'Wretched milliners' bills. They say they have to be settled. It's something like five thousand francs, and at this moment I simply can't . . .'

Hamelin, looking less happy, said, 'Gladly.'

'Sweet of you. Thank you so much.' She went back to Joseph, to mend matters with him. 'Of course, we'll change companions from day to day. Business one day, flirtation the next.'

Away from them, Junot said to Murat, 'I gather you're riding ahead?'

'Yes, I thought I would.'

'Not commanding the escort?'

'I thought the advance guard would be more suitable, in the circumstances.'

Junot looked at him. He got on well with Murat when Murat was not being grand and mysterious.

'You mean, you get first go at the landlord's daughter?'

Murat said grandly, 'Since a certain great lady is rather offended with me for neglecting her, after the first time . . .'

He turned and moved away, as Josephine was moving towards them. She was not close enough to them for his move to seem a deliberate avoidance of her; but she was close enough not to have missed the point of his move.

She said with undiminished gaiety, 'Colonel Junot, I'm arranging partners for the journey. Whom would you like to travel with?'

'Oh, anyone. I really don't mind.'

She looked at him reproachfully. 'Colonel Junot, you are not being gallant.'

'I'm sorry, I just meant . . .' Modest fellow that he was, he tried his best. 'I meant I can't expect to be favoured.'

Her look was still reproachful but also flattering. 'Can't you?'

'I'd be happy to travel with anyone.' His gaze wandered round the room and by the merest chance fell on a certain person. 'Your maid? Mademoiselle Compoint?'

Josephine's eye lost its warmth. 'There!' she cried, moving on. 'I've decided!' The voice was meant for Murat and for Junot and for everyone. 'I shall travel the first day with Captain Charles, because he'll tell me funny stories.'

'Indeed I shall,' said Charles.

It was daylight, but Captain Charles drew the curtains across the windows as soon as the berline had left Paris by the Porte d'Italie.

'I refuse to look out of the windows again until I hear the cobblestones of a town.'

Josephine said, 'Don't you admire nature?'

'It's like Thérèse Tallien, who is, of course, an absolute child of nature. Charming for the first five minutes, but after that rather a bore.'

There is nothing quite so agreeable as to hear people speak ill of one's intimates. 'Thérèse is my best friend. I forbid you to say more than two bad things about her.'

'Two bad things?' Charles gazed in the air and considered which two to choose. 'Well, firstly her husband. Not that one normally meets him, and if one does, he's not with her. And secondly—I must be terribly careful, if I've only got two . . .'

'Her lovers?' Josephine suggested.

'Not all of them, only some—say ten out of the twenty. No, I'm trying to think of the word for her cardinal sin.'

'Indiscriminateness?'

'Worse than that. Enthusiasm.'

Josephine was enjoying herself. 'Yes.'

'She asked me to go to bed with her once. I said, "Darling, it's sweet of you, but I really don't think it's a good idea. You'd be so enthusiastic." '

'Which destroys the pleasure.'

'As I'm sure she'd destroy the second pleasure, the after-pleasure. I told her, "Thérèse, you're so terribly natural, you'd leap out of bed and go round telling everyone all about it. There'd be no one left for me to tell." '

Josephine laughed, out of pure enjoyment. 'That makes three bad things.'

'Allow me three. In order to state the case against naturalness.'

'All right.'

'I am so against it, aren't you? In all its dreary forms, like fields and skies and trees.'

Josephine said, 'So what are you going to look at, all the way to Italy?'

'You. You're so marvellously . . .' He hesitated, in search of the word.

'Unnatural?'

'Artificial,' he said. 'The highest compliment that I can pay.'

They looked into each other's faces for a time, genuinely and sincerely admiring each other's real artificiality.

At last Josephine said, without taking her eyes away from his, 'At least I don't leap out of bed and go round telling people.'

Charles, without taking his eyes away from hers, said, 'Actually, neither do I.'

She said nothing, except with her eyes. After a time he said, 'I do hope we're going to travel slowly, with lots of stops.'

She said, 'I've told them we're to travel slowly.'

In Milan, Napoleon wrote to her:

My life is a nightmare. You are ill, you love me,
I have grieved you, you are pregnant, and I cannot
see you. I have wronged you so much that I do not
know how to atone for it. I accused you of linger-
ing in Paris, when you were ill there. Forgive me,
my dear one, my love for you has robbed me of
my senses, and I shall never recover them . . .

He wrote to Joseph:

I am in despair, I am alone and a prey to my
fears of misfortune. Was I wrong to urge her to
make the journey? A letter from Carnot tells me
she is about to start, though she is not yet fully
recovered from her illness. I beg you to lavish all
your cares on her. I ardently desire her to come.
I need to see her, to press her to my heart. Without
her by my side, I cannot go on. I love her madly.
If she ceased to love me, I would have nothing left
as a reason for living.

Josephine's room at the inn was charming; the landlord
was full of promises that the dinner would be the equal
of anything to be had in Paris; the seven hours spent in
the coach had been not at all unamusing; and she herself,
looking in her mirror, was bound to be pleased by the
brilliance of her own looks. Louise, helping her dress for
dinner, seemed to be not half so well contented.

'Wasn't Joseph an agreeable companion?'

'Dull.'

'Yes, I'm afraid he is rather.'

'After the first half-hour.'

'Why, what happened in the first half-hour?'

Louise was not a girl to be discontented for long. And
she was about to have the fun of telling Josephine: she
and Josephine told each other at least some of their
secrets. She started to laugh. 'Joseph spent the first half-
hour paying me compliments, and not very amusing ones
at that. Then I suppose he thought he'd said enough. He
suddenly stopped talking, and made a bold attack on me.'

'A direct attack?'

'Extremely direct.'

'What did you do?'

'I slapped his face. Hard.'

'Well done.'

'So he sulked and stared out of the window all the rest of the day.'

Josephine said, 'How very boring of him. Tomorrow, you'd better travel with Hamelin.'

Louise said, 'Monsieur Hamelin sat next to me at lunch.'

'You mean—?'

'He was eating his lunch with one hand and squeezing my knee with the other.'

'Louise, you are a problem.'

'I wouldn't be a problem if they weren't.'

'Would you rather have the forwardness of Hamelin or the sulkiness of Joseph?'

Louise said, in her most casual manner, 'I really think I'd be safer with one of the officers.'

'Oh yes?' Josephine was even more casual.

'Captain Charles . . .'

'We'll see.'

'Or Colonel Junot. Unless you want to have the colonel with you?'

Josephine said, looking into a blank corner of the mirror, 'I have no particular preference.'

There was a polite knock at the door. Josephine was dressed quite well enough to receive friends. Louise went to the door and let in Captain Charles, who was dressed well enough for a banquet at the Luxembourg.

He said, 'I thought you should have the best cravat in Europe to escort you down to dinner.'

Josephine said, 'No one but you knows how to tie a cravat.'

He bowed to her. 'Put that line on my tombstone, and I shall die happy.'

Louise, who had stood watching them, said, in a voice which made it quite clear that there was nothing more in her words than could be found on the surface of them, 'Do you need me any more, Madame?'

'No, thank you, Louise.'

Charles, the very pattern of politeness, opened the door for Louise to go, then closed it again behind her. He looked around. 'What a charming room you have.'

'Yes, isn't it?'

'I have the oddest little room. I can't think what Murat was thinking of. And I can't think where Murat has got to.'

'Murat has gone on ahead again. To tomorrow night's inn. He will always be at our tomorrow place.'

'Oh yes, why?'

'Because he doesn't care to meet me.'

'Why not? You're the most meetable person I've ever met.'

Josephine said, looking at the slim Parisian, and enjoying her choice of words, 'Because he thought that I ought to fall in love with his heavy cavalry, terribly Gascon manner.'

'Ludicrous thought.'

'Yes. I disappointed him.'

She was still sitting in front of her mirror. She had to fasten her necklace at the back of her neck. Charles came forward to her, to help her fasten it. He leant forward and kissed her beautiful bare shoulder. She did not seem to mind.

'With the oddest little bed,' he said. 'Quite impossible to sleep on.'

Napoleon said, 'No bed-curtains yet? Where are they?'

Muiron said, knowing that it was not the desired answer, 'Sir, they are still being made.'

'Why?'

The whole thing about becoming a general, Muiron thought to himself, is that you can quite unreasonably ask why, and insist on a reasonable answer. He answered, 'Sir, you said they were to be ready within a week. It is not yet a week.'

'You must do better than I say.'

'Yes, sir.'

'Supposing my wife arrives tomorrow?'

'Sir, she can't possibly do that. Unless carriages can fly.'

'She may be here much sooner than we expect.'

Marmont came to Muiron's assistance. 'Sir, our information is that Madame Bonaparte has only just left Paris.'

General Bonaparte was not in a mood to be reminded of reality. He was in a mood to reprimand his officers for attempting to remind him.

'As in war! A good soldier prepares for every possibility!'

'Yes, sir.' There is nothing else to say when you are reprimanded by a general. And the general was now determined to find another cause for reprimand. The bedroom was splendid, all white and gold and silver, sumptuous and at the same time chaste, erotic and virginal, sensual and marital, burning and cool. It was not possible to imagine a pair of lovers who could quite deserve such a bed or such a room to have a bed in. Everything was perfection.

At the dressing-table Napoleon picked up one of the pair of hairbrushes. 'Silver?'

'Silver plate, sir.'

'Get them changed. I want silver. Solid silver.'

'Yes, sir.'

'Marmont. You'll go to Turin tomorrow.'

'Yes, sir.'

'With a letter to the King of Piedmont. I'll write it in a moment.'

'Yes, sir.'

'When my wife arrives at Turin, on her way here, I want her to be received with the honours usually accorded to royalty.'

Even Marmont, who had known him for a longish time, was taken aback. 'Royalty, sir?' And was immediately sorry that he had questioned the word.

'The King of Piedmont is king only because I permit him to be king. He will do as I tell him.'

Marmont did his best to make amends by saying, 'Yes, sir,' as if what the general had said was the most natural thing in the world.

Napoleon suddenly relaxed and laughed. The inspection was over. He was a human being again. 'And what now? What do I have to do tonight?'

Muiron said, 'Gala performance at the Opera. Given by the grateful Milanese, in your honour.'

'In my honour. But do I have to go there?'

'At least for the sake of La Grassini.'

'Who's La Grassini?'

Muiron and Marmont looked at each other. On subjects unconnected with war and politics, the general was capable of showing great holes in his knowledge; and when he was not on duty, it was sometimes possible to tell him so.

Marmont said, 'Well, second only to you, sir, at this moment La Grassini is the most famous person in Europe.'

'Oh?' He seemed to be interested to learn this.

'In fact, it's possible that she considers herself not to be second to you.'

'Oh?' He was interested.

Muiron said, 'And you must pass the time, sir. Till your wife arrives.'

Louise Compoint looked out of the carriage window at the darkening countryside, and said, perhaps for want of anything else to say, or perhaps for no reason at all, 'It's getting dark.'

Junot said, 'D'you mind?'

'Shall we get to wherever-it-is soon?'

'I don't mind. I'm enjoying myself.'

'Are you?'

They looked at each other. He could see that she was ready to be kissed. He decided to wait just one more moment.

'Go on telling me about Joseph.'

'Why?'

'I'm curious.'

'Oh?'

'You said he "made an attack" on you.'

'Yes, he did.'

'What exactly do you mean? What exactly did he do?' Louise said, 'He moved over and sat next to me.'

'You mean, like this?' He moved over and sat next to her.

'Yes. And then he grabbed me by the shoulders.'

'How? Like this?' He did it.

'Yes.'

'And then?'

'And then he tried to kiss me.'

'Like this?' He kissed her mouth.

'No, he only tried to kiss me.'

'He didn't actually kiss you. Like this.' He kissed her again.

'No.'

'Or like this.' And again.

'No, he didn't.'

'But why didn't he manage to kiss you—like this?' And again.

'Because I slapped his face.'

'But how could you slap his face when he was holding your shoulders, like this?'

'Because I pulled my arms away.'

'Like how?'

'Like this.' But she didn't pull very hard, and he didn't let go.

He said, 'You know, if I'd been him, I'd have held on to you, like this. In fact I'd have put my arms right round you, like this, so you couldn't possibly get away. And, I must say, I'd certainly have kissed you. Like this.'

The enraptured audience shouted for a fifteenth curtain-call, but La Grassini wiped the smile from her face, turned her back on the stage, and set off towards her dressing-room at such a speed that the manager of La Scala had to break into a trot to keep up with her while she gave him her considered opinion of one of her colleagues.

'And tomorrow night I will not take any curtain calls at all if I have to share a single one of them with that tenor. What does he think he's doing, creeping on at the side of the stage and simpering at the audience as if some of the applause was meant for him? There is still some musical taste in Milan. If he went on by himself they would pelt him with rotten oranges. He's not even a tenor, he's a mediocre baritone with a range of one octave. Anywhere above high C he does not sing, he screeches, he howls like a dog. I'd rather have a dog, get me a dog instead, at least the dog would not simper and blow kisses like a village idiot . . .'

Three attendants trotted behind her, burdened with her bouquets. The senders of the bouquets were waiting by her dressing-room door: every one of them at least a count, and some of them very probably princes. They bowed to her in mute adoration. Even without her singing, men would have adored her for her beauty; and even without her beauty, men would have worshipped her for her voice.

She gave them a brilliant smile that swept across them all, and that ended, at its most brilliant, on Marmont and Muiron, who had sprung to attention and given her their smartest salutes.

'Gentlemen . . .'

While the smile was still on him, Marmont stepped briskly forward.

'Signorina Grassini, may I present General Bonaparte's compliments? The general would be most honoured and delighted if you would consent to have supper with him.'

La Grassini said, 'General who?'

Marmont thought, it was only fair. After all, Bonaparte had never heard of La Grassini. He said, enunciat-

ing as clearly as he could, 'General Bonaparte, the Commander-in-Chief of the Army of Italy—'

She had got it. Her smile reached a new peak of brilliance. 'Ah!' she cried, in an ecstasy of delight at having
understood him. *'Il Generale Buonaparte!'*

In the private dining-room at the inn, Junot whispered
to Louise; and Joseph and Hamelin drank their wine in
silence, rather glum, perhaps envious of whispering Junot;
and Captain Charles, as was his duty, amused Josephine.

'The first thing we must do when we get to Milan is
design a new uniform for your husband. Something much
more dashing and much more in the fashion.'

'Yes, but how will we get him to wear it?'

'Oh, that's easy. The Adjutant-General's Department
will issue an instruction.'

'To Bonaparte?'

'To everybody. Then Bonaparte will have to obey it
too. We do it all the time: we exist in order to issue the
most absurd instructions. "With effect from today's date,
all officers of the rank of conqueror and above . . ." '

Josephine laughed, and looked at Louise, whose manner towards Junot was becoming perhaps rather too in-
discreetly intimate.

'Louise.'

'Yes, Madame?'

'Shall we leave the gentlemen to their wine?'

Louise was obviously reluctant to leave Junot's side.
Josephine decided that she must give Louise a short lecture, if not on morals, at least on the virtues of discretion.

The men stood for them to go. Then Junot, in great
good humour—as who would not be, with an excellent
dinner inside him, a bottle in front of him, a woman to
look forward to—said, 'Gentlemen, let each man attack
his own bottle. Except that, dammit, mine's empty already. Buzz me your bottle, Charles, to keep me going
while I shout for the waiter.'

Charles said, 'My dear fellow, please have it. Have it
all.'

'Doesn't the Adjutant-General's Department drink?'

'I'm afraid I have to keep myself clear-headed for tomorrow.'

'Oh, do you? Why?'

'Madame Bonaparte is a delightful woman, but the most demanding travelling-companion. She expects jokes from me at a quite incredibly early hour. Would you excuse me?'

Junot said, 'Sleep well.'

When Charles had gone, Junot said to the others, 'I've always found that a bottle or two make me fitter. For fighting, or for whatever else a man feels like doing. In fact, I propose a toast: to whatever men feel like doing.' He looked at their glum faces, and the sight made him even more cheerful. 'Next week, fighting. Meanwhile, whatever·else.'

Later, in dressing-gown and slippers, tiptoeing along the ill-lit bedroom corridor, Junot turned a corner and came face-to-face with Charles, also on tiptoe, also in dressing-gown and slippers. Neither was pleased to see the other. Each looked at the other warily. Each was seized by the feeling that it was necessary to explain why he was not, at that moment, in bed.

Charles whispered, 'Hullo.'

Junot whispered, 'Hullo.'

Charles was the first to think of an explanation.

'Have you any idea where the . . . ?'

'It's down that way.'

'Is it?'

'Yes.'

'Thank you.'

'Not at all.'

'Well . . . Unless you, yourself—?'

'No, no. Just walking about. Couldn't sleep.'

'Ah.'

'Trying not to wake anyone.'

'Me too . . . Well . . .'

'Good night.'

'Good night.'

Each of them tiptoed on.

Five minutes later, in Louise's arms, Junot said, 'What's Charles doing, creeping along the corridor? As if I couldn't guess.'

She giggled. 'As if you couldn't.'

Junot said, 'He's been quick, hasn't he?'

Louise said, 'She likes them quick.'

Junot said, 'Like you.'

She said, 'Mmm . . .'

Captain Marmont and Captain Muiron, so devoted to their Commander-in-Chief that it hardly even crossed their minds to envy him, escorted La Grassini through the splendid corridors of the Serbelloni Palace.

Marmont said, 'The general is longing to meet you.'

She said, 'As you see, I am hurrying to meet your general.'

Meanwhile Napoleon, in his office, nervously eyed the laid-out cold collation, the champagne bottles waiting in their ice-buckets, the four glasses standing ready for her and himself and his two officers. It was proper, now, for the liberator of Italy to pay his respects to the arts of Italy. It was desirable for him to prove that he was not merely a hero but also a civilized man. He picked up a tidbit and nibbled it, and had to swallow it quickly, to answer a knock at the door.

'Come in!'

La Grassini, who knew how to make entrances, made a particularly good one.

Marmont said, 'Signorina Grassini, may I present our Commander-in-Chief, General Bonaparte?'

Napoleon had seen her beautiful on the stage, and had assumed that stage trickery had helped make her seem so. He was taken aback to find that she was no less beautiful at close quarters. He bowed rather more deeply than he had intended to.

'Signorina, I am most honoured.'

Magnificent, she held out her hand for him to kiss. He kissed it.

She said—regal, commanding—'So you are our conqueror.'

'I hope, your liberator.'

She rejected the word. 'I like conquerors. I don't need to be liberated.'

Napoleon nervously asked, 'Champagne? Do you drink champagne?'

'Always.'

'Muiron—' He made a sign.

'Yes, sir.' Muiron came forward quickly to open a bottle.

Napoleon said, 'We saw your performance tonight.'

'I saw you. In your box.'

'Oh.' Napoleon was conscious that he was not being very brilliant.

'What did you think of me?'

'You were magnificent.'

She dismissed the compliment. 'I was good, but I was not magnificent. It's not possible to be magnificent with that tenor. I am having him dismissed.'

'Ah.'

'He is a fat, stupid Neapolitan pig. I shall never sing with him again. You have good tenors in France.'

'Yes, I believe so.'

'And a good opera house in Paris.'

'Yes.'

'I shall sing in Paris instead. Shall I go to Paris with you?'

Napoleon, totally at a loss for an answer, was saved by Muiron who came to them with two glasses of champagne.

'Signorina . . .'

'Thank you.'

'General . . .'

'Thank you.' He had one short speech ready prepared. He raised his glass. 'I drink to the beauty of your voice—'

'*Alla tua salute!*' she cried, before he could finish the

speech, and took a swig at her glass while he took a sip. He glanced nervously at his officers: he needed some moral support from them. They were standing with ill-concealed smirks on their faces. They were not even drinking: their glasses were still on the table, empty.

'Gentlemen, won't you join us—'

But La Grassini was already speaking to him.

'What did you think of the opera?'

'I admired it greatly.'

'It's not bad. Zingarelli wrote it in twenty-four hours. Specially for me.'

'As a sign of his admiration—?'

She waved away the thought of mere admiration. 'He is in love with me, poor fellow.'

'Poor?'

'I am not in love with him.'

Napoleon prided himself on his next words. They were a well-turned compliment, and they brought Marmont and Muiron into the conversation.

'My officers tell me that all Europe is in love with you.'

'Oh yes,' she said with splendid indifference. 'And now you?'

Now, if ever, was the moment for his officers, his friends, to come to his rescue.

Marmont said, 'Signorina, would you excuse us? We must leave you. Good night, Signorina. Good night, General.'

Muiron said, 'Good night, Signorina. Good night, General.'

Before Napoleon could move to stop them, La Grassini was giving them one of her best smiles and saying, 'Good night. Thank you for bringing me.'

They were gone. He was alone with her, and utterly helpless. She said, 'So. Now. You were saying, the beauty of my voice?'

'Yes.'

'And?'

'The beauty of your person.'

'Good. You shall see more of it.'

She took off the cape that covered her dazzling shoulders. He tried to think of something to say, but nothing came into his mind or into his mouth. It was clearly his duty to take the cape from her and put it down. He managed to do it.

'It is warm in here,' she said.

'Yes . . . More champagne?'

'Yes.'

'And something to eat?' He tried to lead her to the table, but she would not be led.

'No. I shall eat something later.'

'Later?' What did she mean by 'later'?

'I eat a big meal before the opera. And then I don't want to eat again, until maybe in the middle of the night.'

'Ah.'

'Like you? You eat a big meal before a battle?'

He said truthfully, 'I'm not much of an eater.'

'But we shall have supper. Later.'

There was that word again. What could she mean by it?

She had gone on a tour of the room, inspecting it and not admiring it. 'Is this your office?'

'Yes.'

'It is badly furnished.'

'I simply work here. All I need is a chair and a desk.'

'You are a great conqueror, you should show that you are great. Or are you like all the other generals?'

Napoleon, offended, said, 'I am not like any other general.'

'You are a better soldier, perhaps, but you are a soldier. I've met so many. Soldiers have no taste, they have no feeling for beautiful things. To be a truly great man you must have this feeling in you.'

Napoleon, thoroughly offended, said, 'I have a private apartment here. Newly furnished. Beautifully furnished. In the best possible taste, with a great deal of feeling.'

'So why am I here? You simply work here! Am I work?'

He could hardly tell her that she was, in a way, hard work.

In the anteroom, Marmont said to Muiron, 'I'll give you two to one.'

'Make it three.'

'Three's too high. She's a very strong-minded woman.'

'He is not a weak-minded man.'

Marmont said, 'She's a woman. He's a man.'

The door of Napoleon's office opened. Napoleon looked out. 'Muiron—'

'Sir!'

'I want lights in the new apartment. And see that the fires are lit.'

'Sir!'

Napoleon disappeared again.

Marmont said, 'You missed your chance. The bet is off.'

'And this is the bedroom.'

'Evidently.'

'Is it well-furnished?'

'It will do.'

'Have I a feeling?'

'You have the possibility of developing a feeling. Quite a good possibility.'

Napoleon said, 'Now that you've seen the apartment, would you care to have supper?'

But she seated herself on the chaise-longue and commandingly tapped the place beside her. 'Sit down. I must look at you for a time.'

If only out of politeness to a guest, he had no choice in the matter. He sat by her, and she looked at him for a time, studying his face, scrutinizing it as if she would read in it all of his mind and all of his heart.

At last she said, 'You are the King of Italy.'

'In effect, yes.'

'In effect. Effect is everything. Nothing else is important. In the same way, in effect, I am the Queen of Italy.'

'So they tell me.'

'I have had princes before, but not a king. Most kings are fat and old and ugly. You are not.'

'Thank you.'

She said, 'I have decided. I like you. I can love you. You see, I am very direct.'

'Yes.'

'And afterwards we shall have supper.'

Napoleon looked at her, but not as she had looked at him. He was reading not her mind but his own.

'Signorina Grassini, I asked you here tonight to compliment you on your singing, and on your beauty.'

'Yes, I am glad.'

He knew his mind. 'And for a particular reason. My wife will be arriving in Milan very soon. I should like to arrange a series of operas, and concerts, to celebrate her arrival. I should very much like you to sing in those operas and those concerts. You are the greatest, and the most beautiful, singer in the world. I must tell you, my wife is the only woman in the world.'

There was no possibility of mistaking his meaning. Her difficulty was to understand that he meant it. It was the first time in her life that such a thing had ever happened to her.

7. 'MIO DOLCE AMOR'

As her carriage dragged itself up towards the Mont Cenis Pass, towards Turin and a royal reception, Josephine said to Charles, 'After today, I shall travel with one of the others.'

'Must you? Why?'

'We shall be in Italy, where I have a husband.'

'Oh, don't worry about your husband. He's always away conquering somewhere. It's a habit that conquerors get into. They can't get out of it.'

She kissed him lightly on the end of his nose and said, 'My husband doesn't just love me. He adores me. Madly.'

'So do I. Madly.'

'And he is madly jealous.'

'Ah, yes. Well, in that case . . .'

'Yes . . . ?'

'We shall have to be madly careful.'

'Yes.'

Charles said, 'Fortunately, you are one of the great liars of our time. I beg your pardon. One of the great liars of all time.'

'When I have to be.'

'No, darling. You are a great, instinctive, permanent liar. So am I. Except when I say I adore you, and I'm not going to give you up, just because of a husband.'

Josephine said, 'Darling, the husband is your Commander-in-Chief.'

He laughed, so she laughed. He said, 'What fun!'

When the cortège arrived at the Serbelloni Palace, Napoleon was away from Milan—'I told you so!' said Charles—fighting a battle; so Josephine was received, in great

state, by the Duke of Serbelloni himself, Milan's greatest
nobleman, President of the Directorate of what had recently been Austrian Italy and was now reborn as the
Cisalpine Republic.

Josephine was charming, as ever: Serbelloni was enchanted by her. She was queenly, as the occasion seemed
to require, and as she was very easily learning to be: it
was only a variation on her style as the queen of Barras's
salon. And she was, of course, fatigued by the rigours of
her long journey. The duke bowed her to her apartment,
all white and silver and gold.

Now that they were finally in Milan, Josephine judged it
the proper moment to give Louise a quiet word of advice.
She had always been fond of Louise, but it was still notice-
able, sometimes, in some ways, that Louise did need a
hint or two, a helpful hand to put her right, to complete
her training in the manner of polite society. The girl was
still a little too natural.

'Louise, I do think it would be better if from now on
you saw rather less of Colonel Junot.'

'Oh?'

'Much less, in fact.'

'Oh, why?'

Josephine said, in the friendliest possible voice, 'I imagine that in any case Junot will be away most of the
time.'

'With Bonaparte.'

'Yes.'

'He'll be here some of the time. With Bonaparte. Why
should I see less of him while he's here?'

Josephine said, kindly, simply explaining things to her,
'On a journey, one is forced into other people's company.'

'I was not forced. Any more than you were.'

Josephine continued to be kind, and to explain the way
of the world. 'When the journey comes to an end, the
momentary romance comes to an end. This is perfectly
normal.'

Louise said, 'Junot loves me.'

'My dear Louise, soldiers love any woman who will let them love her.'

'No.'

Josephine held back an impatient sigh. She could see that Louise was wearing her obstinate look, which could sometimes harden into a mutinous stare.

'Louise, I am giving you good advice. One should always forget whatever has happened on a journey. I have already done so. I advise you to do the same.' Alas, Louise's face was mutinous already. But Josephine felt it her duty to make every effort. 'Louise, you must understand that here we shall be almost a court, almost a royal court. We shall be looked at. We must set an example.'

Louise said, in a hard low voice, 'Will you?'

Perhaps it was a mistake to have a maid who was also, in some sort, a companion. Josephine saw that it would be necessary to make matters clear, and at the same time make her own authority clear.

'Louise, I do not think that General Bonaparte would approve of his colonel aide-de-camp sleeping with his wife's maid.'

Louise stared at the wall for a time, with a very tight face, and then said, 'Would General Bonaparte approve of his wife sleeping with the Adjutant-General's Department?'

Josephine decided not to scream at her, not to slap the girl's face, not to lose her temper at all. The only lesson to be learnt from the whole thing was that, yes, it had to be admitted, a maid-companion was a mistake.

She said, 'Louise, you are dismissed.'

Louise stopped staring at the wall and stared at Josephine. 'Shall I tell General Bonaparte what happened on the journey?'

Josephine, keeping the firmest possible grasp on her anger, said, 'You are dismissed immediately. You will leave for Paris immediately.'

'Before Bonaparte gets back here?'

As hard-voiced as Louise, Josephine said, 'Yes!'

In the staff officers' mess, Murat was on his third bottle, and therefore becoming unbearably boastful. Luckily for them, Junot and Marmont were each on their third bottle too. The wine didn't make them any more tolerant of Murat, but it did make them laugh at him while they were not being tolerant.

'Marmont. Question for you.'

'Yes?'

'Why is it we don't believe a word Murat says?'

'Junot. About your question.'

'Yes?'

'I quite agree with you. But what's the answer?'

Junot said, 'Answer to question. Because we've known Murat too long to be able to believe him.'

Murat said, 'Are you calling me a liar?'

'I'm calling you an innkeeper's son from Gascony.'

Murat jumped up and flung his glass in the fireplace.

'Junot, are you calling me—'

'Where they may not be liars,' said Junot.

'What?'

'But, by God, they have a talent for exaggeration.'

Murat clapped his hand to his sword-hilt. 'Colonel Junot, I request you to do me the honour—'

But Marmont heard the quick, recognizable step coming along the corridor. General Bonaparte entered, dusty from travelling. They sprang to their feet.

'Is my wife here?'

'Yes, sir. In your apartment.'

'You three will leave with me for Mantua the day after tomorrow.'

'Yes, sir!'

Napoleon glanced at the bottles and did not smile but did not frown.

'Drink your wine. Good night.'

He went, as quickly as he had come. Junot said to Murat, 'And that is the end of that conversation. I told you two days ago, drink your wine and keep your big mouth shut. We're going fighting.'

Josephine was at her dressing-table, in a loose gown, by herself, putting the very last expert touches to her marvellous maquillage. She knew that Napoleon was coming: messenger after messenger had brought news of his approach. Now she could hear him coming, and she laid down her tools. She was ready.

Napoleon came in quickly, came straight to her, clasped her to him in a wild embrace almost before she could rise. A storm of kisses, and a storm of passionate words.

'My darling, my beloved, my adored one, *mio dolce amor,* you are here, you are here at last . . . How are you, are you well, did you have a good journey? No, let me kiss you first, let me kiss you a thousand times, then let me ask . . . Did you get my letters from Mantua? Oh, darling, you'll never know how many letters I wrote you —how many from here, when you were in Paris—you had letters from me every day, but you don't know how many I wrote that I didn't send, I couldn't send, they were mad, mad with love, you'd have thought me a lunatic, loving you madly, to distraction, and hating you because you didn't come and you didn't write to me . . . No, never hating you, but hating everyone and everything that kept you in Paris—hating everyone in Paris, the people you were with, because they were with you and I wasn't, because they could see you and hear you and kiss your hand, and I couldn't . . . Oh my darling . . .'

When the first tempest of kisses subsided for a moment—

'And I was here, I could kiss you only in imagination. I have kissed you in imagination every night since I last saw you, since I left you in Paris—kissed you from head to toe, your lips, your eyes, your breasts, your little belly —oh, most of all your adorable little belly. And tonight I shall kiss you in reality. All tonight, and all tomorrow night. Then I must go back to Mantua. But not for long, we shall never be parted for long again, never, never. I am nothing without you, you are my heart, my soul, my life. I love you more than the world, more than the hope of heaven, more than God himself . . . Do you love me?'

She said, 'I love you.'

He held her to him in an ecstasy of kisses and embraces, then tore himself away from her.

'Let me try to talk like a sane man. Do you like it here? Do you like the rooms? The furniture?'

'Very much.'

He moved restlessly around. The rooms were not perfect. 'You must have more flowers. I'll bring you more flowers—'

'Thank you.'

'Tell me everything. How was the journey? Did they look after you—Murat, and Junot, and Joseph—?'

'Yes, very well.'

'Were you comfortable? Did they find you good inns, good rooms—?'

'Yes, very good.'

'They're good men, they love me, so they must love you.'

'Yes.'

'And you weren't ill? The one thought that tortured me. I imagined you ill. You weren't ill?'

'No, not ill.'

'And how is my son? I know it's a son, it must be, it can only be a son. Is he growing big and strong inside you? Little Napoleon?'

Josephine did not answer.

'Is he?'

Josephine's lip started to quiver.

'Darling? Is he?'

Josephine's eyes filled with tears.

'Josephine? Is he?'

The tears came out of Josephine's eyes and ran down her cheeks. Napoleon stared at her, pale as death, still as death.

'Darling? . . . Is he growing? . . . Is he alive?'

At last she said, in a voice which he could hardly hear,

but he could hear every word only too clearly: 'I thought
I was pregnant. Then I was sure. Then . . . then I wasn't
well. With your letters which worried me so much, telling
me I must come to Italy; and Barras telling me I must
go because you wanted me to go. And then all the prep-
arations for the journey, when I wasn't well . . . Perhaps
it wasn't that, I don't know, I can't really explain. But
suddenly, just before we left, I had a period again. It was
too late to write and tell you. How could I write and tell
you? When you wanted a child so much, and I wanted
a child so much. Perhaps it was all because I wanted so
much to give you what you wanted, too. Perhaps it was
the wanting, and imagination, my imagination, perhaps
I had imagined things. But then, suddenly, it was bleeding, a lot of bleeding, not a miscarriage, no, I wasn't
pregnant, I wasn't pregnant at all, I'd imagined it. And
the journey was all arranged, I couldn't say anything, I
couldn't tell anyone, I had to start on the journey . . .'

Napoleon said, 'I am unforgivable.'

'No . . .'

'I was selfish. I thought of myself.'

'No, it was me, wanting so much to be pregnant . . .'

'I should have loved you more, and made you stay in
Paris.'

'No, I wanted to come here, I wanted to be with you.'

'I was selfish. I thought of myself.'

'No, I wanted, so much . . .'

He put his arms round her, and they stood silent for a
time, he gently holding her, his heart beating against hers.

At last he said, 'Are you well again?'

'Yes. Now.'

'Really well again? Really well?'

'Now that I'm with you.'

He said, 'You know, I've only been married to you for
two days? Till now? And now we're married for another
two days, and then I must leave you again. But we'll be
married for thousands of days, thousands of nights—'

'Yes.'

'And we'll have a son, two sons, three sons, any number of sons. Not imagination, but reality.'

'Yes.'

'Have you had supper yet?'

'No.'

He said gently, 'Nor have I. Come to bed.'

'Yes.'

They kissed, deeply.

He said, 'We'll have supper later. After. In the middle of the night.'

'Yes.'

'We won't even get up for it. Louise can bring it.'

Josephine said—it didn't matter, but it had to be mentioned, sooner or later—'Oh, darling, I should tell you something.'

'Mm?'

'One not very nice thing that happened on the journey.'

'What?'

'Louise misbehaved.'

'Misbehaved?'

'With Colonel Junot. She let him make love to her.'

'Oh?'

'I couldn't have a maid who did things like that.'

'No.'

'And you couldn't have a wife who had a maid who did things like that.'

'No.'

'So I sent her back to Paris. That was the right thing to do, wasn't it?'

'Quite right.'

Josephine said, 'I've got a new maid, an Italian girl, better than Louise. Better-behaved. She can bring us our supper. After.'

Junot marched into the Commander-in-Chief's office and saluted.

'All ready to leave, sir.'

The Commander-in-Chief looked him up and down in a way that meant a reprimand was coming.

'Colonel Junot.'

'Sir?'

'On the journey here from Paris. Bringing my wife.'

'Yes, sir?'

'I'm told there was some misbehaviour.'

'Misbehaviour, sir?'

'Yes.'

'Was there, sir?'

'Don't talk like an idiot.'

'Sorry, sir.'

'You know there was.'

'Yes, sir.'

'You know what happened.'

'Yes, sir.'

'The result is, you've got the girl dismissed.'

'Yes, I heard that, sir.'

'My wife has strong notions of propriety. Quite correctly. And so have I.'

'Yes, I know that, sir.'

'In future you will, at the very least, keep your hands off the members of my household.'

'Yes, sir.'

'That's all. Let's go.'

They marched out, to the carriages that were waiting to take them to the war.

Captain Charles, in his immaculate uniform, entered Josephine's bedroom and bowed.

'Good morning, Madame.'

She was in bed still, but beautifully made-up and charmingly dressed, ready for visitors or anything.

'Good morning, Captain Charles.'

'I saw him leave, on his way to the war. He's obviously going to eat six more kingdoms before breakfast.'

'At least six.'

He came and kissed her hand.

'Thank you so much for inviting me to breakfast.'

'So pleased you could come.'

105

He came and sat on the edge of the bed, without letting go of her hand.

'May I eat you before breakfast? Or after?'

She said, 'Or both?' And they both laughed.

Charles said, 'And he really doesn't know a thing?'

'Not a thing.'

'I complimented you once. I should have put it more strongly. You're not one of the great liars of all time. You are absolutely and without a doubt the most marvellous liar that ever existed.'

Josephine smiled her most seraphic smile. 'Yes,' she said.

8. CAPTAIN CHARLES'S FRIEND

The bedroom of the house in rue Chantereine had been redecorated and refurnished sumptuously and suitably for a victorious commander-in-Chief returning in glory to Paris. The motif was military: the bed was a general's tent, the bedside tables were made like drums.

General Bonaparte himself, at the moment, wore a civilian frock-coat, plain to the point of austerity: a cynic might have suspected it of being aggressively unmilitary and ostentatiously austere. However, the general's manner was verging on the warlike.

'In the name of God, why didn't you tell me?' He brandished a sheaf of papers—invoices, bills, letters demanding payment.

Josephine said, 'But I did.'

'About these?'

'I told you everything I knew about. Absolutely everything.' Her manner was calm and practical. It is foolish to become excited while your maid is doing your hair.

'But these—!' It is impossible to have a scene with your wife while her maid is doing her hair. 'Agathe, get out!'

Agathe went. Napoleon started again.

'But these bring the total to three hundred thousand francs!'

'Yes, you told me.'

'Yes!'

'I didn't know, till you told me.'

'And the house itself is not worth more than forty or fifty thousand!'

'Isn't it?'

'No!'

Josephine continued to be perfectly calm and sensible

and reasonable. 'But darling, you did say that we should have the house redone. While we were in Italy. You agreed. Didn't you?'

'Yes!'

'So I had it redone.' The thing was simple. There was really nothing more to be said.

Napoleon said, 'So the first bills come in. Fifty thousand francs. I show them to you. You are astonished. More bills, a hundred thousand, a hundred and fifty thousand. More astonishment, you didn't know. And now these! Making three hundred thousand! And you simply didn't know! You ordered the decorators to do what they did, they sent you their bills, and now you tell me you simply didn't know!'

Napoleon was missing the point of the whole thing. She explained it to him.

'I wanted the house to be worthy of you.'

'At whose expense?'

'It is our Paris house. And you are the most important man in Paris. Everyone says so. Everyone.'

'Does everyone say I'm the richest man in Paris?'

'Darling, we were in Italy, I wasn't here to see what they were doing. I'd no idea it was going to cost so much.'

'But you told them, regardless of expense!'

'No, darling.'

'I assure you, yes!'

'I told them to be economical, we couldn't afford very much.'

'They've given me the letter you wrote, I have it here!' He pulled a paper from the sheaf, and waved it at her. 'Saying you yourself have enough funds with your agent to cover whatever needs to be done. So you want the whole house redecorated and refurnished, everything hand-made, by the best artists, in the latest style, regardless of expense!'

'I don't remember saying that. When did I say that?'

'In a letter from Passeriano! Look!'

'Oh yes. But I wrote letters after that one.'

'I know you did! I have them! Agreeing payment! From your mythical funds! And you had no funds with your agent! You have no funds at all! Your only funds are mine!'

Josephine, very quietly and sweetly, started to cry.

'I thought you'd like it,' she said, as the first tear began to make its way down her cheek. 'I wanted it to be as pretty as possible. For you . . .'

'And you wanted to give me a surprise!'

A second tear was following the first one.

'Yes . . .'

Napoleon said, in a quite different voice, 'Josephine. Darling. My love. Will you please not cry. But . . .' But there was a knock on the door. 'Come in!'

It was Bourrienne, his private secretary.

'Forgive me. Monsieur Talleyrand is downstairs.'

'Send him up.'

As Bourrienne went away again, Josephine said, 'I can't meet Talleyrand while I'm crying.'

'You don't have to meet Talleyrand. But dry your eyes.' He brought her a large handkerchief. 'I can't bear to see you crying. You know I can't.'

'Darling, I don't cry because I like doing it.' She could say that all the more sincerely because it was perfectly true.

He sat by her at the dressing-table, gentle and husbandly. 'Darling, may we talk like reasonable people?'

'Of course.'

'A husband must support his wife, must give her an allowance, must give her some money to spend as she pleases.'

'Yes, that's right. I understand that.'

'But a wife must not sign bills for her husband to pay without asking him first, and without explaining exactly what it's for. Do you understand that?'

She wiped away the last tear-stain. 'But you were so busy in Italy. I hardly saw you.'

He took her hands and gazed into her soft eyes, still

moist from her tears. 'Josephine. Promise me that you will never do it again.'

She gazed in his eyes and said, 'I promise.'

He was delighted that she was being so docile. He saw that it was best not to be stern with her, but to lecture her gently and lovingly. 'Darling, the only good basis for a marriage is that husband and wife must be open with each other, must tell each other the truth—the truth about big things and about small things.'

'Yes, I agree.'

'Now, last week, I asked you how many new dresses you'd bought since we came back from Italy. You said, "One"—'

'Oh, please don't let's talk about those dresses again.'

He was gentle, but would not spare her the lecture. 'You said "One"—I knew it was twenty, I'd just talked to your dressmaker. Darling, you told me a lie.'

'I wasn't lying, it was just something that slipped my mind.'

'Nineteen dresses slipped your mind?'

'I thought you might be cross with me. I was going to tell you, later, at a good moment.'

'Darling, I shall never be cross with you if you simply tell me the truth.'

Josephine looked at him doubtfully. 'I can't always. You aren't always in a good mood.'

'I shall be in a good mood, always, if you always tell me the truth.'

'Will you?'

'Will you always tell me the truth? Please?'

Josephine said, 'I promise. So long as you still love me.'

Napoleon said, 'My darling, I love you beyond anything you can imagine, and a thousand times more. You are my whole reason for living. The world is beautiful and wonderful to me only because you inhabit it.'

She said, 'And I love you.'

She offered her soft mouth. He hesitated. 'Talleyrand . . .'

'Talleyrand is a cripple. He climbs the stairs very slowly.'

He kissed her mouth.

She whispered, 'Get rid of him very quickly.'

Talleyrand said, 'May I—?'

'Do please sit down.'

'How kind.' He sat, with his stick by his side. 'I shall not detain you long. I simply came to ask your advice—which is given to me immediately, by your clothes.'

'What advice?'

'As your host at the reception tonight, I shall have to make a speech in your honour.'

'Well?'

'So I shall have to refer to you by your rank or title, in association with your name.'

'Ah, yes.'

'I foresaw a difficulty. "General Bonaparte"? "Citizen General Bonaparte"? Or simple "Citizen"?'

'Citizen.'

'So I see, from your clothes. I'm delighted to have your agreement. We may address each other as we please in private; but tonight I shall have several hundred guests, some of whom still believe in the Revolution.'

Napoleon said shortly, 'As I do.'

'Of course. So do I.' Talleyrand was, as always, politely imperturbable. 'Besides, "Citizen" fits in so well with the rest of my speech.'

'What are you going to say?'

'Oh, I shall start with the usual compliments, of which you must be heartily tired—'

'Yes.'

'The Italian campaign, the treaty with Austria—'

'Yes, yes.'

'Of course, the French adore successful generals who win campaigns and make victorious peace treaties. But the question is, what on earth does one do with successful generals when there is peace?'

Napoleon looked at him suspiciously. He had not yet

learned to judge, from the degree of irony in Talleyrand's voice, what was the degree of irony in Talleyrand's mind. He knew how to deal with Talleyrand only by being blunt. 'The general re-becomes a civilian.'

'You anticipate my point. I shall admit—insincerely, of course—to having had a moment of anxiety; anxiety that your greatness, your glory, might seem to be a threat to our doctrine of equality. But my anxiety was unfounded. I was wrong. Personal greatness is, in fact, the triumph of equality: it makes all France, all Frenchmen, greater than they were before.'

'Good.'

Talleyrand inclined his head. 'I'm so glad you like it . . . And I shall point to the lack of ostentation of your dress, the modesty of your way of living . . .' His eye slowly circled the room, ironically, or just possibly not. 'Etcetera, etcetera. Your rejection of military pomp. Your evident lack of ambition . . .'

His eye came to rest on Napoleon. Napoleon said, 'That'll do very well.'

'I had hoped to be in tune with you.'

'You are.'

'Oh, I shall end with a reference to our one remaining enemy: wicked tyrannical England, which will doubtless be defeated by . . . shall I say, by our new hero? Is the word too strong?'

Napoleon said, 'England will be defeated by my going to the East.'

'Ah. The Egyptian adventure.'

'The Egyptian project.'

'I beg your pardon. Project. Will you make any mention of it in your speech?'

'No.'

'I agree. It must be a well-kept secret. And in any case, heaven forbid that we should tell people how England will be defeated. It's so much safer to announce these things after the event.' Talleyrand rose on to his crippled feet. 'When do you put the Egyptian project to the Directory?'

'Tomorrow.'

'It will be agreed within twenty-four hours.'

'So quickly?'

'I speak not as their Minister of Foreign Affairs, but as one who observes the Directors. Paul Barras will clasp you to his bosom tonight. The others, not to be outdone, will bedew you with tears of purest gratitude. And the further away from France you wish to go, the better they will like it.' He made a courteous bow. 'Till very soon, Citizen. I look forward to seeing you at my house, with your Citizeness.'

He limped away towards the stairs. As soon as he was out of sight, Napoleon hurried back to the bedroom. Josephine was still in front of her mirror, now making herself resplendent with jewels, on her fingers, on her arms, in her ears, round her neck, in her hair, round her head.

'Too much jewellery. Far too much. Take it off. Take off at least half of it.'

She looked at him in surprise. 'Why?'

'Because I say so. Because Talleyrand is right. Because of the speech he's going to make this evening. Because of politics. Haven't you got something simpler?'

He threw open her big jewel-casket and started rummaging through it, spilling the precious things. She gave a small shriek. 'Darling, what are you doing?'

'Looking for something more modest, less of a conqueror's wife . . .' He rummaged. A tiara. Necklaces. Earrings. More earrings. Bracelets. Rings. More necklaces. More rings.

'Where did you get these?'

'You gave me them.'

'Not this. Not this.'

'You did!'

'I know what I gave you.'

'So do I!'

Holding up a diamond necklace—'Not this! Where did you buy this? More bills? More bills that have slipped your mind?'

'No!'

'Tell me, then! Where did you get these things?'

Josephine said, after a time, not very willingly: 'They were presents.'

'Presents? From whom?'

'All those princes and dukes in Italy, who wanted to please you, or to save themselves from you, and thought they could do it by sending me presents. Of course, I didn't do anything in return, what could I have done? But I took the presents. Why not? Darling, everyone took presents. You took presents.'

Napoleon, staring at her, jewels cascading from his hands, said, 'Or are they from a lover?'

'No! No!'

'Have you a lover?'

She looked at him, and smiled, and made him wait until the moment when she would finally decide that it was her wish and pleasure to answer him.

At last she said, softly and calmly, 'Yes.'

He stared at her and could not speak.

She said, 'Yes, I have a lover. The most exciting lover in the world. The most jealous lover in the world. You.'

He took her in his arms, in a wild embrace. The jewels spilled to the floor.

'Oh, my darling, forgive me, please forgive me . . .'

In the hall, General Berthier, the soul of exactness, looked at his watch and said to Bourrienne, 'The general is decidedly late.'

'Shall I—?'

'No, no. It isn't a battle. I suppose he's allowed to be unpunctual.'

Junot said to Murat, behind his hand, 'What d'you suppose he's doing—helping her to dress?'

'It takes time, with a woman like that.'

'With a husband like that.'

Murat said, 'I must say she's still a fine woman. Though not quite as fine as she was.'

Napoleon and Josephine appeared at the head of the

stairs, he in his sober frock-coat, she in a simple dress set off by a simple parure: she calmly radiant and serene, he proud and serious and looking remarkably well-pleased with himself.

Joseph Bonaparte, standing by General Berthier, looked up at them and muttered, 'If only he'd married anyone else.'

Berthier gave Joseph an indifferent glance and a non-committal grunt. Berthier had no great regard for his general's wife, but he had even less regard for male civilians like Joseph.

Josephine went in a closed carriage to 100 rue du Faubourg Saint-Honoré, the offices of the Bodin Company, contractors and suppliers to the Army of Italy. The doorman, in accordance with his instructions, showed her straight into the office of Captain Charles, who had resigned his commission in the Hussars in order to serve his country more effectively as a partner of Monsieur Bodin.

Deprived of his gorgeous uniform but still splendidly dandiacal, Charles came forward in a dance-step to kiss Josephine's hand and then to take her into a lover's embrace.

'How marvellous to see you. But why didn't you send me a note?'

'Bonaparte went away this morning on a tour of inspection somewhere. He hadn't told me beforehand. Apparently it was supposed to be a secret. So, the moment he was gone . . . Oh, darling, kiss me. To take him off my lips.'

He kissed her. She wound her soft arms round his neck, wanting more kisses.

'How long will Bonaparte be away?' he asked.

'Ten days, perhaps.'

'Therefore ten nights?'

'Yes.'

'May I have all ten?'

'One or two may be difficult.'

115

'So, eight or nine for me.'

'Yes.' She shivered with delight at the thought.

'Starting tonight?'

'Yes. We'll go to the theatre.'

'And then?'

'And then supper. Just the two of us.'

'And then?' he asked.

'And then,' she said.

He said, 'Heaven.'

She moved away from him, and waltzed round the office, and cried, 'Oh, I feel so free! He may be the greatest man in France, but you've no idea what a bore he is.'

'Oh, yes. All great men are bores. If they weren't, they'd think of something better to do than being great men.'

'Do you know what his idea of love-making is?'

'Something military, done by numbers?'

'He throws me on the bed and then he leaps on me.'

Charles slid an elegant arm round her waist. 'Not like my idea at all.'

'No.'

'I lay you down with the greatest possible care.'

'Yes. And then we laugh.'

'My heavenly Josephine, you are for laughing with.'

'He doesn't laugh.'

'Then he's not merely a bore, he's a silly fellow to boot.'

Josephine said, as though the thought had just struck her, 'Oh, he's being a bore about other things too. You must tell Bodin I need fifty thousand francs quickly. Before Bonaparte comes back from wherever he's gone to.'

'Darling, have you been buying jewellery again?'

'I daren't show Bonaparte the bills.'

'Don't worry. I'm sure we're indebted to you for fifty thousand francs.'

'Oh, at least. And tell Bodin I've written to the Minister of War, so he owes me for that too. But the other letters, the ones to people in Italy, he mustn't use those just for the moment.'

Charles raised an eyebrow. 'I'll tell him, but may I tell him why not?'

'I have a terrible feeling I'm being watched.'

'By Bonaparte?'

'No—but by someone, one of his brothers perhaps, perhaps Joseph.'

'Darling, you're so much cleverer than Joseph.'

'Yes, but he hates me. It might be dangerous if he found out anything.'

Charles kissed away her fears. 'I promise you, Bodin and I will both be as discreet as if we were both your lovers. Oh, would you like the money now? I doubt if we have it in the house, but I can send a man for it, if you have half an hour. And if you do have half an hour, shall we start to celebrate the great man's departure?'

She thought of the bedroom, not large, but charmingly, elegantly furnished, on the floor above the offices. The thought was tempting, but she had her social duties.

'Oh, darling, I can't. I promised Paul Barras. I'm late already.'

Charles saw her to the door, and said, 'Best respects to Barras, from Bodin and myself.'

'No. I shall be discreet too.'

'You might ask him where Bonaparte will be going to, with his next expedition. The Bodin Company would like to know. We exist to serve the army. At least, to supply the army.'

'I'll try.'

'You're so good at asking. Shall I bring the money to-night?'

'Please.'

'Till then.'

'Yes.'

'The theatre.'

'Yes.'

'Supper.'

'Yes.'

'And then.'

'Yes.'

'And we shall laugh.'

117

'Yes.'

'What fun.'

She went on to Barras's reception. It seemed to her that every time she visited Barras now there was a slightly higher proportion of beautiful young men around the place, and a slightly lower proportion of beautiful young women. Not that it mattered: Paul had always taken pleasure in all varieties of pleasure; and anyway, Thérèse had moved on to Ouvrard the banker, and Josephine herself was agreeably busy.

Barras greeted her. His manner was becoming daily more fantasticated. 'Welcome, O Queen of Paris!'

'Paul, darling, do you love me as much as ever?'

He was at the same time gallant and perfectly truthful. 'As much as ever I did.'

'In spite of your . . .' She glanced at the young men. 'Your new tastes?'

'An additional taste, not a substitute. My bed is still as open to you as it is to them.'

'Am I invited?'

'You have a standing invitation.'

'So tell me something, Paul.'

'Anything, except one of my secrets.'

'It's just that it'll be so much easier when Bonaparte is away.'

'He is away now. Isn't he?'

'I mean, abroad. A new campaign. An expedition.'

'Ah.' He looked at her and smiled. 'Bonaparte hasn't told you his plans?'

'He has hinted at things, but not told me.'

'I'm delighted he's so conscious of security.'

She said sweetly, cajolingly, in a voice that no one else could hear, 'Paul darling, you can tell me. Is it England? Or Egypt? Is he really going to Egypt? Darling, I am his wife.'

'Do you want him to go?'

'If he goes anywhere, I want him to go quickly.'

'Yes, I'm sure you do, but why? Your debts? The Bodin Company? Or Charles?'

'All three, perhaps.'

Barras said, 'You worry too much. Darling, why should you worry? A husband must pay his wife's debts: it's the law. You have nothing to worry about. The Bodin Company—your connection is perhaps not quite legal, but it's certainly normal. Our armies must be supplied, and by contractors like Bodin. Who better than you to recommend which contractors should get which contracts?'

She said, 'Bodin pays you, too. They all pay you.'

'My dear, I am so splendidly corrupt, no revelation could shock anyone.'

It was true: his corruptness had become so open and unconcealed that he was admired for his frankness and praised for his honesty.

'Your only danger is your husband finding out about Charles—and myself, I suppose: your occasional lover, when both of us feel like a change.'

She said softly, 'My past and future lover . . . Tell me. Is it Egypt? And when?'

He smiled into her eyes, and she knew he was going to tell her. He could never, for long, resist the pleasure of giving away someone else's secret.

'As the head of the Directory . . .'

'Yes, Paul, I know. But I swear I shan't tell a soul.'

'Well, if anyone is going to Egypt, he must sail from France before the English find out about it, or Nelson and the English fleet will catch him, and sink him, and all his army.'

'I see.'

'Also, if anyone is going to Egypt, he must land in Egypt before the Nile floods. So he must leave France very soon indeed.'

'Thank you, Paul.'

He bowed. 'I shall look forward to any reward.'

As they were at the point of being ready to leave the house in the rue de la Victoire—which had been the rue

Chantereine until the municipality renamed it in honour
of France's great general—Josephine suddenly burst into
tears and said, 'I want to go with you.'

'But you *are* going with me.'

'Only as far as Toulon.'

'Yes.'

'But I want to go with you to Egypt.'

General Bonaparte was in fine boisterous spirits, as
always when he was off to the wars. He roared with laughter, gave her a jocular slap on the bottom, and planted
three great kisses on her cheeks to dry her tears.

'Did you hear that, Marmont?'

'Yes, sir.'

'Would you believe it! The silly girl wants to come to
Egypt!'

She said plaintively, 'Why shouldn't I come?'

'Are you taking your wife, Marmont?'

'No, sir.'

He turned to Josephine. 'And Marmont has only been
married two months. No, we'll send for wives when it's
safe for them to come.'

She said, 'I want to come now.'

'My darling, I've laid it down, no wives till we've won
the campaign.'

'But you're the Commander-in-Chief, you can do whatever you please.'

'I have to set an example.'

'But you'll be a long way away from me. And all those
beautiful Egyptian women.'

Tears were dribbling out of her eyes again. Marmont
discreetly withdrew from the room as the general put his
arms round his wife and started the task of petting her
back to her normal good spirits.

'My dearest, it never enters my head even to look at
another woman.'

She knew that was true. She also knew that she thought
it rather dull and boring of him, never to look at another
woman. She would have found it much more satisfactory
for him to look, and for other women to look at him, and

for herself to see what was happening and to show her power over Napoleon by calling him back to her side, and making him say he was sorry, and making him show he was sorry by bringing her a beautiful present.

Since she knew him to be totally, tediously faithful, why was she unwilling to let him go to Egypt alone? Since she did not find him in the least amusing, why was she suddenly so anxious to be with him? Since her friends and her pleasures were in France, why did she feel such a strong impulse to leave France? Why on earth was she crying, when there was nothing to cry about?

Napoleon said, 'As soon as it's safe in Egypt, I'll send for you to come out and join me.'

She wondered, But is it safe for me in France? Wouldn't I be safer anywhere else?

He said, 'Give your letters to Paul Barras or anyone at the Directory, they'll send them out by the first ship. The letters may take a month or two getting there. It can't be helped.'

She thought, But with Barras and my other friends so near, and Napoleon so far, it is very possible that I shall behave badly, and worse than I really seriously mean to behave: because I have never been good at seriously meaning things, and I have never been good at resisting temptation.

He said, 'I've arranged for Joseph to pay you a monthly allowance, from my funds. And remember, you're not to sign any bills. Joseph will deal with everything.'

She realized why she had to be with Napoleon. He was her strength. He protected her. He would protect her, against the whole world and against his own family. The other Bonapartes hated her. Joseph hated her. They thought her foolish and fickle and ruinously extravagant. With Napoleon so far off, they would do their best to ruin her one way or another.

And her Paris friends would not do anything to save her: they were not the kind of people who helped people.

He said, 'You must go to Plombières for the summer, to take the waters. The waters there are very good for fertility. And you know what I want more than anything in the world. And what you want, too, as much as I do. A child. Our child. Our son.'

He was so longing for a child. It was useless for her to insist on Egypt. It was pointless for her to try to be anything but docile and obedient to his will. And, certainly, a summer in Plombières would be very agreeable. Her friends from Paris could come and visit her there—Thérèse Tallien, and Charles, and Barras, and so many others. Charles might, perhaps, be too busy with Bodin to get away from Paris for more than an occasional week-end; but it was not so long till September, and in September she would move back to Paris, and would be able to see Charles as much as she wished.

She was back in her normal good spirits. Napoleon was relieved, and pleased, and very loving. He could not be happy unless she was.

9. FAITHLESS JOSEPHINE

On the ship, on deck, at night, a fine starlit night, Napoleon stargazing, as Bourrienne, his school-friend, his secretary, came up to him—

'Do you believe in the stars, Bourrienne?'

'No.'

'I asked Marmont that once, in Italy. He gave the same answer. I agree with you both. But I believe in my star.'

'Destiny?'

'I used to call it luck. Now I know that it is more than luck. Destiny is knowing how to catch the luck as it flies. As I am doing now.'

They stood silent for a time, looking at the sky. Then Bourrienne said—since the moment seemed right to ask the question he had been wanting to ask—'How long shall we be in Egypt?'

'Six months. Or six years.'

'Six years?'

'Barras and his Directory are fools. They continue to exist as a government only because of what I did for them in Italy. Italy was my luck. Since then, they've been afraid to give me anything, for fear of making me greater than they are. But they have been afraid to refuse me anything. I say "Egypt"; they say, "Yes, do go to Egypt." They think this is their luck: it gets me out of the way. But it's not their luck: it's mine. So—either six months, a lightning campaign, then back to France to smash the Directory. Or six years, to build my own empire in the east. I must catch the luck, wherever it flies. As others did, in their day. Alexander the Great conquered Egypt. Julius Caesar conquered Egypt.'

Napoleon, apocalyptic, stared at the stars. Bourrienne, an ordinary mortal, stared at Napoleon.

Josephine wrote from Plombières:

> I beg of you, dear Barras, please do keep me informed about yourself, and also about Bonaparte when you have news of him. I am upset at being separated from him: I have a sadness that I cannot shake off. I only wish that your doctor would prescribe the waters of Plombières for you, so that you would come here and take them too. It would be really most obliging of you, to be ill in order to cheer me up.
>
> I am sending you a letter for Bonaparte, which please send on to him at once. You know how angry he gets if he doesn't hear from me all the time. His last letter to me was very sweet and very touching. I really am fond of him, despite his little faults.

Colonel Junot, dirty, dog-tired, with a throat like an oven and a head like a red-hot brick, slogged through the burning sand and pushed into the Commander-in-Chief's tent. The sentry tried to stop him. Junot's throat was too parched and his temper too vile for him to care about remembering the password.

'Get out of my way, I'm Colonel Junot, I need a drink.'

General Berthier, the meticulous mathematician, was at work on his maps.

'Where's Bonaparte, then?'

Berthier didn't look up from his maps. 'He's coming. You can report to me.'

Junot said, 'I estimate we have lost another five hundred men today. Perhaps six hundred. Making roughly two thousand in the last three days. In that oven of hell. Heatstroke. Thirst. Suicides. Men going mad. It's not like Italy. Where's the wine?'

Berthier said, 'You will come to understand that war is a matter of reckoning.'

The voice of the sentry outside. Napoleon giving the password. Napoleon coming in. Napoleon as inhumanly energetic as ever.

'Meal ready? Good. Shall we sit down? Junot, your report?'

Berthier answered for Junot. 'Nothing that changes anything.'

Napoleon said, 'We shall beat the Mamelukes tomorrow, and be in Cairo two days after that.'

Berthier, professional and practical, corrected him. 'Two or three days.'

'Two or three. And all Egypt is ours. Berthier, some wine?'

'No, thank you, sir.'

'Junot?'

'Yes. Staggering around that damned desert all day . . .'

Napoleon was suddenly elated at the thought of Cairo, at the thought of taking and ruling that mighty and mystical capital city, stronghold of the Mameluke beys; he was not listening to Junot's grumbling or to Berthier's careful pessimism—

'And then we'll send for our wives. And our friends. And actors from Paris, and singers, musicians, artists. We'll make it a civilized capital, a European capital . . .'

He was in the mood to make boisterous jokes, bad jokes.

'Berthier, whom will you send for? Since you haven't got a wife? The beautiful Madame Visconti, I suppose? With or without her husband?'

Berthier, very red in the face, said, 'Sir, you know that Madame Visconti would willingly come without her husband, but cannot.'

'My clever Chief of Staff, who falls in love with a married woman.'

Berthier sat silent, his face burning with resentment against the man he worshipped, on behalf of the woman he loved.

'Junot? Whom will you send for?'

'I'm clever enough not to fall in love with anyone.'

'Not clever. You agree with me, Berthier?'

'Yes, sir.'

'Love one woman only, Junot. Then you'll know what love means.'

'You reckon.'

'I know it.'

Junot said, 'Going to bed with them is all right. Falling in love with them is bloody stupidity, for a soldier.'

'We deny that—don't we, Berthier?'

'Yes, sir.' Berthier delighted to find that Napoleon and he were fighting on the same side again.

Junot said, 'Well, I say falling in love is bloody madness, for men like us.'

'How do you know?'

'I've seen. I've seen what happens.'

Napoleon warmed to the argument. 'Berthier, are you any worse a soldier for loving Madame Visconti?'

'No, sir. Not at all.'

Junot said, 'He's not a soldier, he's a Chief of Staff. And his Madame Visconti's married to someone else. He just dreams about it. It's not real. He doesn't know the first bloody thing about reality.'

Napoleon was triumphant with the question that was in itself a victorious statement.

'All right. Am I a soldier?'

'Yes.'

'I am married to my wife. Am I any worse a soldier for loving her? For loving one woman only?'

Junot sat silent.

'Am I?'

Junot sat silent.

'Well? Junot? Am I?'

'No. You're no worse a soldier.'

'No worse. Thank you.'

'But that's not real either.' Junot got up from the table and flung the bottle into the wall of the tent because it was empty. 'I mean, look at Marmont, married two months and then comes out here, doesn't know when he's going to see her again. First thing he gets is a letter from a friend telling him she's playing around with someone else. That's not marriage. It's not fair. It's not fair on either side. That sort of thing's bound to happen. Look at you. You talk about marriage as if you knew all about it. What do you know? You've been married to Josephine, what, two years and a piece? Eight hundred, nine hundred days. How many of those days, how many of those nights, have you been with her? One hundred? Out of nine hundred? Couple of days at a time, and then off to the war again? That's not marriage. It's not fair on you, it's not fair on her. So what happens? Naturally! I mean, it's to be expected! Madame bloody Marmont, and Madame bloody Bonaparte—I'm not blaming them, we're all flesh and blood! Aren't we?'

It came into his mind that he was not saying exactly what he would have said, or at least not using exactly the same words that he would have used, had he been sober.

He said, in an altered voice, 'I'm just trying to explain why I think soldiers are bloody fools to get married when they don't have to.'

Napoleon, very quietly, said, 'Junot.'

'Sir—I'm sorry. I didn't mean it. I didn't mean anything. I was drinking before I got back here. I'm a bit drunk.'

'Junot. What did you mean?'

'I just meant it's not fair on women, being left alone.'

Napoleon rose to his feet, took his glass, and smashed the bowl from the stem, on the edge of the table.

'Junot. Tell me the truth. Tell me.'

Junot silent again.

'Junot. Old friend. Comrade-in-arms. Brother. Tell me the truth.'

Silent still.

'Colonel Junot, I order you to tell me the truth.'

'No.'

'Do you love me? Junot, *do you love me?*'

'Yes!'

'Tell me the truth!'

Junot said, 'You're a fool.'

'Yes! I want the truth! . . . On the way to Italy. You were with them. You were sleeping with her maid. Louise. Louise Compoint. You saw. What did you see? . . . Louise came to me, in Paris, and told me. I didn't believe her. Captain Charles—was it Charles?'

'You want to know?'

Eyes sunken, black, glittering. 'I must know.'

Junot said, 'I saw Charles going into or coming out of your wife's bedroom every night of that trip. I was having her maid, he was having your wife. I didn't tell you because I didn't want you to know. But if you want the truth, well, that's it. And he's gone on having her since, in Paris. Every time you went away. Everyone knows this, except you. Yes, we love you. We loved you by not telling you. But, for God's sake! Everyone knows.'

Napoleon turned to Berthier.

'Is that the truth? Is it?'

'Yes.' Honest Berthier. Faithful Berthier.

Junot said, 'It wasn't as if it was anything new. I mean, Paul Barras—'

'Barras?'

'She was his mistress before she married you. He's gone on having her since. We all know that.'

'Is that true? Berthier?'

Berthier who could not tell a lie. 'Yes.'

Napoleon said, 'Murat? They told me that Murat had boasted . . . ?'

Junot, sober enough to give a comrade the benefit of the doubt, 'No, not Murat, you don't want to listen to that, he's just a Gascon, he's just a big talker, you can't believe it.'

'But Charles.'

'Yes.'

'And Barras.'

'Yes.'

Then Junot said, 'Your fault. You shouldn't have married and then left her alone so much. You can't do that, with that kind of woman. You can't blame her. Your fault. You were a fool.'

Napoleon struck his fists against his head, and fell to the ground, and lay there writhing, convulsively, like an epileptic in the throes of the *grand mal*.

'Josephine!' he cried in his agony, like a dying man.

10. PAULINE

Much the pleasantest place in Cairo of an evening was the Tivoli Egyptien, a close copy of the Tivoli in Paris, a pleasure-garden with coloured lights strung among the greenery, with tables where officers could eat ices and drink wine and watch the acrobats and the jugglers and listen to the military band. But at the Paris Tivoli every officer had a woman on his arm or sitting at his side. At the Cairo Tivoli, alas, the officers sat with other officers, and for that reason, if for no other, devoutly wished themselves in Paris.

Colonel Junot looked across at another table and said, 'Now who the devil is that?'

Napoleon and Lieutenant Eugène de Beauharnais looked where Junot was looking. A waiter was showing a young French officer to a table. He had with him a young woman, deliciously pretty, slim, blue-eyed, blonde. She was laughing, showing the whitest imaginable teeth. And she was saying something in what was undeniably French.

Junot said, 'Eugène, do you know who she is?'

'I've seen her here before.'

'She's gorgeous.'

'Yes.'

'French? Yes, of course, she must be, with that voice. Even without the voice. You only have to look at her.'

'Yes, I'm sure she's French.'

'What's he, a lieutenant? That's no problem. I'll soon get rid of him.'

Eugène said, 'I think she's his wife.'

'Oh. More difficult.'

'At least, someone told me she was his wife.'

'What the hell's he doing with a wife out here?'

'I gather she smuggled herself out, disguised as an officer.'

Napoleon spoke at last, and said, 'I thought I had given orders that all officers' wives were to be left behind in France at the regimental depots.'

Eugène said quickly, 'I'm not absolutely sure she's his wife, sir.'

'Junot.'

'Sir?'

'Find out who she is.'

'A pleasure.' Junot jumped to his feet and went off towards the blonde young woman's table.

Eugène said, 'I'm sorry, sir. I suppose I should have reported it.'

'Yes.'

'I did know of your order, sir. I just didn't think about it.'

The boy was so serious and so ashamed of himself that Napoleon laughed and then was sorry he had laughed.

'Eugène, you take me too seriously. I'm not going to punish anyone, least of all you. I only wish we had more wives out here. They would make us more civilized. We need women here—not whores, they're just machines; but cultivated women, to soften us, to improve our morals and our manners. Or soldiers revert to being savages.'

He looked at Eugène, who sat with downcast eyes, his cheeks now burning red not from shame but from embarrassment. He said, very gently, 'Eugène, if you are thinking of your mother—'

'I can't help it, sir.'

'You are too young to understand what has happened between Josephine and myself.'

'I am not too young, sir. I am seventeen. I do understand it, sir. I'm sorry.'

Napoleon said, still gently, 'Are you apologizing for thinking about it?'

Eugène kept his eyes fixed on the table. 'I have offered you my resignation as your aide-de-camp, sir. I should be grateful if you would accept it.'

Napoleon looked at Eugène and wondered how it was possible that Alexandre de Beauharnais, a cynical rake, a cowardly soldier, and Josephine de Beauharnais, also not famous for her attachment to the notions of faithfulness and loyalty, could have produced a son who was brave, naïve, and the very soul of honour.

He said, 'Your mother is the most charming, the most civilized woman I have ever known. For reasons of which you are aware—whether or not you understand them—I no longer consider her to be my wife. But this makes no difference in my attitude to you. I shall always consider you to be my stepson, my adopted son; as I shall always consider your sister Hortense to be my stepdaughter. That is all there is to say about it.'

Eugène mumbled, 'Will you divorce my mother?'

There was a great burst of laughter from Junot and the blonde young woman. Junot had risen from her table, grinning at the blonde young woman's husband, and was coming back towards Napoleon. Napoleon said, more sternly, 'Eugène, you are right to love your mother, whatever she has done. Kindly remember that you are not responsible for her faults.' He was not looking at Eugène, but at the blonde young woman.

Junot was still laughing as he came back and said, 'Madame Pauline Fourès, wife of Lieutenant Fourès of the Twenty-second Light Infantry. Want me to arrest them?'

'Ask them to join us for a glass of wine.'

'Better idea.' Junot went off again.

Napoleon said, 'Eugène, do you read novels?'

'Yes, sir, sometimes.'

'If I were the ruler of France, I would ban all novels. They give a false idea of life. I don't believe in romantic love: it doesn't exist in the real world. In novels, a man falls in love, and stays in love with the same woman all his life. However much he's away from her, he never wants to go to bed with anyone else. And the heroine does the same. Romance. It is not true to life. It is not in human nature.'

'You were in love with my mother, sir.'

'Yes.'

'Can't you forgive her?'

'We are not characters in a novel. We are human. We live in the real world.'

He rose. Junot said, 'Sir, may I present Madame Fourès and Lieutenant Fourès.—Don't worry, he's not going to shoot you.—The Commander-in-Chief.'

Fourès rigid in the position of attention. 'Sir!'

Napoleon was looking at the blonde young Madame Fourès. She gave him a heavenly smile. He bowed. 'Madame . . .'

Junot said briskly, 'Well. Sit down. Let's get chairs. Let's get glasses. Have some wine.'

Lieutenant Fourès marched into General Berthier's office and saluted.

'Lieutenant Fourès, Twenty-second Light Infantry, reporting, sir!'

He stood stiffly to attention, waiting for permission to stand at ease. It did not come. He continued as he was, arms pressed to his sides, heels glued together.

Berthier said, 'Lieutenant Fourès, your commanding officer speaks highly of you, as a brave and resourceful officer.'

It seemed he was expected to say something. He said, 'Sir.'

'Consequently you have been selected for a most important mission.'

Again he had to say something. 'Thank you, sir.'

'To carry urgent dispatches to the Directory in Paris.'

He couldn't stop his face from falling. 'Sir?'

Berthier ignored the question-mark. 'As I imagine you know, the English fleet is now in control of the Mediterranean.'

'Yes, sir.'

'Getting to France will be difficult, and may be dangerous. You will need all your bravery, and all your resourcefulness.'

'Sir.' There was nothing else to say.

'You will collect the dispatches from the Commander-in-Chief's secretary, Monsieur Bourrienne. You will proceed with them to Alexandria, where you will report to Colonel Marmont. Under his instructions, you will embark on the courier ship *Chasseur*, which will take you to Italy. You will proceed overland to Paris.'

'Yes, sir.'

Berthier said, 'Any questions?'

There was only one question that he could ask, of any importance. Would he get another night or two with Pauline, or just a few hours?

'Yes, sir—one question. When do I leave, sir?'

Berthier said, 'Now.'

Napoleon gave a small dinner-party, in his private dining-room in Elfi-Bey's palace, for a few of his closest colleagues and friends: General Berthier, General Murat, Colonel Junot, Monsieur Bourrienne. Also present was Madame Fourès.

The Commander-in-Chief, normally a man who led and dominated the conversation at table, sat silent throughout the meal, for some unknowable reason. Normally a man who ate a small dinner, on this occasion he ate nothing. He did, however, devour Madame Fourès with his eyes.

She was having a very good time. Even with Napoleon unspeaking and unmoving, there were four gallant men vying with each other to pay her compliments, leaping from their seats to be the first to fetch her whatever she wanted. A beautiful woman enjoys being admired. She was a very beautiful woman. She was by far the most beautiful French woman of the few that there were in Egypt. She was being greatly admired, and was greatly enjoying it.

She said, 'Yes, well, it's nice here. But I do envy Fourès, going back to Paris. I've never been to Paris. You should have sent me with him.'

Berthier said drily, 'It's hardly a pleasure trip.'

She had drunk her coffee. Junot was the first to notice this, and to jump up. 'Can I get you some more coffee?'

As he took her cup, Pauline asked Berthier, 'Where do you suppose he is now?'

'He?'

'My husband.'

'At sea, somewhere between Alexandria and Malta.'

She laughed, not unkindly, but at a memory which had become a good joke. 'I hope it's calm, he's a terrible sailor. I'm not, I don't mind anything. On the way out, with me stowing away like that, he'd wondered what he was going to do about feeding me. What happened was, I ate all his rations, while he just lay on his back and groaned.' She looked impishly at Murat. 'And I thought men were supposed to be strong.'

'Strong in other ways.'

Junot said, pouring coffee at a side-table, 'No, we're the weaker sex. Which is why we need women to support us.'

Berthier made a little bow to her and her sex in general. 'What man would be brave enough for childbirth?'

She smiled at him to thank him. 'Yes, that's right. Not that I know much about it yet. But I'm sure I shan't just lie on my back and groan.'

Junot said, 'Your coffee, Madame.' He stumbled as he was putting the cup down. The coffee spilt on to her dress.

'Oh!' She jumped up.

'I'm sorry—'

'No, it doesn't matter—'

'Clumsy, I caught my foot just as I was—'

'It won't stain, if you've got some hot water—'

'Hot water, yes, I'm sure we have—'

'I should do it straight away—'

Junot, so penitent, so woebegone, turned urgently to the others for help. 'Murat, hot water—do you know where—?'

Murat was brisk, soldierly, efficient. 'Would you come with me, Madame?'

Junot went with them to the door. 'If it doesn't come out, of course I'll be only too happy to—I mean, the least I can do is buy you a—'

They were gone. Junot came back to the table and poured himself a brandy, and drank it, and looked at Napoleon, who had sat silent all this while.

'Well,' Junot said, 'I've done my bit.'

Murat said, 'Hot water in this one. Sponges and so on. Towels. Is there anything else you'll need?'

'No, you just leave me to get on with it. I'll come back when I've done it.'

He bowed and went. She took her dress off and inspected the stain, and put it over the bowl, and poured hot water over it, and looked at it again.

She heard the door, and turned. General Bonaparte had come in. He was coming towards her. He made her a stiff little bow. She was amused and not in the least surprised. She looked at him, smiling at him, waiting for him to say something. Since he didn't say anything, she broke the silence by laughing—not at him, but at the whole situation. She found it funny. It was funny, the way things happened in life. Life was funny. She liked it that way. She enjoyed having funny things happening.

She said, 'Why did you have to get him to spill coffee on me? It's a nice dress.'

He said, 'I'll buy you a thousand dresses.'

She laughed again, pleased. 'I'm glad you can speak. Instead of just staring at me—'

'You are worth staring at.'

'—and sending me presents.'

'Did you like the presents?'

'Oh, yes, I always like presents. Whoever they're from.'

'They were from your most devoted admirer.'

He was so serious, she had to make fun of him, and be mock-serious. 'Yes, I did actually understand what you were getting at.'

He said, 'I should explain . . .' But he didn't know how to explain. She helped him.

'Look, you met me that night in the Tivoli Gardens. Then you sent my husband away. Then you sent me all those presents. Then you invited me to dinner. Honestly, it doesn't need explaining.'

His face relaxed, but his voice was still serious. He said, 'I should explain, I fell in love with you when I met you in the Tivoli Gardens.'

'Really?'

'Yes.'

She said gently, 'That's nice. I'm glad you fell in love with me.'

He was no longer awkward, but still anxious. He said, trying to hide his fear of her giving the wrong answer, 'I hope that you may be able to love me.'

He knew why he was fearful: because he knew that her answer would be the truth. She was not a woman who deceived herself or deceived anyone else. The truth came straight out of her, directly, perfectly naturally, like water from a spring.

She said, 'Well, I thought about it. Of course. When I saw what was happening.'

'Did you decide?'

'Yes.' He was seized with a violent hope that she had decided in his favour. But had she? 'Yes, I decided, a Commander-in-Chief is more important than a lieutenant.' She laughed. 'That sounds mercenary, doesn't it? I don't mean it that way. I don't mean "richer", I just mean "more important". In every way.'

His heart was beating violently, with a fierce happiness.

She said, 'And I thought, you're nice-looking. And quite young. And it's silly to miss a chance when you get one. I never do, on principle. Fourès was the nephew of the lady I worked for. He fell in love with me, he asked me to marry him, he could have asked me to do something else but he didn't. It was a big chance for me, I took it. This is a bigger one. I think you've got to take your luck, don't you? I've never refused a piece of luck. You'll see.'

He said, 'I think we suit each other.'

She looked at him with her honest eyes. 'Yes, I think we do.'

He put his arms round her, diffidently, gently, and kissed her.

'You are adorable.'

She said, 'Say nice things to me. But don't say them unless you mean them. I can't stand that.'

He said, 'I adore you.'

'I'm glad.'

They kissed again.

'I want you to live with me as my wife.'

She raised an eyebrow, half-comic, half-serious. 'What does that mean?'

'As if you were my wife.'

'What's your real wife going to say? I know she's in Paris, but she's bound to find out sooner or later, isn't she? Or don't you mind? If you don't, I don't.'

'I no longer consider her to be my wife.'

'You don't love her any more?'

'No.'

'Truth?'

'Truth.'

She said, happily, 'Well, that's all right, then. Do they expect us back at the dinner-table?'

Her eyebrow was raised again, but this time it was purely comic.

Napoleon said, 'They'd be greatly surprised.'

She looked at her dress, on the bowl, on the wash-stand; and she looked across the room at the magnificent double bed. She said, 'Yes, the moment I saw that bed, I thought, "Oops, this is going to be it." '

Napoleon laughed, out of amusement and out of sheer pleasure. 'You're funny.'

'Quite funny sometimes.'

He took her by the hand and led her slowly to the bed. They were sure of each other now, there was no anxiety and no haste. They sat on the edge of the bed, facing each other and smiling, like old friends who were also in love with each other. They started to undress each other, slowly.

He said, 'And your husband?'

'Well, it's better having him out of the way. He'd have minded.'

'And you don't mind? For yourself?'

'I'm practical.'

'Yes.'

'You can promote him for carrying important dispatches.'

'Yes.'

'Are they really important? If you tell me they are, I won't believe you.'

Napoleon said, 'There's nothing in them that the Directory doesn't already know—that the English don't already know, that the world doesn't already know . . .'

'Why the English?'

'In case he gets captured.'

'Will he?'

'I don't know. But in case.'

'But he'll never know they weren't important, will he?'

'No.'

'That's all right, then.'

They went on smiling at each other and undressing each other. Then, very happy, they climbed into the great bed.

Brigadier-General Marmont, not long ago a captain, recently a colonel, now commanding the port of Alexandria, was peacefully signing his mail, towards the end of the day, when his lieutenant aide-de-camp rushed in, positively panic-stricken.

'Sir!' He remembered he hadn't shut the door, and ran to shut it, then ran back to Marmont's desk. 'Sir!' He remembered to lower his voice to a wildly urgent whisper. 'Lieutenant Fourès is here!'

'Who?'

'Lieutenant Fourès.'

'He can't be.'

'He is!'

It was not the first time Marmont had seen one of his officers run quietly mad, from the heat, and the flies, and the longing for France.

Marmont spoke firmly, as he had learnt to do in these cases. 'Lieutenant Fourès is on a boat somewhere in the Mediterranean.'

'No, sir. He's here.'

'Here?'

'Just outside. In my office. He wants transport back to Cairo.'

Marmont took the shortest way to find out whether the man was mad or not. He marched out to the outer office. Lieutenant Fourès jumped up and saluted him.

'Sir!'

Marmont pulled himself together as fast as he could.

'Fourès?'

'Sir!'

'What the devil are you doing in Alexandria? You're supposed to be on your way to France!'

'Yes, sir!'

'Why aren't you?'

'We were captured, sir. By an English cruiser. The second day out.'

'Captured?'

'We put up a good fight, sir. But they were ten times stronger than us. We didn't stand a chance.'

'So you were captured.'

'Yes, sir. That's right, sir.'

'Well? Why aren't you a prisoner?'

'The English sent me back, sir.'

'Why?'

'On parole, sir.'

'Yes, I heard you. Why?'

'I don't know, sir.'

'What do you mean, you don't know? Didn't they tell

you why?' Marmont was still doing his best to conceal the simple fact that he was still flabbergasted.

— 'No, sir. They took all the others off to a prison camp in Turkey. But they dropped me on the coast quite near here. And they wished me luck. I couldn't understand what they were saying, but there was one of them who spoke French, and he wished me luck, and he said they all did. All the English. He said, all the whole English nation.'

Marmont stared at him, speechless.

Fourès said, 'Perhaps they liked me.'

'Perhaps they—!' Marmont managed to restrain the fury which had taken the place of the flabbergastedness. 'Well. So you're here. How nice for you.'

'I ought to get back to Cairo, sir. To report to General Berthier.'

'We'll see. You need a meal first, and some sleep. Rest for a day or two.'

'I'd like to get to Cairo, sir, as soon as I can. If you can let me have transport.'

'We'll see.'

'I have a wife in Cairo, sir. Of course, I'd like to see her, and tell her I'm still alive.'

Marmont said, 'I shall let you know when I can send you to Cairo. Go and find yourself some food and a bed. Come back here tomorrow.'

'Sir!'

When Fourès had gone, Marmont said to his aide-de-camp, 'I can't hold him here for ever.'

'No, sir.'

'Cairo, as fast as you can.'

'Yes, sir.'

'Tell General Berthier the English have a first-class spy system in this country; and also an over-developed sense of humour.'

Berthier sat at his desk. Lieutenant Fourès marched in and saluted.

'Lieutenant Fourès, Twenty-second Light Infantry, reporting, sir!'

Fourès saw that Pauline was in the room, at a distance, with a civilian who looked like a lawyer. She smiled a greeting. He did not dare speak to her.

Berthier said, 'Lieutenant Fourès, what are you doing in Cairo? You're supposed to be on your way to Paris.'

'We got captured, sir. By an English cruiser. The second day out.'

'Captured?'

'They were ten times stronger than us, sir.'

'Why aren't you a prisoner?'

'I don't know, sir.'

'Don't know?'

'I had to give my parole, sir.'

'What parole?'

'Not to fight against the English for the remainder of this campaign.'

'You should not have given your parole.'

'Well, if I hadn't, sir, I wouldn't have been able to fight against them even after this campaign, because I'd have been in a prison camp in Turkey.'

Berthier said, 'Lieutenant Fourès, you are posted to Upper Egypt. Where there are Arabs but no English.'

'Sir—may I speak to my wife, sir?'

'You may not.'

Fourès said, 'Sir, I have heard certain things already. I think perhaps I have been made a fool of.'

Berthier said, 'Your wife has applied for a divorce, under the laws of France, which are valid for French troops serving abroad. This gentleman here is a civil commissioner, with the power to grant divorces.'

Fourès stared at his wife. She said, 'It's all arranged, darling. So you might as well look cheerful.'

He could not look at her any longer.

'*She's* applied? On what grounds?'

Berthier said, 'Cruelty.'

*　　*　　*

Eugène stood, very stiff and red-faced, in front of his stepfather's desk, and said the speech that he had learnt by heart.

'Sir, I am proud of being your stepson, and of being your aide-de-camp.'

'Well?' Napoleon was not in an easy or patient mood.

'Sir, one of my duties is to ride as your escort, when you go out in your carriage, through Cairo.'

'Yes. Well?'

'With Madame Fourès by your side, sir.'

'It is one of the duties of the aide-de-camp of the day.'

'Sir, I request permission to resign the position of aide-de-camp. My mother is still your wife, sir.'

Napoleon said, after a time, with no kindness in his voice, 'I do not give permission.'

'Sir—', Eugène was flushing even redder, and preparing to be obstinate.

'You are excused escort duty when Madame Fourès is with me.'

'Thank you, sir.'

'But you will behave towards Madame Fourès with all possible respect.'

'Yes, sir.'

Napoleon fixed his eye on Eugène's, forced Eugène to look him straight in the eye. He said, slowly and clearly, so that there could be no possibility of mistaking his meaning, 'She is to be treated with the respect due to my future wife.'

Josephine, nervous, unhappy, in a bad temper because Barras was making fun of her, and the subject was not the least bit funny—

'I shall divorce him, and marry Charles.'

Barras laughed again. Why should he laugh? It was absolutely not a laughing matter. But he laughed, and said, 'Darling, you're not such a fool.'

'I will not stay married to a man I don't love.'

'Most women do.'

'A man I never see!'

'Most women long for that.'

'Paul. Be a friend. Help me. Advise me. What shall I do? I'm in love with Charles—seriously, deeply—'

'New words, for you.'

'I am really in love.'

Barras said, not laughing, but looking as if he might laugh again very soon, 'Love is the most wonderful thing in the world, for the rich. Monsieur Charles is lovable. Is he rich?'

She said impatiently, 'I don't care about money.'

'Yes, that was the big problem of having you as a mistress. It must be one of the big problems of having you as a wife.'

'I would marry Charles if he had nothing.'

'And give him your debts as a dowry? How much do you owe at the moment?'

'I don't know.'

'What's the price of that new house you've bought? Malmaison? Two hundred and seventy thousand? You've signed the contract. You've got no money. Who's going to pay for it?'

'Bonaparte can pay.'

'After you've divorced him? No, my dear girl. You can't do it. And you mustn't.'

She said pettishly, 'Mustn't? You can't tell me I mustn't.'

'I've told you your reason why you mustn't. Your debts.' His voice hardened. 'I'll tell you my reason. The Directory is falling apart. There has to be a new form of government soon. I can manage to stay at the head of it, if I have a strong right arm with a sword. The best right arm—the best sword—would be Bonaparte, back from Egypt. Your husband. My friend.'

She made a face. 'I am not a politician.'

'You are a very good politician when you want to be.'

'I don't want to be, now.'

Barras sighed. 'If you stay on the emotional level, which I find boring . . . Third reason. Charles does not wish you to divorce Bonaparte, and has not the slightest desire to marry you.' She had, after all, asked for it.

In a tight, harsh voice, hating Barras, she said, 'Charles loves me.'

'Yes, darling, and will continue to love you. So long as you're Bonaparte's wife.'

'No!'

Her colour was coming and going. She was not a reasonable woman. Barras took great care to be at his most reasonable.

'Darling, why is Charles employed by the Bodin Company? Because you are his mistress, and you can write letters to important people. Why do important people pay attention to your letters? Because your husband is—'

'Charles loves me for myself!' The words came out as a kind of muffled scream.

Barras did not vary his polite smile. 'In that case, since you ask my advice, I give it. Marry him. And live on bread and cheese and kisses.'

She said, 'He is coming here, this evening. Soon. Wait. You'll see.'

Barras bowed. 'I am always ready to learn something new.'

'You will learn.'

When Charles arrived he brought gaiety into the room, and lightness, and charm, and if not immediate amusingness, at least the feeling that life was really an essentially amusing business.

'Dear Madame. My dear Barras. What marvellous news from Egypt. Another great victory. Bonaparte is quite incredible.'

Josephine said, loudly, unsmilingly, 'Barras advises me to divorce Bonaparte and marry you.'

Charles looked at her. Was it a joke? He looked at Barras. Barras was a joker. Could this be one of his jokes? But neither was smiling. It was to be hoped that it was a joke. But it would not be safe to treat it as a joke. Barras had advised it. He would reply to Barras—a serious, sensible reply, but given with a certain lightness, a certain amusingness, in case the whole thing was a joke. It must be a joke. Barras could hardly be serious.

'My dear Barras, always delighted to take your advice, on anything except marriage. The idea is charming, but total madness. It's simply not a practical proposition. Why on earth should Josephine and I want to kill the goose that lays all those lovely golden eggs?'

He turned to Josephine with a smile, to invite her agreement. She struck his face with her open palm, as hard as she was able.

He said, 'But darling, I thought you understood . . .'

He saw her face: the face of a woman whose love has been destroyed in a moment.

In Cairo, Pauline and Napoleon were getting ready for bed: already as connubial and used to each other as a long-married couple.

He said, as carelessly as he could, 'Oh, I'm going on a journey tomorrow.'

'Oh, where to?'

He didn't answer.

'Is it a military secret? Or are you allowed to tell me?'

'No.'

'Am I allowed to guess?'

'No.'

'Can I ask, will it be for long?'

He said, carefully, 'We shan't be parted for long.'

'Good.'

'Yes.'

'We'd better get to bed, then.'

'Yes.'

He went to her and put his hand on her slim belly. 'You're not pregnant yet?'

She said cheerfully, 'Not for want of trying.'

'No.' He smiled because she was smiling, and because the trying had been such a pleasure.

'My fault or yours? I don't know much about these things, do you?'

'Not much.'

'I thought it just automatically happened, unless you took precautions. I mean, usually.'

'I thought so too.'

'Have you ever got anyone pregnant?'

'No, I haven't.'

'Fourès and I always used to take precautions. But anyway, I've never been pregnant. So it could be you or it could be me.'

'Yes.'

'Or just luck. I've known couples, first time, straight off, bang! Pregnant. When they didn't want it. Other people, they do want it, they go on for years, hoping. Then suddenly it happens, for no reason.'

'Yes.'

She said comfortably, 'Well, we'll go on trying. I like trying.'

'Yes.'

'It ought to happen, we both want it and we're both lucky people. Look at your luck, against the Turks.'

'That wasn't luck, that was a brilliantly fought battle.'

She was pleased: she had got him out of being touchily vain about his military skills. Now he was only jokily vain. That was all right.

'Well, brilliant or not, it was what you wanted, wasn't it? A great triumph.'

'Yes, I admit it was a great triumph.'

They got into bed and lay facing each other, fondly, in each other's arms.

After a time she said, 'Am I allowed to say I've guessed where you're going?'

She was herself all truth, all honesty. He could not tell her an untruth.

He said, 'I'm taking Berthier with me, and Murat, and Marmont, and Eugène, and two or three others, that's all. I would take you, but the journey's rather dangerous. I've left you some money. You'll get it tomorrow, from Junot. And I've left orders that Junot is to bring you to join me as soon as possible. As soon as it's safe.'

Her mouth was against his ear. She whispered, 'You're going to France.'

He did not answer.

She drew her head back and looked at him. 'That really is dangerous. With all those English ships.'

He said, 'That's the only reason I'm not taking you with me.'

'You could smuggle me aboard. Disguised as an officer.'

'No.'

'But I'll see you soon.'

'Soon.'

'In France. Sorry, I didn't say that. I won't say it to anyone else.'

She went back into his arms again, closely, her cheek against his, her soft body against his.

She said, 'You do know I love you.'

'Yes, I do know.'

'One last try?'

'One more try.'

11. NAPOLEON'S HOMECOMING

Josephine was dining at the Luxembourg, with her friends the members of the Directory, when the news came by military telegraph that General Bonaparte had landed on the south coast of France, at Fréjus, and was hurrying northwards to Paris.

She went very pale. She hoped the paleness would be taken as a sign of her feeling an almost unbearable joy at her husband's return.

Her mind was very clear. She knew what she had to do. She said it to Barras.

'I must meet him on the road. I must go now, immediately, as fast as I can. It's the right thing to do, isn't it?'

'The only thing to do.'

'If his brothers get to him first—Joseph, or Lucien—'

'Then you're done for.'

'They'll tell him lies about me, wicked lies—'

Barras said sweetly, 'Darling, you needn't worry so much about the lies. But if they tell him the truth, you're done for.'

'Yes, they've been spying on me—they know—they know about you, too—'

'I do hope not. I need Bonaparte as my friend.'

She clutched his arm. 'Paul, you'll help me—you'll tell him, you'll swear to him—'

'Of course, but who believes what I say? What matters is what you say, and how soon you can say it.'

'His family have always hated me, they've always wanted a divorce—'

'As you did.'

'I can't let him divorce me now!'

'No, I agree, you can't.'

149

'I'll take Hortense with me—that's a good idea, he's fond of Hortense—'

It was more than a good idea, it was a stroke of genius, it was the move that would turn the whole course of the game and snatch a last-minute victory against all the odds. Bonaparte loved Eugène but he doted on Hortense. She was the daughter every father would have wished to have: sweet, pure, angelically pretty. It was impossible to look at her and think ill of her mother: surely, only a saint could have produced someone with so candid a gaze, with such totally innocent blue eyes. And, during Bonaparte's time away, she had grown taller and slimmer and more beautiful: she was fifteen now, and on the brink of becoming a most desirable young woman. She would melt her stepfather's heart, if anyone could, and even if her mother failed to do it.

Josephine made her apologies to the Directors—who understood perfectly well what she had to do—and hurried to the house in rue de la Victoire, calling for her maid.

'Agathe, pack my clothes for some days, I'm leaving tonight, I'm leaving now. And find Hortense. Tell her to come here quickly, quickly—she has to go with me—'

Hortense came running. 'Mamma, what is it?'

'Hortense, you must get ready—we heard the news at dinner, Bonaparte has landed in France—we must leave as soon as we can, we must meet him on the road.'

In his carriage, travelling northwards, Napoleon said, 'The timing is perfect. Austria and Russia at war with us again—a corrupt government in Paris, incompetent commanders in the field—and I return from my triumphs in Egypt and Syria.'

Berthier said, 'Should we mention Syria? It was hardly a triumph.'

'All they know is what they've read in my dispatches. In my dispatches, Syria was a triumph.'

'Hm.'

'And in Europe they have nothing to show but defeats.'

'One or two victories.'

'Nothing compared with me. The moment is right for me. I shall seize the moment.'

'To take charge of the whole of the French Army?'

Napoleon was patient with good, honest, slow Berthier.

'No. To take charge of the whole of France.'

In her carriage, speeding southwards, Josephine bit deep into her lip and drove her fingernails into the palms of her hands.

'Faster! Oh, why can't he drive faster?'

'Mamma, he is driving very fast.'

'He must go faster. I must get to Napoleon before anyone else does.'

'Mamma, what does an hour matter, or even a day?'

'Hortense, you don't understand. I'm a million francs in debt.'

Changing at Lyons to a lighter and faster carriage, a two-seater with room for only himself and Eugène, Napoleon said, 'Tell him to take the road through the Bourbonnais.'

'Yes, sir. Though the Burgundy road might be quicker, sir.'

'There are more big towns on the Bourbonnais road.'

'Big towns, sir?'

'For the people to line the streets and cheer me.'

Josephine said, 'Why haven't we met him yet? We can't have passed him on the road without seeing him!'

Hortense said, 'Do you think he can have taken the other road?'

'No, no. He always preferred the Burgundy road. He never took the road through the Bourbonnais.'

When she arrived in Lyons, she discovered that she was wrong.

When he arrived in Paris, at his house, he called out 'Josephine!'

He turned to Eugène and said, 'I shall not be unkind.

But, you understand, it must be a divorce. She must move out of here today, to Malmaison. You will take her there, and see that she is properly settled there with everything she needs.'

'Yes, sir. I understand, sir.'

'Where is she? Josephine!'

Agathe and the other servants came quickly, flustered.

'Welcome home, Monsieur—'

'Agathe, where is Madame Bonaparte?'

'She went to meet you on the road, Monsieur. Didn't she meet you?'

'On the road? What road?'

'The Burgundy road. She was sure you would be coming that way.'

He turned to Eugène.

'Your mother is out of luck.'

On the road back to Paris, two days to Lyons therefore two days back again, Josephine still cried from a hoarse and aching throat, 'Faster! Faster!'

But, she thought, 'His brothers have spoken to him by now. I have lost my last chance.'

From the moment of Bonaparte's return the house in rue de la Victoire lost all its elegance, its softness, its femininity. It became a military headquarters, full of hard, tanned-faced men in uniform, and orderlies running in and out with messages, and anxious politicians clamouring to see Bonaparte, and being ignored or told to wait.

He himself commanded everything, though he had gone back to posing as a civilian again in his grey frock-coat.

'Berthier will sound out the General Staff. Under his supervision, Murat will sound out the cavalry officers; Lannes, the infantry; Marmont, the artillery. To make sure that they will all be solidly on our side when we decide to strike.'

Berthier said, in his dry practical voice, 'They will be.'

'Is there any other question we should decide now?'

Talleyrand said, 'Two questions, possibly related. Paul Barras.'

'Barras must go.' Napoleon was terse.

'You don't think we need him? At first? Until we can do without him, after the first few days?'

'No.' Napoleon grew even terser.

'I simply mention the thought. He is longing to believe that he is one of us. He could be useful, in his way.'

Napoleon said, 'Whether we need him or not, I will not have Barras in any government of mine.' His voice did not give permission for further debate.

Talleyrand said, 'And a possibly related question. Madame Bonaparte. Your wife.'

Berthier gathered his papers together. 'That's outside my province. I'll go and start organizing the army.' He went.

Napoleon said, 'The question is already decided. I shall divorce her immediately.'

Again, he forbade discussion. But Talleyrand said, mildly, innocently, 'May one ask why? Why divorce?'

Napoleon's two brothers were more than ready to tell him why.

Lucien said, 'Because she's a whore.'

Joseph said, 'We have given Napoleon proofs—undeniable proofs—'

'Of her adultery—'

'Repeated adultery—'

'Compound adultery—'

Joseph said, 'I was blind in Italy. I didn't see what was happening. But now, her adulteries are completely beyond dispute. Do you wish me to go into details?'

Talleyrand mildly disclaimed any such desire. 'No, no. I had imagined that perhaps you had a political reason, of a sort that I could understand.'

Joseph flushed. 'It's a stain on the honour of our family.'

'Ah, yes. Of course.'

Collot the banker—blunt, burly, pugnacious—looked

at the brothers and said, 'I don't give a damn for your Corsican honour. Is a divorce going to help us, or not?'

Lucien jumped up, at his most Corsican. 'Monsieur Collot, is the question of the divorce any concern of yours?'

'Monsieur Bonaparte—all three of you—I am putting up the money to finance your *coup d'état*. If I'm financing it, I want a say in how it is run.'

Napoleon stopped his brothers from answering, and gave the answer himself. 'It is run by me, and by no one else.'

Collot said, 'You're cleverer than your brothers. Think. Is this the moment to parade your domestic quarrels?'

'It is more than a quarrel.'

'I was phrasing it politely. All right, I'll put it plainly. Is this the moment to proclaim to the people of France that from your wedding-day till now, regularly, all the time, other men have been screwing your wife?'

Napoleon stared straight in front of him, and said in a hard tight voice, 'I am going to get rid of her.'

Collot said, 'Talleyrand? You're the only sensible man we've got. What do you think?'

Talleyrand said, 'Oh, I agree with the Bonapartes.'

'What?'

Talleyrand said to Napoleon, 'I entirely agree with Joseph, and Lucien, and yourself. I urge you to get rid of her. Not because of her adulteries, but because she commits them so publicly. You should not have an indiscreet wife . . . It may be asked, who knows of her indiscretions? Our circle. A few hundred people perhaps, in Paris. To the rest of Paris—to the rest of France—you are a popular hero with a charming helpmeet. I also agree with Collot. I urge you, for the moment, to preserve the illusions of the French people. When you are in power, as you will be very soon, you can do as you please. Rulers have that privilege. But you are not yet in power.'

Napoleon said, between his teeth, grindingly, as if he were grinding his teeth, 'I shall never forgive her. I shall never speak to her again.'

Talleyrand made a little bow, directing it towards the inevitable, whatever it might be.

'So long as you are sure of that.'

Napoleon cried, in a sudden white-hot rage, 'If I were not sure of myself, I would tear my heart out and throw it on the fire!'

They were silenced by his rage. He looked round at them and said, 'The question is decided.'

It was midnight when Josephine, worn out by travelling, got back to the house in rue de la Victoire. The first thing she saw was all her trunks, all her bags, all her belongings, piled high in the hall, near the front door, ready to be taken away.

Agathe said, 'He says you're to go and live at Malmaison. And never come here again.'

'Agathe. Where is he?'

'In the bedroom, Madame.'

'I must talk to him.'

'He says he won't see you, Madame.'

But Josephine was already running towards the stairs.

Agathe would have told Josephine, but Josephine had gone so quickly, she could only tell Hortense.

'He's locked himself in the bedroom. So that she can't get in. So that he can't see her.'

Josephine ran to the door of the bedroom, but stopped a moment before she got to it. There were mirrors to look into. She must look tired and tragic and repentant, but she must also look beautiful. She inspected herself in different mirrors, by different lights. She removed from her cheek one tear-mark too many. She adjusted a curl on her forehead. She decided what she would do. It was better to speak to him straight away, travel-stained as she was, but while she still had the emotional tension and fatigue of her journey to give her words more power and more pathos.

She went quietly to the bedroom door and tapped on it, gently, almost timidly.

'Napoleon . . . ?'

She waited. There was no answer.

She tapped again, a little louder, in case he was asleep.

'Napoleon . . . ?'

No answer. But she could hear that there was someone in the bedroom, a man, Napoleon, walking about, starting to pace up and down, not near the door but somewhere beyond the bed, by the window. Quietly, almost silently, pacing up and down.

She tapped again. She knew he could hear her. No answer.

'Napoleon?'

She knew he could recognize her voice. No answer.

She tried the handle. It turned, but the door would not open. The door was locked.

She called more loudly.

'Napoleon!'

No answer.

She said, pleadingly, caressingly, not loud but loud enough to be sure that he could hear her words—

'Napoleon. Please let me in. Please let me talk to you. Please . . . I drove all the way to Lyon to meet you, I wanted to see you so much, after so long. Oh, darling, I haven't seen you for so long. Please let me in.'

She waited. No word from him. He was still pacing.

'I must have taken the wrong road, wasn't that silly? I was so sure you'd come through Burgundy, because that was the road you took before, the way you took when you travelled with me. And when I got to Lyon and found out I was wrong, I nearly died. I was so longing to see you. And I wanted to explain. Darling, let me come in and explain . . .'

No word from him. Still pacing.

'Napoleon. Napoleon. Darling. Can I ask you? Has Joseph, has Lucien, either of them—have they been telling you things about me? None of it's true, darling, not one word of it's true. I can explain, won't you let me come in and explain?'

The pacing was as regular as a metronome, the footfall as inevitable as the drip of a leaking tap. She felt suddenly that she couldn't bear it, it must stop or she would run mad, she would scream. She must not let herself scream.

'Napoleon, I can't bear it if you won't speak to me. Don't let me in if you don't want to, but come to the door and speak to me. It's just to hear your voice. Napoleon, come to the door and say my name. Just say my name. The name you gave me. Your name for me. Josephine. Please say it. Say "Josephine", that's all. That's all. "Josephine". Darling, *please* say it.'

She must not scream. She sobbed. She could not stop herself from sobbing. She could not stop herself from falling to her knees, at the foot of the door, sobbing helplessly.

'Napoleon, I am on my knees to you . . .'

She no longer knew what she was saying, between the sobs. The words came out of her, brokenly, disjointedly, uncontrollably, but out of her old instinctive and habitual lying, untruths as passionately sincere as truth.

'Oh, darling, Napoleon darling, I know I've been foolish, I know I've been childish, but nothing more, nothing more than that, whatever anyone has told you, it's not true, it's simply not true, I swear it's not true. Oh darling, I shall die if you don't believe me, I shall die if you don't speak to me, Napoleon, speak to me and tell me you believe me, Napoleon. I love you, I love you, please speak to me . . .'

She collapsed against the door and slid down it to the floor, prostrate, sobbing, with great painful sobs that racked her whole body. Hortense came in and found her there, and knelt by her and cradled her in her arms.

'Mamma . . .'

'I shall die . . .'

'No, Mamma. No . . .'

'I shall die . . . Tell him I shall die . . . Tell him I love him . . .'

Hortense gently put her mother down, and rose, and knocked on the door, and stood at the door, waiting.

'Father. You once told me to call you "Father". If

you won't speak to her, will you speak to me?' No answer. 'Will you listen to me?' No answer. 'Father, you are killing her, do you want to kill her?' A sound of some kind in the bedroom, not words, but an indefinable sound made by a man's voice. 'Father, she loves you, I know she does. And you love her. Do you want her to die?' Another sound, perhaps a man stumbling, blindly, knocking into furniture. 'Father, she is dying at your door.'

She listened intently, straining her ears. She thought she heard footsteps, stumbling footsteps coming slowly towards the door.

She whispered, 'Mamma, stand up . . . !'

She knelt down again, quietly, but as quickly as she could, to help her mother to her feet.

Josephine sobbed again, but silently, heartrendingly, sobs which were more like deep shudders, her eyes tight shut, her head on Hortense's shoulder.

Another whisper. 'He's coming . . . !'

'No, he won't, he won't . . .'

Then they heard the key turn in the lock, and Josephine opened her eyes.

Then they heard and saw the handle turn.

Then Napoleon came out of the bedroom, crying, tears running down his face, without making any sound.

Josephine went forward to him, her legs hardly supporting her, and threw herself into his arms, her head against his breast.

'My love . . .' It was all she could say.

He held her, profoundly moved by her distress, holding her to support her, to save her from falling, but not loving her.

He said, quietly, with no hatred, no unkindness towards her, 'I can never forgive you.'

'I love you . . .'

He said, 'You have killed my heart.'

Hortense whispered, 'Father, she is dying of unhappiness. Please be kind to her.'

He looked at Hortense, and she understood, and went quietly out of the room, leaving the two of them alone, he still holding her but not embracing her. There was no warmth in his arms.

She found a little voice to ask, 'Let me come in . . .'

'No.'

'I'm dying . . . Let me lie down . . . Somewhere . . .'

He silently supported her to a couch, and laid her down on it gently, and stood looking down at her. She dared not look at him.

He said, 'I loved you more than any woman has ever been loved.'

'Yes.'

'I have no love left in me. I cannot love you ever again. Nor anyone, ever again.'

She acknowledged her crime. 'Because of what I have done.'

'That is what you have done.'

She said, haltingly, with difficulty, because the thought was a new one to her, 'So I find what I want most in the world, as I lose it. Your love.'

He said, still without unkindness, 'You found other men's love.'

'No . . . ' She found a way of telling him that was nearer the truth than ever before, which was the truth mixed with some lies: she could never help telling some lies, but a kind of virtue came into her: she felt virtuous at the really most unusually high proportion of truth that there was in what she said.

'No, I've been foolish, I've been stupid, I've been mad. Barras—that was to help you, I thought it would help you, I was stupid—you didn't need my help, I needed yours. I never loved Barras, I never cared for him, I hate him . . . The other—the other was madness, but I'm a woman, a foolish woman, it wouldn't have happened if you'd been there. We were married, but it wasn't a marriage. I'm weak, I needed your strength, but you weren't there. I'm no good by myself, I'm no good without you, but you left me alone so much. Oh, darling, you shouldn't have left me alone . . .'

He thought of the desert, and Junot drunk, and Junot telling him whose fault it was.

She said, 'You're too kind to me, you should hit me, you should kill me. I'll go to Malmaison, I'll go now, you'll never have to see me again. But because you loved me, because you loved me once, do one thing for me before I go, because I love you. Kiss me once. Please. Kiss me good-bye.'

At last she dared to look up at him, with her beautiful tear-stained face, with her beautiful quivering mouth, offering it to him, asking him to touch it with his own mouth, for the last time.

He couldn't refuse her modest request. He bent down and kissed her. Her arms slowly went up to him and slid round his neck.

Lucien Bonaparte, striding into the house the next morning with news for Napoleon—bounding up the stairs to the bedroom, knocking on the bedroom door—

'Come in!' Napoleon's voice, full, buoyant, cheerful.

—Lucien, going into the bedroom, finding the two of them in bed, side by side, Napoleon very cheerful and pleased with himself—

'Good morning, Lucien!'

—Joséphine in a marvellously pretty nightdress, her hair newly done, her face newly made-up, even more pleased with herself—

'Good morning, Lucien!'

An utterly charming smile. She could afford to smile, now. Lucien could only stare.

Early in the morning of the day of the *coup d'état*, Collot, the banker, gave Talleyrand two million francs in bank-notes.

'Since the easiest way with Barras is to bribe him.'

Talleyrand looked admiringly at the notes. 'That should be enough, even for Barras.'

'Who are you taking with you?'

'Admiral Bruix. A splendid sea-dog. I represent right,

the admiral represents might: which may be more persuasive, today.'

Barras kept them waiting, then arrived in a great hurry, apologetic, unusually nervous.

'I'm so sorry, I hadn't expected you, I was in my bath . . . My dear Talleyrand. My dear Admiral. Delighted to see you.' He was undoubtedly extremely nervous. 'What can I do for you? You've come from Bonaparte, I suppose?'

Talleyrand gave his most charming smile, to put Barras more at his ease. 'Yes, I bring a letter.'

A little bow, as he handed the letter to Barras. He was pleased to see that Barras was starting to look more confident.

Barras said, 'Well, has he decided to be sensible? Is he coming in with me?'

Talleyrand said, 'Not a letter from Bonaparte. A letter to him. From you. For your signature.'

Barras, with the letter unread in his hand, stared at Talleyrand. 'What?'

Talleyrand said, with constant charm, 'The letter is your resignation from the Directory, and your pledge to quit political life. I should tell you; of the other four Directors, two are on our side and two are at this very moment being placed under arrest by our troops . . . My dear Barras, may I ask you to trouble yourself to go to the window? If you look out, you'll see some of Bonaparte's cavalry, commanded by his good friend General Murat. If you listen, you'll hear distant drums, coming steadily nearer. Bonaparte's infantry, in great numbers. And you must know, as well as I do, Bonaparte would be happy to have you shot, for more than one reason.'

Barras, ghastly pale, said, 'I am to sign this letter?'

'Yes.'

'May I read it?'

'Since you are to sign it, do please read it.'

Talleyrand courteously walked apart, with Bruix, to let Barras read the letter at his ease.

Bruix said, 'Will he sign?'

'Of course.'

'Are you going to give him the two million?'

'I hate waste, don't you? Shall we discuss afterwards what's best to be done with the money?'

He turned to look at Barras, who was already going to a desk to find pen and ink.

'There, what did I say?' He almost yawned. It was still a good deal earlier than his normal hour for waking. 'Bruix, tell me, what do you usually do on the day of a *coup d'état*? I tend to stay at home and play cards.'

Some time later, Junot got back to Paris, and hurried to report to Bonaparte, full of honest apologies.

'We couldn't get through on the first ship, we were stopped by the English, we had passports but they took us off and sent us back to Egypt—'

Bonaparte, the First Consul, the ruler of France, wouldn't listen to the apologies, but hugged him in his delight to see him again.

Junot said, 'And you've done it. What you said you would. Taken charge.'

'Yes.'

'Congratulations, sir.'

'Thank you.'

Junot said, awkwardly, 'I must give you one private message. I brought Pauline back. Madame Fourès. As you told me to. She's in Paris. She'd like to see you.'

Napoleon said, after a time, 'Give Madame Fourès my sincere regards. Tell her I shall make her an allowance. I shall provide for her. But cannot see her. I shall do everything in my power to ensure her happiness. But cannot meet her ever again.'

PART TWO

JOSEPHINE
IN LOVE

12. MADEMOISELLE DUCHESNOIS,
MADEMOISELLE GEORGE

The First Consul was working late, in his palace at
Saint-Cloud. He had a terrible appetite for work. Whichever of his great houses he was in—Saint-Cloud or the
Tuileries or Fontainebleau or Malmaison—his habit was
the same. He would snatch a hasty dinner at six or seven
o'clock, eating whatever food was readiest to his hand,
never sitting at table for more than twenty minutes. Then
he would go back to his study and shut himself in, by
himself, and write out, in his almost illegible handwriting,
the principles of a simplified tax system for the whole of
France, or his instructions for the drawing up of a new
criminal code, or his proposals for an honorific order to
be called the Legion of Honour, or his outline of the cur-
riculum to be followed at provincial universities. It was
not so much that he was the ruler of France: but he
seemed to be—very successfully—ruling France single-
handed.

Meanwhile, his wife and the members of his entourage
ate their dinners at a more normal pace, and gossipped,
and played whist and backgammon, and yawned, and
went to bed and slept. And Napoleon went on working.

There were one or two who stayed awake for him:
Constant, his first valet, who attended to his personal
needs; Roustan, his Mameluke, brought from Egypt, who
guarded his door and his life.

Constant—in any case, the best valet in France—had
one exceptional talent. It was for putting at their ease,
simply by his own natural cheerfulness, the occasional
visitors who came to call on the First Consul when he
was working late in his apartment. Even the most timid

were reassured by Constant's honest healthy face with its friendly jolly smile.

However, he was having much more than the usual difficulty with Mademoiselle Duchesnois. In the carriage, all the way from the Comédie Française to Saint-Cloud, he smiled and chattered in the jolliest possible way, but he failed to win an answering smile or to get a single word out of her. She sat very upright, which showed off her figure to advantage: a well-moulded figure, for those who liked slender women, as the First Consul did. She looked straight in front of her, except that once or twice, at something Constant said, she turned on him her great dark beautiful eyes: eyes like a startled doe's, fearful but at the same time submissive.

There was a story that her childhood had been unhappy. There was a story that she had been a servant, and then a prostitute, and that one of her customers had somehow got her taken on at the Comédie. What was certainly true was that some old sadness had left its mark on her: and this sadness had helped to make her the new great tragedy star, the new queen of the national theatre.

Constant, still smiling in the hope of calming whatever fears she might feel, led her through a room to a wall with a hidden door, up a spiral staircase to another door at the top, through the door to the landing of the First Consul's private apartment.

Roustan faced them, dark, fierce, turbaned, a scimitar by his side. Constant gave him a friendly nod, and turned to Mademoiselle Duchesnois to explain him.

'Roustan. He won't hurt you. Unless you actually try to kill the First Consul.' His big smile, to show that he was making a joke.

Was there a tiny response from her, a flicker of something in her eyes? He couldn't tell. He gave her a specially encouraging smile, opened a door, and invited her to go in.

It was a bedroom. There was a long sofa. There was a vast double bed. She looked at them apprehensively.

Constant made a little bow, to excuse himself for a

moment, and went to another door, and knocked and went in.

Napoleon was at his desk, scribbling. Constant approached him.

'Excuse me, sir.'

Napoleon did not stop scribbling.

'Sir, Mademoiselle Duchesnois is here.'

Still scribbling—'What time is it?'

'Eleven, sir.'

'Tell her to wait.'

Constant bowed—for form's sake: Napoleon did not look at him—and went back to the bedroom. Mademoiselle Duchesnois was standing in the exact spot where he had left her. Her eyes were afraid that it was Napoleon coming in. Her eyes were still timorous when she saw it was Constant. He gave her his encouraging smile.

'The First Consul apologizes, he hasn't quite finished his work yet. Would you mind waiting for a moment? Do please sit down.'

He placed a chair for her. She sat. He left her there, sitting very upright.

At midnight, when he came back into the room, she was still in the same chair, and in the same position. He gave her a smile and a little bow as he crossed to the study door and knocked and went in.

'Excuse me, sir. It's midnight.'

'Well?' Still scribbling.

'Mademoiselle Duchesnois is waiting.'

'Tell her to take her clothes off.'

A bow, and back to the bedroom. She timorously looking at him.

'The First Consul apologizes, he has a little work still to finish, he'll be with you very soon, would you be so good as to get ready . . . ?'

He went to the bed and turned the covers down, to make sure she understood what he meant.

At half-past two Constant stirred himself out of a doze, listened at the bedroom door, and hearing nothing went in.

Mademoiselle Duchesnois, stripped down to her shift, was sitting in the bed, as uprightly as she had sat in her chair. Constant gave her a very special smile, to compensate her for two and a half hours there. He went to the study.

'Excuse me, sir. It's half-past two in the morning. What do you want done with Mademoiselle Duchesnois?'

Eternally scribbling. 'Send her away.'

Constant went back to the bedroom.

'The First Consul apologizes a thousand times . . .'

It was impossible to tell whether she was disappointed or grateful.

Mademoiselle Raucourt, also a great actress, came to Saint-Cloud in the daytime, to see Josephine, not Josephine's husband. Mademoiselle Raucourt had had famous lovers in her time, and still had some pretensions to beauty: but she was fifty, and the time of lovers was over, and the time of playing the younger heroines of classical tragedy. She was teaching those parts to her pupil, Mademoiselle George.

She said, 'The footman will announce us to Madame Bonaparte. We shall go in, you on my left but one pace behind me. As soon as I stop and curtsey to Madame Bonaparte, you will do the same. You will remain in the curtsey position until Madame Bonaparte tells you to rise. After that, when you are standing, you must hold yourself very straight, chin up, head held high, bosom thrown well forward, stomach held in.'

Nature had already done wonders in throwing Mademoiselle George's bosom well forward. She was really remarkably well-developed for a girl of her age.

'And you must look at Madame Bonaparte, but do not speak unless she asks you a question. If she does ask you something, answer her very clearly, paying great attention to your vowel sounds and to the musicality of your phrasing.'

As it happened, Madame Bonaparte was so charming

and so welcoming, they hardly had time to show the perfection of their curtseys.

'Dear Raucourt!' she cried, as the two of them bent their knees to her. 'No, please don't, we are old friends, we've known each other far too long to stand on ceremony.' She raised Raucourt to her feet. 'And, of course, you've met Madame de Rémusat before—'

'Dear Madame . . .'

'Mademoiselle . . .'

'And this is your new protégée?'

Mademoiselle George was still deep in her curtsey, eyes cast down, motionless. Josephine looked at her with kindness and admiration.

'My dear child . . .'

Her hand helped to raise George to her feet. George remembered to stand very straight. Josephine's eyes were examining her, approvingly.

'She's very beautiful. How old is she, Raucourt?'

'Sixteen.'

Josephine said, 'Sixteen.' At sixteen she had been the prettiest girl in Martinique. At sixteen she had come to Paris and married Alexander, which had been delightful for at least the first three months. 'Shall we sit down? Raucourt, you shall sit by me. And Mademoiselle—?'

Raucourt said, 'George.'

'George.'

'A stage name: I renamed her myself, after her father's first name.'

Josephine said, 'Mademoiselle George shall sit there, so that we can admire her. What's your real name, child?'

She had been asked a question. She replied very clearly. 'Marguérite-Joséphine Weymer.'

Josephine smiled at the child's sharing a name with her, and said to Raucourt, 'And you've taught her—?'

'Everything I know.'

'In tragedy?'

'She has the face and the figure for tragedy.'

Josephine looked at George again. 'Yes, I agree.'

Raucourt said—moving with all possible speed towards what she had come there hoping to say—'She is perfectly formed for the great tragic roles. A miracle of nature. As, let us say, Mademoiselle Duchesnois is not.'

Josephine, kindness itself towards everyone, said, 'Raucourt, you mustn't be unkind, simply because Duchesnois was not your pupil.'

Raucourt made one of her splendid stage gestures, signifying her resolve to tell the truth even if it cost her her life. 'I may be difficult to please. But I confess I find Mademoiselle Duchesnois positively plain.'

Madame de Rémusat, with a sharp clever face, said, 'Duchesnois has gracefulness, and eyes, and a voice.'

Josephine said, 'I agree with you, Claire. And she makes me cry. She makes the whole theatre cry.'

Raucourt, in her most impressive tones: 'Madame Bonaparte, if Duchesnois makes you cry, this child will break your heart.'

'I do hope so.' Josephine turned to George. 'When shall we see you?'

It was a question. George was about to answer it. But Raucourt, magnificent, took the stage.

'Madame Bonaparte, the troubles we have had. We were promised, categorically promised, that George would make her début before Duchesnois. But Duchesnois, I don't know how, seems to have influence in high quarters. She is brought forward, we are put back. She makes her début, she gives fifty performances, she shows herself in no less than four different roles, while we are still kept waiting. She becomes the idol of Paris, simply because they have not yet seen George. I must ask myself, who is to blame? Who is the enemy?'

Madame de Rémusat said, 'Duchesnois is in her twenties. It seems logical for the elder actress to make her début first.'

Raucourt threw her eyes up to heaven. 'Ah, Madame, if I could think it as simple as that! But, I assure you, I know only too well! You would hardly believe the currying favour, the running to important people, the using her friends to bring influence to bear, that Duchesnois has done!' She turned to Josephine. 'Madame Bonaparte, all we ask for is justice. Could you help to get permission for this child's début very soon?'

Josephine said doubtfully, 'The controller of the theatre must give permission.'

'You could order it to be given.'

'I don't think I could. The First Consul could.'

Raucourt's eyes went up to whatever is higher than heaven. 'Ah! The First Consul! It goes without saying! The First Consul can order anything and everything! If only you would persuade him, dear Madame!'

Josephine, always willing to help, indeed always helpful when there was no great effort needed, and no inconvenience to herself—'He's here, in the palace. Shall I ask him if he can come and meet—?'

George cried out in a sudden panic, though the question was not asked of her. 'Oh, no, Madame! Please don't!'

'Why not?' Josephine was amused.

'It doesn't matter about my début. It really doesn't.'

'Wouldn't you like to meet the First Consul?'

'No! He frightens me, I'd behave like an idiot. I don't mean he frightens me, I mean I'd be frightened to meet him. Not because he's frightening. I'm sure he isn't frightening. But because he's such a great man.'

Josephine said, smiling at the girl's panic, 'He'll be there at your début. He always goes to débuts.'

'Yes, Madame, but that's different. If he's one of an audience I don't have to think about him. But here. Please. No. I couldn't bear it.'

Raucourt, majestic, moved in with a few well-chosen words.

'Of course, we do very much hope that the First Consul will attend George's début, when it finally takes place. Duchesnois has her admirers. They're paid to applaud her. No doubt they'll be paid to hiss this poor child. But if you and the First Consul would deign to applaud . . .'

Josephine looked kindly at the poor child. 'Will you recite for me?'

'If you wish, Madame.'

'I should like it.'

George looked to her teacher for instructions.

'Clytemnestra.'

Josephine was mildly surprised. 'Is she old enough for Clytemnestra?'

'I have trained her in the maternal emotions. My belief is that she will excel as a mother.'

George went to a little distance, and turned to face them, and gave them Clytemnestra's great speech to her husband King Agamemnon. Acting, she ceased to be a beautiful child: she became a superbly beautiful woman.

The dressing-room after the début was impossibly crammed with stage people and society people, all trying to reach George and to embrace her, while she stood silently weeping tears of purest joy.

Raucourt trumpeted, to anyone who would listen, and even if no one could hear, 'What can they say now? What can Duchesnois and her gang say to that? A triumph such as I have not seen in thirty years at the Comédie Française! A triumph such as no one has ever seen before! She was marvellous, marvellous! She will be the greatest actress in the world!'

The dresser tried to push through to Raucourt, but had to give up and scream her message.

'Mademoiselle Raucourt!'

'What?'

'General Murat!'

'Who?'

'Murat! From the First Consul!'

'From the First Consul? Where?'

'In the corridor!'

Determination gave Raucourt the strength to fight her way out. The corridor was full of people trying to fight their way in. She had another great battle before she finally reached Murat. He was lounging, puffing a cigar, calm and magnificent.

'Hullo, Raucourt.'

'Was the First Consul pleased?'

'The First Consul sends his compliments. He thought she was splendid.'

'Ah . . . !' Raucourt was in ecstasy.

'I must say, she's a beautiful girl.'

Still in ecstasy: 'She will be the greatest actress in the world!'

Murat said, 'Who's keeping her?'

'I beg your pardon?'

'I imagine she has a rich admirer who keeps her. I just wondered who it was.'

Raucourt was the image of matronly pride, rejecting the vile insinuation. 'Mademoiselle George is my pupil.'

Murat grinned. 'Yes, you had admirers, in your time. D'you want to tell me about this girl, or not?'

Raucourt was no longer a matron but a queen.

'General, would you convey my sincerest thanks to the First Consul for his most kind message?'

The effect would have been more successful if Murat had not spoilt it by bursting into laughter and slapping her on the bottom.

After the theatre, Napoleon accompanied Josephine to their bedroom.

Josephine said, 'I thought she was excellent. I'm so pleased, for her.'

'Who?'

'Mademoiselle George. Didn't you think so too?'

'Yes.'

'And such a figure, at sixteen. I'm only afraid she may grow fat.'

'Yes, a very good figure.'

'I thought you liked women to be slim.'

'Oh, I do.' He looked at her as she took her clothes off. 'Like you.' Her figure was still beautifully slender and supple, even though she was forty.

She said softly, 'Are you coming to bed?'

'I have two or three hours of work to do yet.'

'Not tonight.'

'I must.'

'Darling, not every night.'

'France needs a new constitution, its system of justice needs a new code, its education needs a new pattern, its coinage needs a new design . . .'

'France can wait a day or two.'

'France can. But I can't.'

She went to him and put her soft arms round his neck. 'France may need. I need. I need you.'

He said, gently, 'Later.'

'Doctor Corvisart is giving me a new medicine. He says it'll make me start having periods again.'

'Yes, Corvisart told me.'

'We'll have a child.'

'I hope.'

'I'm sure of it. We will have a child.'

'It would solve a good half of my problems.'

'Believe that we will.'

He said, 'Corvisart does not say that you will start having periods again. He says it is possible that you will.'

'It must happen. I know it'll happen.'

He released himself from her arms, ready to go.

She said, 'Has Corvisart examined you?'

She had said the wrong thing: she knew it immediately. She knew that she had lost him, at least lost him from her bed that night, by saying it. But she had not been able to stop herself from saying it, in the hope of making him believe that her barrenness was possibly his fault, or at least making him believe that it was not necessarily entirely her fault.

He said coldly, 'Corvisart examines me often. Too often.'

She had to go on with it, and make it worse. 'I mean, to make sure that you yourself—'

She had lost the night with him. It was more important to make him uncertain.

He said icily, 'There is no reason why I should not have children.'

'Corvisart says that?'

'Corvisart says that.'

She tried to bring him back to her. 'Oh, darling, I'm sure of it. I simply meant, in case Corvisart could help, with a medicine . . .'

'The only person I need help from is you.'

She came back close to him. Now she could say it.

'So come to bed.'

'Later.'

She knew, better than most women, how to offer her body without seeming to offer it, without making a gesture of offering.

She said, as if it were a serious, loving thought, 'You love my body.'

'Yes.'

'I love yours.'

'Yes. Later.'

'I shall be awake.'

He said, politely, 'I shall make love to your body as soon as I can.'

He kissed her, but only on the cheek, and turned to go, but turned back again to say something else. An afterthought.

'The times when I work very late in my study—through the night, almost: till three, or four, or five—it might be better for you if I slept upstairs.'

It was a prepared statement, posing as an afterthought.

She said, 'Better? No. Why?'

He was acting, as she had been. But he had not known that she was acting. She knew that he was.

He said, rather lamely, 'Whatever time I come in, you wake up. I disturb your rest.'

'I'm the lightest sleeper.'

'Yes.'

'But that's good. It's a protection for you. If anyone tried to get in, I'd hear him.'

'Darling, wherever I am at night, Roustan sleeps across my door. No one could get past Roustan.'

She said, 'Yes, I know, but it's a double protection, with me. And there are so many people who want to kill you. There are conspiracies, you know there are.

Royalists. Extremists. Foreigners. Hired assassins. I'm a very good watchdog, to wake up and bark.'

She tried to sound as practical as possible, and then as loving as possible. 'And I like waking up when you come in at night. And I like waking up in the morning, to find you in my bed. Promise me you'll always come back here, however late it is. You won't sleep up there.'

He said, 'I promise.' But she knew he was lying.

Mademoiselle George had the prettiest little apartment in the rue Saint-Honoré. After the theatre she went back there with Clémentine, her dresser, who the moment she crossed the threshold became her confidential maid.

George had played Clytemnestra again, and been a wild success again, and been applauded by the greatest man in France again.

'And when I said,

> "Achilles, how can woman e'er repay
> The noble deeds that you have done today?"

I didn't look at poor Talma, I don't know why, but I looked straight at the First Consul's box, and our eyes met, I assure you they met—'

She stopped, because she was startled to see a strange man in her drawing-room. A pleasant-looking man, with a jolly smile which assured her that he intended no harm.

'Forgive me, Mademoiselle. Your footman was so good as to let me in. May I introduce myself? Constant, first valet to the First Consul.'

'Oh!'

She knew that famous young actresses should not give exclamations of surprise. She just couldn't help it.

He was saying, 'Could I possibly . . . ?' And he was glancing, with just enough meaning, at Clémentine.

George said quickly, 'Clémentine, would you make us some tea? If Monsieur Constant would—?'

He bowed. 'You're very kind.'

Clémentine, who had dressed other actresses before

George, went to the kitchen to make tea. George said, to pass the time, 'The First Consul was in the theatre tonight.'

'Yes.'

'It's the third time he's seen my Clytemnestra.'

'Yes.'

His smile said, she was not to worry, he understood everything. He said, 'You're not acting tomorrow evening.'

'No, it's a comedy tomorrow.'

'May I beg you, on behalf of the First Consul, to allow me to take you tomorrow evening to visit the First Consul, who wishes to congratulate you personally on your great success?'

She repeated mechanically, 'Tomorrow evening?'

'If I could call for you at eight o'clock? Here? Or at the theatre? As you wish?'

The marvellous thought came into her mind that she was going to be the First Consul's mistress: she was going to spend the next night in the arms of the ruler of France.

It was not the kind of thought that she would wish to keep to herself. She said, 'At the theatre.'

When he had gone, she asked Clémentine, 'What shall I wear, for the First Consul?'

Clémentine had seen everything in her time. She said, 'What does it matter what you wear?'

George considered that it did matter. She decided on a virginal effect: very little make-up, a white muslin dress, a lace veil, a cashmere shawl; a simple necklace, nothing more than a gold chain and a gold medallion; and a modest ring.

She was sitting in her dressing-room, staring at herself in the mirror, adding a tiny touch to the almost-nothing make-up, when Mademoiselle Volnais came in. George was delighted to see her, at such a convenient moment. Volnais was seventeen, and very pretty, and was wearing a gorgeous dress, and was quite the most outrageous gossip of the whole lot of them.

Volnais said, 'Hullo! I heard you were here. You didn't come in to see the show?'

'No.'

'Nor me. Or perhaps just a bit of it. I have a friend calling for me at nine.'

'General Junot? Of course.' Everyone knew about Volnais and General Junot. It had been a sensation at first, but by now it was impossible for Volnais to find any one who had not heard the news.

Volnais did her best to make some kind of effect. Her only hope these days was to overdo it. 'Poor Junot, he's so mad about me, he won't leave me alone for a single night. Who are you meeting?'

The question was thrown in casually. George replied equally casually.

'Oh, no one.'

'Prince Sapiéha?'

'No, no one.'

'Darling, I always tell *you* things.'

'No, honestly, I'm not meeting anyone.' George yawned ostentatiously. 'I'm tired, I think I'll go home to bed.'

Clémentine came in. 'Carriage waiting for you at the stage door.'

Volnais was delighted: she thought George was trying to hide something, she thought she had caught George out. She rose quickly.

'Good night, darling. Have a nice time at home in bed.'

George knew that she had gone to spy on the carriage at the stage door, and try to see who was in it, and what coat-of-arms was on it.

But then George felt suddenly frightened, really frightened.

She said to Clémentine, 'I think I'd rather go home.'

'Are you crazy? The First Consul?'

She had suddenly lost all her confidence.

'He only wants to congratulate me.'

Clémentine looked at her with a fine cynical eye.

'You mean, congratulate you before? Or afterwards?'

At Saint-Cloud, Constant led her through a room, to a wall—were they walking into the wall?

'Where are we going to?'

'To the stairs. Don't worry. You'll see.'

Constant pressed a panel, and a section of panelling swung back. It was a hidden door, hiding a spiral staircase.

He said, 'There! Isn't that clever?'

At the top of the stairs, there was the famous bodyguard, Roustan: everyone had heard about Roustan. Constant said, 'He's a friend, he won't hurt you. Unless you actually try to kill the First Consul.'

She knew it must be an old joke of his: he was so pleased with it.

He opened a door, and invited her to go in, and followed her in.

It was a bedroom. She had supposed it would be a bedroom. She had expected something more voluptuous, more exotic, more in the style of the Arabian Nights. But it was quite a nice bedroom.

Constant gave her his encouraging smile, and went and tapped on another door, and went in.

She decided she wasn't really frightened at all. She took her shawl off and draped it carefully—it was an expensive shawl—over the arm of the big sofa.

She heard the door opening, the door where Constant had gone out. It wasn't Constant coming back. It was the First Consul.

She was pleased to see that he was smartly dressed: green uniform with red facings, white satin knee-breeches, silk stockings. That was really very considerate and respectful of him; he could so easily have come in wearing just a dressing-gown, or less. He was a handsome man, particularly for someone so important. She wondered whether she should curtsey to him or not. She decided not to.

He came towards her, smiling a very charming smile. She smiled at him, through her veil. He took her hands, still smiling into her eyes, still not saying anything, and sat her down with him on the sofa, side by side. He took her veil off and threw it on the floor.

'Oh!' She hadn't meant to say it, but she did.

'Why "Oh!"?'

'My veil.'

'What about it?'

'It might get trodden on.'

He picked the veil up.

She said, 'Thank you.'

He looked at it, holding it up.

'Who gave you the veil?'

'Prince Sapiéha. Do you know him? He's a Pole. A Polish nobleman who lives in Paris.'

He looked past her, at the shawl on the arm of the sofa.

'And the shawl? Prince Sapiéha?'

'Yes. He's terribly rich, he likes giving me things.' She felt very confident. She laughed. 'He's funny. All he's ever done is kiss my hand.'

Napoleon stared at her, and stood up, holding the veil, and ripped it violently to pieces, and threw the pieces on the floor.

'Oh!'

He said violently, between his teeth, 'Don't lie to me!'

'I wasn't—!'

He picked up the shawl and ripped it to pieces.

'Oh!' She jumped up.

'You hear? You must not lie to me!'

He threw the shawl down and went to her. Face hard like iron. Eyes burning. She wondered if he was going to hit her. It would have been terrifying if it hadn't been so exciting.

He stared at the slender gold chain and medallion round her neck.

'And the necklace? Sapiéha?'

'Yes.'

He took it in both hands and tore it apart and threw it on the floor. She was sorry he had to break it, but the passionate brutality was really rather enjoyable. What on earth would he do next?

He stared at her hand, at her one modest ring.

'And the ring?'

'No, that's not from Sapiéha, that was given me by Mademoiselle Raucourt, it was a present for my début—'

'Don't lie!' He had seized her hand. He was pulling the ring off.

'It was! Really it was!'

He threw the ring on the floor and stamped on it with his heel, ground it into the floor.

'Honestly, you ask Mademoiselle Raucourt, she'll tell you!'

He marched to a bedside table, picked up a small handbell and rang it.

She supposed it must be for Constant to come and take her back where she came from.

She said, 'I don't mind so much about the other things. But you ought to have listened to me about the ring.'

He said nothing.

Constant came in and waited for orders.

Napoleon said, 'Before Mademoiselle George leaves, bring a white cashmere shawl, a large lace veil, a gold necklace with a medallion or something similar, and a ring. Diamond.'

'Yes, sir.' He went.

Napoleon, calm again, gentle, said, 'You must have nothing except what comes from me. Do you understand?'

She smiled at him, and gave a good imitation of Constant. 'Yes, sir.'

'And you must never lie to me. Do you understand?'

'Yes, sir.'

He came and looked into her face. His gaze travelled down to her shoulders, to her dress.

'And the dress?'

'No, I bought that—' she stopped, and laughed. 'I was

going to say I bought it myself. I suppose Prince Sapiéha'll pay the bill. He pays all my bills. He's really rich.'

'Richer than me?' Napoleon was amused.

'How rich are you?'

'I am . . . comfortably off.' He looked at the dress. 'When did you buy it?'

'Today.'

'For me.'

'Well, I thought I ought to do my best to look virginal.'

'You did very well.'

'You want the truth?'

'Always.'

'Normally Sapiéha sits up all night somewhere, gambling. He doesn't bother me much.'

'Ah.'

'I honestly don't know why he thinks it's worth his while.'

'And before Sapiéha?'

'Consul . . . Do you want me to call you "Consul"?'

'No.'

' "General"?'

'No.'

'Well; whatever you are—you've never been an actress.'

She didn't quite know why, but this amused him enormously. He said, 'I spend a great deal of my time acting.'

'Well, I can tell you, you get paid a lot more for it than we do at the Comédie Française.'

He said, laughing, 'I deserve it. I'm playing to a much bigger audience.'

He was starting to enjoy himself, genuinely. They were both enjoying themselves.

He asked, 'What's your name? Real name?'

'Marguérite-Joséphine.'

'Hm . . .'

She wondered if she'd been right to tell him the second half. But if he wanted the truth, he'd get it.

He said, 'I like your name. But I shall call you Georgina.'

He came to her again, and looked in her face again, then looked down at her dress again.

She said, 'Are you going to tear it?'

'No, I'm just going to throw it on the floor.'

Josephine sat in her bed as the hours went by: haggard, miserable, sleepless, waiting.

At five in the morning Napoleon rang for Constant, who came in with new shawl, veil, necklace, ring. Napoleon took them one by one from Constant and put them on her: the ring on her finger, the necklace round her neck, the shawl round her shoulders, the veil over her head. He gently kissed her on her forehead, through the veil.

'Till tomorrow. I mean, till tonight.'

She was very happy.

As Constant took her to the hidden staircase, he said, 'Congratulations.'

Napoleon, in green uniform, white knee-breeches, silk stockings, entered Josephine's bedroom as quietly as he could. She was awake, sitting up in bed, looking unwell and old. He made a stiff little bow to her, but said nothing. She said nothing, but stared at him. Her eyes were an accusation.

He started slowly to unbutton his uniform, without speaking.

She could not bear the silence any longer. She said what she knew she should not have said; but she could not stop herself from saying it.

'Was she pretty?'

Napoleon made no reply and showed no emotion. He stopped slowly unbuttoning his uniform. He started buttoning it up again.

She knew that she had made a terrible mistake, a mistake that could never be put right.

When his uniform was fully buttoned up again, he said, 'Since you take it like that, Madame, do please continue to sleep in this room, which is your room. I shall sleep in mine.'

He made a stiff little bow to her, as he had done when he came in. He went, as quietly as he had come. She sat in her bed, staring into a future which promised nothing but unhappiness.

13. GEORGINA

At the end of the play, George was so happy and excited she simply couldn't keep still, and very nearly tore her costume while Clémentine was helping her take it off.

'I always act so much better when the First Consul is there in his box. He inspires me, I give of my best, I really do. But wasn't that terrifying, in Act Five?'

'Wasn't what terrifying?'

'Didn't you see it?'

'No.'

'But you must have heard the applause, in the middle of the act.'

'I was in here, getting your things ready.'

'Well, you know my line: "Cinna is at my feet! Others will kneel there yet!" '

'Yes.'

'Well, when I said it, everyone burst into mad applause and looked up at the First Consul's box, as if I meant him—as if I meant that *he* was at my feet. And they shouted for me to say it again, and I had to say it again, and they applauded even more, and I absolutely didn't know where to look, and they shouted for me to say it yet again—'

Mademoiselle Mars and Mademoiselle Bourgoin burst into the dressing-room, almost as excited as George was.

'Well!'

'Darling, you were marvellous!'

'But how did you manage to stay so calm?'

'We did so admire you, you didn't turn a hair!'

George was all wide-eyed innocence. 'Tonight? In the play? When do you mean?'

'George!' they cried. 'You know perfectly well what

we're talking about! You were wicked, absolutely wicked! It was sensational!'

Wide-eyed still. 'Oh, did you think so?'

Mademoiselle Raucourt walked in, with a brow like thunder and a voice like thunder.

'Well!'

'Oh, Mademoiselle Raucourt, wasn't it terrifying, what happened in Act Five?'

'Yes! It was!'

Raucourt turned her baleful eyes on to Mars and Bourgoin. They vanished.

George said, in a small voice, 'It wasn't my fault. I didn't know where to look.'

Raucourt said, 'I will tell you where you should have looked. At Talma and Monvel, who were on the stage with you. Not at the audience. And not at one particular member of the audience!'

'Did I?'

'You did.'

'It was only when they applauded so much.'

Raucourt said, giving each word the force of a hammer-blow: 'You will never do such a thing again, not even for the sake of applause. We live by applause, but there are some things which we do not do.'

George mumbled, 'I'm sorry.'

'As soon as you are dressed, you will apologize to Talma, and to Monvel.'

'Yes . . .'

'I only wish you could apologize to Madame Bonaparte.'

George was surprised. 'Madame Bonaparte?'

'She was sitting next to her husband. As you must have known perfectly well.'

'I didn't think of it.'

'Everyone else in the theatre thought of it.' Raucourt looked at the silly penitent child with ineffable disdain. 'Mademoiselle George, the acting profession has its dignity, even though we are great men's mistresses.'

* * *
185

George went to Saint-Cloud that night, devoutly hoping that Napoleon wouldn't mention the play, and above all wouldn't mention Act Five.

Her hopes grew. He was charming to her. He seemed untroubled, positively carefree.

He was smiling, almost laughing, when he said, 'You were very good tonight, Georgina.'

She said nervously, 'Oh, did you really think so?'

'You must have seen me leading the applause.'

'When?'

'At the end of each act.'

She sketched a little curtsey.

'I am very grateful for your approval, which is most flattering to me.'

Napoleon stared. 'What sort of language is that?'

'I'm trying to talk like a countess. Now that you're letting all the countesses come back from abroad.'

'Talk like Georgina.'

He started undressing her, slowly, carefully, gently.

She tried to put no meaning at all into her voice. 'Did Madame Bonaparte like me?'

He said, with no meaning in his, 'My wife has always admired your acting.'

'Tonight? In Act Five?'

'Ah. Perhaps not.'

'I'm very sorry about Act Five.'

He continued, still gently, to undress her. He was looking at her hooks and buttons, not at her. After a time he said, 'There is a rumour in Paris that you are my mistress. I can't stop the rumour, so I have decided not to do anything about it. In France, the ruler's wife must be irreproachably well-behaved—as my wife is. But the French quite like their ruler to show that he is human.'

She said, 'In Act Five tonight I was a bit too human.'

'Yes. I have forgiven you. It didn't matter. And I don't discuss you with Josephine.'

'I met her once.'

'So I believe.'

'She's very beautiful.'

'She is a very charming woman.'

'I really wouldn't like to do anything that would annoy her—'

But he had suddenly gone away from her. He was away on a new subject, in a new voice, all animation, all enthusiasm.

'Yes, you were good tonight, Georgina. But Talma! Ah, Talma was sublime! The greatest actor in the world! What power! What command! The way he controls an audience with his voice, and with his eye! Every single person there feels that that eye is on him! He dominates, we are his slaves! If he gave a sudden call to arms, we'd follow him to death!'

She giggled. 'Lucky there aren't any calls to arms in the parts he plays.'

'Do you know, Georgina, if I were not what I am, and what I will be—I would choose to be Talma. I could do it.'

'I'm sure you could.'

'Of course I could. Like everything else, it's a question of determination. The will to persevere. The energy to persevere.' He came to her and seized her hand. 'I'll read you a scene. We'll read a scene together. Your big scene with Talma. Come on!'

'What, now?'

'Now!'

'I'm not dressed for it!'

She was dressed only for lovemaking or sleep. But he was already pulling her towards the study, excited by his thought. He had found a new game.

'You were good tonight, Georgina, but you still need more rehearsal. I'm not at all sure about some of your inflections.'

In the study, he let go of her hand and went to the bookshelves, looking for what he wanted.

'Corneille, the plays of Corneille, C, C—'

'Look, I've got a rehearsal tomorrow—'

'C, C—of course, right up at the top—'

He quickly climbed a library ladder, on little wheels, for pushing along the shelves—

She said, loud and clear, 'I've got a rehearsal tomorrow morning. Early. Very early.'

Up the ladder, scanning the shelves, he said, 'Georgina, could you give me a little push?'

'Big push, if you want one.'

She pushed the ladder.

'That's enough!' He found the book he wanted. He found the place he wanted. 'Now. Corneille. Cinna. Act Five.'

'Oh! Please! Not Act Five!'

'I insist on Act Five!' He struck a pose, great actor at the top of the ladder. 'Now. I shall be Talma as Cinna, and also Monvel as Augustus. You will be you, in the part you played tonight—'

'I don't want to!'

'Who is the ruler of France?' he cried.

'Bully!'

'The ruler of France as the Emperor of Rome! Augustus speaks!' He put on his great-actor voice. ' "Your soul surrenders to sweet love too soon!" '

She shouted, 'No! I won't do it!'

She ran at the ladder, and holding it pushed it as fast as she could, along the shelves, across the room. Napoleon held on for dear life.

'Georgina! No! Stop! That is not in the play!'

Josephine was in the small drawing-room, with Madame de Rémusat, each sitting at her embroidery. A footman came in with a sealed note on a silver salver. Josephine took it and opened it and read it, and thanked the footman, who bowed again and left the room. Josephine rose and went to the fireplace, and put the note on the fire and made sure that it was consumed by the flames.

She said, 'Mademoiselle George is with him.'

Madame de Rémusat said nothing. There was nothing to be said.

Josephine went back and sat at her embroidery again, but with her hands tightly clutching each other.

'I shall go and catch them together.'

'No, Madame—!'

'I am his wife! I have the right to enter his room!'

Madame de Rémusat said, more calmly but no less urgently, 'I beg you not to do it, Madame.'

Josephine was twisting her hands, each hand twisting the other in turn. 'Shall I tell you the women he's had, the last two years? And I've put up with it, I haven't said a word. Singers, actresses? I can tell you every one of them. And how many nights.'

Claire de Rémusat admired the best of Josephine and despised the worst of her. She said incisively, 'Madame, a wife should not spy on her husband.'

'A husband should not bring cheap women into his wife's home! Should he?'

'No.'

'Is there a worse insult than that?'

Josephine was half-deliberately and half-unconsciously agitating her own emotions, exacerbating her own feelings of jealousy and resentment, provoking a nervous crisis in herself in order to create some justification for her doing something stupid. Claire de Rémusat took it to be a large part of her duties to prevent Josephine from doing anything irretrievably stupid.

'Madame, if I were a husband, and my wife paid her servants to spy on me, I should find the situation intolerable.'

'And *my* situation? Isn't that intolerable, too?'

Claire's voice was cold, as healthy and as sobering as cold water. 'You create your situation yourself. If you didn't spy, you wouldn't know: so there would be no situation.'

'The whole of Paris knows!'

'Not from him.'

'You saw, at the theatre tonight! I must fight her! I must fight this woman George!'

'Madame, you are the first lady of France. It is not for you to fight actresses.'

'I must fight this one.'

'I beg of you to be a realist, Madame. Paris is full of husbands who go to bed with actresses. If Mademoiselle George, or any other, boasts of being the First Consul's mistress, no one thinks the worse of him for it, and no one thinks the worse of you. It does no harm to your position. The important thing is your position.'

'He has been seeing George too often, for too long now. I must put a stop to it.'

Josephine was illogical and obstinate, but Madame de Rémusat's obstinacy was stronger: it was founded on her principles.

'Madame, we are of the old nobility, we should understand these things, for what they are worth. The only danger to you is if the First Consul forms a real attachment to a lady of rank; if he appears in public with her instead of with you, if she becomes in some sort his official mistress; if he acknowledges her children as his own. But what is George? An actress, a fashionable prostitute. Very beautiful. Very young. I suppose she excites him sexually. I suppose she is good in bed.'

She stopped, because Josephine gave a sudden violent scream.

After the scream, a whisper. 'As I was . . .'

Claire's words had been knives in her heart.

She ran to a mirror to stare at herself. She was a marvellously well-preserved forty. She was a beautiful forty. But she was forty. George was sixteen, becoming seventeen.

She picked up a candlestick and thrust it into Claire de Rémusat's hand. She said, 'I am going to get rid of her. And you are coming with me.'

The ladder game was over. Napoleon came down the ladder, laughing, tottering.

'I'm giddy. I'm fainting.'

'I'm exhausted. Pushing you. You're getting heavy.'

'I shall have to lie down.'

'Me, too.'

They flopped down on to the big rug in front of the fire. They lay there together, fond and starting to be amorous but not very active about it yet. Touching and kissing—

'Do you love me a little, Georgina?'

'I think I love you too much.'

' "Your soul surrenders to sweet love too soon . . ." '

'Yes . . .'

'Why too much? What's wrong with loving me?'

'Well, I'm only a plaything, aren't I?'

'My favourite plaything.'

She smiled at him. 'That's nice.'

Josephine led the way, through corridors, through a room. Claire de Rémusat thought they were going to walk into a wall; but Josephine pressed a panel, and a door opened in the panelling, to show a spiral staircase. Claire instinctively drew back. Josephine silently commanded her to follow.

Napoleon was lying on the rug, on his back, taking his agreeable ease while George leaned over him giving him occasional fond kisses. He laughed, for no obvious reason.

'What's funny?'

'Mm?'

'You just thought of something funny. Tell me.'

'I thought . . . I thought, tomorrow, my dear brother Joseph, so pompous now, and other people, Talleyrand, and my Ministers of State, will come to see me in this room. And while they're boring me to death, I'll look at this rug, and think to myself, Georgina and I made love on that rug last night.'

'Who said we made love on it?'

'Me.'

'We haven't yet.'

'We're going to. Aren't we?'

'Yes.'
'Now?'
'Yes.'

Josephine, leading the way—Claire de Rémusat close behind her, holding up the candlestick—moved very cautiously and very quietly up the spiral staircase. There was a sound from above: perhaps a footstep, perhaps a voice, from somewhere near the stairhead door.

Claire was, in any case, against the whole enterprise: it could do no good, it could do a great deal of harm. Napoleon would have one of his terrible outbursts of rage. Josephine would be reviled, rejected, perhaps repudiated. She herself would lose her job as lady-in-waiting. Her husband would lose his job as Superintendent of the Palace. They could not afford to lose their jobs.

And, in any case, Claire was afraid of the dark, and afraid of secret passages and hidden staircases. And she was terrified of Roustan, who slept across his master's door, his scimitar by his side.

The sound from above—footstep, voice, whatever it was—froze her blood, and her limbs. She could not move. She could only listen. She heard the sound again. Impossible to tell what it was. But there must be someone, a man, perhaps more than one man, on the landing, near the head of the staircase: perhaps waiting for them, to spring out at them and kill them.

Josephine, one step above her, looked down at her by the trembling light of the candle.

Claire, without any voice at all, framed the words, 'What was that?'

Josephine managed to whisper. 'Probably Roustan.'

Still voiceless—'Roustan!'

Josephine whispered, 'He'll probably cut our throats.'

Claire's mouth opened wide in a scream of terror, without any sound coming out. Her limbs were unfrozen. She turned and ran back down the steps as quickly as she could, but as silently as she could. The candle blew out, but she was glad to be in the dark: the assassins were less likely to see her and seize her and murder her.

When she got back to the lighted rooms she still ran, clutching the useless candlestick. She could not believe she was safe until she was in the little drawing-room again, in her own chair, in front of her own embroidery. What had happened on the staircase had been the worst thing that had ever happened to her in all her life.

Josephine came back into the room, quickly, with a high colour, with a strange strained voice.

'You left me in the dark.'

Claire could still hardly speak.

'I . . . I apologize, Madame . . .'

Her heart was still jumping up and down, wildly, out of control.

Josephine looked at her, and suddenly laughed.

'On those stairs—you looked so terrified!'

'Yes . . .'

'You still look terrified!'

'Yes . . .'

Josephine was laughing. Claire gave one laugh, a nervous laugh.

Josephine was laughing more and more: not hysteria, but the release from tension. Claire felt it too: she laughed again, and again.

Josephine collapsed into her chair, laughing, crying, 'It was so silly! Wasn't it silly! Weren't we silly!'

Napoleon looked at the rug which had supported his lovemaking the previous night, and then raised his eyes to look at Talleyrand.

'I've decided. Emperor.'

'Ah.'

Napoleon raised his eyes higher still, up to the topmost bookshelf and the works of Corneille.

'Emperor. Like the rulers of Rome. Like Augustus.'

'You know my preference. The French are accustomed to a king.'

'France is a Republic, as Rome was. Rome became an empire.'

'You don't find "Emperor" too—' Talleyrand chose the word fastidiously—'too grandiose?'

'The French are fond of grandiosity. And I am not the nineteenth Bourbon. I am the first Napoleon. I am entitled to be grandiose.'

'Indeed you are.'

'Emperor. My decision is still secret. Not a word of it to anyone.'

'I understand.'

'Particularly my family.'

'I do understand.'

'My dear brother Joseph will be here in a moment. I want you to help me deal with him.'

'A pleasure—I hope.'

Napoleon threw his hands up in the air. 'Talleyrand, what am I going to do with my family?'

'I suppose you can't resettle them in Corsica?'

'I would if I could.'

'Short of that—'

'They want more! Always more! Joseph comes here every day, wanting more for himself! And Lucien, and Louis . . .'

Talleyrand said, 'The two necessary things for the stability of France are that you should become a hereditary monarch; and that you should outlive all your brothers—'

'I shall take care to outlive them.'

'—so that there is no possibility of any one of them becoming your successor.'

Napoleon paced the room, in high discontent.

'Lucien might have made a successor. But the fool has married that Jouberthon woman, against my instructions. I must have a moral leadership in France. The people have a right to expect virtue in their leaders. I try to restore morality, and my brother goes and marries his whore.'

Talleyrand looked closely at his fingernails. 'Forgive

194

me—I myself, quite recently, on your instructions, married my own whore.'

'You're my Foreign Minister, you have to receive ambassadors, you need a hostess, your hostess must be your wife.'

'Yes, I do see, the case is different.'

'Quite different.'

'Joseph is respectably married.' Talleyrand could not resist a private joke. 'Though, of course, he does run after actresses.'

'Joseph is useless.'

'I'm so glad you agree . . . Louis is splendidly married, to your own stepdaughter.'

'He hates Hortense and she hates him. The whole marriage was a mistake. She refuses to live with him.'

'She has my sympathy. Oh, may I ask—?'

'What?'

'Is Louis syphilitic?'

'No.'

'There is a strong rumour.'

'He was cured.'

'I'm so glad. It suggests a possibility.'

Napoleon burst out, 'I am the ruler of France, and I can't control my own family! I offered to adopt their son! Hortense wouldn't hear of it! Louis wouldn't hear of it! I will pass a law making me master of my own family!'

It was not the best possible moment for Joseph to arrive; and Joseph did not make things any better by staring at Talleyrand as if a hostile look would be enough to drive Talleyrand out of the room. Talleyrand smiled charmingly and said, 'Would you care to pretend that I'm not here?'

Joseph was so full of what he had to say, he did not care to waste time on evicting Talleyrand. He faced Napoleon and struck a manly posture which made it quite clear that he was in no sense an inferior.

'I gather that you are going to make yourself king.'

'Do you?' Napoleon did not admire the manly posture.

'Or Emperor.'

'Do you?'

'Aren't you?'

'The adoption of either of those titles would require a change in the constitution of France. The constitution of France can be changed only by a new law proposed by a senator and passed by a vote of the senate. No such new law has yet been proposed by a senator.'

'All new laws are written by you.'

'That is fortunate for France.' Napoleon's voice was a growl. Talleyrand was mildly surprised, but rather more amused, to see that Joseph did not take warning from the growl. But then, Joseph had foolishly come to believe that Joseph was a person of some importance.

Joseph said, 'Since you have, as I believe, decided to become king, or Emperor—'

He waited for a challenge. It did not come. He went on.

'And since I am your elder brother, and therefore the head of the Bonaparte family—'

Again he waited. Again there was no challenge. He went on.

'As head of the family, I have discussed the matter with Lucien and Louis, with our mother, and with our sisters. It is my duty to the family to ascertain what titles we will each of us assume, when you are king or Emperor; what the order of precedence will be, in the new kingdom or empire; and what the order of succession to the throne will be.'

The moment had to come at last. Talleyrand looked up at the ceiling and pretended he wasn't there.

Napoleon had done with growling. Now, the lion roared, and rose, and leapt.

'Good God, anyone would think we were inheriting a crown from the late king our father! If I take the crown —if I take it—do you know how it will have happened? I saw the crown of France lying on the ground! And I picked it up with the point of my sword!' He marched to the door and pulled it open, wide open. 'You may be my elder brother! You may be the head of a family! You are not the head of mine! Get out! Come back when you have learnt who you are!'

Joseph stood scarlet-faced and confused and uncertain. But to stand there was to choose a course of action, and he had no choice. He marched out of the room, doing his best to be manly, head held high, not looking at Napoleon. Napoleon slammed the door after him.

Talleyrand said, 'I hope I helped you deal with him.'

Napoleon grinned. 'If you hadn't been here, I might have lost my temper.'

Talleyrand thought to himself, an actor needs an audience; and for that scene, he, Talleyrand, had been the only possible audience. To appreciate the acting, it had been necessary to know the secret: that it was acting.

They went out to the woods beyond Vaucresson. It was autumn, but a fine warm day, fine enough for her to sit under a tree and for him to lie with his head in her lap, looking up at her.

'Georgina . . .'

'Why are you looking at me all the time?'

'I've never seen you in daylight before.'

'I'm not sure that you should.'

He said, making fun of her, 'Daylight is not entirely unfavourable to you.'

'Glad you think so. If you think so.'

'Georgina, we don't lie to each other.'

'I think I look better with all that stage make-up on.'

'It makes an effect, on the stage.'

'That's where I live. On the stage.'

'As I do, on my stage. But we are also ourselves.'

'I suppose.' She was doubtful.

'You are you. No longer a tragedy mother. Yourself. Young.'

'Do you like me because I'm young?'

'No. Because you're you.'

She said, 'Do you like me because I don't want anything? I'm sorry, Talleyrand said that to me. It's not really true. He's clever, but he's not always right. I do want something.'

'What do you want? Whatever it is, you can have it.'

'I can't.'

'What do you want, Georgina?'

'You.'

They walked hand in hand through the woods. The leaves were starting to fall.

He said, as if he were starting to recite a poem, 'Woman was given to man—'

'Oh, was she?' She had thrown off her sentimental melancholy. She was in high spirits again, and ready to argue with him if he wanted an argument.

He said, 'Was she what? Given to man?'

'I just wondered if that's the best way of putting it.'

'Georgina. Listen. And learn.'

'Always willing to learn.'

'Woman was given to man . . .'

'Go on, it's the next bit I want to hear.'

'For his pleasure. And for him to get children.'

'You mean it's him that gets the children, and not her.'

'Georgina, are you being difficult?'

'Just trying to learn.'

Napoleon said, in his role of teacher, 'They understand these things better in the east. In Egypt.'

'Yes, I'm sure they do.'

'Nature . . .' He was pondering a ponderous statement. She said, 'Yes, well, Nature was a man, wasn't he?'

'Nature made women our slaves. But civilization—'

'Ah, yes, that's the trouble. Civilization is a woman.'

He said firmly, 'Civilization encourages the fantasy that women are our equals.'

'You the great thinker. And that's the great thought?'

'Yes.'

'Shall I tell you my . . . well, not great thought, but favourite thought?'

'Do.'

'Well, every now and again you send for me to come and see you.'

'As often as I can.'

'And I think to myself—I'm an actress, I'm quite famous, I could live on what they pay me now, I don't want to but I could. And anyway, there are lots of other people offering me necklaces and earrings and so on. I'm independent. I'm free. I don't have to say "Yes" when Napoleon sends for me.'

'But you do.'

'Ah, that's not thinking. That's feeling.'

They came to a little pavilion in the woods which seemed to belong to Napoleon: so many things belonged to him now, it was difficult to know what didn't. Constant had got there before them, and laid out a delicious cold lunch for them, at a table on the balcony; and he stood ready to help them to food and wine, and after helping them went and lurked discreetly behind a convenient tree.

At the end of the meal, she said, 'Mmm . . .'

'Was it good?'

'Very good. I think it's the moment to give you . . .'

'Give me what?'

'What you asked for.'

'When did I ever ask you for anything?'

'You did once. You don't remember, but you did.'

She took off the slender chain which was round her neck, with a miniature which had been hidden by her corsage.

He said, 'Your portrait.'

'Yes. I had it done. For you.'

He looked at it, and wrinkled his brow. 'Hmm.'

'Yes, I know it's not marvellous.'

'You're more beautiful than that.'

'It's my fault, I've got no patience, it's not very amusing sitting there doing nothing. Give it me back, then.'

'No.' He put it in his pocket.

'I'll have another one done.'

'Yes, I'd like more than one.'

'I'd like one of you in exchange.'

'I'm sorry, I didn't bring one with me.'

'But you will give me one?'

'Yes.'

'You see, I do want things.'

'Small things.'

For no apparent reason, she looked long and hard at his hair. She said, 'I'll have something else to be going on with. Have you got a pair of scissors?'

'Why do you want scissors?'

'Never you mind. I bet Constant has got scissors. Call him.'

'Constant is miles away.'

'No, he's not, he's behind that tree over there. Call him.'

'You have the stage voice. You call him.'

She called, in her biggest Clytemnestra voice, and Constant came quickly, while Napoleon asked, 'But why scissors?'

'I want a lock of your hair.'

'Georgina, I'm losing my hair enough already—'

'Just a little bit. Just a little lock.'

'No!'

'Just two or three hairs—'

Constant was with her, smiling. 'Yes, Mademoiselle?'

'Constant, have you got a pair of scissors?'

Of course he had a pair, in his pocket.

'Thank you, Constant. Go back to your tree.'

She took them, and brandished them, and menaced Napoleon with them.

'Just two, or three, or four—'

'Two! At the utmost!'

'Bend your head over, then.'

He did not immediately obey her.

'Georgina, if I do this for you, will you do something for me?'

'Will I do what?'

'In your mother parts, on the stage, somehow, for me, you're still not quite enough of a mother.'

'What do you want me to do about it?'

'There's a wise old woman in the Faubourg Saint-Antoine. I'll give you the address. You can go and see her. She's supposed to be a great expert on these matters. I think we should make you a mother, in real life. I think you and I should, between us, get a child.'

She said softly, 'I'd like that. What I am saying? I'd go mad with joy. Bend your head over.'

That evening, late, Napoleon, returning to Saint-Cloud, found Josephine alone in her small drawing-room, sitting at her embroidery but not working at it. He bowed politely.

'My dear, I apologize for my absence from your reception earlier this evening. The day went on longer than I had expected.'

She was twisting her hands, each hand twisting the fingers of the other.

She said, not looking at him, 'Did you shoot well?'

'Shoot—?'

'I understand you went to Butard for a day's shooting.'

'Yes.'

'Did you shoot well? What did you shoot?'

'Various animals.'

She said, in an unnaturally high, cracked voice, 'May I hope that you shot Mademoiselle George?'

She still did not look at him, nor he at her. He took to pacing the room, his head on his chest. She sat, her hands eternally twisting.

At last he said, 'Josephine. We have been married for eight years now.'

'Yes.'

'There was a time . . . for a time . . . I loved you.' His voice was flat, precise, mathematical.

'Yes.' Her voice spiritless, lifeless.

'I am no longer capable of love. I can no longer love, in any real sense of the word. Women have become meaningless to me. I can no longer give my heart to a woman. A momentary distraction. That's all.'

After a time she said, dully, 'That's all?'

'That's all.'

She could not bear it. She could no longer control herself. Everything she felt mounted up in her and shouted at him, 'You are my husband! And I am your wife! Your wife! Your wife!'

Napoleon started slowly walking round the room, smashing it up, smashing ornaments, small furniture, china, glass, anything that came to his hand, kicking them over, flinging them to the ground or at the wall or at a mirror. And while he was smashing, words came out of him, slowly, brutally, grindingly—

'When you were my wife, you were a whore! I kept you as my wife to get a child! You failed! You no longer play the whore, but you are barren! I will no longer have an old barren whore as my wife!'

14. JOSEPHINE MARRIED

Josephine sat in her drawing-room, silent and apprehensive, waiting for Eugène to come back from his interview with the First Consul. Hortense was with her, and Claire de Rémusat: both silent, in sympathy.

At last Eugène came in. Josephine looked at him but did not dare to ask him.

Eugène said, finding it difficult to say—

'He is going to divorce you. He says he does not mean to be cruel, but he has made up his mind to divorce you, and nothing can change that now. He says it will make no difference to Hortense's position, nor to my position. I told him, if he divorces you I shall resign everything and go with you wherever you go. Don't cry, Mamma.'

But Josephine was softly weeping, at the thought of a husband who was casting her off and a son who loved her so much.

Hortense said, 'Let him divorce you. And Louis can divorce me, I want him to. We'll go away together. We'll go and live at Malmaison, you'll be happier there. Or we'll go back to Martinique. We'll be happier where there aren't any Bonapartes.'

Josephine wept, at the thought of a daughter who loved her so much.

Josephine said, 'I don't know what to do. Eugène, what shall I do?'

'I agree with Hortense. You'll never be happy, married to that man.'

Her son loved her and her daughter loved her, that was marvellously consoling. But they were not telling her what she wanted to be told. She turned to the other person. Claire was her friend. Claire would tell her.

'Claire? Advise me. You're so sensible.'

Claire was so clever. She would know what Josephine wanted. Hortense and Eugène were angels, but they assumed that what Josephine said she felt was what she actually felt. Claire would not make that mistake.

Claire said, 'The dignified thing for you to do is to retire to Malmaison, and write him a letter saying that you agree to the divorce.'

Claire had not given the right answer.

Josephine said, 'What else am I to do?'

'The less dignified thing?'

'Yes.'

Claire said, 'You can stay here, and tell him that you are entirely at his disposal—that you will do whatever he wishes, whenever he wishes.'

'Yes.'

Claire said, 'That you will be totally obedient, totally compliant, totally submissive.'

Claire had given the right answer.

Napoleon's manner towards her was not in the least unkind—was, in fact, almost over-considerate. He was sorry that he had lost his temper with her. He very much wanted to arrange the separation, and the subsequent divorce, in a very practical and reasonable and perfectly friendly way, friendly on both sides. There was absolutely no reason why they should not continue to be good friends. He was willing to make a great number of concessions to her—was willing to give her pretty well whatever she asked for: he was willing to agree to almost anything, for the sake of peace and quiet, and an end to the emotional strife of the last few years, the incessant quarrels, jealousies, recriminations, hysterical outbursts.

He was, at the moment, somewhat confused and disturbed. Why had she suddenly, at this meeting intended to settle everything, become so totally submissive?

He said, patiently and kindly, 'You understand, the reasons are entirely political. I am becoming Emperor. I am founding a hereditary empire. The question of the succession is therefore supremely important. You are forty now: whatever Corvisart may say, it seems highly unlikely that you will become pregnant again. But I must have a direct heir to my throne.'

Her head was delicately bent, indicating submission. 'Yes, I do understand.'

'The divorce will be embarrassing for me personally, and painful for me.'

'You must do whatever is best for France.'

He was taken aback. She had said what should have been one of his lines. He moved on to his next statement.

'I shall, of course, provide for you handsomely . . . richly . . .'

Her head still gracefully bent. 'Whatever you say. It doesn't matter to me.'

'I am fond of you. Very fond. I want you to be happy.'

'That isn't important. Compared with other things.'

'No. Exactly.' He felt curiously helpless. What does one do, when one wishes to persuade another person of something, and finds that the other person is trying to persuade oneself of exactly the same thing? And, what is more, the other person is using one's own arguments?

Josephine said, with a beautiful meekness, 'I'll do whatever you wish, whenever you wish. You must decide everything: where I must go, and when I must go. You have only to say the word.'

'Thank you.' He had only to say the word. He would say it, when he wished. Not now: now would be too cruel.

She said, 'Since the separation and divorce have nothing to do with our personal feelings—'

'Nothing at all.'

'May I tell you . . .' She raised her head and looked at him at last, but the submissiveness was still there, in her eyes. 'I do know that you don't love me any longer. I accept that. I know you're fond of me, but I accept that your love for me has died . . . I love you more than I ever did. Which is why I want whatever you want.'

'I see.' He thought his response feeble and foolish.

She said, 'Because I love you, I was jealous. Foolishly

jealous. I've learnt my lesson now. I suppose it doesn't matter now, now that we're divorcing. But I've learnt that you must do whatever you want. Whatever happens, I shall never be jealous again.'

He thought to himself that Josephine's upbringing had been at fault; and, of course, her first marriage, which was, of course, not her fault; but that she was, essentially, a good woman, in herself.

Murat drank a glass of wine, while George, mostly behind a screen, changed into her costume for the play.

Murat said, 'I must tell you, he's very cross with you.'

'Oh, is he?'

'He sent for you last night. You didn't come.'

George said, innocently, 'He's so cross with me, he sends the Governor of Paris to come and tell me he's cross?'

'Yes.'

'He must be really cross, mustn't he?'

'And to tell you that he wants to see you on Friday night.'

George said, 'Well, if it's so important that he tells the Governor of Paris to tell me—'

'It is important. To him.'

'Did he say that?'

'Yes.'

'All right, then. Friday. Governor of Paris, would you tell him that?'

'And he wants to know, why not last night?'

George came out from behind the screen, a tragedy queen but making a comedy face, wrinkling up her nose, wrinkling her brow.

'Why not last night? Yes, well, I got worried.'

'What about?'

'I'm supposed to keep him happy. And I try to. But I suddenly got the feeling that perhaps I was mucking up his marriage.'

Murat said, 'My dear George, we're all in favour of mucking up his marriage.'

'Oh, are we?'

'But anyway, you don't have to worry about that. It's all over. The marriage.'

'Oh?'

'It's all decided. Hasn't he told you? He's going to divorce her.'

Caroline Bonaparte, as Talleyrand once remarked at least half-admiringly, had the head of Machiavelli on the shoulders of a beautiful woman. She had committed a foolishness once in her life: she had fallen in love with Murat—that was not the foolishness, any girl might easily have done that—but she had insisted on marrying him, against everyone's advice and against Napoleon's instructions. The fact that Napoleon had ordered her not to had made her even more determined to do it; and when she was determined to do something, she did it.

It must be said that her Machiavellian head was an extremely pretty one, and was much admired, not only by her husband Murat. It must also be said that, Napoleon excepted, she was twice the man that any one of her brothers was.

She was in Napoleon's study, making Joseph seem ineffectual by comparison, and making even Napoleon feel tired by the sheer relentless pressure of her energy.

She said firmly—she said everything firmly—'And there is one thing that I will not have.'

Napoleon said, 'Only one?'

'You are making Joseph and Louis princes and highnesses—'

Joseph quickly put in, 'Naturally, as his brothers.'

'But you are not making your sisters princesses and highnesses.'

Napoleon had had almost enough of explaining. 'A wife takes her title from her husband. That is the general rule, and has been, for many centuries.'

'So Julie will be a princess and a highness, because she's Joseph's wife—'

Joseph put in, 'Of course—'

'And Hortense, because she's Louis's wife, even though she never goes anywhere near him—'

Napoleon explained again, more irritably—'The wife of a prince is a princess, whether she is near him or not.'

'But not me!'

A great fatigue and a great feeling of boredom came over Napoleon. Was this the price of empire, then? To spend half of every day listening to foolish people who had set their foolish hearts on foolish titles?

He said, 'Caroline, if I make you and your sisters princesses—'

'And highnesses—'

'And highnesses, will you leave me in peace?'

'Yes.'

'All right. Thank you. Be what you want. You can go.'

He had himself done a foolish thing. By giving way to Caroline, he had given encouragement to Joseph. Joseph was striking that damned silly pose again.

'One last point—'

'Make it quick. I'm tired.'

'Caroline and I represent your entire family in saying we trust that your divorce will take place very soon.'

'Oh yes, why?'

'We trust that there is no question of Josephine becoming Empress.'

'Oh yes? Reasons?'

'You're going to divorce her.'

'I know that. Reasons?'

Joseph was puzzled. 'Because you're going to divorce her.'

Napoleon growled, 'What has the coronation got to do with the divorce?'

'Everything, surely.'

'Nothing!'

Joseph, failing to follow the argument, had to fall back on assertion.

'Napoleon, we, your family, could not possibly give our agreement—'

Napoleon shouted at the top of his voice, 'Your agreement! Do I need your agreement?' He walked ten paces while Joseph sat silent, ten paces away, then swung round at him. 'The divorce will take place when I wish, not when you wish! I need only one person's agreement, and I have that already! Josephine agrees to my divorcing her whenever I please! And that is when I shall do it!'

In bed with Napoleon, happy and peaceful after making love, she said, 'I just didn't want to feel I was being a nuisance.'

'Georgina, you are never anything but a great pleasure.'

'You know, coming between man and wife. I don't think people should do that. And I admire your wife so much. She's my idea of a great lady.'

'Yes. Don't worry. She's told me she'll never be jealous again.'

'Murat says you're going to divorce her.'

'Not your fault.'

'I'm glad of that.'

'Nor hers. It's just that I need a son.'

She pressed her face into his shoulder and said, 'Sorry I haven't been able to oblige. It would have been a beautiful bastard.'

'Yes, I'm sorry too.'

'Though it wouldn't have been a good idea, would it?'

'I'd have liked it.'

'Would you have liked the scandal? The gossip? You know me. I'd have boasted. I'd have shouted it from the stage.'

Napoleon did not answer, but jumped out of bed and put his dressing-gown on.

She said, amused, uncomplainingly, 'You never lie still for long, do you?'

He was brisk. 'Georgina. Speaking of scandal and gossip.'

'Mm?'

'I have—how shall I put it?—I have pulled off a most remarkable trick.'

'Nothing new for you to do that.'

'This one is really rather exceptional. I have persuaded the Pope to come to Paris for my coronation.'

She raised both eyebrows and whistled in admiration. 'Well, you can't do much better than the Pope.'

'I must make my crown sacred and inviolable. I must be anointed as Emperor by the Vicar of Christ on earth. The Pope has agreed. He's coming. With six cardinals, ten bishops, God alone knows how many chaplains and priests. Paris will be overrun with them. And while the Pope's here, I can't have any scandal. Any gossip. I can't risk it. I've got to be very respectable, for a time.'

She took the thought in and considered it. 'So I shan't see you.'

'For a time.'

'How long, do you think?'

'A time. While the Pope is here.' He came and kissed her fondly. 'It can't be helped. I must be a moral man, a virtuous spouse—'

'So no divorce?'

'For a time. I need Josephine as my hostess, to be charming to the Pope, and all those princes and dukes and ministers who are coming to see it all happen. There'll be receptions, banquets, all sorts of things. I'm no good at public events, I never look as if I'm enjoying them. She does.'

Georgina said, 'I'm glad she's going to be Empress. She'll enjoy that. Even if it's only for a time.'

'Yes . . . Afterwards, I can divorce her whenever I please. Whenever it's most convenient. It's not as if we'd been married in church. There wasn't any church marriage in those days. Two minutes in the Town Hall of the Second Arrondissement, by an Acting Registrar with a wooden leg. It can be undone in two minutes. But she's been with me over eight years now, and I'm not the best possible husband. She deserves to be Empress, for a time.'

Pope Pius VII, and his cardinals and bishops and priests, were lodged with suitable magnificence at the Palace of

Fontainebleau, before the final ceremonial stage of the journey to Paris.

Josephine, Empress-to-be, was, naturally, received in audience by His Holiness. She came to the audience room looking marvellously nun-like and devout. She knelt and kissed the Pope's finger.

'Holy father . . .'

'My daughter . . . Please sit down.'

'Holy Father, may I stay on my knees while I tell you something? There is something I think I must tell you.'

'Do you wish to confess to me, my daughter?'

'I don't know if it's really a confession. But I think it's a dreadful sin. And it's a secret, a terrible secret: at least, I don't believe you can possibly know it. And it troubles me so much, I can't sleep for thinking of it.'

'If it troubles you, tell me, my daughter.'

'Holy Father, I am to be crowned in Notre-Dame with Napoleon. We are to receive your holy blessing, as Emperor and Empress, as husband and wife. But we are not married.'

'Not—?' The Pope was, for the first time for a long time, startled by someone telling him something.

'We are married in the eyes of the law, but not in the eyes of the Church. You will remember the wicked days of the Revolution, Holy Father: there was no Church in France then, there was only civil marriage, without God. And then Napoleon went to Italy, and then to Egypt, and he was always so busy, fighting his wars and governing France, so we kept postponing the moment .. . . But we cannot receive your blessing, Holy Father. For all these years we have been living in sin.'

Talleyrand, summoned by urgent messengers, was waiting in Napoleon's study. Napoleon rushed in like a whirlwind.

'Talleyrand. I need you. Where's Berthier?'

'Coming.'

'Why is he never here when I want him? Why do I have that fool as my Chief of Staff?'

'Because he believes in you.'

'He will believe in my fist—'

Berthier arrived, red-faced and out of breath.

'My apologies, Sire—'

The 'Sire' did a great deal to mollify Napoleon. It was premature, perhaps, but there was no great harm in that.

'Berthier. Talleyrand. I need you both. Tomorrow afternoon. And get me Fesch. Cardinal Fesch. I need him too. Or there will be no coronation the day after.'

Berthier stared. 'No coronation?'

'So the Pope tells me, and for once I must accept what the Pope tells me. No coronation. I shall not be "Sire". Unless I do what he tells me. Well, we'll keep it as private as possible. You two will be my witnesses.'

Berthier said, still goggling, 'Witnesses to what?'

Napoleon's smile was grim, but was also appreciative, in a way.

'Josephine has pulled off a most remarkable trick. We are going to be married.'

Those present in the private chapel of the Tuileries were Cardinal Fesch, Napoleon's mother's stepbrother, which was one of the reasons why he was a cardinal; Marshal Berthier, Chief of Staff to the First Consul; Charles-Maurice de Talleyrand-Périgord, Minister for Foreign Affairs; and the bride and bridegroom, kneeling side by side.

Fesch had hastily renewed his acquaintance with the marriage ceremony.

Napoleon and Berthier had not enjoyed the ceremony. Josephine and Talleyrand had.

Whether the bride and bridegroom had enjoyed it or not, they were married.

George said, insistently, 'I said you can have the tickets. Have them, Mademoiselle Raucourt. Really.'

'George, you are mad.'

'You can have them. It was nice of him to send them. But I don't want to see the coronation.'

'Anyone else would give her ears—'

'Well, I don't want to give my ears, I need them, I'd look silly without them.'

'You should see him crowned.'

'What does it matter? Am I the best actress in France?'

Mademoiselle Raucourt said, with some sharpness, 'The best young actress.'

'That's what I meant.'

'Yes, you are.'

'So I don't look at the past, I look at the future.' She put on her stage presence. ' "Cinna was at my feet! Others will kneel there yet!" ' She laughed, to try to make Raucourt laugh. 'They say the Tsar of Russia is handsome.'

'I believe, very handsome.'

'There's a French theatre in Moscow. Shall we go to Russia?'

Josephine was ready for her bed that night, and about to get into it, when Napoleon came into the room. She had not seen him since their wedding that afternoon. He had not spoken to her at the wedding: his only words had been his responses to Fesch; and he had left the chapel as soon as the ceremony was over, with a formal bow to her, but without a smile or a backward look.

She did not dare to speak to him now. It was for him to speak first, and to say whether or not he hated her for what she had done.

He spoke at last, slowly and weightily.

'Tomorrow, in Notre-Dame, the Pope will anoint us, and bless us, but will not crown us. I have no intention of making it appear that my crown depends on the will of the Pope. I shall take my crown and place it on my own head, myself.'

His hands took an imaginary crown from the air, and held it up, and brought it to his head, and his head received it.

He said, 'Then you will kneel before me, with clasped hands.'

She understood what he wanted her to do. She knelt before him, in her nightdress, and clasped her hands.

'I myself shall go to the altar, and pick up your crown, and come back to you, and place the crown on the head of the Empress Josephine.' Her head received the imaginary crown. 'We shall then move in solemn procession to the great throne, and be blessed.'

She stayed kneeling. She would stay there until she had his permission to rise. She would do whatever he wanted: she would be totally submissive.

He moved away from her, and started slowly to unbutton his coat. He looked at her. She returned his look, with a soft question in her eyes, with a hope in her eyes.

He came to her and raised her courteously to her feet, and led her to the bed. He smiled at her. He undid another button on his coat.

He said, 'My dear, it is, in a sense, in an important sense, our wedding night.'

15. FRANCOISE

General Duroc, Grand Marshal of the Palace, came to the end of the first part of the list he was reading out to the Emperor, and stopped. The Emperor continued to pace about the róom, chin deep down on his chest, hands clasped behind his back, without speaking.

'Shall I go on with the clothes, Sire?'

'Go on with the clothes.'

Duroc read out, from the second part of the list:

'In addition to the aforementioned, Her Majesty the Empress has during this last year purchased one hundred and thirty-six dresses, seventy-three corsets, eighty-seven hats, five hundred and twenty pairs of gloves, nine hundred and eighty pairs of shoes—'

'Purchased?'

'Yes.'

'But not paid for.'

'For the most part, not paid for.'

'What's her dress allowance? Three hundred and sixty thousand francs a year?'

'Yes.'

'And what is she spending, or owing?'

'Four times as much.'

Napoleon paced. Duroc said, 'Shall I move on to the jewellery?'

'No.'

'Will Your Majesty speak to the Empress?'

'No.'

'Does Your Majesty wish me to speak to the Empress?'

'No.'

'Sire—what, if anything, am I to do?'

Napoleon said, 'Knock twenty per cent off the bills and pay them.'

'Twenty—?'

'All right, twenty-five per cent, thirty—whatever you think fair. They should be pleased to have the Empress's custom, without wanting profit as well.'

'Yes, Sire.'

'They should be proud to have her custom. Do you know what men are ruled by, Duroc?'

'Honour. Loyalty. Patriotism.'

Napoleon had the highest regard for Duroc as an excellent soldier, a first-class administrator, the very soul of honour and loyalty and patriotism. He had no great regard for Duroc as an observer of human nature.

'Men are ruled by vanity. All men. And Frenchmen most of all. The French don't want liberty or equality, those are things they don't understand. They want glory. Splendour. Pomp. It makes them feel important to have an Emperor who has never lost a battle. It makes them feel important to have an Empress who is the best-dressed woman in the world. If they have provided the dresses or the gloves or the shoes, they can be additionally vain about that. This whole court is part of the pomp. Why do you suppose I invented all these titles—you Grand Marshal of the Palace, Talleyrand Grand Chamberlain, Murat Grand Admiral—good God, a Grand Admiral who rides a horse?'

Duroc, noble fellow, still believing the best—'Sire, not all men are vain.'

'Duroc. Tell me honestly. If I said to you—as I might do, as I may do—"Duroc, you've served me well, I create you duke"—what would you feel?'

Duroc thought for a time, to give an honest answer.

'I'd be proud, and pleased.'

'Pride and pleasure are when someone tickles your vanity. Let Josephine have her dresses. I must tickle her vanity too. I have to ask her a difficult question.'

Napoleon visited her in her rooms and found her choosing, from a great choice, what jewellery to wear that evening for dinner. He told her that he had to ask her a question. She was in her charmingly submissive mood, as she sat trying on different necklaces and rejecting each one of them in turn.

'You know you have only to ask, and I shall say yes.'

'You are the best of wives.'

'Not the best. But I try to be.'

'My dear, as you grow—I should say, as we grow older, we become fonder of each other.'

She smiled at his reflection in her mirror. 'Fonder all the time.'

He said, seeking to expand his statement, 'We become more good-humoured. More tolerant.'

'Tolerant?' The word put her on her guard. She hoped she had not shown that it had put her on her guard. She thought that Napoleon had not noticed—he was so busy, making the moves by which he would arrive at the result he had planned.

He said, 'There was a moment when we spoke of divorce.'

She corrected him gently. 'When you spoke.'

He accepted her correction, almost gratefully. 'A moment of crisis. I suppose every marriage has a certain number. The moment is over. I've dismissed the thought from my mind.'

'Thank you.' She was sweet and sincere.

'Things are going far too well with us.'

'Yes.'

'Except for one thing.'

She misunderstood him: it was the only thing she could usefully do. 'Can I try to please you better, in one thing?'

He said, rather too hastily, 'You do understand, there is no question of a divorce.'

'Darling, if you say so, of course I understand.'

'But you do also understand, it is of paramount importance for myself, and for you, and for France, that I should have an heir to the throne.'

'Yes, I do understand.' She was now not merely on her guard: she had transformed herself into a thousand watchful eyes.

'And my family are useless. I can't even find a suitable king for Italy. I create a new kingdom; someone's got to be crowned king of it. I suppose it'll have to be me.'

There was no harm in his words yet. 'You are the best possible king.'

'With you as queen, of course.'

'If you say so.'

'But if only I had a son—if only we had a son . . .'

She thought, He said 'if only I', then corrected it to 'we', as if he meant an apology. It was not an apology, it was a manoeuvre.

He asked, 'Who knows that you are past childbearing?'

'Am I?'

'Corvisart says so.'

'Does he?'

'Categorically.'

'Then Corvisart knows.'

'Does anyone else?'

'I have not told anyone.'

He said, 'And Corvisart keeps a secret.'

She couldn't resist it. 'Does he? He told you.'

'Good God, I'm your husband, he's my doctor, I've made him a baron, I pay him like a prince, he had to tell me! He had to tell me you've been deceiving me with false hopes! For years now!'

She lowered her head. 'The hopes were mine, too.'

Her tears were so well-trained, they sprang to her eyes of their own accord when Napoleon was angry. He had never learnt to be indifferent to her tears.

'Josephine. My love. Will you please not cry. I'm trying to help you. I'm trying to ask you . . .'

Now it was going to be said, what he had been trying to say, what he had come to her room to ask her, the difficult question. She had delayed his asking it. She could delay it no longer. But, at least, by delaying it she had made him declare the importance of the question.

He said, 'Suppose someone else—a woman of good stock, of good family, were to become pregnant . . .'

'Pregnant?'

'Suppose.'

'Who? What woman?'

'I simply say, "Suppose" . . . And suppose I were sure —not the slightest doubt—that the child was mine . . .'

'Yours?'

'Yes.'

'Who is this woman?'

He was becoming impatient. She was giving him no help at all. A wife should help her husband. 'There is no woman! And no child! I simply say "suppose"! Will you please suppose!'

She said—docile, ready to be helpful—'If you tell me to.'

He took to pacing the room again. She was glad to see him pacing. It meant that they had fought a drawn game. The second game would start in a moment, as soon as he had decided on a new gambit.

He said, 'I must have a successor who will be acceptable to France. The French don't want my brothers, don't want my nephews, don't want—forgive me—your son, Eugène, who is splendid but who is only my stepson. They want a child of mine to reign after me as Napoleon the Second.'

'Yes, of course.'

'My legitimate heir.'

'Legitimate?' The word was a warning and an indication.

He said, not looking at her, 'Suppose. Suppose. Suppose that you were to appear to be pregnant, while this other woman, this hypothetical other woman, is pregnant. Suppose that you were to appear to give birth to a child, when this hypothetical child is born. You would, so far as the world would know, be the child's mother. You would go on being Empress. And France would have what it most needs.'

She sat silent. Her silence was what would most discompose him.

He said, 'I've spoken to Corvisart; he pretended to be shocked, but the ethics of his profession go down before reasons of state. He would keep the secret.' He looked at her—with some surprise, she thought, almost timidly. 'Are you shocked?'

'No.'

'Would you agree to it?'

She phrased her answer very carefully. 'I always say yes to whatever you ask, if it's best for you, and for France.'

He was greatly relieved, and really rather touched by her answer. He came and kissed her fondly. She was a good wife, after all.

'Thank you, my dear. Well. Have you chosen your necklace yet? Shall we go down to dinner together, like a fond old married couple?'

She gave him her fondest smile. 'In a moment. I must repair the tear-marks. I can't think why I cried.'

He said, 'I shall wait for you in your boudoir. I shall expect you in a moment.'

'Oh, if Madame de Rémusat is there, would you ask her to come in?'

He said, fondly, 'Don't let her see the tear-marks.'

'I shan't.' A fond brave smile.

He went. She repaired her face. Claire de Rémusat came in.

'Your Majesty—?'

Josephine, hard, nervous, urgent. 'Claire, he has a new mistress. A woman of good family. It's dangerous, I can tell it's dangerous. I must find out who she is.'

That evening after dinner she played backgammon with Talleyrand. She often did. Talleyrand had the courtier's art: he gave her a closely fought game, an exciting game, and he let her win at the very last moment, without showing her that he was letting her win, and without letting her see how he was managing to do it.

He said, 'I believe the crowning of a King of Italy is a spendidly colourful ceremony.'

'Is it?'

Talleyrand threw the dice, artfully casual. 'I am the

strangest person. Last year I wanted your husband to be King, not Emperor. Now that he is Emperor, I don't want him to be king.'

She was looking across the room at Napoleon. She said softly, 'A great Emperor. A great king.'

'Yes, I agree. The greatest man on earth. Such a pity he isn't lazy.'

She wasn't listening to him. Her eyes and her mind were on the other side of the room with Napoleon. She was straining to hear what she could not possibly hear: what Napoleon was saying to the ladies of the court as he passed from one to another. It was a habit he had recently adopted: every evening in the salon, a short conversation—no, hardly as much as a conversation: but a short polite talk with each of them in turn. He claimed that it relaxed him, it civilized him, after a day spent talking politics or planning war.

It had occurred to Josephine that his speaking to each of the ladies in turn might also be the best possible cover for his speaking words of particular significance to one particular lady.

He was moving on to the clever and bewitching Madame Duchâtel, lady-in-waiting to the Empress, wife of one of the Emperor's financial counsellors—a charming man but thirty years her senior, and often away from Paris in the performance of his duties.

'Madame Duchâtel . . .'

'Your Majesty . . .'

There were women who said that her nose was a tiny fraction of an inch too long; but no man favoured with the brilliance of her smile would have dreamt of agreeing with such a malicious judgement.

Napoleon said, 'Your beauty, as ever, is . . .' He searched for a word.

She did her best to help. 'Indefinable?'

'Incomparable.'

'Oh, what a shame.'

'Why?'

'I should have liked to hear a comparison.'

221

'Give me time to think of one.'

'How long will you need?'

No one could overhear them. They were having a short polite talk, as he had done with the other ladies.

He said, 'I shall have thought of one by midnight.'

She said, 'I shall look forward to it.'

Josephine was looking at them—rather too intently, Talleyrand thought. He said, 'I beg Your Majesty's pardon. I had forgotten your strength.'

She brought her eyes to Talleyrand and the board. 'At backgammon?'

'As the Emperor's wife. I am talking politics, and you have a mind above politics.'

'Ah.' She smiled, but her eyes were straying back towards Napoleon.

Talleyrand said, 'May I ask Your Majesty to observe that I am bearing off one of my men on my six point?'

Caroline, also of the opinion that Napoleon had been talking to Madame Duchâtel quite long enough, took the direct way to put a stop to it.

'Napoleon. I am longing to play whist. Will you partner me? Shall the Bonapartes challenge the world?'

Caroline took his arm and led him briskly towards the card tables. Murat, as brisk as his wife, timed his own arrival at Madame Duchâtel for the merest moment after Caroline had taken her brother away.

'Madame Duchâtel. May I join you?'

'Of course, if you wish.'

'For your own sake. The Empress has been watching you with a great deal of attention.'

'Oh? Shouldn't she watch?'

'If the Empress should be jealous . . .'

She laughed. She had the most delicious laugh in the world.

'When the Emperor speaks to me, shouldn't I speak to him?'

'I admire you.'

'For my incomparable beauty?'

'Yes. But.'

'How can there be a "but"?'

'Even more for your coolness.'

Her eyes sparkled, with the fun of it. She whispered, to make fun of him. 'Prince Murat, you don't imagine that—how shall I put it?—that I am having an *affaire* with the Emperor?'

'If you're not . . .'

'I'm afraid I'm not.'

Murat was never a man to waste what might be an opportunity. At least it was an opportunity to ask.

'Then I shall try to persuade you to have an *affaire* with me.'

She was enjoying herself. 'Really?'

'Yes. With no "but".'

'Is there room for another feather in your cap, Prince?'

'I'll throw the others away.'

'And your wife, too?'

'Ah. Well.'

'You can't throw the Emperor's sister away.'

Murat said—as he said more than once in his life— 'Wives are politics. Mistresses are love.'

'Oh, isn't everything politics?'

'Not you.' He gave her his most irresistible look: it was positively an ogle. She answered with her most charming smile.

'Prince, you are paying court to me, in order to make the Empress believe that you are the one who is paying court to me; and also in order to show the Emperor your zeal on his behalf. I'm so sorry that the zeal is misplaced.'

At the card table, Caroline had recruited Claire de Rémusat to join them. It only remained to choose a fourth. This was not proving easy.

'Duroc, then. Or Berthier.'

Napoleon objected. 'I've been with them all day.'

'If you refuse everyone I suggest, we shall never play whist.'

'I've been with men all day. I need civilizing.'

'Claire and I will civilize you.'

'It takes at least three to do it. Ask . . .' He looked

around the room. 'Who?' He said to Madame de Rémusat, 'Ask Madame Duchâtel to join us.'

Madame de Rémusat obediently rose and went to do what she was told.

Caroline said, 'Is that a good idea?'

Napoleon was good-humoured again. 'My dear Caroline, I am a mighty monarch, I shall play whist with whom I please.'

'But Madame Duchâtel?'

He said, not loudly but with great clarity of utterance, in the voice he used when he wished something to be understood once and for all, 'A lady-in-waiting. A woman of the highest possible reputation. If you think anything else, you are totally mistaken.'

They were awoken by an urgent knocking at the door, and the agitated voice of Madame Duchâtel's maid.

'Madame! Madame! Wake up, Madame! It's six o'clock!'

The maid did what she hardly dared to do: came into the room, to make sure that they woke.

'Six o'clock, Madame!'

Napoleon woke and cried 'What?' and leapt out of bed naked, all in a single instant. The terrified maid averted her eyes from His Majesty's person.

'Constant sent me to tell you—Madame!'

She ran out of the room before she could be found guilty of *lèse-majesté*.

'Six!' He grabbed his drawers and his dressing-gown.

'What . . . ?' Madame Duchâtel was less willing to wake. He went to her.

'Darling, we were fools, we fell asleep. Not fools, it was marvellous, but we were fools not to wake sooner. I must get back as fast as I can, as best I can. I adore you. Till tonight.'

An embrace, not long but strong. He tore himself away from her. She gave a happy sigh and settled to sleep again.

There was no one to be seen in the corridor. He set

off at a brisk stride, almost a canter, looking around, fearful that servants might suddenly appear in doorways.

At an angle in the corridor there was a closet, like a large cupboard, with glass windows in its door, and a curtain inside. As Napoleon came up to the angle, spying round the corner to make sure that he was not spied on, he suddenly saw a pair of large dark eyes, a woman's eyes, looking out at him from the closet, from behind the window, from behind the held-back curtain. He stopped and stared at the eyes. The eyes stared back at him, terrified, for the tenth part of a moment. Then the curtain was drawn, and there was nothing more to be seen.

Napoleon did not stop to inquire. The corridor was clear: he cantered on. When he was gone, the curtain was held back again, and the dark eyes looked out again, still terrified.

Napoleon, safely in his room but still unsafe because he had been seen, described her to Constant while he lathered his face for shaving.

'A young woman. A girl. A maid, I suppose. One of Josephine's maids.'

'Can Your Majesty give a closer description—?'

'I have done. A maid.'

'Dark or fair?'

'Dark, I think. Yes. She had dark eyes. I think she had. It was dark.'

'Pretty or plain?'

'I didn't stop to look. Pretty, I think. The eyes were big, and dark.'

'Françoise.'

'You know her?'

'Yes, Sire.'

'Find her. Now. She can't have spoken to Josephine yet. Josephine never wakes before eight o'clock at the earliest. Get hold of her and tell her, if she wants to continue working here—or anywhere in France—'

'Yes, Sire. I know what to tell her.'

'Put the shaving-bowl down somewhere. Roustan and I will manage.'

'Yes, Sire.'

Napoleon was energetic and revengeful. 'I'll give this female spy a sermon myself. Bring her to see me. This afternoon.'

'Yes, Sire.' Napoleon was ready for the razor. Constant handed it to him. Roustan held the mirror so that the Emperor could attack his beard in the best possible light. 'Would Your Majesty do something for me, while I'm gone?'

'Do what?'

'As I have tried to teach Your Majesty? Shave upwards?'

Napoleon majestically swept the razor down one cheek, from cheekbone to chin.

'I do not have enough time to shave upwards.'

Talleyrand was, as always, doing his best to make the Emperor see reason. Berthier was, as always, waiting for the Emperor to decide what he was going to do, so that he himself would know what he had to organize. Until then, he was prepared to remain silent. One talker like Talleyrand was enough.

Talleyrand said, 'I beg Your Majesty to consider. We are, at this moment, at war with only one country: England. I am in hopes that the rest of Europe will come to forgive France her good fortune and her great glory.'

Napoleon was terse. 'I have considered this.'

'But if the same head wears the two crowns of France and Italy, then Austria will not forgive. If Austria, then others.'

'The old monarchies. They have no strength compared with mine. I am the new principle. The child of Revolution. The welcome liberator.'

Talleyrand made a polite inclination. 'Indeed, Your Majesty is the most welcome man in the world, except in other countries.'

Napoleon laughed. 'Talleyrand, why do I have you as my Minister?'

'Because you enjoy an uncomfortable truth—not often, but sometimes.'

'I am a man who can be told anything.'

'Then we must talk more often.'

The Emperor continued to show that he was amused. 'If I didn't know you better, I'd say you were like a woman.'

A bow. 'I accept the compliment.'

Napoleon said to Talleyrand, 'I shall take the crown of Italy myself because there is no one else.'

Talleyrand shrugged his shoulders delicately, to show how little he thought of his own suggestion. 'In the last resort—one of your brothers?'

'Talleyrand, you've had a thousand mistresses in your time. I have only one mistress: Power. I've caught my brothers trying to flirt with her.'

'Ah, yes.'

'That is not permitted.'

'I withdraw the suggestion. However—'

'Austria will go to war with me?'

'Yes.'

'Is that good, or bad?'

'Bad.'

'Why?'

Talleyrand said, 'You will win.'

'Is that bad?'

'The rest of Europe will be frightened into going to war with you.'

'I shall win.'

'I imagine.'

'Is that bad?'

'Sire, when an English prizefighter retires unbeaten from the ring, he opens an academy of boxing, or takes a public house and serves drink to his old admirers. Emperors can't do that.'

There seemed a momentary possibility that he might have persuaded the Emperor to see reason, since the Emperor was silent for a moment. But the possibility was never a likelihood.

'Talleyrand. Do you wish me to continue to be Emperor?'

Talleyrand chose to avoid the question of whether or not he wished it. Personal wishing was of no importance. 'It is necessary, for France.'

'I am Emperor because I give France glory, which is what France wants. Appetite comes with eating. I must continue to give glory.'

'And when you retire from the ring?'

'My son will inherit a great empire.'

Talleyrand inclined his head. 'Ah, your son. Yes, Sire.'

'I shall have a son, sooner or later.'

'And will your son continue to give glory?'

Napoleon said, coldly, simply, as a matter of fact: 'There will no longer be any enemies.'

'I understand.'

'Do you understand this?' Napoleon's voice was rougher.

A discreet tap sounded at the door. Constant came in.

'Forgive me, Sire—'

'What is it?'

'The person Your Majesty wished to see has arrived.'

'Person?'

Constant came and said it quietly into his ear. 'The maid.'

'Ah.' Napoleon indicated the door of his bedroom. 'I'll see him in there. Ask him to wait.'

'Yes, Sire.' Constant went, without the trace of a smile on his face.

Napoleon turned back to Talleyrand. 'I have four hundred thousand reasons for going to war. However, I shall not go to war with Austria. But if Austria should choose to go to war with me—Berthier?'

Berthier said, 'We shall be ready to march.'

Constant said, 'Sire, this is Françoise.'

Françoise, blushing very red, dropped down into a deep curtsey. Napoleon stared at her, menacingly. She, no doubt feeling the force of his eyes, stayed in the curtsey, with her head bowed.

'Get up.'

She did, but with her head still bowed, her eyes still lowered, her cheeks still glowing.

'Look at me.'

She did, but only because she did not dare disobey his order.

'So you took it into your head to spy on me.'

'No, Sire.'

'You spied on me.'

'Sire, I was doing what Her Majesty the Empress told me to do.'

'What did Her Majesty the Empress tell you to do?'

'To hide there. And watch.'

'Watch me?'

'No, Sire.'

'Watch whom, watch what?'

'Watch to see if anyone came out of, or went into, any of the bedrooms.'

'And did you see anyone?'

She was silent.

'Out with it! Did you?'

She said, turning her eyes to the wall, 'I saw Your Majesty go into Madame Duchâtel's room, soon after midnight. And I saw Your Majesty come out again at six in the morning.'

'You saw.'

'Yes, Sire.'

'And what did you think?'

'Sire, I was told to watch, but—'

'But what?'

'I wasn't told to draw conclusions.'

'Look at me!'

She looked at him. Her eyes were very big and very dark.

He looked hard into her eyes so that she would not dare to lie. 'Did you tell Her Majesty the Empress what you had seen?'

'No, Sire. Constant had talked to me by then.'

'But did you tell her?'

'No, Sire.'

'What did you tell her?'

'I told her I'd seen nothing, Sire.'

'Was Her Majesty pleased that you had seen nothing?'

'I think so, Sire.'

'Why do you think so?'

'She gave me five louis, Sire.'

'Five what?'

Her blush deepened, if that were possible. 'I beg your pardon, Sire. I mean five napoleons.'

Napoleon turned to Constant, quickly, almost as if to catch him smiling at the poor girl's lapse. The renaming of the currency was, after all, very new.

'Constant. Ten napoleons.'

'Yes, Sire.' Constant went to a drawer to get them.

'Well, Françoise.' He fixed her with his eyes again. 'Has Her Majesty told you to watch again? Tonight?'

'Marianne is to watch tonight, Sire. I am to watch tomorrow night.'

Constant brought to Napoleon a rouleau of ten gold coins. Napoleon made a brusque gesture at the maid.

'Give them to . . .' It was to be supposed that he had forgotten her name.

'Yes, Sire.'

She said, 'Thank you, Sire,' and was going down into another curtsey, but another imperial gesture forbade it.

The Emperor said, 'Constant, you can go. I must deliver my sermon to this young lady.' Constant bowed and started to leave. 'She will keep you informed of which nights she is on duty.'

Françoise said, 'Yes, Sire.'

Constant smiled at Françoise, accepting her as a future fellow-conspirator, and bowed again to his Emperor, and left him to deliver his sermon. Napoleon, perhaps rehearsing it, paced about the room. Françoise waited, apprehensive, prepared for a stronger reprimand, but no longer actually frightened. It did seem to her that the Emperor was not quite her imagined ogre.

Napoleon said, 'The sermon.'

'Yes, Sire.'

'A lesson in history. You may not have learnt history.'

'No, Sire.'

Napoleon, taking a deep breath for a long speech, said, 'The Court of the Bourbons, before the Revolution, was riddled with immorality. The queen had lovers, the nobles had mistresses. When the aristocracy is corrupt, it corrupts the whole nation.'

She stood silent, listening and perhaps learning.

'After the Revolution, the Directory fell into decadence and vice. A decadence which enfeebled the whole nation. I had to destroy the Directory, destroy that whole régime, and create a new one. A régime based on order. On discipline. On moral values. The importance of the family. The sanctity of marriage. The Empress and I are in complete agreement about this. Our court must set an example to the whole nation. There must be no hint of the decadence and the corruption which ruined the old régime.'

He paused, perhaps for breath, perhaps for thought. There did not yet seem to be anything for her to say.

'The Empress has a duty to see that immorality does not happen. She is right to set people to watch. She must make sure that my laws are obeyed. Is that clear?'

There was something for her to say at last. 'Yes, Sire.'

Napoleon, for no apparent reason, started to unbutton his jacket.

He supposed that she was about twenty. She was really a very pretty girl: her eyes were remarkably big and extremely dark.

He said, 'It is also true that the Emperor himself is above the law. He decrees, but he need not obey. I must explain to you, I am not subject to the same rules as common mortals. I am not subject to any rules. I am not a common mortal.'

He threw off his jacket, on to the floor. He went to her and took her by the shoulders, to compel her obedience.

He said, 'If you ever tell the Empress what you have seen, this last night, then I shall tell the Empress what you have done.'

He took her into a strong embrace. She was not quite sure what she should do, but she did know that the Emperor was the greatest man on earth, and was not to be refused.

He called on Josephine before dinner. She was being dressed by her maids. One of them was Françoise.

'Good evening, my dear.'

The maids all fell into curtseys at the sight of the Emperor. Françoise was as burningly blushing as she had been before. He spared her by not looking at her. And Josephine was enchanted to see him. She wanted him all to herself. She commanded the maids to leave.

'No, they can stay, one word with you, that's all . . .'

He held her hand, and took her aside, so that the maids could not hear.

'It came into my mind . . . If I finish work not too late —it's impossible to say at the moment, but I'll try . . . Might I pay a call on you, tonight?'

She was in heaven at the thought. 'Please try.'

'I shall try.' He made a courteous little bow. 'My dear. I shall see you in a moment, at dinner. Shall I send Madame de Rémusat in?'

He went without waiting for an answer.

In the boudoir, Madame de Rémusat and Madame Duchâtel were waiting, as ladies-in-waiting must do.

Napoleon said, 'Madame de Rémusat, I think the Empress would like to see you.'

Madame de Rémusat went to the bedroom. As soon as she was gone, Napoleon said to Madame Duchâtel, 'Not tonight. But tomorrow night.'

16. MADAME DUCHATEL

He was standing staring out of the window, though it was dark and there was nothing to be seen. Madame Duchâtel said softly, 'Come back to bed.'

'I must leave you. I have work to do.'

She screwed her eyes up and focused them to look at her clock. 'At three in the morning?'

'Three in the morning is a time like any other time.'

She sighed. 'For emperors, perhaps.'

'And I must be careful of your reputation.'

'And of your own.'

He laughed, but quietly, as if he might be heard. 'Creeping along the corridors at night . . . ?'

She said, as she had said before to him, 'Darling, if you are seen in the corridors at night, you are still the Emperor, nothing can change that. But if I am seen, then I am no longer a virtuous woman, I am no longer fit to be at your morally respectable court. You do want me to be virtuous, don't you?'

He came and kissed her, lovingly, tenderly. 'I want . . . What do I want?'

She said, 'Me.'

He said, 'Yes. But. Beyond that, what? Do I know what? . . . I am a successful ruler because I have more common sense than any one else, and because I make decisions faster than anyone else. But with you, I have no common sense, and I can't make a decision.'

She said, calmly, sensibly, 'Your decision is to be my secret lover.'

'I am your secret lover because that is all I can be.'

She was very calm. 'I have a husband. An old jealous husband.'

'Whom I send away on business as often as I can, but . . .'

She was the calmest woman in the world. 'But you have a wife.'

'Even more jealous.'

'And you can't send her away.'

'No. I can't.'

'So we must be secret.'

He walked away from her, to the window, and raised his fist almost as if he felt the need to break the window, at least to break something, as if something had to break.

'And Josephine watches. Her eyes bore through the back of my skull. That is not my idea of relaxation. Why can't she understand that I need to talk, freely, openly, with a woman who is not her? Why does she try to cut me off from half of the human race?'

Madame Duchâtel, more sensible than Napoleon, smiled. 'If she believed that it was only talk . . .'

He said, almost irritably, 'I also need, sometimes, what every man needs sometimes.'

'Yes.'

'I am not so entranced by the act of love that I think it, as a thing in itself, vastly important. You see, I know myself.'

'Yes.'

'I need, occasionally, the softness of a woman's arms. An hour's talk every evening, an occasional hour together at night. I spend my day being told that I'm the most powerful man in the world. Why can't I have what I need at the end of the day?'

She said, 'Because we are in the situation that we are in.'

'I must change the situation.'

'Are you as powerful as that?'

He came back to the bed, and kissed her, and sat looking down into her face, not knowing whether to ask her his question, because he did not expect that she would give him the answer he wished. But he had to ask her the question.

'Suppose . . . suppose you were to become pregnant.'

She was so sensibly shaking her head. 'Darling, I take very good care not to become pregnant.'

'Suppose.'

She smiled, as one does when a supposition is absurd. 'Then I suppose that my husband would not believe that he was responsible. I suppose that your wife the Empress would be more than suspicious. And I suppose that the child would be beautiful, but unfortunately, the image of you.'

'Yes. Well?'

'I suppose I should find myself divorced, changing my name, running away from Paris, living in an obscure village . . . Why do you want me to suppose?'

'A thought I had.'

'Not a good thought for me.'

'No.'

'Secret mistress is better.'

He said, 'But not what I need.'

She said, lightly but carefully—as everything she said was carefully considered and carefully worded—'Then you must make a decision.'

'Yes.'

'And decide whether to make your wife more unhappy, or less.'

He said, half saying it but half asking her, 'I imagine that she is unhappy now.'

'Because you don't love her.'

'Does she say that? To you? You are with her more than I am.'

'She believes that there is someone else, that you are in love with someone else—she doesn't know who it is, she suspects us all, she suspects everyone at your court. Perhaps any one of the ladies-in-waiting, perhaps more than one, perhaps all of us. She suspects you of monstrous gargantuan appetites. You must know, she understands everything in terms of love, desire, bed. You no longer love her in those terms—no more than once a month, and then it seems merely a politeness. Therefore you must

235

—in those terms—love someone else, you must be making love to someone else . . . Last night, Claire de Rémusat and I went into her room. She was staring at herself in the mirror, tears streaming down her cheeks. "I am growing old! I am no longer beautiful! The Emperor doesn't love me!" '

'Is that true? She said that?'

'Yes.'

'Last night?'

'Five hours ago.'

He said, sadly and soberly, 'Poor woman.'

'Yes.'

They lay in each other's arms, giving each other human warmth and lovingness.

She said, softly, in his ear, 'Great ruler, most powerful man, you will have to decide.'

Napoleon made a decision, not on the question that Madame Duchâtel had in mind, but still, a decision of some importance; and he went to call on Josephine at her breakfast-time, in order to tell her what he had decided.

She was sitting up in her bed, ready to receive visitors, even her husband: hair charmingly curled, face newly painted, lips brightly smiling. One would have said, from a short distance, a young woman.

'Good morning, my dear. You're looking very beautiful.'

'Thank you.'

'Very.'

'Did you come to tell me that?'

'The compliment was spontaneous. I simply came to see you.'

'It's lovely to see you.'

They smiled at each other.

'And to say . . .' But there he stopped.

After a moment she saw that he would like her to ask, gently, 'What did you come to say?'

She could tell that he was grateful for her help, and

that he wished her to go on helping him. He had something to say which he thought should be said diffidently, under persuasion to say it.

'Darling, you may remember a notion I had . . .'

'You have so many.'

'A theory, a hypothesis . . .'

'Remind me.'

'About a hypothetical woman . . .'

'Ah. Yes.'

'And a hypothetical child.'

'Yes, I remember.'

'Last night I considered it more deeply.'

She had to go on helping him towards his answer, whatever his answer might be.

'What did you decide?'

'I decided that it was not a good idea.'

Her relief was so great that she could have screamed. She kept her fixed smile and made a safely neutral sound, somewhere between 'Ah' and 'Oh'.

'So I came to tell you.'

Now that he had decided against what she would most bitterly have fought against, she could take credit for not having opposed it.

She said softly, 'You do know that I would have agreed.'

'Yes, you're the best of wives.' He was willing to give her some credit, in order to get more for himself. 'But it was a bad thought—'

'For a good reason.' She was willing to give him credit, but perhaps not as much as he wanted.

He said, 'The reason was good but the thought was a bad one. It would have meant my being unfaithful to you—'

'Darling, I'd have understood. Knowing the reason.'

'It would have meant my making love to someone I didn't love—'

'It would have meant your getting what you long for. What I can't give you.'

'It would have been a betrayal. A betrayal of you.'

'No, it would have made us feel that I had helped you
—that it was my child, because I had helped you.'

'But another woman's child, by me—'

'I would have become its mother. I would have made
myself believe myself its mother.'

Napoleon was annoyed. He was not getting half enough
credit for having rejected the idea, while she was taking
twice too much, for not having rejected it.

He said, 'You should be pleased that I can't bring myself to be unfaithful to you.'

Her eyes were all innocence and love. 'I simply want
what is best for you.'

How could she be so imperceptive, to fail to see that he
was demanding not love but gratitude? The whole point
of telling her was to make it clear to her that he had, for
her sake, made a considerable sacrifice. But she was behaving as if the sacrifice was hers. His intention had mis-
fired. He abandoned it.

He said crossly, 'It wasn't a practical notion.'

'Wasn't it? I would gladly have kept the secret.'

'There would have been rumours, very difficult to deny.
There would have been disbelief, from the mere fact of
your age.'

It was an unfair blow, and he knew it.

She said, 'Yes. . .'

'Everyone knows, we've been married ten years without having a child, you're forty-two, you're a grandmother.'

'Yes. . .'

'It would hardly seem likely . . .'

'No. . .'

'Well, would it? At your age?'

'No, I agree, my age . . .'

She started crying. How dared she? How could she
be so lacking in understanding? He had very naturally
expected gratitude, and all he got was a crying wife. It
was exasperating.

'Good God, it's nothing to cry about! We all get older!
You're still a beautiful woman!'

'Still . . . ?'

Now she was turning his words against him.

'Yes, still! Still! In the same way as I am still your husband, I still love you! What more do you want? There's no reason for you to cry! There's no reason for you to sit staring in your mirror at night—"I'm not beautiful, I'm getting old, he doesn't love me!"'

As soon as he had said it, he knew that he had made a terrible mistake.

She had stopped crying, on the instant.

She said, 'Who told you I said that?'

'No one. I imagined it.'

'Did you?'

'I imagined you sitting there crying, because you foolishly believe I don't love you.'

'You imagined.'

'I've known you long enough now to be able to imagine.'

'Long enough.'

She was turning his words again. He felt entitled to be angry again.

'Yes! Long enough!'

He stiffened into an attitude of cold controlled anger. 'If you cannot be pleased with what I have told you, I must ask you to think about it. I hope and believe that you will decide to be pleased.'

He marched out, virtuously and justifiably angry.

After a time she sent for Madame de Rémusat and Madame Duchâtel. When they came, she said to them, 'Last night, in this room, I said something which you two heard, you two only. You were the only people in this room when I said it. It has been repeated to me this morning by another person.'

They were standing close together, she could look at both of them without moving her eyes.

Madame de Rémusat instinctively turned her head to look at Madame Duchâtel.

Madame Duchâtel met Josephine's eyes. She was as

polite as a lady-in-waiting and as coolly composed as an
Emperor's secret mistress.

'Your Majesty, that hardly seems possible.'

'Doesn't it?'

Josephine stared at her, but there was nothing more to
be learnt by staring. In any case, there was nothing more
to be learnt. She knew now who her rival was. She knew
that she could not hope to prove it, and that there was
nothing to be gained by proving it. She knew that there
was nothing she could do but be silent, and endure, and
seek comfort in tears.

Napoleon said, 'If I speak to her, she cries. If I look at
her, she cries. If I tell her not to cry, she cries. What am
I to do?'

Caroline said, 'Let her cry.'

'It does not make my life very amusing.'

Caroline shrugged her shoulders. 'Avoid her.'

'She's my wife, poor woman.'

'Ignore her.'

'She's the Empress.'

She looked at her brother coldly. If he wanted com-
miseration, he would not get it from her. He would get
from her not what he wanted but what he needed: a calm
and rational view of his situation, and good practical
advice on what to do about it.

'Divorce her. Then she will cease to be the Empress.'

He was silent for a time, brooding. At last he said,
'We Bonapartes were not made for marriage.'

'Or we should have married each other. Like the kings
and queens of ancient Egypt.'

'Yes, we both have the same temperament. We don't
need much love.'

She thought, If our energies and our ambitions had
been harnessed and coupled by a different relationship,
then we would have ruled the whole world by now. Failing the possibility of marrying each other, they had both
made bad matches. Josephine and Murat did not want

to rule the world: they simply wanted the titles, and the trappings, and the applause.

Josephine, tears in her eyes, as always now, said, 'He is a monster of wickedness, why shouldn't I reproach him? Why shouldn't I cry? If I left him in peace, he'd feel free to give himself up to every possible kind of vice. A hundred mistresses, a thousand, no woman would be safe from him. He already believes that because he's Emperor he can have any woman he pleases. If I allow it, if I turn a blind eye to it, he will corrupt the whole world.'

Madame de Rémusat felt uncomfortably honoured to be the Empress's confidante, and devoutly wished that the Empress had chosen somebody else. There was no reasoning with Josephine at her moments of believing that Napoleon was all heathen wickedness and she herself his sacrificial victim. There was nothing to be done but listen to the almost-hysterical babble.

'And it's not only Madame Duchâtel. You saw Napoleon last night, talking to Laura Junot. It's why he sent Junot to Italy. She'll be the next. You'll see. Watch them this evening. You'll see.'

Indeed, that evening, in the salon, Napoleon was in a mood of rough good humour, joking with young Madame Junot. He had known her since she was a child, he took the privileges of an old friend; and he enjoyed it when she answered him back with more spirit than the other court ladies would have cared or dared to show, in a conversation heard by the entire court.

'Whatever you may tell me, Sire, the fact remains that I am his wife, and not you. I shall write to him and insist on an explanation. I am entitled to do so.'

Napoleon laughed. 'My dear Laura, the gossips have been putting mischief into your head.'

'But who put it into the gossips' heads?'

'Whoever put it there, why listen to mischief?'

'Because Junot is my husband.'

Napoleon was still laughing, but there was something of the bully in his laugh.

'Laura, wives must not think badly of their husbands, or they may make them worse.'

She was not to be bullied, not even by the Emperor. 'Wives are entitled to know what their husbands are doing.'

'They're entitled neither to know nor to care. If Junot amuses himself in Italy, what's that to you?'

'A matter of some importance.'

'A trifle! Which you wives think important, when you know it; and which is nothing, when you don't.'

He was no longer laughing and no longer in a good humour. It was clear to those who saw and heard him that he was no longer defending Junot against Junot's wife; he was, without looking at the Empress, defending himself against her.

At least, it was clear to everyone except Laura Junot, who refused to be put down.

'Sire, when I am told by those who have come from Italy—'

'You should not listen.'

'Shall I not ask my husband—'

'Do you want to know what you should say on such occasions?'

He was almost shouting. His voice was hoarse. He was oddly red in the face.

She was angry, too, and did not try to conceal it.

'What should I say, Sire?'

'Nothing! Or if like the rest of your sex you must speak, let it be to give your approval. But I recommend silence.' He was breathing hard. 'There is a grand old proverb, Madame: "The hen should be silent in the presence of the cock".'

He turned abruptly away from Laura, to deny her the last word.

Josephine had heard it all. No one near her dared to look at her, except Madame de Rémusat, who was afraid for her. A sob rose up in Josephine's throat and had to make itself heard before her hand could get to her mouth to stifle it. For fear of the sobs that would follow, she ran out of the room.

Napoleon scowled blackly at everyone and at no one.

Claire de Rémusat made him a hurried curtsey. 'Would you excuse me, Sire? I think Her Majesty is not well.' She followed Josephine out.

Napoleon said loudly, as if he wanted Josephine to hear, a hundred yards away, as she ran to her bedroom, 'Well, whatever it is, it certainly isn't morning sickness.'

The members of the court avoided his eye, and prayed for the evening to end quickly.

In the warmth and comfort of her bed, in the middle of the night, bodies no longer urgent and active but minds still active, Madame Duchâtel felt inclined to talk, and Napoleon felt inclined to listen to her.

She said, 'If you decide that the Empress no longer means anything to you, then the situation is not what it was before.'

She waited, in case he felt inclined to say something. He said nothing. She went on.

'Until now, you have wanted me; but you have also, perhaps more strongly, wanted to keep up appearances. If you no longer feel the need to keep up appearances, then the situation is totally different from what it was.'

She waited. She went on.

'If you now feel strong enough, as Emperor, not just to be above the law, but to show that you are above the law, that you can break your own rules because they don't apply to you . . . If you feel sure enough of this, then you will feel sure enough to announce it.

'I don't mean an official bulletin. I mean, an Emperor can announce something simply by letting it be understood. He can, if he wishes, almost without a word, let it be understood that the Empress is still the Empress but is only the Empress . . . that someone else, who is not the Empress, is nevertheless more important, as a person, as a woman, to the Emperor.'

It was time to make a pause. She had said a great part

of her meaning: she had gone a great distance beyond anything she had ever said before. He could not stop her now, and reject her meaning out of hand. If he did not, she would go on, and go further.

He did not speak. She went on, with growing confidence.

'If this were to happen, then of course my husband would cease to be of any importance to me, because your strength would also be mine. You do understand—of course you do, you understand everything—that in our society a woman may love a great man, but so long as the love is secret, the woman's strength is only the strength of her husband. But if the great man acknowledges the love, if he announces it, then she takes her strength not from her husband but from her lover . . . And you do understand that without your strength it is difficult for me to continue, wearing one face by day, and another face at night . . .'

She had explained herself enough. It was time to offer not explanations but persuasions, without making them seem to be persuasions. Napoleon loved her because she combined a warm body and a cool mind. Her mind must continue to show itself cool.

'I should like all this to happen. I should like to be your helper, if it's possible to help you. I should like to be your partner, if anyone can be your partner. I want to be your mistress, because I love you. I'm proud to be your mistress, but, oh, darling, I do want to be able to show my pride . . .'

She knew that she had said enough, and that it was time for him to say something. She felt his cheek, and kissed it softly, in the dark.

'Did you hear all that? Or have you fallen asleep?'

'I heard every word.'

She said, not quite truthfully, 'It wasn't to persuade you, but to ask you. To ask you to make a decision.'

'Yes, I know.'

She wondered if she should say it, and decided to say

it. 'I'm feeling lazy and loving, may I say one word of persuasion?'

'Yes.'

She said, 'I do think I could help you.'

His answering voice came from the same distance, the same closeness or remoteness. 'Yes, I know.'

She had done what she could. She had worded it as well as she could. He had not stopped her. He had listened, and he was still lying in her arms. She was pleased.

Napoleon found Josephine in her little drawing-room, with Madame de Rémusat, and begged Madame de Rémusat's forgiveness: there was something he had to say to the Empress alone.

Even when they were alone, he seemed to find it difficult to say. He paced, while she sat patiently, warily waiting.

'My dear . . . We know each other well enough to speak frankly to each other.'

'Yes.' Warily. So many conversations had begun this way, to end in tears or hysterics or storms. Ten years of marriage is a long experience of conversations with another person.

'You may have felt, for some time now, that I have been . . . what shall I say . . . moody, not in the best possible temper.'

He gave her a chance to say, 'No, you have been consistently charming.' She did not take it. He went on.

'This is partly due to the fact that I have great problems on my mind—the situation in Europe, the likelihood of a new war with Austria, perhaps with Prussia, with God knows whom. Perhaps, at last, an invasion of England. As you are aware, I've been working fifteen hours a day, since plans must be made for whatever is possible . . .'

He gave her a chance to say, 'Yes,' and it happened that she obediently said, 'Yes.'

He was encouraged by this. He took a deep breath and said:

'And partly due to the fact—I must tell you frankly—that my mind has also been occupied by the thought of another woman. I have done nothing about it, but I must tell you that this other woman has been much in my mind.'

Her only policy was silence and a hurt look in her eyes.

'Because this woman has been so much in my mind, I have had to make a decision, an important decision, for myself, for her, and also for you.'

Silence. Hurt, pleading look. There was nothing else she could possibly do.

'I tell you this because I should be grateful to have your consent.'

Silence. How could she consent till she knew? He must say it. He must say the name.

'The woman is Madame Duchâtel, whom I admire greatly, whom I esteem . . .'

He had said the name. Silence.

He said, choosing his words with great exactness, 'I have come to the conclusion that much as I admire Madame Duchâtel, I do not admire her strongly enough to want her as my mistress: that if I were to take her as my mistress, if I were to announce this, as one can announce these things, not officially, but by letting it be known . . . then I believe that she would try to help me —politically, perhaps, and politics are difficult enough already without any help from women. I have a horror of petticoat government. Your great advantage, my dear—you don't give a damn about politics.'

She was ten years younger, twenty years, she was the youngest and the happiest woman in the world, though she did not dare say it.

He said, 'I have not told Madame Duchâtel my decision. I feel, myself, that it would be better if she were to retire from the court. And I feel that it would be better—since she is a member of your entourage, not mine; and since, in any case, I shall shortly be leaving for the camp at Boulogne—if you, rather than me, were to speak to her on this subject.'

Her cup was overflowing. She said, 'If you wish me to.'

She thought, How right I am, to know nothing of politics, and not ever to suggest that I can be any help.

The day after Napoleon left to inspect the troops at Boulogne, Josephine sent for Madame Duchâtel and asked most solicitously about her health, in the kindest possible way. The Empress always felt a keen anxiety about the health of her ladies-in-waiting. The ceremonial life of the Tuileries and Saint-Cloud, even of Malmaison, imposed a certain strain on the constitution of the imperial attendants, in particular the younger people. Once this strain started to show its effects, it was highly desirable that the person should guard against any possibility of the effects becoming permanent—by leaving the court for a time, at least, and taking a course of treatment at some such place as Plombières (the Empress's own favourite, when she herself found herself at less than her best) or Aix-les-Bains.

Madame Duchâtel seemed surprised by Her Majesty's kind inquiries, and by Her Majesty's thoughtful suggestion.

'Your Majesty, I am not ill.'

Josephine was mild but firm. 'I agree, you are not ill. But you are not well.'

'Your Majesty, I feel perfectly well.'

'Allow me to know better than you do. You are tired. Your duties here have been tiring.'

'Your Majesty, I have not found them so.'

'I assure you, you need a rest. You need to take the waters at a spa.'

'No, Your Majesty.'

It is not proper to contradict an Empress. Josephine decided to forgive the impropriety: it was a sign of the deterioration in Madame Duchâtel's health.

'It is clear to me that you need quite a long rest. Your

husband will understand. I should think that he will be pleased. I have never felt that he greatly cared for your living at court.'

Madame Duchâtel's hands were trembling: another symptom of nervous debility. She said, in a voice which was hardly that of a healthy woman, 'May I ask Your Majesty . . .'

Josephine was quick to reply, and was graciousness itself.

'If you wish, I will gladly take it on myself to explain to your husband.'

'That is not what I wanted to ask.'

'Ask.' Josephine was ready for any suggestion. It was for the questioner to decide whether she preferred the Empress to continue being gracious, or not.

Madame Duchâtel asked, in a hard clear voice, 'Did Your Majesty choose to wait until the Emperor had left for Boulogne, before noticing that I was ill, or not well, or tired?'

'Yes.' Josephine was still smiling.

'I had imagined so.'

Still smiling. 'Yes, I waited. Because the Emperor told me to wait. I do not question his decisions. I advise you not to question them.'

Madame Duchâtel was a brave woman. She still met Josephine's eye, and challenged her.

'I do not know of any reason why the Emperor should have made such a decision.'

Josephine, the winner, was kindness itself, to answer so gently.

'Nor do I. But I obey, without asking for reasons. Would you be so good as to leave in the morning?'

Napoleon came back from Boulogne ten days later, and re-entered his study, and was met by General Duroc.

'Hullo, Duroc. How are you?'

'Very well, Sire. How was Boulogne?'

'I could see across the Channel to England. God knows if I can ever get there. How is my wife?'

'Very well, Sire.'

The desk was covered with neat piles of papers that needed urgent attention. He sat down to start urgently attending to them.

'And Madame Duchâtel?'

Duroc said, 'Gone.'

'Did you give her the miniature? The portrait of me?'

'Yes, Sire.'

'Good.'

'You can see for yourself, Sire.'

Duroc picked up from the desk an envelope, and opened it, and took out a frame, gold, with diamonds, and showed it to the Emperor.

'She kept the portrait of yourself, Sire. But returned the gold frame, with the diamonds.'

Having made such a decision, how can a man ever know whether or not the decision was a mistake?

17. ELEONORE

Eléonore Dénuelle de la Plaigne was an extraordinarily pretty girl with dark curly hair, the daughter of an extremely pretty mother with dark curly hair—who was perhaps no more respectable than she should have been; and of a handsome father who lived by business speculation of one sort and another—perhaps no more honest than he might have been. Monsieur and Madame Dénuelle, so shrewd in other ways, committed the imprudence of marrying their daughter to a good-looking young army officer who was absolutely a swindler and a confidence man and who foolishly allowed himself to be caught and condemned for it. However, the Dénuelles had earlier taken the wise precaution of sending Eléonore to school at Madame Campan's establishment, at St Germain-en-Laye.

To have been at Madame Campan's school was an insurance policy in itself. Madame Campan had herself been a lady-in-waiting to that unfortunate Queen Marie-Antoinette. The Empress Josephine's daughter Hortense had been one of her pupils, and the Empress's nieces Émilie and Stéphanie, and, most important of all, the Emperor's own youngest sister Caroline, now Princess Murat. As a member of such a distinguished company, a girl could not come to any real harm, at least not for long.

Eléonore, with a husband in jail, went to see Madame Campan. Madame Campan wrote to Caroline. Eléonore wrote to Caroline. Eléonore went to see Caroline, and poured out her shallow little heart.

'Caroline—oh, I know I mustn't call you Caroline, it just slipped out, I mean Princess, I mean Your Highness . . . But if it were possible for you—for Your Highness—to give me some sort of a job, any sort of a job, I really would be so grateful . . . Revel took all my money, what little money I had. Then he forged things, and they sent him to prison, but of course I didn't get my money back, he'd spent all that already. I had absolutely no idea what to do. Then I thought of Madame Campan, and she thought of you, she thought perhaps you might remember me, she thought perhaps you might have . . . well, some sort of vacancy in your household, as one of your ladies, or anything. I really don't mind what I do. I just don't want to starve.'

Caroline looked at her appraisingly. She really was a sensationally pretty girl: made to be desired by men, and made to satisfy men's desire.

Caroline said, 'I shan't let you starve.'

'Oh, thank you, Caro—I mean, thank you, Princess. Honestly, I'll do whatever you want me to—'

Caroline sent for Murat, as a doctor calls in a specialist to give his opinion. She hardly needed a statement of his opinion: the look in his eye was enough when he first sighted Eléonore across the room.

'Who's the girl?'

'She was at school with me, she married a scoundrel, she hasn't a sou to her name. Come and look at her more closely.'

'Yes, I will.'

She took him to Eléonore.

'Darling, I'd like you to meet an old schoolfriend of mine. Eléonore, may I introduce my husband?'

Murat's eyes inspected the big soft eyes, the small soft mouth. He turned to Caroline.

'Yes, I entirely agree.'

Eléonore had no idea what he meant, but it sounded as if he approved of her, and as if they had some kind of vacancy in mind for her. She was happy.

When they explained to her what they had in mind, she was still happy. When Napoleon came to the house, and she was presented to him, she thought him really very attractive, for an Emperor. When she was taken to visit him at the Tuileries, late one evening in February, she was fully conscious of her good fortune.

She was shown into his study. Napoleon was working at his desk. He did not rise: she had not expected him to rise. He went on working: she had been warned not to be surprised if he went on working.

His valet, Constant, said, 'Mademoiselle Dénuelle, Sire.'

He looked up briefly. She was cloaked and hooded, against the February weather and against possible spies.

'Do sit down. Is it cold out?'

'Yes, Sire.'

'Would you like a glass of wine? Of cognac?'

'Of wine, please.'

'Give Mademoiselle Dénuelle a glass of wine.'

He went back to working, with his papers and his maps, while Constant mutely invited her to sit in an armchair near the fire, and brought her a glass of wine, and smiled and bowed to her and left the room.

She sipped the wine, slowly, making it last until Napoleon decided that he had, for a time at least, finished his work.

He coughed, almost nervously. His manner was more awkward than she would have imagined.

'I think my sister Caroline spoke to you.'

'Yes, Sire.'

'And explained.'

'Yes, Sire.'

'Then I don't have to explain.'

'No, Sire.'

'I hope it wasn't inconvenient, your coming here.'

'No, Sire.'

'I shall make a more convenient arrangement, for the future.'

'Whatever you wish, Sire.'

'You understand, I am extremely busy with my work.'

'Yes, Sire.'

'The best thing would be for you to have a house of your own. Close at hand. Where I can call on you when I have a moment to spare . . . an hour to spare, for an hour's conversation . . .'

'I understand, Sire.'

'What else? Ah yes. I believe you are married to a Monsieur Revel?'

'Yes, Sire.'

'Do you want a divorce?'

'Yes, please, Sire.'

'I'll arrange it.'

'Thank you, Sire.'

'I think we shall be able to talk to each other more easily if you don't call me "Sire" all the time.'

'What would Your Majesty like me to call him?'

'I shall have to decide.'

'Yes, Sire.'

'Not "Sire". And not "Your Majesty".'

'I'm sorry.'

'You do realize, I want us to talk freely.'

'Yes.'

It sounded so bald, without the 'Sire'.

He said, 'Are you feeling warmer?'

'Yes.'

'Would you like to take your cloak off?'

She rose and took it off and put it on her chair. She stood there, waiting for whatever might come next.

He said, 'As it happens, I am exceptionally busy tonight.'

She said, seeking always to please, 'Would you like me to go away?'

He moved abruptly to a door which was not the door she had been shown in at. He opened the door, wide. She could see that it was the door to a bedroom.

He said, 'Shall we go . . . into the . . .'

She was not certain whether it was correct for her to precede him through the doorway into the bedroom. But he held the door for her, and invited her to go through

253

first, so she did. Similarly, in the bedroom, he invited her to enter the bed before he did.

She was installed in a charming little house in the rue de la Victoire, not at all far from the house that Napoleon and Josephine had lived in when he was only a general and the Empress was only a wife.

Caroline supervised the choice of the furniture, to suit Napoleon's taste rather than Eléonore's: since Eléonore had no particular taste, but merely desired to please, she was pleased with the furniture because it was found to be pleasing. General Duroc, Grand Marshal, made all the arrangements and paid all the bills. Prince Murat, Grand Admiral, came to inspect the rooms and to give his approval. She showed him round.

'And this is my private sitting-room. Isn't it charming?'

'Yes. Charming.' Murat was for some reason looking at her, more than at the room.

'I can't tell you how grateful I am to the princess.'

'And to me, I hope.'

'Of course. And to you.'

'I recommended you for the job.'

She smiled at him. 'I am deeply grateful.'

'May I claim my reward?'

It had become a flirtation. She was enjoying it.

'What reward do you claim?'

He looked into her eyes, rather longer and rather more closely than the princess's husband ought to have done. Then he looked away, towards a decanter on a silver tray.

'Wine? May I?'

'Oh, yes, please do have some wine. I should have thought of it sooner. I'm so delighted you called.'

He went to pour wine. 'I was passing.'

'So few people call.'

'My dear Eléonore, so few people are supposed to know where you are.'

'Yes, I feel almost like a nun.'

'Not quite like a nun.'

'I said almost. Not quite.'

It was the kind of talk she enjoyed, the only kind of talk she understood: the handsome man indicating, by his eyes and by the tone of his voice rather than by his words, that he found the girl extremely desirable; the girl indicating that she knew this, and was pleased that he desired her.

Murat said, 'The few of us who call must call more often.'

'Whenever you like.'

'When the Emperor isn't calling?'

Murat was the kind of man she understood, the kind of big vain swaggerer and boaster and liar that had filled her parents' drawing-room throughout her childhood, and her own drawing-room through her brief career as a wife. Murat was not at all unlike Monsieur Revel who had married her and swindled and forged and gone to prison: except that Murat was a marshal and a prince and Grand Admiral of France.

He came back to her with two glasses of wine.

She said, 'I've been here two weeks, the Emperor has called twice.'

'He is not very ardent.'

'He is exceptionally busy.'

'I say it's an insult to a beautiful woman.'

'He makes me doubt whether I'm beautiful.'

He raised his glass. She raised hers in reply. He said, 'You are exceptionally beautiful.'

They drank from their glasses. As they lowered the glasses, her mouth was not far away from his. He leant forward and kissed it. She drew away from the kiss, but slowly, and only after it had happened. She smiled.

'Your reward?'

'Second part of my reward.'

She said, 'But he is the Emperor.'

'Oh yes, he's the Emperor, no doubt about that.'

'Your Emperor.'

'Yes, so my wife keeps telling me.'

He looked at her with admiration beyond the level of normal flirtation. Madame Campan had trained her to be a lady, but undoubtedly Eléonore's mother had brought her up to be a whore, inside marriage or outside it. She had the lusciousness and sheen, and the invitingness, of a ripe fruit almost ready to drop.

'Is there anything else I ought to see?' He looked away, at a closed door. 'What's through there?'

'My bedroom.'

'May I see?'

'The Emperor may see.'

He grinned at her, in appreciation. 'Caroline says you're not clever. I think you're clever.'

She laughed. 'Prince, you recommended me for the job. I want to keep it.'

They were both pleased. They had become fellow-conspirators.

'What's he like, with you? I never think he understands women.'

'As you do?'

'I understand women like you.'

He poured more wine, to encourage her to tell him. She did not need any encouragement.

'Well, he comes here . . . And he looks at me . . . And he looks at the clock . . . And he says something, not very interesting. And I say something rather stupid. And he looks at the clock again, because he's exceptionally busy . . . And we go in the bedroom. And he looks at the clock.'

She started giggling. Murat waited to be told what was funny.

'Do you know what I did last time he was here? When he fell asleep?'

'No, what?'

'Well, of course, we all know he's the greatest man in the world. And perhaps it's my fault, I expect it is. But honestly, don't you think, sometimes, that great men are . . . ?'

'Not very amusing?'

'Boring?' She giggled again. 'Is that treason?'

The next time Napoleon came to call on her, he fell asleep again, and she did again what she had done the last time. She crept out of bed and tiptoed to the clock, and silently opened the glass on its face, and turned the minute hand forward by forty minutes.

Then she tiptoed back to bed, and gently prodded him, and whispered.

'Napoleon . . .'

'Mm?'

'It's half-past two.'

'What?'

'You said you had to leave at half-past two.'

'Already . . . ?'

'Yes. I just looked at the clock. It says half-past two.'

He struggled out of bed, and reached for his clothes. He was exceptionally busy. He had work to get back to.

Talleyrand was always delighted to see the Empress looking well; and she was looking particularly well at that time, in those halcyon days after her victory over Madame Duchâtel and her husband's victory over his imperial Germanic rivals. He saw a good deal of her in the evenings at court: he was still her favourite opponent at backgammon: and he still said things to her, not for any specific or immediate purpose, but in the belief that some good would come, some day, of something he had said and she had happened to remember.

On that evening in May, he said, 'Yes, the Russians are charming and unreliable. The Germans are unreliable and uncharming. But the negotiations are going well.'

'I'm so glad.'

'The only difficult person I have to negotiate with is your husband.'

She gave him a smile of sympathy and words of consolation. 'Napoleon says you're a great minister.'

'My talent is to make things move smoothly. His is to decide which way they shall move.'

'And which way are they moving?'

'Smoothly, towards a new war.'

'Are they? Why?' She did not particularly wish to know why; but Talleyrand clearly wanted her to ask.

'Because we have four hundred thousand bayonets, and you can do anything with bayonets except sit on them.'

She was feeling quietly contented, she wanted Talleyrand to feel contented too.

She said, 'Napoleon would make a great Emperor· of Europe.'

'Of the world.'

'Of the world. Yes.'

'I agree. If only the world agreed.'

She said, 'The world may come to agree.'

'Your husband employs me to make peace after his wars. I should infinitely prefer to make it beforehand.'

'Ah, but then the victory would be yours, not his.'

He threw the dice, and made his move. 'I have a hope remaining.'

'Which is?'

'You, Your Majesty.'

She said, gently, 'Talleyrand, you know I never try to influence him.'

'You are at peace with him.'

'Yes.'

'That is an influence. When his life is peaceful, there is still a chance of peace.'

Caroline came into the room, and went to Napoleon to ask his forgiveness for her late arrival. He was in a forgiving mood: things were going well for him: and she was his favourite sister.

'My dear Caroline, you are always forgiven.'

'I've been seeing a friend, I must tell you—' She stopped, as if to make sure that she could not be overheard, and took Napoleon's arm, and led him away to a corner.

'What friend?'

'Eléonore.'

He smiled ruefully. 'Does she hate me for neglecting her?'

'She adores you.'

'Does she?' He was sceptical.

'She knows how little time you have.'

'Good, I'm glad she knows that.'

'But yes, she feels neglected. You haven't been there for weeks.'

'No, I haven't.'

'She wonders if she's done something wrong.'

Napoleon looked at his sister and said, 'Caroline, what did they teach you and her, at that school of Madame Campan's?'

'How to be ladylike. And how to be beautiful.'

'She is both those things.'

'Yes.'

'The best school in France? Is that all? But you have a brain, and she hasn't.'

'Eléonore is not a fool.'

He threw up his hands, not in exasperation but in a confession of failure: a failure which was of no particular importance.

'She has the body of an angel and the mind of a child. She has learnt to make love but not conversation. We have nothing to say to each other, so we go to bed. The physical union is not a bond between us. There is no bond. We are still just as much strangers as we were when we first met. She is a remarkably beautiful girl. It was kind of you to think of her for me. But she is not what I need.'

Caroline said, with a controlled excitement in her voice, a hint of triumph: 'She has done what you needed.'

'Oh? What's that?'

'Shall I change your life for you, with three words? . . . Eléonore is pregnant.'

Napoleon stared at her, and put his hand out and

reached for the back of a chair, to steady himself, or he might have fallen.

He sent for Fouché, who understood exactly what he wanted, and who came back a very few hours later with a sheaf of neatly tabulated reports.

'Lastly, Sire: the list of visitors to Mademoiselle Dénuelle's house, with dates and times.'

'Full? Accurate? Are you sure?'

'Any house where Your Majesty calls is under my constant surveillance.'

'Whether I like it or not?'

'I am Your Majesty's servant.'

'Yes.'

'Responsible for Your Majesty's safety.'

'Yes. Who gave you the names?'

'I have had the house watched night and day, as a matter of routine, Sire. And Mademoiselle Dénuelle's footman is in my pay.'

Napoleon growled, 'Everyone is, except me.' But he took the list from Fouché, and opened it to look at it.

Fouché said, 'Your Majesty will note the name of the most frequent visitor.'

Napoleon went to call on Eléonore, and kissed her on the cheek, and told her that he was delighted with the news. She looked at him doubtfully. His face was not showing much delight.

'Are you pleased? Really?'

'Yes.'

'I didn't know if you would be.'

'Delighted.'

'I'm glad you are.'

'Of course, it must be a secret.'

'Yes, I thought that.'

'My wife must not find out.'

'Yes, that's what I thought.'

'I'll speak to Duroc. He can arrange for you to have the best possible care, the best possible doctors . . .'

'Thank you.'

'You're—what—two months gone?'

'Yes, just over two months.'

'So the child will be born in December.'

'Yes, it ought to be.'

'I shall almost certainly be away then, in one country or another.'

She smiled faintly. 'There wouldn't be much you could do.'

'In fact I may be leaving Paris quite soon. But you must stay here in this house. I'll increase your allowance. Of course, I'll provide for the child . . .'

'You're very kind.'

He was kind, perhaps, but gruff and reserved. He paced about the room, not looking at her, staring at the floor, as if there were some great weight on his mind.

He said, 'I'm sorry I haven't seen you more often.'

'I'm sorry too.'

'You must have been lonely here.'

She didn't answer the question, if it was a question. She said, 'I was very pleased when Princess Caroline suggested . . . what she suggested. I am very pleased. If you're pleased.'

Napoleon chose to persist. 'But you must have been lonely. With so few visitors. Have you had visitors?'

'Some.'

Not looking at her. 'Who?'

'Princess Caroline, of course.'

'Yes.'

'And two of her ladies-in-waiting, the ones who were in on the secret.'

'Yes.'

'And General Duroc, to arrange things.'

'Yes.'

'And your valet Constant, to tell me when you were coming, or when you couldn't.'

'Yes.'

'And you. When you came.'

'Yes.'

'That's about all.'

He said, 'No one else?'

'I don't think so.'

'Murat?'

'Oh yes, Prince Murat.'

'He came here?'

'With Princess Caroline.'

'And without?'

'Once or twice.'

'By himself?'

'Once or twice.'

'No more than that?'

'I don't think so.' She knew what he was asking her, now.

He asked, 'How long ago? Two months ago? Just over two months?'

'Not as long as that.'

He shouted at the top of his voice, 'Liar!'

He was looking at her at last, staring at her, staring through her. His eyes were like knives.

She said, 'He called for a minute sometimes, when he was passing. Out of politeness.'

Napoleon ground his words out. 'I have a list of his visits, with their dates, and how long he stayed.'

'Why?'

'Why did you say "Once or twice", when he came here a dozen times? Why did you say "Not as long as two months", when he came here two months ago? Why did you say "He called for a minute", when he stayed for an hour?'

She was not a coward. She faced him.

'Because I didn't want you to think I was having an *affaire* with him.'

'When you were.'

'No!'

'Murat does not call on young ladies out of politeness.'

'He flirted with me, he tried to make love to me, he didn't succeed.'

262

'I've known Murat ten years now. When did he not succeed?'

'With me.'

'Why did you allow him to call here?'

'How can I refuse a prince?'

'How can you refuse a prince anything?'

'I did.'

'Liar!'

His face was ghastly white. He was trembling, not with rage, but with some extreme anguish.

She found a stubborn courage. 'Murat did not go to bed with me. The child is yours.'

'Tell me the truth. What does it matter to you? Tell me!'

She said, 'All right, what does it matter? I've never been able to talk to you, because you don't listen. You think I'm silly. Well, Murat's silly too, in the same kind of way. But he's amusing, to me. He flirts with me. I like being flirted with. But he's not the Emperor. He's not what I'm paid for. And I didn't want to lose my job. So I didn't go to bed with him.'

He said, still staring through her, 'I have longed for ten years to get a child. I have longed for ten years to prove that I can get a child. The future of France—no, more than that: the destiny of Europe hangs on this point.'

The pulses in her forehead had started beating like drums. There was nothing she could do but say the same thing over and over again, with a desperate obstinacy.

'The child is yours.'

'How can I be sure? How can I be sure, beyond all possibility of doubt?'

'The child is yours. I swear it.'

'I have been married for ten years. Marriage has taught me one thing: that women are liars.'

'The child is yours!'

'Is it? Is it?'

*   *   *

263

In September, Napoleon prepared to set out for Mainz, to take command of the Grand Army. He gave instructions to Duroc, who took notes.

'When her child is born, you and I will be in Germany, or Poland, or in our graves.'

Duroc was cheerful. 'The arrangements are made, Sire. Whatever happens to us.'

'The birth will have to be registered.'

'That is arranged, Sire.'

'Get a reliable man. There must be no mistake in the registration.'

'What wording do you want, Sire?'

'If it's a boy, he is to be called Léon.'

'Léon. Yes, Sire.'

'Half of her name, and half of mine. Because I am only half sure, and cannot be more than half . . . Mother, Mademoiselle Eléonore Dénuelle, of independent means . . . Father . . .'

Duroc suggested, 'Father unknown?'

'No. Father absent.'

18. COUNTESS WALEWSKA

He was at Pulstuk, on the road to Warsaw, when a courier sent by Caroline brought him the news. Eléonore had given birth to a son on 13 December, at 29 rule de la Victoire. The child's birth had been registered at the Town Hall of the Second Arrondissement: Léon, son of Mademoiselle Eléonore Dénuelle, of independent means, twenty years of age; father absent.

There was no need for Napoleon to take any action: everything had been arranged. He moved on through deep snow and thick mud to Warsaw, where the Poles were waiting to adore their liberator and to celebrate his arrival.

Prince Joseph Poniatowski gave a ball at Pod Blacha, his great house in Warsaw: Poniatowski, nephew of the last King of Poland, when Poland was still a kingdom, ten years before; Commander-in-Chief of the Polish Army, when there was still a Polish Army, before Austria and Prussia and Russia had torn the kingdom to pieces and made Poland nothing more than a geographical expression.

For Poniatowski's ball, five hundred of the great men of Poland—the officers, the officials of what was once, and would be again, Poland—brought their brilliant uniforms out of hiding and out of mothballs. Their five hundred womenfolk—princesses, countesses, baronesses at the very least—had new ball-dresses made, of the greatest magnificence. The Polish aristocracy had always been half-French in its education, in its tastes, in its style of life. French was the language of polite society. Warsaw was always almost a second Paris. Now Napoleon had come there, with the whole Diplomatic Corps of Europe hurrying after him, through the snow and mud, in their gaudy carriages: and Warsaw became Paris itself, became the capital of Europe. Wherever Napoleon was, was the centre. Paris without Napoleon was a desert, inhabited only by the Empress, and Princess Murat, and General Junot, who against his will had been left as governor of the city, and perhaps a few dozen others, of no great importance.

Even Talleyrand, limping and listless, had been forced to come to Warsaw, as Grand Chamberlain of the Empire, as Napoleon's Foreign Minister, created Prince of Benevento, now also appointed Governor of Poland and Commissary-in-Chief to the Grand Army. He hated the journey, but enjoyed the arrival. Poniatowski was, of course, an old friend: all European aristocrats from before the Revolution were friends of Talleyrand's. Poniatowski's sister, the still beautiful Countess Tyskiewicz, had been a close friend, some said more than a friend, in those days when Louis the Sixteenth and Marie-Antoinette were on the throne. It was not to be supposed that they were anything more than friends, after a parting of nearly twenty years, now that they were both on the wrong side of fifty; but the countess invited Prince Talleyrand to be her guest at her house in Warsaw, and the Governor of Poland gratefully established his headquarters under her roof.

In one or another of his functions, it was Talleyrand's duty to announce the Emperor's arrival at Prince Poniatowski's ball. He himself, having received instructions which were not totally clear, imagined that the announcing must be a perquisite of his position as Grand Chamberlain: so he dressed himself in what he had brought from Paris, through all that mud and snow: his absurdly ornate Grand Chamberlain costume.

He had arranged with Poniatowski that at a given signal the music should stop. He had let it be known to his friends what the sudden silence would mean. His friends had told their friends. The whole company of a thousand knew what was going to happen.

He thought to himself, in his tired, amused way: 'I am good at it, because I can keep a straight face. He is good at it because this kind of acting has become second nature to him—indeed, he hardly any longer knows the difference

266

between acting and reality. He is starting to believe himself to be as great a man, as great a more-than-man, as they, foolish people, believe him to be. This is not the moment for me to tell them, or to tell him, that he is only a man. I am here in my hieratical function. I shall say what I am here to say, keeping my face straight.'

He said, loudly, 'His Majesty the Emperor.'

Trumpets sounded. Napoleon appeared, wearing the simple plain green uniform of a colonel of the Guards: the only plainly dressed man of the hundreds of men in the room. Talleyrand thought yes, of course, it was an old trick; but the old tricks were always the best.

Five hundred men bowed to him. Five hundred women went down into a curtsey. As they rose again they gazed at him with hero-worshipping curiosity; and he, traversing the great semi-circle with his eyes, returned the gaze of each one of them.

Poniatowski strode forward.

'Sire, we greet you as the Emperor of the French; as the greatest hero of our times; as the brilliant conqueror of the armies of Austria and of Prussia; but, above all, as the liberator of our country, our beloved Poland.'

Napoleon gravely acknowledged the greeting.

'Prince Poniatowski . . .' He looked round again. 'No music? No dancing? I had been told it was to be a ball.'

'Your Majesty wants music?'

'Yes.'

Poniatowski raised his arm. The orchestra struck up a waltz. No one moved, waiting for the Emperor to move.

'Would Your Majesty care to dance? Every woman here would think it an honour beyond all expressing . . .'

'I do not wish to dance. But I wish them to dance.'

Because he wished it, they danced.

Murat, standing with Marshal Lannes, inspected the dancers.

'Hm, with women like these, I could have a good time as their king.'

Lannes cocked an eyebrow. 'You, King of Poland?'

Murat was carelessly grand. 'The Emperor has the thought in his mind.'

'Oh, yes? Who put it there?'

'It seems a fairly obvious thought. For services rendered.'

'As the Emperor's brother-in-law?'

'I'd make a great deal better king than any of his brothers.'

'Murat, your horse would make a better king than any of his brothers.'

Lannes was an infantryman: he didn't much care for the cavalry. He was a Gascon, and didn't much care for other Gascons. He was short, and not particularly handsome: he thought Murat a mountebank and a conceited fool.

He turned away from Murat and saw a beautiful woman, not dancing but walking, on an old man's arm.

'Hey, who's that one?'

'What one?'

'That one in white.'

Murat deigned to look, for a moment.

'Not my kind of thing. You have her.'

'D'you think that's her husband, or her grandfather?'

'What's the odds? They're all mad to go to bed with us. We're their liberators. Their gods.'

'Their king?'

'I'm considering it.'

Lannes said, 'So far as I'm concerned, Poland is mud, snow, filthy villages, black bread, rotten potatoes and no wine. You want it, you can have it. I'm going to find out who that white woman is.'

Talleyrand brought Count Malachowski to the Emperor: Malachowski, the great and venerable elder statesman of Poland.

'Sire, Count Malachowski wishes to thank you for appointing him head of the Provisional Government—'

Napoleon said sharply, 'Under your supervision. Is he clear on that point?'

Talleyrand smoothed it over. 'Of course, with my close cooperation—'

'Supervision. You understand that, Count?'

Malachowski bowed. 'Indeed, Sire.'

'Your first task, with Poniatowski, is to raise me an army of twenty thousand Poles.'

'You shall have them, Sire.'

'Half of Poland is still occupied by the Russians.'

'You will beat them, Sire.'

'Yes. When I have beaten them, we will see about the future of your country.'

He looked away, having said what he had to say. The Poles were not to expect liberation as a gift, but were to work for it as a reward.

Talleyrand said, 'Sire, the members of the Provisional Government fully understand that nothing can be decided yet, about the future of Poland—'

He broke off, because he saw that the Emperor was not listening. Napoleon was staring fixedly at a woman in white, a short distance away, walking slowly round the room, on the arm of a man of seventy. The room was full of beautiful women, but this woman was worth staring at: fair-haired, blue-eyed, young—not more than twenty? —but with an expression of high seriousness that was almost sadness. She was all in white: white satin and white tulle. One would have said, the priestess of a new secular order, vowed to simplicity, chastity, all forms of purity.

Talleyrand turned to Malachowski with a smile and a shrug, to apologize for Napoleon's preoccupation.

'Forgive me, Count. There will be better opportunities.'

Napoleon, still staring at the white woman, said, 'Talleyrand.'

'Sire?'

'Get me Duroc. Or Poniatowski. Where's Poniatowski?'

Duroc had just been buttonholed by Lannes.

'Duroc, you're supposed to know everybody—'

'Who d'you want to meet?'

'I rather like the look of that one in white.'

'Not a chance there. Married—'

'To him?'

'And devoutly religious.'

'Murat says they're all mad for us.'

Duroc grinned. 'Murat says that because he doesn't care who it is so long as it's a woman. But I'm afraid that one isn't for Murat. Nor for you.'

Poniatowski hurried to the Emperor.

'Your Majesty, you required—?'

'Poniatowski. Who's that woman in white?'

Poniatowski looked, and saw her, and smiled. The Emperor had remarkably good taste.

'One of your greatest admirers, Sire. And one of our most ardent patriots. Countess Walewska.'

'Who's the man she's with?'

'Her husband, Sire. Count Walewski. Also a great patriot.'

'Poor woman.'

Poniatowski looked at the Emperor in surprise, not that he should think such a thing, but that he should say it.

'Does Your Majesty wish me to present them?'

'She is not dancing. I should like to see her dance.'

'Your Majesty does not himself wish to—?'

'No. I wish to see her dance.'

Talleyrand limped up to Duroc.

'Marshall Duroc, the Emperor wants you.' He looked, and saw Poniatowski going towards the woman in white. 'But you may no longer be needed.'

Poniatowski came back to Napoleon in some confusion and some dismay.

'Your Majesty, Madame Walewska begs your forgiveness—'

'For what?'

'She implores your forgiveness. But she does not wish to dance.'

Napoleon's expression, fixed, stern, did not change.

'Present her to me. If she wants my forgiveness.'

'Gladly, Sire. And her husband?'

'No.'

As Poniatowski went back to her, Duroc reached Napoleon.

'Did you want me, Sire?'

'Stay near me. I may do.'

As she came towards Napoleon she cast her eyes down, so that she would not have to meet his gaze.

'Sire, may I have the honour of presenting to you Countess Walewska.'

She curtseyed, her eyes still cast down. Poniatowski bowed again, and discreetly moved away. Others, taking his example, edged aside to give the Emperor more room, but their eyes were on the Emperor, and on her: the first woman to be presented to him, and at his request.

She rose, and looked at him at last, and waited for him to speak. His eyes were hostile. His manner was stiff, his words curt, almost deliberately discourteous.

'White does not go well on white, Madame.'

She looked at him. She was not afraid of him. She was ready to reply, but he prevented her, by speaking again, quickly, as if he did not wish her to reply.

'This is hardly the reception I expected in your country, Madame. I wished you to dance, you refused to dance. Why? I speak to you, you refuse to answer. Why?'

'Your Majesty—'

Again he prevented her, while seeming to deny the prevention.

'I am eager to hear your explanation, Madame.'

She said, 'I have sworn to wear no colours—to wear only white, or grey or black—and I have sworn not to dance, no matter who asks me or who wishes it, until the day when Poland is a free and independent kingdom again.'

His voice took on an even greater harshness.

'Is a woman's oath so absolute?'

'Yes, Your Majesty.'

'I have not found it so.'

'I swore the oath not for a man's sake, but for my country.'

271

'So you cannot please your country's liberator by dancing?'

She said, 'I shall dance for you when all Poland is free and great—as you can make her free and great. It lies in your power to re-create our nation. When you do, all Poland will dance.'

'I shall do as I think best.'

'Your Majesty, you are a great statesman as well as a great general. You must know that an independent Poland is essential to the peace of Europe.'

He would not relent. The sternness of his face was almost a scowl. 'Madame, when I choose to speak to a beautiful woman, I do not expect to be lectured on politics.'

She said—very simply, but there were two meanings in what she said—'I have nothing else to say, Your Majesty.'

He caught at the second meaning. 'You have no other subject of conversation?'

'None.'

'But you can answer questions.'

'Yes, if you wish.'

'How old are you?'

'Twenty.'

'How long have you been married?'

'Two years.'

'Have you a child?'

'A son.'

'How old?'

'Almost one.'

'His name?'

'Antoine.'

'Do you love him?'

She said, 'Yes,' but with a hesitation.

'You seem uncertain.'

'I love him, but I hardly see him.'

'Why?'

'He is in the care of my husband's sisters.'

Again, the harsh 'Why?'

'Because they are Colonna Walewskis, and the Colonna Walewskis are an ancient and noble family, and they wish to bring him up as a Colonna Walewski.'

He said, staring at her, 'Why are you married to a man fifty years older than yourself?'

She said calmly, without self-pity, 'Because my family is not quite so noble, nor so ancient, nor so rich.'

His voice was gentle, for the first time. 'I am sorry for you.'

She said, always calmly, steadily, her eyes meeting his steadily: 'Your Majesty, make Poland free, and I shall be the happiest woman in the world.'

'I admire your patriotism.'

'It is all I have.'

He said, with a gruff humour, 'So if we talk again, you'll lecture me again?'

'Yes, Your Majesty.'

'We shall see.'

He turned and summoned Poniatowski, who came quickly forward.

'Your Majesty . . . ?'

'Prince Poniatowski, if Madame Walewska is an example of womanhood, then you are certainly a great nation.'

She said, not with a conscious modesty, but with the same simplicity and directness that she had said everything else, 'I am one of many, Your Majesty.'

'Are you?' He looked at her as if to read in her face whether she expected another compliment. He could read no expectation there. He said brusquely, 'We shall meet again, Madame.'

As Poniatowski led her away, there was a murmur from those who had been watching, admiringly or enviously or curiously. Her friends clustered round her, burning to know what Napoleon had said to her, what she had said to him: why he had chosen her, whether he had talked commonplaces or war or love.

Duroc said, 'Do you wish to meet other Polish ladies, Sire? They are all dying to be presented. And I suggest that it might be polite not to confine yourself to only one.'

Napoleon did not appear to have heard him. He was still looking at Countess Walewska, the centre of an ever-growing group of questioners and admirers, Polish and French.

'Duroc.'

'Sire?'

'Fetch me Berthier.'

Duroc hurried away. Napoleon stood staring at the countess's circle. Major Louis de Périgord, young, handsome, a well-known lady-killer, had been introduced to the countess, and appeared to be doing his best to charm her with smiles and oglings and amusingnesses and a series of overblown compliments.

Berthier came to the Emperor.

'Sire?'

'Berthier, Major Périgord is seconded to your staff?'

'Yes, Sire.'

'Send him back to his regiment.'

'Yes, Sire. Immediately?'

'Tonight.'

Early the next morning, Constant, going into the Emperor's room with hot water and towels, found the Emperor already out of bed, in his night-drawers, standing staring out of the window.

'Good morning, Sire.'

No response. Constant put the jug down on the washstand.

'Are you ready to wash yourself, Sire?'

No response. Napoleon started to pace the room. Constant went to the window and drew back the curtains.

'I have brought your hot water, Sire.'

No response. Constant picked up the jug and poured the water invitingly into the basin.

'The hot water is here for you, Sire.'

Napoleon was suddenly aware of Constant's presence.

'Ah! Good morning, Constant.'

'Good morning, Sire. I have your hot water here.'

Napoleon came to the bowl and washed his hands and face. Constant stood by with the towel. Napoleon took it, dried himself, gave it back to Constant; then sat down and stared into vacancy.

'Are you ready to shave yourself, Sire?'

No response.

'Shall I call Roustan, Sire?'

No response.

'Do you wish to shave yourself now, Sire?'

No response. Napoleon jumped up and paced the room again.

'Constant. Fetch me Marshal Duroc.'

'Now, Sire?'

'Now.'

'Yes, Sire.'

Constant got almost as far as the door.

'Constant.'

'Yes, Sire?'

'Pen. Ink. Paper.'

Constant almost released a sigh. It really was time that the Emperor learnt where things were to be found. He went to the writing-desk and pointed them out.

'Pen, Sire. Ink. Paper. Here, Sire.'

Napoleon came to the desk and sat down. Constant looked at him with prudent curiosity: the Emperor was in a particularly funny mood this morning. The Emperor was staring at the paper. Constant gave him a little bow, and went to fetch Duroc.

Napoleon dipped his pen in the ink and wrote:

I saw no one but you, I admired no one but you, I desire no one but you. Tell me you will come to me soon.

N.

In her small private sitting-room in the Walewski house, the countess poured coffee for her great friend Elzunia Abramovicz. Elzunia had taken the privilege of a great friend and called to see the countess almost earlier than was socially thinkable. There was a good reason for the earliness.

'I simply had to be first. I warn you, the whole of Warsaw is going to call on you today. Everyone is eaten up with longing to know what the Emperor said to you last night.'

'The whole of Warsaw asked me that last night.'

'But you didn't tell them.'

'There's nothing to tell.'

Elzunia made a moue. 'I think it's rather horrid of you not to tell me. I am your best friend.'

'Elzunia, I told you.'

'Yes, but did you?'

'We spoke of Poland, and patriotism. He said I was lecturing him. He was quite right. I was.'

'And that's all?'

'All.'

'The whole of Warsaw thinks that something else was said.'

'The whole of Warsaw, as always, is mistaken.'

Elzunia looked at her out of the corners of her eyes. 'The whole of Warsaw is consumed with curiosity to know what will happen next.'

'Next?' She looked at Elzunia in some surprise. 'How can there be a "next"? I was presented to the Emperor. He spoke to me for two minutes, perhaps. Others were presented to him, after that. He spoke to them.'

'Hardly spoke.'

'They were presented.'

'He didn't look at them. He was looking at you.'

She sat silent for a time, not looking at Elzunia. Then she said, choosing her words to state her meaning precisely, 'It is possible that the greatest man in the world admired me for a moment last night. If so, I am greatly flattered. But it is not possible for there to be any question of "next".'

Elzunia giggled. 'You really think it's not possible? For him, or for you?'

'Elzunia, please may we talk about something else?'

Elzunia had to wait quite five minutes before she could recover from her disappointment. After five minutes the maid came in.

'Forgive me, Madame . . .'

'Yes, Marysia?'

'Marshal Duroc is here, Madame. He asks if he may see you.'

'Duroc?' She had no need to ask. She knew who Duroc was.

'Yes, Madame. The Emperor's Grand Marshal.'

She only wished that Elzunia had not been in the room. Elzunia was silently buzzing with excitement.

She said, 'Give my apologies to Marshal Duroc, and tell him that I am not dressed to receive visitors.'

'If he asks to wait, Madame?'

'Simply tell him that I am not dressed to receive visitors. He will understand.'

'Yes, Madame.' Marysia went out.

Elzunia was appalled. 'You can't say that to the Grand Marshal!'

'I do not receive visitors until I am dressed.'

'You received me.'

She smiled. 'But you told me yourself, Elzunia—you're not a visitor, you're my best friend.'

'But aren't you dying to know what he—what the Grand Marshal—has to say?'

'I do not break my rules for a Grand Marshal.'

'But he comes from the Emperor!'

'I do not know that he does.'

They were silent, Elzunia looking at her, she looking into space.

Elzunia said, 'The Emperor wants to see you. I'm sure of it.'

'If he does, he can address himself to my husband.'

The maid came in again, with a letter on a salver.

'Madame, Marshal Duroc asked me to give you this.'

She took the salver to the countess and offered it. The countess looked at the letter but did not touch it.

'Madame, he asked me to ask you to read it.'

The countess still looked but did not touch.

'He is waiting, Madame.'

'Waiting for what?'

'I suppose, for an answer, Madame.'

The countess took the letter, broke the seal, and opened it. She read:

> I saw no one but you, I admired no one but you, I desire no one but you. Tell me you will come to me soon.
>
> N.

Her face slowly flushed with indignation and pride: pride at being admired by the greatest man in the world, but injured pride, insulted pride, at his believing that she could be addressed in such words. She crushed the letter in her hand and held the hand tightly closed.

'My thanks to the Grand Marshal for bringing the letter.'

'Yes, Madame. Is he to wait, Madame?'

'No. Tell him there is no answer.'

'She said *what?*'

'Simply that there was no answer.'

Napoleon strode to his writing-desk, sat down, picked up his pen, and forthwith began to write a second, longer, letter.

'Go back to Madame Walewska, at an hour when she will receive you. Give her this, yourself, in private. Insist that she reads it, in front of you. And explain to her what it means.'

She read the letter, while Duroc watched her.

> Have I displeased you, Madame? I thought I had the right to hope the contrary. Was I wrong? Have

I deceived myself? Are you more reluctant, as I become more eager? You have destroyed my peace of mind! Give me a moment of joy, of happiness. My poor heart is ready to adore you. Is it so difficult to get an answer from you? You now owe me two.

N.

She said, 'Marshal Duroc, I do understand what it means.'

'May I therefore hope for an answer?'

'There is no answer.'

'The Emperor is most anxious to have an answer. In fact, he suggests that you now owe him two.'

'You have read the letters, Marshal Duroc?'

Duroc flushed. 'No, Madame. But I am aware of their contents.'

She said, 'Is it part of your duties as Grand Marshal to run this sort of errand for the Emperor?'

Duroc's face flushed a deeper red, but he answered her directly and sincerely. 'Madame, the Emperor is the greatest man on earth. I am his devoted servant. I am proud to run any errand for him.'

She said, more softly, 'Yes, I can understand that.'

'I worship the Emperor,' Duroc said. 'I cannot see how any man, or woman, can fail to worship him, or can refuse to do whatever he wishes.'

'Tell the Emperor that I, too, believe him to be the greatest man on earth. That I am married, with the blessing of the Church, to Count Walewski. And that I worship God more than I worship the greatest man.'

Only Talleyrand, in a chair, was at his ease. Duroc shifted nervously from one foot to the other. Napoleon, incapable of stillness, strode back and forth without stopping. Talleyrand, however, was positively enjoying the problem that had been put to him. In any case, he enjoyed problems, the more difficult the better. But this problem was a splendid challenge both to his old reputation as a successful seducer and to his newer reputation as a consummate diplomat.

'May I ask one more question? The elderly husband was at the ball last night. Do we know, is he continuing to stay in Warsaw, or retiring to his estate?'

Duroc said, 'He's been at political meetings all day. He'll be at his house this evening. I'm told he is proposing to stay in Warsaw.'

Napoleon said, impatiently, 'Are you suggesting I'd do better to write to the husband?'

'No, one should never write to the husband. Only to the wife.' Talleyrand gave them the fruits of thirty years' experience, going back to the days when adultery was a favourite occupation for gentlemen.

'I've written to her four times. Twice this morning, twice this afternoon. With no result. What do I do now?'

Talleyrand said, 'We considered appointing Count Walewski to be a member of the Provisional Government. We rejected him on the grounds of age. We had already chosen Malachowski, the grand old man of Poland. One dotard is enough for any government, even a government which is only provisional.'

'Yes? Well? Shall we make him a member? What good would that do?'

'I think it's not necessary. The point is that Count Walewski shares the patriotic hopes and aspirations of the Provisional Government.'

'Well?'

'And the Provisional Government, Your Majesty tells me, is under my supervision.'

'So?'

Talleyrand, a great actor, disliked being rushed to the conclusion of a scene: it spoiled the dramatic effect. He made a deliberately slow turn of his head and body, to look at his Emperor before speaking.

'Sire, I must ask you, do you urgently and overwhelmingly desire to have this lady in your arms?'

'Yes.'

Talleyrand said, as if it were the most natural and most

obvious answer in the world, 'Then I shall summon an emergency meeting of the Provisional Government.'

She was by herself that evening, in her sitting-room, when Walewski came in.

'Marie. Prince Poniatowski and Count Malachowski are here.'

'In the salon? Shall I come down?'

'No, they wish to see you here. In this room.'

'To see me?'

'Yes. In private.'

She knew that it must be something to do with the Emperor. Her husband's manner was never anything other than stiff and formal, but at the moment it seemed positively unfriendly. She supposed that he suspected her of having encouraged the Emperor—that the gossip of Warsaw had come to his ears already. No doubt he had heard of Duroc's four separate visits to the house during the day. He was an old man, and immensely proud of the family name.

She had nothing to hide from him.

She asked, 'Do you know why they wish to see me?'

His manner was at its most disagreeably pompous. 'I gather that the Emperor has expressed a desire to meet you again, to continue the conversation he had with you last night. I gather that he sent one of his most senior officers to propose this. And I gather that you, for some unaccountable reason, have gravely offended the Emperor by refusing to agree to his proposal. I must ask you—why?'

She said, after a time, 'I did not know that I had offended the Emperor.'

'Marie. Why?'

He was an old man. It was better to leave him believing whatever he believed.

She said, 'If the Emperor is offended, I shall be willing to send my apologies through Prince Poniatowski and Count Malachowski.'

She had said the correct thing. But he was petulant.

'You realize that this has not improved my own position *vis-à-vis* the Provisional Government.'

'Yes.'

'Nor *vis-à-vis* the Emperor. And whatever his birth may have been, he is now of a rank greatly beyond ours.'

'Yes.' There was no good purpose to be achieved by saying anything else.

'We owe him the respect paid by the nobility to a reigning monarch.'

'Yes,' she said listlessly. 'I shall apologize.'

Whatever she said, it made no great difference. He was stiffly dissatisfied with her behaviour, which had been unworthy of a Colonna Walewski.

'Very well. I shall bring the prince and the count here. But I myself shall prefer not to hear your apologies.'

He brought Poniatowski and Malachowski, who bent over her hand in turn, wearing the faces of great statesmen charged with making great decisions. Walewski left them with her. The statesmen were silent, as if they knew what had to be said but did not know how to begin.

She broke the silence. 'Am I to suppose that you understand what my husband does not understand?'

Malachowski said heavily, wagging his great head, 'Madame, it is best that your husband should not understand.'

'May I ask why I have become a matter for the Provisional Government?'

'Because the Emperor is offended.'

'Am I not offended?' she cried. 'I have his letters to me! Read them!'

She took them from a drawer, and offered them, with both hands.

Poniatowski said quietly, 'Marie, we are—'

'Aware of their contents?'

'Yes.'

She cried, 'Are you not offended? As Polish noblemen? As Poles, whether noble or not? The Emperor desires me! He wants me in his bed! He says it to me, in these letters!

Says it to me as plainly as if he were a drunken soldier and I were a woman of the streets!'

They were known to be brave men. Poniatowski was a soldier whose courage was undisputed. He did not dare look at her. He said, 'Marie, is it true that the fourth—the most recent—of the letters says, "Your country will be dearer to me, when you take pity on my heart"?'

'Have you read the letters, then?'

'A copy of the fourth letter has been read to us. Is it true that it contains those words?'

'Yes, it is true.' She had no intention of winning an argument by denying the truth.

Poniatowski said, 'Marie, you are the daughter, the sister, the wife of Polish patriots. Their one aim in life is the restoration of our ancient kingdom. Nothing—nothing in the world—matters one thousandth part as much as that.'

Malachowski said, 'Madame, I have watched a great deal of history in the making. I assure you, little causes can produce great effects. Authority is vested in men; but so long as men are swayed by their passions, women will have the power to change the course of history, for the better or for the worse. They can change it by their influence, at a precise moment in time: and soon, at a certain moment, Napoleon Bonaparte, Emperor of the French, will decide the fate of Poland.'

Poniatowski said, 'Napoleon, who loves you.'

She turned to Poniatowski and said, 'I do not love him.'

'Did you marry for love?'

She was silent.

Poniatowski was a friend, but friendship had ceased to matter. He said, 'You married out of respect for the wishes of your family. You did what you thought to be your duty. You have a larger family: your country. Will you do your duty to Poland? Or do you think that your likes and dislikes are more important?'

Malachowski said, 'Poland will exist again, if Napoleon decides that Poland shall exist. We are a Provisional Government, a puppet government, ruled by Napoleon.

We have no power to determine what shall become of Poland. He has.'

Poniatowski said, 'And if he desires you—as he does—and if you can meet his desire, then the power may be yours. The decision may be yours.'

She had no time to speak, and nothing to say. Malachowski said, 'Perhaps the decision may be yours. Perhaps an influence on the decision. How can we tell? But we do know that if you refuse this chance, you will have done nothing, and less than nothing, for Poland.'

She looked at them. There was nothing in their faces but a command.

She said faintly, 'Must I?'

Their faces said that she must.

She said, 'Must it be me?'

Poniatowski said, 'You are the one he desires.'

There was horror in it for her, but a kind of glory, too. She felt like a soldier going to his necessary death: for some good reason, for his country's sake, not yet blindfolded, boldly facing the firing squad.

19. MARIE

She was ready before the appointed time. She waited in
her room, sitting bolt upright, not sewing, not reading,
hardly even thinking. Her dress was dark grey, simple,
severe. Her fur-lined cloak and hood were by her side,
ready for her to put on when she had to go. It was January,
and bitterly cold.

On the stroke of ten, Duroc came to her. A deep bow.
'Madame . . .'

Without her intending or wishing it, a big tear came
out of one of her eyes, and rolled down her smooth fair
cheek. Then another tear, from the other eye. She tried
to stop them, by an effort of will-power.

Duroc, out of the corner of his eye, saw the tears, and
in his heart was sorry for her.

At the Grand Palace, the Emperor was in a fury of
impatience.

'Constant!'

'Sire?'

'What time is it?'

'Just after ten o'clock, Sire.'

Napoleon fingering his hair in front of the mirror,
smoothing it down, adjusting his collar, striding out into
the anteroom.

'Constant! What time is it?'

'A quarter past ten, Sire.'

She had to arrive at last. Warsaw was not such a great
city, it was not so far from the Walewski house to the
palace. Napoleon heard her coming. He stood in his bedroom, rigidly facing the open doorway to the anteroom,
staring straight through the anteroom to the doorway
where she would enter.

The door by which she would enter was closed. Constant opened it to Marie, cloaked and hooded still, on the arm of Duroc. Constant bowed deeply.

'Madame . . .'

He gave her his most respectful but most encouraging smile. Then he saw her tear-stained face, and was deeply sorry for her. It came into his mind, not for the first time but more strongly than ever before, that his master was a monster.

She let go of Duroc's arm. For a moment it seemed as though she might faint or fall, with no one to support her. Constant quickly offered his own arm.

'Madame . . .'

She took it, blindly, without looking at him. She was looking through the open doorway into the bedroom, where Napoleon was waiting for her.

Duroc, his duty done, bowed and excused himself.

'Madame . . .'

Constant led her slowly to the bedroom. She was trembling, but she held her head up high and she looked at Napoleon as she went towards him.

'Sire . . . Madame Walewska.'

Napoleon bowed.

'Good evening, Madame.'

Constant gently withdrew his arm from her grasp. Napoleon came to take her hand and kiss it with formal courteousness. Constant withdrew to the anteroom, silently closing the doors.

She shuddered and swayed. Napoleon had let go of her hand. He caught it again, for fear she might fall.

'Do, please, sit down, Madame.'

He supported her to a sofa. He stood close to her, looking down at her. Now that they were alone, she could not look at him. Again, noiselessly, she was starting to weep.

He said, 'Why didn't you answer my letters? Was it so difficult a thing to do? Is it so terrible to have an Emperor fall in love with you?'

She could do nothing but weep.

He said, gently, 'Please don't cry. What is there to cry about?'

The tears still came out of her eyes. He sat beside her and took her limp hand and kissed it, and spoke to her in a quiet voice.

'Marie . . . Do your friends call you Marie? . . . Marie, if I could cry I would be crying too, but tears of joy. I have not slept since I first saw you, I have not eaten, I have not had one single rational thought, I have done nothing but long for this moment. I had no right to suppose that you would long for it too. I hoped that you would come here willingly, without sadness. But, above all, I hoped, I prayed, simply that you would come here. Marie, I have heard of men dying for love, but I have never believed it before, I have never felt it before. There was a weight on my heart, a crushing weight, crushing my heart, breaking it, killing me, and only you could lift it, only you could let me live.'

The tears had stopped. She found her voice.

'How should I have come here without sadness?'

'Is it sad to have a man so much in love with you?'

'No. My sadness is in coming here.'

'Isn't there some kind of happiness in being greatly loved?'

'Not happiness.'

'Some kind of pleasure at least? At least, a compliment?'

'A compliment I don't deserve. Why *me?*'

He said, with a kind of desperate earnestness, 'Marie, I did not choose to fall in love with you.'

She looked at him, at last, her eyes as full of earnestness as his. 'We are both unfortunate.'

'Am I a misfortune, to you?'

'Yes.' She did not seek to be unkind. It was necessary to tell him the truth.

'Am I an ogre, to you?'

'No.'

'But an Emperor. A tyrant.'

She said, 'I cannot return your love.'

287

He sat for a time without speaking, looking at her, still hooded and cloaked, as if hood and cloak were protectors of her virtue.

He said, 'Take your cloak off. Let me see what I love and cannot be loved by.'

He gently helped her to her feet. She stood passive and let him undo her cloak and take it from her shoulders. He looked at her dress.

'Dark.'

'I told you why.'

'I shall hope to see you in colours yet.' He walked away from her, to put her cloak down, then turned and faced her from a distance, as if it were easier for him to speak strongly when he was not softened by her closeness.

'Is it because I am Emperor, that you cannot love me?'

'Because you are not my husband, and I am not your wife.'

'Do you know what love is? Love for a man?'

'I know what loyalty is.'

'What do you feel. When your husband holds you in his arms? Do you feel love?'

She did not yield an inch. 'I am married to him.'

He cried, with a sudden violence, 'You are his slave! Sold to him at an auction! An eighteen-year-old virgin to a sixty-eight-year-old goat! I tell you, such a marriage is obscene! And if you tell me it was blessed by the Church, I say that the Church must look again at what it blesses and what it does not! Religion should not sanctify such crimes against humanity!'

'I was not forced to marry him. I agreed to it.'

'At eighteen? You can plead ignorance! He can't!'

He was wilfully refusing to understand what was perfectly clear. She tried once again to make it clear beyond all mistaking.

'Whatever you think. Whatever his age. I am married. It is not possible for me to be married to more than one man.'

'Be married to me, then.'

'You have a wife.'

'No. I have an Empress. Be my real wife. My Polish wife.'

She looked at him hard. 'Your Polish mistress? Your Polish woman?'

He cried, 'What must I do to convince you that I love you more strongly, more profoundly, than I have ever loved before, ever in my life? I have never loved before! Till now, I have not loved!'

She was not to be deceived by words. She said, 'That is not true.'

He walked the room for a time, chin on his chest, brooding.

He said, 'I feel it to be true. You're right, it isn't true. It's not a lie, but a forgetting. I have loved, once. This is the second time.'

He came to her and took her hand, and sat with her again, to talk to her in a quiet, tired voice.

'I was as mad for Josephine once as I am for you now. Twelve years ago, when I was young and knew nothing except the use of artillery in siege warfare. Josephine was all woman—all charm, all grace, all sympathy, all subtlety, all sexual knowledge. I didn't die for love of her: she took me into her bed, and she married me. But afterwards I died of jealousy. She turned my heart to a stone, to rock, to iron. But we were married.'

He went on speaking, after a time, still holding her hand.

'When you're the great man of a great country, you can have any woman you please. Women throw themselves into your bed, out of vanity or greed or ambition or fear. I am not one of those who cannot rest without a woman in their arms. I know the pleasure of a moment for what it is—a moment's pleasure, and gone. I have had women in my bed, and my heart has still been as iron as Josephine made it. I have felt nothing in my heart, from then till now. Then I was an awkward young general. Now I'm an awkward Emperor, not far this side of forty. But my heart has come alive again, because you, too,

289

are all woman, of a different kind of woman: you are all
goodness, all nobleness, all purity.'

She said, 'What would become of my purity, in your
bed?'

'What will become of your goodness, if you condemn
me to die?'

'You will not die, whatever I do.'

'I believe that my life is in your power.'

'I can make you suffer, perhaps, for a time. I can't
make you die.'

He cried, not loudly but in a muted anguish, 'You do
not know what love is! You do not know what love can
do!'

She did not doubt that his anguish was real; but his
arguments did not convince her. She said, 'If you went
to bed with a woman you loved, but who did not love
you, and you knew that she did not love you . . . would
it be the pleasure of a moment for you, or less than a
moment, or more than a moment? Would it be a pleasure
at all, since the woman would feel no pleasure? Or would
it be only a triumph?'

'You would come to love me.'

'Why?'

'Love creates love. My fire would warm you. My love
would make you love.'

She said, with careful gravity, 'I have been brought up
as a Pole in occupied Poland, where your kind of love
does not exist. We have only one adoration, one passion,
one thing we live and die for: our country. Everything
else is practicality and survival. Yes, I was sold to the
highest bidder; but if he had not been a great Polish
patriot, then my family, and I myself, would have spat on
his bid. My marriage is a double loyalty: through my husband, to Poland . . . You are our liberator, we hope our
friend. I am told to go to bed with you, for the sake of
that hope. I am told this by the leaders of my nation, the
men whose word is law to me; and I will do anything
for Poland. I will go to bed with you, if you wish. But I
will not deceive you. I admire you above all men, for

what you are and what you have done. I do not feel for you what you call love. If you say so, I will throw myself into your bed.'

They looked into each other's eyes, deeply. He looked for any sign of deceit, even a trace. He found none.

He jumped to his feet. He marched to the door and threw it open.

'Constant!'

Constant leapt out of a chair. 'Sire?'

'Fetch Marshal Duroc. Madame Walewska is leaving.'

Napoleon came back to her, with her cloak, holding it for her to put it on.

'Since I undid it, may I fasten it again?'

She said, 'Thank you.'

'You will come here again. Promise me that you will come.'

'Promise me that you will free all of Poland.'

He smiled. 'I promise that I will not go to bed with you unless you yourself wish me to.'

'Then I promise to come here again.'

'Thank you.'

He took her hand and raised it to his lips, with a respectful love.

Elzunia Abramovicz paid a call on Marie, at a more reasonable hour than her previous one. She was thrilled to learn that Marie had visited the Emperor, but disappointed to learn that the visit had not been a great event in the history of the world. Marie made it sound positively dull.

'The Emperor was charming, and courteous.'

'And you discussed politics? Really?'

'I went to see him at the request of politicians, in order to discuss politics.'

'Was that what the Emperor wanted to discuss?'

Marie said severely, 'Elzunia, I went there with the knowledge and consent of my husband. I am not a light woman; and the Emperor is a serious-minded man.'

Elzunia sighed. 'Forgive me. I'm an incorrigible romantic.'

'Yes.'

'I'd hoped that the Emperor was in love with you, and that you would fall in love with him. A grand passion. Both of you struck by lightning.'

'That was a very romantic hope.'

'Oh, I know, but wouldn't it have been marvellous? Well, I'd have thought it marvellous.'

Marie smiled at Elzunia's foolishness. 'You want things to happen that don't happen in real life.'

'Yes, of course, don't you?'

'No.'

Marysia, the maid, came in, and announced two callers: Countess Tyskievicz and the Prince of Benevento.

Madame Tyskievicz sailed in, a splendid galleon.

'Marie, my dear, I brought the prince to meet you. You know he's staying in my house.'

Talleyrand, limping forward to tender his devoirs to Marie and Elzunia, explained, 'I have been Madame Tyskievicz's humble admirer—'

'Prince, you were hardly humble.'

'Devoted admirer, then, since—'

'Oh, we never mention years.'

'My dear Madame, we never even think of years. We think of days. I was about to say, since the days—'

'—when France had a king, and Paris was the only place in the world for a woman.'

'Ah, Madame, only we who lived then know how sweet life can be.' He turned to Marie and Elzunia. 'You are young, you are fortunate in everything but that.'

Madame Tyskievicz said, 'We are making a round of visits, because the prince is giving a ball.'

He gently corrected the statement. 'Madame Tyskievicz is giving a ball, on my behalf.'

'Very well, I am giving it. But Elzunia is to do all the arranging of it.'

'Very gladly.'

'Elzunia, we must go into a corner and talk. And the prince is not to hear. It must be a surprise for him, too.'

Talleyrand, left with Marie, begged and was given permission to sit.

'Do you care for parties, Madame? I adore my own, when other people give them. Even though I myself am not a dancer.' He smiled at Marie. 'I saw you at Prince Poniatowski's ball, Madame.'

'I was there.'

'You were more than there: you were celestial, in white. I'm sorry we were not introduced. For you, I would even have attempted to dance.'

She said, 'I don't dance.'

'Then I would have attempted to amuse you. As I attempt to amuse the Emperor, who equally does not dance.'

She smiled. 'Attempt? Don't you succeed?'

'He remains resolutely and passionately serious and high-minded. I admire this, but must wish him otherwise.'

'Why?'

Talleyrand was at his most charming and most self-deprecating. 'Madame, I am a diplomat. I spend my life saying things I don't mean, in order to gain a point. The Emperor invariably says what he means, and means what he says, and has no thought for whether a point is gained or not. It makes my deceptions more difficult.'

'But if you were to do as he does?'

He raised his eyes in mock despair. 'Diplomacy as I understand it would cease to exist.'

'Which—forgive me, Prince—might be a good thing?'

'An excellent thing. But if truth and sincerity are to become the fashion, it will create a vast amount of unemployment among Foreign Ministers.'

She laughed. He was succeeding in amusing her. 'Prince, you malign yourself.'

'In order to have the pleasure of complaining about my problems. May I give you an example?' But he stopped himself before he began. 'Forgive me. I was about to talk politics; which I should not do, to a beautiful woman.'

She said quickly, 'I should like you to talk politics.'

He had only needed her permission. 'Well, then, my complaint against the Emperor. I must tell you, I seek to persuade him that we need an alliance with one other great power.'

'Isn't France greater than all the rest put together?'

'Ah, Madame, but there is that island of barbarians, protected by what they are pleased to call the English Channel.'

'You think England is the enemy?'

'The permanent enemy. The others are only temporary.'

'Russia is the enemy too.'

'Temporary, momentary.' He waved a careless hand. 'We have defeated the Austrians, Austria now begs to be our ally. We shall shortly defeat the Russians, and Russia will beg to be favoured instead of Austria.'

She said, strongly, 'The Emperor cannot wish to make an alliance with Russia.'

He replied, with a little bow towards her sincerity, 'Madame, you are talking principles, I am talking politics.'

'Are they so different?'

'You are talking—what shall I say?—like the Emperor. For me, the two have nothing in common.'

She accused him. 'Prince, you are pretending to be a cynic.'

'Not at all: I am claiming to be a realist. A Russian alliance would have great advantages for us. France would dominate western and central Europe: Russia would safeguard our eastern frontier.'

'And what would become of Poland?'

'May I continue, Madame? I shall mention Poland later . . . France already controls the coastline of Europe, with the exception of the Baltic. Russia would seal off the Baltic. The blockade against England would be complete.'

'Russia would demand a great price for this.'

'Perhaps worth paying. Last but not least: if we cannot defeat England in England, then with Russian help we can defeat England in India.'

She felt the blood coming to her cheeks. 'May we now mention Poland?'

He said, 'I assume that it would be necessary to let Russia keep her part of Poland.'

'It may be necessary, but it cannot be permitted.'

He raised his eyebrows in polite query. 'Why not, Madame?'

She said, vehemently, 'It would be a crime against my country. It would be a denial of what is right and honourable.'

He was as calmly detached as ever. 'I do not see war—or peace—in those terms. It is my complaint against the Emperor that he seems to agree with you.'

She caught her breath. 'Does he?'

'However, I hope to persuade him. For me, the alternative—an alliance with Austria—has fewer advantages. It would turn Russia from being a temporary enemy to being a permanent one. And Austria is a not very powerful power.'

'But with Austria, and with a strong new Kingdom of Poland as an ally—'

'Yes, I agree, our eastern frontier would be moderately safe. There is something to be said on both sides.'

She knew that her cheeks were still bright with the uprush of her emotion. She was afraid that her voice might be trembling. 'There is only one honourable course for France.'

'Madame, I am concerned not with the honour of France, but with the safety of France.'

'You are French.'

'I have that good fortune.'

'The Emperor is French, but more than French. He is universal.'

Talleyrand considered this, and gave his opinion. 'I admit, his temperament is hardly French. He is romantic, not realist; visionary, not practical; ruled by the heart, not by the head. Yes, I suppose he is universal—or Corsican, it's much the same thing.'

She said, keeping her voice as steady as she could, 'And the Emperor will decide. Not you, Prince.'

He smiled affably. 'Yes, the question is in the balance, and the Emperor will decide, one way or the other. He will decide, for reasons which to him will seem all-important, and to me will seem supremely trivial.'

He rose from his chair, and smiled again, and sighed, and made his apologies.

'There. And all that, simply to show you that I have problems. I am afraid I have wearied you. Forgive me. I usually say these things to the Emperor, who is a less sympathetic listener.'

Madame Tyskievicz responded to the signal he had given by rising from his chair. She came quickly towards them.

'Marie, I must take the prince away, we have twenty calls to make. May I take Elzunia, too? She has promised to do all my work for me.'

'In arranging the ball?'

'It will be the most important event that ever happened. Elzunia will make it happen.'

Talleyrand, bending over Marie's hand, said, 'Madame, I am more than enchanted to have made your acquaintance. Please try to believe that I also have some sincerity. I do what I think best for my country.'

'Then you do what everyone must do.'

He said, 'And I sincerely regret that my country is not yours.'

After they had gone, she sat in silence for half an hour, without moving.

When she had made her decision, she rang for Marysia.

'Madame?'

'Do you know, is my husband in the house?'

'Yes, Madame, he is.'

'By himself?'

'Yes, I think so, Madame.'

'Ask if it would be convenient for me to see him.'

'Yes, Madame.'

* * *

At night, Duroc brought her to the palace, and to the Emperor's anteroom. Constant showed her into the bedroom, where the Emperor was waiting.

'Sire . . . Madame Walewska.'

Napoleon bowed.

'Good evening, Madame.'

He came to take her hand and kiss it with formal courteousness. Constant withdrew to the anteroom.

She was wearing her cloak and her hood, covering her bright hair and her dress.

Napoleon said, 'Let me take your cloak.'

'No . . .'

She unfastened it herself, and took it off, and put it down. Her dress was rose-pink. She had jewellery round her neck and in her hair.

He looked at her. He said in a whisper, 'Thank you, Marie.'

She said, 'I have forsworn all my vows, and sworn new ones. I will wear colours, if they please you. I will dance, if it pleases you. I will do whatever pleases you.'

He stood gazing at her, and could not speak.

She said, 'But you must understand, I cannot be the wife of two men. If you want me, I am yours. If I am yours, then I can be no one else's. I have told my husband this. I have told him that I am offering myself to you; and that if you take me, I shall be your woman, not his, and he must forget me, or think of me as dead. I shall not see him again, nor shall I see my child. I cannot divide myself: if I am to be yours, I must be yours alone.'

She said, more strongly, 'I am what I am, I am Polish, it's not possible for me to stop being Polish; but I shall be what you asked me to be, here in this room. Do you want me, as your Polish wife?'

He went to her and gently took her in his arms. She looked into his eyes, neither afraid nor ashamed, now that she had made her decision. She offered him her mouth, and they kissed, a long kiss.

20. 'MY POLISH WIFE'

At three in the morning, in his tent at Eylau, he wrote to Josephine:

My dear,
Yesterday there was a great battle. I won it, but I lost a great number of men. The Russian losses were even greater, but that is no consolation to me. I am very tired, but I write you these two lines to tell you that I am well and that I love you.
Yours ever,
Napoleon

Two nights later he wrote to her again:

My dear,
I write you a line. You must have been very anxious. I have beaten the enemy in a fight to be remembered, but it has cost a great number of brave lives. The countryside here is covered with dead and wounded. I am appalled by the sight of so many victims. Do not worry about me. It will all soon be over, and the happiness of seeing you again will make me forget my troubles. I am in excellent health.
Adieu, my dear. A thousand kisses.
Napoleón

His losses had indeed been great. He took his precautions, dictating letter after letter, at enormous speed, to his secretary Méneval.
'Letter to Talleyrand in Warsaw. "Dear Prince, You are a splendid party-giver. Make your parties more splen-

did than ever before. There must be no loss of confidence amongst the Poles." Letter to the Minister of Police, in Paris. "Dear Fouché, You will receive by the same courier my bulletin on the battle of Eylau. You will immediately arrange public festivities to celebrate this victory. My sister Caroline will help you organize them. Paris must be as gay and glittering as possible, in order to keep up public morale. No one is to be allowed to believe any bulletin put out by the enemy, or any accounts which make it seem that we have suffered heavy losses. The figures I give in my bulletin are to be believed." '

Méneval said, 'Do you think they can be believed, Sire?'

'Why not? A big lie is more convincing than a small one.'

When he had finished, he walked into Berthier's office, and found Marshal Lannes there, red-faced, bursting with rage.

'Sire. May I speak to you?'

'Not now.' Napoleon could guess the reason for the rage. He did not want to waste his time pacifying Lannes.

'Sire. I have been waiting half an hour to speak to you.'

'I have been busy.'

'Sire. I am a Marshal of France. I wish to speak to you.'

'Speak to my Chief of Staff.'

Lannes threw a murderous look at Berthier. 'I have failed to obtain satisfaction from your Chief of Staff. I must come to you, Sire. I have the right to do so.'

It was easier to let Lannes speak than to quarrel with him about his rights.

'Well, Marshal Lannes. Speak.'

'I've read your bulletin on the battle, Sire.'

'Yes, well?'

'It does an injustice to Marshal Augereau and myself.'

'Lannes, when you are Commander-in-Chief you can write your own bulletins and do justice to whom you please.'

Lannes's face went even redder. 'Why do you write a bulletin which is a pack of lies?'

'Not lies. Propaganda.'

'Why do you give all the credit to Murat? Who came up at the last moment! One cavalry charge, that's all! When Augereau and I had been fighting there all day!'

'The cavalry charge gave us the victory. Murat led it. He is a brave man.'

'What Frenchman is not brave?'

'Some are less brave than him.'

Lannes's face was scarlet. 'Me?'

Berthier thought for a moment that Lannes might be going to strike the Emperor.

Napoleon, with the same hard hostile face, said, 'No. Not you.'

Berthier thought for a moment that Lannes might be going to seize the Emperor by the throat. He stepped forward.

'Sire, Marshal Lannes is not well. Shall I have him taken to his quarters?'

'No.'

Lannes said, into Napoleon's face, 'There are twenty thousand brave Frenchmen lying out there dead in the snow. My men, and Augereau's. They are the ones who gave you the victory. Because each one of them killed more than one Russian. They're lying out there with twenty-five thousand Russians. But the only name you name is Murat! That circus rider, with his pantomime clothes! Why? Because he's your brother-in-law? Because he's one of your family? Are you going to make him king, too, like your brothers? What are you warming up for him? The throne of Poland?'

Napoleon stood silent. Lannes shouted into his face, 'Come on, out with it! Are you making him King of Poland? Or do you want us to go on fighting for you?'

Napoleon's face was made of stone.

'Marshal Lannes, I distribute glory as it suits me. All glory, all success come from me.'

Lannes, breathing hard, stepped back and looked at

him. 'Because you march through blood, you think yourself a great man. I tell you, the blood of one Frenchman is worth more than the whole of Poland.'

'Marshal Lannes, if you are not satisfied, you have my permission to go back to France.'

'No. You need me.'

Berthier gave a small sigh of relief. They were still staring at each other like enemies; but the quarrel was over.

He moved his headquarters to the castle of Finckenstein, and he sent for Marie.

He wrote to Josephine:

I have received your letter of the 12th. I see from it that your health is good, and that you are happy at the thought of going to Malmaison.

The weather has changed to fine: I hope it will continue so.

There is nothing new to report from here. I am very well.

Yours ever,
Napoleon

When Marie arrived, he ran to embrace her.

'My dearest, you've come, you've come . . .'

'You sent for me, so I came.'

'I'm afraid it's not much of a place, compared with Warsaw. I've tried to make it fit for you.'

'If it's fit for you, it's fit for me.'

'No, I'm a soldier, anything more than bare boards is luxury. But, for you . . .'

They stood, smiling at each other. In their happiness, they could find nothing to say but commonplaces and repetitions. He kept saying, 'Thank you so much for coming.' He kept saying, 'I'm so happy you've come.'

They had dinner together, just the two of them. Constant bringing them the dishes and then retiring to a distance.

He said, 'What do they think of the battle, in Warsaw?'

'That it was a victory.' She wondered why he asked.

'Good.'

'Wasn't it a victory?'

'Yes. Someone had to win. It's better to win than to lose. But only just.'

'But you won.'

'Just.' He was silent for a time, brooding. 'There was a snowstorm. No one could see what was happening. Each man killed the nearest Russian, or was killed by him. I suppose the Russians are used to fighting in snow. We're not.'

'But the Russians retreated.'

'I rode across the battlefield the next morning; and I felt the full horror of war . . . Yes, they retreated. So I shall have to fight them again.'

'And beat them.'

'Yes. When I'd hoped to have beaten them already . . . Marie. Tell me the truth. What do they say of me now, in Warsaw?'

'You are still—and always—our liberator. Our hero. What else?'

'Next time, the victory will be complete.'

She said, 'Yes. And all Poland will be free.'

He pushed his plate aside. 'May I change the subject? Murat. You've met Murat. What do you think of him?'

She thought for a moment.

'He has a great reputation as a very brave man.'

'He deserves it. But what do you think of him?'

'He is a great talker.'

'Yes, he deserves that too.'

'He talks. He tells everyone that you have promised to make him King of Poland.'

'Does he?'

She smiled. 'I know you by now. When you say you change the subject, you don't change the subject.'

He said shortly, 'I have not made any promises, to Murat or to anyone else. I do not make promises until I can carry them out. When I've beaten the Russians I shall make not a promise but a decision. I am a realist. I'm practical.'

'Are you? Always?'

'I've learnt to deal with things as they happen. Each day has its own necessities.'

She said, 'I think you are two men, at war with each other. One ruled by the head, one by the heart.'

He softened, and smiled, and reached across the table for her hand.

'My dear, my darling. Today is the heart's day. You are here. There is no necessity for anything but joy.'

Later, when they lay in the great four-poster, relaxed and loving and happy, he said, 'If you had all the world to choose from . . . what a thing to say, in a draughty old castle . . .'

'I can answer. I would choose to be here with you.'

'I love your answer, but it's not an answer to my question.'

'Ask me your question.'

'If you had all the world to choose from, whom would you choose to be King of Poland—if there were a Kingdom of Poland?'

She did not have to consider her reply. 'There is only one man. Prince Poniatowski.'

He said neutrally, 'Ah, yes, Poniatowski.'

'He is the nephew of our last king. He is a good leader, and a good soldier.'

'And a good Pole.'

'Of course. Would I choose a foreigner to be my king?'

He kissed her. 'Darling. Beautiful Marie. Beautiful Polish-woman, Polish patriot. You have chosen a foreigner to be—'

She said, 'My husband.'

'Yes. Your husband.'

She said, 'I am ruled by my heart.'

Napoleon received a letter from Josephine, and replied to it:

I don't understand what you say about women.
Are you jealous? You have no reason to be. I love
only my little Josephine, sweet, sulky, capricious,
and always lovable except when she is jealous: then
she becomes an absolute devil.

I assure you, I am much too busy planning my
new campaign against the Russians to have any time
for thoughts of women.

You must not think of travelling out here this
summer. Polish inns and army camps are no places
for an Empress. I long as much as you do for our
reunion and for a peaceful life, but that must wait
until I can come home to you.

Very best love. My health is good.

Napoleon

In the light of dawn, Constant helped Napoleon put on
his uniform for going to war again. Marie was with them.

'You mustn't come outside: it's too cold for you, at
this time in the morning. You can watch us leave from
the window.'

'Will you look up at the window?'

'Yes.'

'One look. For one moment.'

'Then you must go back to Warsaw.'

'And wait. Yes.'

'Is your . . . ' He corrected himself. 'Is Count Walewski
there?'

'He is at his estate in the country.'

'Where shall I find you?'

'I have his permission to use the house in Warsaw.'

'But he will not see you.'

She said, 'We shall not see each other, ever. That is
agreed.'

He was dressed. He said, 'I shall catch the Russians
in a few days, and beat them, and the war will be over,
and then . . . ' He turned to Constant. 'Get yourself ready.
We leave in fifteen minutes.'

'Yes, Sire.' Constant turned and bowed to Marie. 'May I say good-bye, Madame?'

She smiled at him. 'We shall see each other again soon.'

'I very much hope so, Madame.'

He bowed again, and went.

Napoleon said, 'Constant told me last night that you are an angel.'

'Constant is a flatterer, like his master.'

'He also told me that I myself have been a good deal more angelic, since I have known you.'

She said simply, 'You make me happy, so I try to make you happy.'

He was simple and sincere, like her. 'You are everything I need in a woman.'

'I am your woman for as long as you need me.'

He said, 'You do know it's impossible for me to marry you, legally marry you? Or I'd take the Pope by the scruff of the neck and shake him like a dicebox until he pronounced two divorces and gave his blessing to one new marriage.'

She said, 'Yes, I think you would. I like the thought. Yes, I do know it's impossible.'

'Emperors are not allowed to marry for love.'

'I don't ask for marriage. I don't ask for anything.'

'For my love?'

'I don't ask. I hope for it.'

He said, 'You do also know that at first I didn't love you, it wasn't love. I simply wanted you, with a sexual desire that was like torture, like agony, like death. I, for whom sex is not a great necessity and sometimes not much of a pleasure.'

She said, 'You do know—of course, you know—that at first I didn't love you.'

'Yes.'

'I do now.'

'I do now.' He kissed her. 'I have trained myself not to regret the past, and not to wish it otherwise.'

'So have I.'

'But if I had married a better woman, I might have been a better man: better because happier. You have made me happy, so perhaps you have made me better.' He cried out in a sudden passion, 'Let me regret for a moment! Things should have been otherwise!'

She would not give him permission to regret. 'You mean, I should have been born a dozen years earlier, and been French, and met that awkward young general—'

'Yes!'

'Be happy with what has happened.'

He accepted it. 'Yes.'

She moved gently out of his arms. 'Don't think of me till after the battle. Then think of me just for a moment. Send someone to tell me that you've won, and that you are alive and well. You see, I do ask something of you. But that's all.'

'I shall do more than that.'

'Send someone. That will be enough.'

He looked at his watch. 'Duroc has arranged a carriage for you, and an escort.'

'Yes.'

'I must go.'

She had fetched a small box from a drawer.

'May I give you something? Will you look at it, after the battle?'

'Before, and during, and after.'

'After.'

She opened the box and gave him what was inside. He looked at it.

'A ring.'

'You needn't wear it. But please keep it with you.'

'With a strand of hair twined round it. Your hair.'

'Yes.'

'Your bright hair . . . And an inscription.'

'You can't read it in this light. Read it after the battle.'

'What does it say?'

'You will read it.'

He asked again, 'What does it say?'

306

'It says, "When you shall cease to love me, do not forget that I love you".'

He put the ring on his finger, and took her in his arms. 'My love . . .'

In Warsaw, three weeks later, Talleyrand came to her house.

'Did the Emperor send you?'

'To Warsaw, Madame, though not to you.'

'But you've come from the Emperor. How is he? Is he well? Do please sit down. Tell me everything.'

'He is extraordinarily well.'

'Of course I know that. I just wanted to hear it again. And I know he's won his great victory, and the Tsar has met him to ask for peace. So you have your peace at last.'

'Not my peace, Madame.'

'Well, we have peace, the Emperor has peace.'

'Yes, he has his.'

'So tell me. What have you come to tell me?'

He was not smiling. He said, 'I have come to offer you my very humble apologies.'

'Prince, you have nothing to apologize for.'

She was puzzled, not so much by his words as by his manner. For the first time in her knowledge of him, he seemed to be completely serious and completely sincere.

'Madame, for the first time in my life I am ashamed of my own skills at deception and persuasion.'

She said, gently, 'Diplomacy is an honourable profession.'

'I no longer think so, Madame.'

There was a strange look on his face: not quite self-disgust, but certainly self-distaste.

'Believe me, Madame, my motives were not entirely dishonourable. I deceived you into believing that I favoured a Russian alliance, which in fact I did not; and into believing that you could influence the Emperor into rejecting this alliance—which in the event you could not. I did what I did, partly in order to persuade you into the Emperor's bed: it is one of my functions to provide him with playthings. But my greater motive was to have your influence on my side, supporting what I supported: the rejection of the Russian alliance, and the creation of a Kingdom of Poland. I sacrificed you, Madame, for my purposes. The sacrifice was in vain.'

She had become very pale. She asked, 'What has happened?'

'The Emperor and the Tsar, those two great gods, have redrawn the map to indulge their Olympian fantasies. Russia is to be allowed to keep its half of Poland. There will be no Kingdom of Poland, but a tiny Duchy of Warsaw. It will be ruled not by a Pole, but by the ruler of Saxony.'

'Saxony?'

'Yes, Madame: so that the Emperor can take much of Saxony to help create yet another vassal principality for yet another of his foolish brothers . . . I now see, Madame, that he conceives of Europe as one vast estate, with himself as its landlord and his family as bailiffs. I now see, Madame, that his ambition has no end: he must go on until he is landlord of the whole world. I do not think it my duty to serve this ambition. From now on I am, in a word, against him, Madame. And I am distressed by the thought of the harm I have done to your life. The word "apology" is too weak; but I beg you to accept my apologies.'

After a time, she said softly, 'You are mistaken, Prince. You have done no harm to my life. There has been no sacrifice. I have a new loyalty. I am his wife. His Polish wife.'

21. THE GRAND DUCHESS KATARINA

Constant helped the Emperor to put his clothes on again, then left the room.

Napoleon looked at Corvisart and said, 'Well?'

'As I've told Your Majesty a hundred times before . . .'

'Tell me again.'

Corvisart was blandly confident, inspiring confidence. 'I see no reason why Your Majesty should not become a father.'

'You see no reason. But might there be one?'

'Doctors are like generals. We are better at explaining things after they have happened.'

The Emperor was not so easily satisfied. Questions were to be answered with something better than a joke.

'Corvisart. Tell me. Am I capable of getting a son?'

'In my opinion, yes.'

'Why have I never got one?'

'The Empress has been infertile for some years now.'

'But the others? The others who would have been only too glad to get pregnant by me? You've inspected them, too.'

Corvisart said, with nothing in his voice to indicate an opinion, 'Mademoiselle Eléonore Dénuelle has a son.'

'Is it mine? Do you think it's mine?'

Corvisart kept to the undeniable fact. 'The child resembles you.'

Napoleon growled, 'When I believe it's mine, it resembles me. When I have doubts, it resembles Murat, or anyone else. How can I tell? Why can't you tell?'

'Your Majesty, medical science is permanently in its infancy.'

'Murat has a horde of children.'

'The Dénuelle child may still be yours.'

'But probability is on Murat's side.'

'I've known a great number of children born improbably.'

Napoleon looked at him with dark suspicious eyes. All doctors were charlatans. Most doctors were ignorant fools. Unfortunately it was necessary sometimes to consult a doctor, Corvisart was the best of a bad lot: but could even he be trusted to know the truth, and to tell it?

Napoleon said harshly, 'Corvisart, I've made you a baron, I'll give you any title you want . . .'

Corvisart bowed. 'Sire, I can give you nothing but simple advice. To get a child, believe that you can get one.'

The advice was too simple. He brushed it aside. 'Eléonore may or may not have slept with Murat, her child may or may not be mine. But Madame Walewska is a pure woman. She is purity itself.'

'Yes, Sire.'

'I have been sleeping with Madame Walewska for more than a year now. She had a child by her seventy-year-old husband. But by me, nothing! Why not me?'

Corvisart raised his shoulders expressively. 'If I knew the answer to that question, Sire, I would be greater than an Emperor.'

Caroline came to see him, dragging Fouché behind her. Caroline was the last person Napoleon wanted to see. He knew that she would attack him, and he knew that he would not be in a position to counter-attack. Nothing put him in a worse temper than being forced to fight on the defensive. He could not reply to her arguments. He was reduced to being rude to her.

'Caroline, you're a clever woman, please don't talk like a fool.'

'Napoleon, you're a decisive man, please make up your mind.'

'I make decisions when they are needed.'

'All except this one.'

'It is not yet needed.'

She turned to Fouché. Napoleon had wondered when she would turn to Fouché, to reinforce her.

'Fouché will tell you. He has reports from his agents.'

'From his informers.' He stared bad-temperedly at Fouché. 'What do your informers tell you, that Caroline wants you to tell me?'

Fouché had a thick wad of reports in his hand.

'Sire, there is a great and growing anxiety throughout France at the lack of a direct heir to the throne.'

'Do they suppose I'm going to die?'

'You risk your life so often, Sire. There is always the possibility.'

'And because of that, I must divorce, and remarry, and get a son?'

Fouché bowed to him. 'Sire, the people of France believe it to be your duty.'

Caroline said, 'And you yourself know it's your duty.'

It was almost too irritating to be told what his duty was, and to be told that he knew it, when, of course, he knew it perfectly well. He swung round to strike at Caroline.

'Why should you of all people want me to have a son?'

'If you're killed in your next battle, who will succeed you? There must be someone to succeed.'

He looked at her malevolently. 'I have other informers, besides Fouché's. If I had been killed in the Polish campaign, you would have tried to seize the throne for yourself and Murat.'

She returned his look perfectly calmly. 'Yes, I was ready to do that. It would have been a crisis. France would have needed a soldier.'

'A soldier, yes. But not a cavalryman.' He was pleased to see the shaft strike home. 'My dear sister, I'm giving you a kingdom. Because you're my sister, and because you have a brain. Because Murat will please the Neapolitans: they love opera, and he's a whole opera in himself. And because, in Naples, he can do no particular harm.

Kindly be content with your kingdom, and leave my Empire alone.'

She said, rather huffily, 'I only want what is best for you and for France.'

When she had gone, Napoleon held out his hand towards Fouché.

'Let me look at those reports.'

'I brought them in the hope that you would want to look at them.'

Napoleon took them, but as if they were things of no particular importance.

'Fouché, you understand, I am not going to ask the Empress for a divorce.'

'I understand, Sire.'

Napoleon said, dropping the reports on to his desk, 'It would be different if the Empress herself believed it to be her duty.'

Fouché considered what he should do, and decided. Two days later, he paid a call on the Empress.

'Dear Fouché . . .'

'Your Majesty. Most kind of you to receive me.'

'Not at all, you always have something fascinating to tell me. And Madame de Rémusat? Or not?'

Fouché made an apologetic bow. 'Forgive me. I should prefer not.'

So Claire left the room, and the Empress invited Fouché to sit down.

'Is it gossip? I do hope so.'

'Not exactly, Your Majesty.'

It must be, if not gossip, then at least information. Fouché knew everything. Sometimes, if it suited him, he would tell what he knew.

'Oh, Fouché, is it true the Polish woman has arrived in Paris?'

'Madame Walewska? Yes, Your Majesty.'

'I'm so glad. I'm told she has a soothing effect on the Emperor. Where's she staying?'

312

'The Emperor has taken a house for her in rue de la Victoire.'

Josephine said, without showing any special interest, 'And how is her health?'

He said, without showing that he knew what the question meant, 'She is in normal health.'

'I'm so glad.' She smiled, to thank him for the information. 'What else?'

'Hardly gossip, but public opinion.'

She was on her guard. 'Tell me.'

'Your Majesty, I have long been devoted to your interests.'

The beginning boded ill. She gave him a specially charming smile. 'Yes, Fouché, we've known each other since you were one of the leaders of the Revolution.' The smile was to show that she remembered very well that the Revolution had condemned her to death.

He smiled back at her. 'And one of the leaders of the movement that ended the Revolution.'

'Yes, you have the great gift, Fouché: you are always on the winning side.'

He modestly acknowledged it. 'I survive. As some of us do.'

'You and I.'

'My devotion to you is unalterable. As a fellow-survivor.'

He looked at her, in case she wished to speak; but she waited for what he would say next. It was time for him to declare himself.

He took a long letter from his pocket. 'Which is why I have dared to write you a letter, concerning your present position, and that of the Emperor.'

She said, as if politely puzzled, 'My present position is Empress. I can hardly hope for more.'

He bowed in agreement. 'And the Emperor is at the height of his fame and his power. Master of France and of Europe.'

'He, too, can hardly hope to improve his position.'

Fouché said delicately, 'His present position. But he owes France a future.'

The word 'future' told Josephine what Fouché had come to say to her. She continued to seem puzzled. 'You mean, an even greater Empire?'

'An inheritance, and someone to inherit it. A successor. A dynasty.'

'Ah!' She seemed relieved that Fouché meant nothing more than that. 'The Emperor has the question in mind. He will decide. As he always does.'

She implied that there was nothing more to be said, though she knew that Fouché would say a great deal more.

'Your Majesty, the Emperor's throne would be based so much more securely if there were an heir to it.'

'There will be one.'

'A direct heir.'

'Direct or not, does it matter?'

Fouché rather overdid the gloomy wagging of his head. 'Your Majesty, we have lived through one Revolution. I hope never to have to live through another.'

'I, too. But why?'

'As Minister of Police, I know what the public thinks.'

'Dear Fouché, the public can hardly think it before you know it. But again, why?'

'The public trembles—as you and I do—at the thought of a new Revolution. The public fears—as I do—that there will be one, when the Emperor is suddenly removed from us, and his brothers and sisters and brothers-in-law, and whoever else, all fall to fighting for the throne. There will be anarchy again, and perhaps a new Reign of Terror.'

Josephine said lightly, almost laughing, 'The public trembles too easily. The Emperor will appoint a successor.'

Fouché shook his head, refusing even to smile. 'The appointment will have no force, unless the successor is the Emperor's son.'

'The Emperor has no son.'

'And will have none, Your Majesty, unless you yourself make it possible.'

314

It was a thought for her to take with absolute simplicity, with her eyes very wide.

'Monsieur Fouché, I am not the person who decides.'

He said, 'Your Majesty, your present position is great and glorious. I beg you to look at it from the point of view of the French people. Your subjects love you as much as the Emperor does. Consider how much more they will love you; how much greater your glory will be; how much more secure the throne will be, and therefore how much more secure your own future—which at this moment lies at the mercy of a stray cannon-ball, a random musket-shot. If the Emperor were struck down today, tomorrow, by some dreadful accident, then the governance of France might pass into the hands of those that do not love you. But it is in your power to safeguard your position, to make it permanent and rich and rewarding: if you yourself, of your own free will, choose to make the great sacrifice, and allow the Emperor to remarry and have a son who will reign after him.'

She thought, how very like Fouché: he had pretended to appeal to her patriotism, and had in fact appealed to her strongest desire, for continued wealth till the end of life: never to be poor again.

She said, as if it were hardly to be believed, 'Are you the Emperor's messenger?'

'The Emperor would be gravely displeased if he even suspected . . .'

'Yes, so I must suppose.'

'It is simply that as minister responsible for the maintenance of public order, I took it upon myself . . .'

'Of your own free will?'

'Yes, Your Majesty. May I beg you not to inform the Emperor of this interview?'

She added a touch of coldness to her voice. 'I shall not inform anyone.'

'Your Majesty is most kind. And may I beg you to read my letter, which explains my reasons at greater length . . . ?'

'You may leave it. I cannot promise to read it.'

When he had gone, she rang for Madame de Rémusat, who came in to find the Empress on the edge of hysteria.

'Claire. The Emperor sent that man to tell me he wants to divorce me. What am I to do? I must write to Hortense. Hortense must come here straight away. The Emperor loves Hortense, he'll listen to her. And Talleyrand —I must talk to Talleyrand, he hates Fouché, he'll help me, he'll advise me . . . Claire, it's a plot. A plot against me. Fouché is in league with the Bonapartes. They've always wanted to get rid of me. It's simply a plot to get rid of me. How can Fouché say the things he said? How can I allow the Emperor to have a son? Napoleon can't have a son! Everyone knows that! He can't!'

She was still a little pale when it was time to dress for dinner, so she gave her cheeks just a touch more rouge than usual. At dinner she was as charming as ever, if not very talkative. After dinner she played backgammon with Talleyrand, and told him her news. Talleyrand was most interested to hear it.

'Fouché, of course, creates the opinion which he then reports as opinion. His agents go into a café, buy drinks for an ignorant peasant, trick him into agreeing that black is white—and behold, the public has spoken.'

'Should I reply to his letter?'

'I suggest, briefly and coldly. Fouché is not a gentleman. He still has the weakness of the middle class: he can be put in his place.'

She nodded. 'Yes.'

'His approach to you is unseemly and ridiculous. Emperor and Empress may discuss these matters, without the intervention of a policeman.'

'Yes, of course.' She looked across at Napoleon, who seemed to be joking, was certainly laughing loudly, playing cards with Caroline and Murat and one of Caroline's ladies-in-waiting.

Talleyrand said, 'You should show the letter—and your reply—to the Emperor. Making the assumption that he knows nothing of what has happened.'

'He must know. Or Fouché would never have dared to do it.'

'Your Majesty, I do advise you, assume that the Emperor does not know, and therefore that he will be shocked.'

Napoleon laughed even more heartily at something Caroline had said to him. Josephine looked at him again. 'He is in an unusually good mood tonight.'

'Then perhaps he does know. In which case he will be at a worse disadvantage. He will have to pretend that he does not know, and therefore will have to pretend to be shocked.'

Napoleon came to see her that night, just as she was on the point of going to bed. Her maids made quick scampering curtseys and left the royal pair alone as quickly as they could.

'It is only to say good night. Shall I call them back?'

'No, I am ready for bed.' She went to him. 'Good night, dear Napoleon. And thank you for coming to say good night.'

She put up her forehead to be kissed. He kissed her forehead. She went towards the bed. He had said good night, he had kissed her, he was free to go, she made it clear that she expected him to go. But he did not seem to want to go.

He said, 'I thought the evening was very agreeable.'

'Yes, very.' She seemed mildly surprised at his starting a conversation. Out of politeness, she did not get into her bed yet.

'I hardly saw you before that. Did you have a good day?'

'Yes, a very good day.'

'I apologize for always being so busy. I know I should spend more time with you.'

She said sweetly, 'I know that you want to. And that's enough for me. So long as I know it.'

'You are the best-natured woman in the world.'

That was his way of leading up to something. She decided to use it as her way of leading up to something quite different.

She said, 'Is it my good nature? I think it's just that we've been married twelve years. We've come to suit each other's natures.'

'Yes.'

'Even when we're not together, we feel together.'

'Yes.' He was unusually acquiescent. Why?

'We know each other so well now: the good things about each other, and the not-so-good things: that we're sure of each other. We can't surprise each other. Is that good? I think it is. It's peaceful. I'm very happy. I look forward to the next peaceful twelve years.'

'Yes. So do I.'

Whatever he had come in to say, he had missed his chance. He had let her take the initiative.

She said, calmly, offhandedly, 'Oh, Fouché came to see me today and ordered me to divorce you.'

The bombshell burst with a most pleasing effect. Napoleon jumped in the air.

'What?'

Josephine smiled. 'Would you care to read his long, long letter? And my terribly brief reply? They're on the dressing-table.' Napoleon was staring at her open-mouthed. She liked that. 'I found it difficult to know whether to be shocked or amused. In fact, I was shocked. So I decided to be amused.'

His jaw was still hanging down. He managed to ask, 'Fouché did what?'

'Instructed me to divorce you. As Minister responsible for the maintenance of public order.'

'How dare he?'

'Darling, please don't encourage me, or I shall start to be angry with him.'

'Weren't you angry? You had every right to be angry!'

She opened her eyes wide. 'Darling, how can one be angry with a vulgarian like Fouché? With a policeman who tries to come between an Emperor and an Empress? He's ridiculous.'

'I shall dismiss him.'

'No, darling, he's useful to you. As a policeman.'

Of course, he had to say what he said next. 'I must hope Fouché didn't suggest that I myself—'

'No, no, he made it quite clear. It was entirely his notion. He had taken it upon himself.'

'I shall make it very clear to Monsieur Fouché what he may take upon himself, and what he may not.'

'Darling, would you read Fouché's letter? And give him my reply? If you agree with my reply?'

She went to the dressing-table and picked up the two letters and handed them to him. He had no choice but to say, 'Yes, of course, if you wish.'

'So that I shan't ever have to think about it again. Good night, darling. Don't be too hard on Fouché. He's stupid, that's all. He doesn't understand.'

This time she really got into her bed, and settled herself, and gave him a soft sleepy smile, and was obviously ready to close her eyes the moment he left the room.

But, for some unexplained reason, he did not leave the room. He stood shifting from one foot to the other. He said, 'Josephine . . .'

'Mm?'

'You're right, Fouché doesn't understand how much we love each other.'

'No . . .'

'It may be necessary, politically necessary, not now, but one day, some time, I don't know when . . . for me to provide an heir to the throne . . . In which case, because we love each other so much, you yourself would of course want to take the initiative . . . You yourself would voluntarily step aside . . . if it became necessary, politically necessary . . .'

Josephine said, lazily, almost sleepily, but perfectly clearly, so that not a syllable was lost on him: 'Darling, we were married in a dreadfully shabby town hall by an acting registrar with a wooden leg, and then married again by a Cardinal of the Church. Our marriage, and our coronation, were blessed by the Pope. Can I step aside from

319

that, and all those years of being the wife of General Bonaparte, First Consul Bonaparte, Emperor Napoleon? Voluntarily step aside? Of course I can't. No woman could. Oh, perhaps, if I didn't love you. But I do.'

He tried again. 'So you want what is best for me. Politically.'

'Darling, you understand politics, I don't. If something is best for you, one day, some time, whenever it is, then I'm sure you'll order it to be done, as you always do; and I know that I shall obey, as I always do. But I shan't be able to tell lies about it. I shall want everyone to know that I am obeying your orders against my will. That I am the unhappiest woman in the world. That you have broken my heart.'

He stood there like a naughty schoolboy caught red-handed and with nothing to say for himself. But she knew him. Her words had considerably moved him, and she knew it.

Talleyrand, wearing his most judicious air, said, 'I entirely agree with you, Sire. You should dismiss Fouché.'

'And appoint in his place—?'

'The only man capable of filling his place.'

'Who's that?'

'Fouché.'

Napoleon laughed. It was a good joke because it was a good judgement. 'So long as he keeps his nose out of my bedroom.'

'And out of what he calls public opinion.'

Napoleon demurred. 'His reports on public opinion are interesting.'

'Sire, our friend Fouché is eternally a man of the Revolution. His idea of making policy is to organize a mob under your window, shouting for a divorce. But a ruler who gives way to the mob a first time will give way a second time, and a third—when the mob demands a new régime and a new ruler. It is for you to decide policy, Sire. It is for such as myself to carry it out—secretly, in the ancient tradition of diplomacy.'

'Secretly and speedily.'

'Diplomacy takes time.'

'I want this thing settled, finished, done with.'

'Sire, you are in the prime of life. You can afford a little time.'

Napoleon stopped pacing, and stood and looked at him piercingly.

'Talleyrand, what would you have done if I had been killed in the Polish campaign?'

'Died of fright, Sire.'

'Exactly.'

'Sire, I understand your wish to press forward with this affair. But not even you, Sire, can make an instant marriage with someone of royal rank. And a divorce, without the new bride standing ready, would demean both the Empress and yourself. It would seem that you were divorcing for the usual reasons. As you know, Sire, royalty does not commit anything so commonplace as adultery. A royal divorce must be as calmly political as a royal remarriage.'

'Read me the list again.'

Talleyrand took a piece of paper from his pocket.

'I think at our last discussion we agreed to strike out the King of Saxony's daughter. She is thirty, and excessively plain.'

'Out.'

'We are left with three possible candidates. The two sisters of the Tsar: the Grand Duchess Katarina—'

'Catherine.'

'I believe, in her own language she is called Katarina. Aged twenty. And her younger sister the Grand Duchess Anna, aged fourteen.'

Napoleon said decisively, 'Catherine.'

'The third person is the daughter of the Emperor of Austria: Maria-Luisa, aged eighteen. She is reputed to be very handsome.'

Napoleon said again, 'Catherine.'

'Ah.'

'Talleyrand, I know by heart all your arguments against a Russian alliance.'

'It is for you to decide, Sire.'

'I have decided. Catherine.'

Talleyrand laid down the piece of paper, and acted a sigh. 'That will indeed take time.'

'Why? The Tsar is my friend.'

'The Tsar's mother—who is equally, of course, the mother of the Grand Duchess Katarina—considers you, Sire, to be a vulgar plebeian upstart Corsican monster.'

Napoleon laughed, grimly enjoying a joke which was not new to him. 'As you do, Talleyrand? Don't you?'

Talleyrand made a little bow. 'Sire, I consider that your beginnings are no longer of any great importance.'

Napoleon enjoyed that too, and enjoyed giving curt commands to an old aristocrat. 'Catherine. Arrange it.'

'I must ask, Sire: are you willing to risk a rebuff?'

'There can be no question of a rebuff. I shall marry Catherine. Arrange it.'

There was nothing more to be said. The thing was decided.

Hortense had been sent for. She was at Plombières, taking the waters. She came hurrying to her mother's side. Josephine fell into her arms.

'Hortense, darling! Oh, I'm so glad you've come!'

'Dearest Mamma . . . How are you?' She gazed into Josephine's face. 'You've been crying! Why have you been crying?'

Josephine clutched her, emotional, almost hysterical. 'Hortense, he wants to get rid of me!'

'Mamma, he's been saying that for ten years now.'

'But this time he really does. This time it's dangerous. It's not the same as before. He doesn't want to divorce me. He wants me to divorce him. Because I love him. Because it would be best for him. Don't you see how dangerous that is?'

Hortense looked over her mother's shoulder at Madame de Rémusat, whose face confirmed what she supposed.

'Mamma, do please calm down.'

'How can I? With this threat hanging over me!'

'What threat?'

'That I must divorce him!'

Hortense dearly loved her mother, and sometimes found her irritating almost beyond endurance. The two of them had been through this scene fifty times before, with Josephine refusing to be sensible, refusing to take a practical view of the situation, refusing to recognize what was in her own best interests.

'Mamma, if he really wants you to divorce him, then divorce him.'

'Hortense, how can you say that? You're as cruel as your brother!'

'Does Eugène say the same thing? I'm glad to hear it.'

'I wrote to him asking him to help me. He wrote back the most cruel letter, simply saying that I must be sure to get a good settlement out of the Emperor, and that he and his wife will be very glad to have me live with them after the divorce.'

'Mamma, that's not a cruel letter. That's simply sensible. Eugène loves you as much as I do. We want you to be happy.'

'How can I be happy, if I divorce Napoleon?'

'Mamma, you *don't* love Napoleon.'

'Yes, I do.'

'All he's ever done is make you unhappy.'

'And happy. Very happy.'

'Mamma, no one can love a Bonaparte. No one can be happy with a Bonaparte.'

'I am. I love him. I mustn't lose him.'

Hortense sighed. How can one reason with a fractious child who denies and contradicts everything?

'Mamma, darling, what do you really care about? Position? No, not really. You're like me. We don't care about being queens and empresses—at least, we don't care about the titles. It's nice to be rich and have beautiful houses and lots of servants, that's all. That's what you *really* care about. Well, if you divorce him he'll give you enough money. He'll have to. You'll be rich for the rest of your life. Divorce him, and live in Italy with Eugène. Or with me. We'll buy a house somewhere. We'll be happy. You can't go on letting Napoleon make you unhappy like this. Get rid of him. He's a monster.'

'No! I tell you, I love him!'

Her eyes were flooded with tears. It was useless trying to make her see what was truth and what was self-deception.

Hortense said, wearily, 'I suppose you want me to talk to him.'

'Yes, he's fond of you. He'll listen to you. Talk to him today. As soon as you can. Please, Hortense. Quickly. I'm frightened of what may happen.'

'Frightened?'

'Hortense, he'll do anything to get rid of me. I know he will. He'll poison me. He's capable of anything.'

Hortense glanced at Claire de Rémusat, who shook her head.

'Mamma. I'm quite sure that you are imagining things—'

'No!'

'—and that the Emperor wouldn't dream of harming you—'

'Yes! You don't know him as I do!'

'—but if it makes you feel any better, I'll see him as soon as possible. Where is he now?'

Josephine looked quickly around, as if fearful that someone else might hear.

'He's gone to see that Polish woman. In rue de la Victoire.'

'Mamma, are you spying on him again?'

'He's my husband! Why shouldn't I spy on him?'

Napoleon looked out of the window, into rue de la Victoire.

'Do you like the house, Marie?'

'Yes, I do. Thank you.'

'If there's anything that should be done to it, tell me, or tell Duroc . . .'

'Nothing needs to be done. Except for you to come here every day.'

'As I do come here. As I shall come here.'

'Yes. Thank you.'

She went to the window, and stood by his side, and looked out with him.

'What are you looking at?'

'I lived in this street once. Not here. At Number Six. I can't quite see it, through the trees.'

'On the other side.'

'Yes. It was Josephine's house. I moved into it when we married. It was rue Chantereine in those days. I went off to Italy from Number Six. When I came back, they'd renamed the street rue de la Victoire, in honour of my victories.'

'And you lived at Number Six again?'

'Till I became the ruler of France, with an official residence, a palace or two . . .'

She said gently, 'Were you happy at Number Six?'

'Happy and unhappy, both to the point of madness. Enraptured and tortured by my love for Josephine.'

He came away from the window, as if he were trying to put the old rapture and the old torture out of his mind.

Marie said, 'She was stronger than I am. I can do neither of those things to you.'

'Both.'

'No.' She smiled at him. 'Thank you for saying it. But it was only politeness.'

He took her hands. 'It was a poor compliment and a false one. With you there's no torture, there's only happiness. But I love you as strongly as I loved her.'

'Perhaps.'

'In a different way. She was all woman, woman of one kind, the enchantress, the mistress. You are all woman of another kind: the saint, the angel.'

He kissed her, then walked away from her, as if he could not look at her while he said, 'I have decided. I am going to divorce her.'

Marie said, 'You can't.'

'Why can't I?'

'You are married in the eyes of God. As I am.'

'What God?'

He turned and looked at her at last.

She said steadfastly, 'Napoleon, you and I are sinners, and we know it, and we know that God knows it, and we hope that God may forgive us. But you can no more divorce your wife than I can divorce my husband.'

When he came back to the Tuileries the day was growing dark. He found Hortense waiting for him in his study. He embraced her fondly.

'When did you arrive?'

'This afternoon.'

'Why did you arrive? Of course, I'm delighted to see you. But is there a reason?'

'My mother asked me to come.'

His face darkened. 'Ah. Well. How are you? Are you reconciled to that husband of yours yet? If not, why not? What's wrong with you both?'

She faced him squarely. 'If you are asking "why" questions, I shall ask you one. Why did you marry me to the least of your brothers?'

'Not the least,' he said gruffly. 'Louis is less foolish than some of the others.'

'Why did you marry me to Louis?'

'Does your mother say it was my doing?'

'All Bonaparte marriages are your doing.'

'No. Your mother married you to Louis. She wanted to make sure of keeping me, by bringing you into my family too. It was to be another bond between us.'

They stood silent, both thinking the same thought. Hortense said it. 'I am separated from my husband, and you are going to divorce your wife. So much for bonds. And so much for good intentions.'

Napoleon stared into the fire, and spoke in a low voice, almost as if to himself. 'I must have an heir, or after me France will fall into anarchy. I must have a son. We are at the mercy of a blind fate. There was a son, who could have been my son.'

'What son? Whose son?'

'Yours.'

She stared at him. 'Mine?'

'Your son who died. Louis's son—not mine, of course not mine. But people believed it was mine—because you obviously did not love your husband, because I obviously did love you: love you as my stepdaughter. But common people believe the worst of great people. I have two reputations in the mouth of the world. Do you know what they are?'

'I know at least one of them.'

'One is, that I am impotent. Because I have failed to get a child. The other is, that I am a monster of lustfulness who has bedded every woman within reach, including my three sisters, and you. And that your son, your dead child, was my child. Half Europe believed it. Didn't you know that?'

Her voice was trembling, she didn't know why. 'I heard the rumour. I tried to put it out of my mind.'

'I kept it in my mind.'

'Why?'

'Who am I to deny a rumour? Denials are never believed. If the child had lived, I would have had my agents encourage the rumour, I would have had them confirm it. I would have adopted the child legally, and the whole world would have come to suppose that I was the real father. And the boy would have reigned after me, as Napoleon the Second.'

'And my reputation?'

'There are a thousand things more important than reputations.'

She almost smiled. 'Yes. I do know that. I apologize. It was a stupid thing to say.'

'Yes.' The word was harsh, but he touched her cheek gently, to show that he loved her and that he wished to be friends with her.

She asked, 'And if my son had lived, and been made your heir, you would not have wanted to divorce my mother?'

'Fate. If your mother had had a child, a son, by me, as I hoped . . . If I had had a child that could have passed for hers . . . If your child, little Napoleon-Charles, had lived . . .'

He was staring into the fire again, holding on to the chimney-piece. His face was white, his forehead suddenly covered with sweat.

She said quickly, anxiously, 'Sire, are you unwell? Shall I call Constant?'

He did not seem to have heard her. He said, 'Hortense, do you remember—you're old enough to remember, of course you remember—the house in rue Chantereine? There, I loved your mother more than any woman has ever been loved. I loved her beyond my hope of heaven . . .'

He half-turned, and staggered, and almost fell, and clutched at his stomach, as if he were stricken by a sudden violent cramp.

She cried in alarm, 'Sire, you are ill! I must fetch your servants!'

'No!'

She looked at him. His face was twisted with pain.

He said, 'No . . . Josephine . . . Your mother . . . Tell your mother I want her . . .'

Josephine came quickly, in her gown and her parure, ready dressed and bejewelled for the evening. Constant opened the door to her. She flew to the bedside. Napoleon was on the bed, in shirt and breeches, twisting and turning, groaning, doubling up as if crippled by muscular spasms.

'Darling, what is it? Shall I send for Doctor Corvisart?'

He looked up at her, and his eyes streamed with tears.

'My poor Josephine!' he cried.

As she bent over him, he reached up convulsively and threw his arms around her, and pulled her down on to the bed in a frantic embrace, crushing her in his arms, crushing her dress, crushing her marvellous coiffure, knocking the tiara out of her hair.

'Josephine!' he cried. 'I shall never leave you!'

Napoleon and Josephine lay naked in each other's arms, weeping, their faces bathed in their own tears and in each other's.

'My poor Josephine . . .'

'Don't leave me . . .'

'I shall never be able to leave you . . .'

'Please don't leave me . . .'

'I shall never leave you . . .'

In the morning they woke early. He did not ring for Constant at once, but got up and put on his dressing-gown, and opened the shutters to let the sun in, and padded quietly about the room, doing nothing in particular.

She sat up in the bed, bright-eyed and smiling, happy at his recovery.

'Are you really feeling well now?'

'Better. Much better.'

'I'm so glad.'

He grinned ruefully. 'Tired.'

'Darling, we hardly slept.'

He went to her and kissed her fondly.

He said, 'You are not to believe that I wish to divorce you.'

'I don't believe it. If you tell me not to.'

'I shan't divorce you.'

'And I shan't divorce you.'

He said, 'Unless I'm forced to.'

'I shan't force you.'

'Unless I'm forced to by necessity. By fate.'

She still kept her mouth as smiling and her eyes as bright. She said, 'But darling, you are the master of your fate.'

'Sometimes.'

'Always.'

He sat on the bed and took her hands, but did not

329

look at her. He said, 'I used to think so. I'm no longer sure of it. There is still the same difference between me and other men: they make mistakes, and I do not. But once I did not believe that accidents could happen. I now admit the possibility of accident, which can have the same effect as a mistake.'

He moved away and padded about the room again, aimlessly. 'Believe me, I have no wish to change my life. As we grow older, marriage becomes a matter of habit, of convenience. The words are not uncomplimentary. Pleasant habit. Agreeable convenience.'

He stopped and looked at himself in a cheval-glass, from the front and then from the side. He was balding. He was getting fat.

He said, 'What would I be doing with a girl whom I don't even know, who doesn't know me, who hasn't learnt by experience what I need in a woman—when I need to be with her, and when I need to be without her?'

Josephine looked at him looking at himself. She said gently, sliding the question smoothly over the threshold and into his mind, 'Whom were you thinking of marrying?'

After a moment he answered her, rather too abruptly. 'No one. I had no one in mind. No one at all.'

22. JOSEPHINE LOST

General Caulaincourt, the newly appointed French Ambassador to Russia, was a soldier and a diplomat, son of an aristocrat who had fought as a Revolutionary general; was himself a staunch supporter of the Empire; was the trusted servant of the Emperor, and the confidant of Talleyrand. The combination was remarkable, and would hardly have been possible, had not Napoleon and Talleyrand both known that Caulaincourt was the soul of honour, and would betray neither of them.

In the great salon, as far as possible from the orchestra, so that they could hear each other, and from the rest of the company, so that they could not be overheard, Talleyrand and Caulaincourt talked.

Talleyrand said, 'I have already written privately to the Tsar, suggesting that he should seem to favour the notion of the Emperor marrying his sister.'

' "Seem to"?'

'Yes.'

'Only "seem"?'

'I should like the Emperor to have reason to hope.'

'But no more than that?'

'I have suggested to the Tsar, secondly, that there should be some reservations, some difficulties to be overcome: particularly, the Tsar's mother will have to give her consent, which will not be easy to obtain; so that Napoleon is kept hopefully waiting.'

Caulaincourt made a grimace. 'Will the Emperor enjoy waiting?'

'No.'

'Why do you want him to be kept waiting?'

'Not waiting. Hopefully waiting. There's a great difference.'

'Hope but not fulfilment? Are you against a Russian marriage, in the end?'

Talleyrand waved aside the thought. 'My dear Caulaincourt, I only wish that Napoleon would ask for the hand of every princess in Europe, all at the same time. No one makes war where he hopes for marriage. At last we'd be at peace.'

'Unfortunately, he can only ask one at a time.'

'But you do see why I have no great desire for the negotiations to be concluded too speedily. As soon as the Emperor marries one great power, the others will rebecome potential enemies.'

'But he must marry soon.'

'So he tells me.' Talleyrand was very nearly guilty of yawning, as if the subject of the Emperor's marriage had suddenly begun to bore him. His jaded eye lit up again as it fell on a splendidly dressed foreigner, at a distance. 'Oh, do you know the Prince of Mecklenburg?'

'We haven't met.'

'I must introduce you immediately. A great friend of the Tsar's mother—therefore he may be useful to you. And even for a hereditary prince, quite remarkably stupid.'

Caulaincourt laughed. 'Then he may indeed be useful.'

'Oh yes. A meddler. I think we should encourage him to meddle, if only we can guide his meddling.'

He started to limp towards the prince, but stopped for a moment and turned to Caulaincourt, who was following.

'Forgive me if I overdo it. He has a passion for titles.'

They arrived at Mecklenburg, who greeted Talleyrand with the smallest and stiffest possible bow, such as is due from a great hereditary prince to a prince whose family is ancient but not royal.

Talleyrand spoke undeterred: 'Prince, may I have the honour of presenting to you one of my closest colleagues, General the Count of Caulaincourt, the Emperor's Master of Horse, and new Ambassador to the Court of St Petersburg?'

Something stirred in the prince's eye. 'Delighted.'

'Your Highness . . .'

'Caulaincourt leaves for Russia—I think, tomorrow?'

'Tomorrow.'

'Ah.' Mecklenburg acknowledged the information.

He took Talleyrand aside for a private word, to ask his advice.

'My dear Prince, of course.'

'In confidence.'

'Naturally.'

Mecklenburg weighed his words with the greatest care. 'I came to Paris with a purpose in mind, a particular purpose . . .'

'I am at your service, if I can help.'

'On behalf of a friend of mine, a very important friend, I can't tell you the name . . .'

'I would not dream of asking it.'

'The question is delicate, extremely delicate. I'm sure I can rely on your discretion . . .'

'Absolutely.'

'The fact of the matter is, that my very important friend has requested me to make private inquiries, and to . . . how shall I put it? . . . to ascertain the truth about the Emperor's powers.'

'Military? Political?'

Mecklenburg looked darkly around, and said, with a wealth of meaning, 'No.'

Talleyrand managed to keep his face straight, and to convert a laugh to an 'Ah!'

Mecklenburg said, 'His powers as a man.'

'Ah, yes. I understand.'

'There are rumours.'

'Indeed there are.'

'But are they true or false?'

Mecklenburg obviously required a weighty reply. Talleyrand gave it.

'Prince, in these matters, an opinion is hardly worth more than a rumour. There are, of course, two people who are in a position to know the truth—or falseness—

of what you have heard. One is Doctor Corvisart, who is pledged to secrecy by the Hippocratic oath. The other is, of course ... Would you care for me to arrange an interview with Her Majesty?'

Josephine was at her most charming with Mecklenburg. She received him alone, in her boudoir. She poured tea for him. She gently encouraged him through his initial hesitations.

'The question, Your Majesty, is delicate, extremely delicate.'

'If I can help to answer the question, whatever it may be ...'

'I think perhaps I should start by explaining ... But I imagine I hardly need to explain. I take it that Your Majesty is in the Emperor's confidence.'

'The Emperor and I have no secrets from each other.' She gave him her sweetest smile.

'That is what I had assumed, or I would hardly have dared ...'

'No secrets at all.'

'Of course.'

'Not even on ... what might be thought delicate questions.'

'Naturally.'

'Naturally. We've been married so long now.'

'Exactly. I therefore take it that Your Majesty is well aware of the negotiations which are on foot ... the somewhat premature negotiations, but these things have to be arranged in advance ... for the Grand Duchess Katarina of Russia to become Your Majesty's successor.'

After a moment, during which she controlled herself admirably, she said, 'Yes, I am well aware.'

'I imagine that Your Majesty has in effect approved the choice.'

'I think the choice would be an excellent one.' She could not resist adding, 'From the Emperor's point of view.'

He nodded sagely. 'Certainly, from his point of view. But, from the other side . . .'

'Oh, aren't the negotiations going well?'

'There are problems.'

'I'm sorry to hear it.'

'One of them being . . . the delicate question.'

She said softly, 'Do please go on, Prince.'

His voice became even more important. 'A friend of mine—a friend in a very high position, the equal of yours, Your Majesty—and who is, necessarily, deeply involved in this affair . . . I have been asked not to mention her name . . .'

'I understand.'

He bowed. 'Thank you.'

'Your discretion does you credit, Prince.'

'Thank you . . . This friend has heard rumours.'

'There are always so many rumours.'

'A particular rumour, which would be disturbing if it were true . . . That the Emperor, in one sense, one very important sense, would not be likely to . . . the sense I refer to is the physical sense . . . would not be likely to make a successful husband.'

Josephine looked at her teacup for a long time.

At last she said, without raising her eyes, 'The rumour your friend has heard is that the Emperor is impotent.'

'Exactly. Thank you.'

She continued her examination of her teacup. He waited. He quite understood that she had to decide whether to honour him with her confidence.

She raised her eyes and looked at him, with the frank wide-open gaze of a woman who is speaking nothing but the truth, whatever the cost.

'Prince, you know of course that I was married before.'

'Indeed.'

'And had two children by my first husband.'

'Indeed.'

'My darling boy Eugène, now the Viceroy of Italy. And my darling girl Hortense, now so unhappily married to the Emperor's brother Louis. Two beautiful children, and each of them born . . . you will understand what I mean . . . each of them conceived without any delay.'

He nodded his head. 'Yes . . .'

'When I married General Bonaparte I was still young, very young, and in perfect health.'

'Yes, I'm sure.'

'Naturally I hoped—what young wife does not?—I hoped, I expected, that our union would be blessed: that I would have children, as easily as I had done before.'

'Naturally.'

'But nothing happened.'

Mecklenburg's eyebrows went up into his hair. 'Nothing?'

She said, with the utmost simplicity and truthfulness, 'I was disappointed. Immediately. And have gone on being disappointed. Have I answered your question, Prince?'

He inclined his head in deepest gratitude. 'Yes, Your Majesty.'

'I have never told this to anyone. I must ask you not to repeat it.'

'I swear never to repeat it.'

'Except, of course, to your friend.'

'Except, of course . . .' He was greatly relieved that she allowed him the exception.

'I would never have told you, were it not that I think it better for the Grand Duchess to marry the Emperor, knowing what the marriage will bring, and what it will not bring. So that my own disappointment cannot happen again.'

'Your Majesty is most kind.'

Josephine said, 'Perhaps I have put it too strongly. The Grand Duchess may very well be happy with the Emperor. He is capable of feeling pleasure, and to a certain extent of giving pleasure. It's simply that . . . how can I best express it . . .?'

Mecklenburg waited, while she found words to express it.

She said, 'It is like water.'

Napoleon called in on Josephine that night, for a connubial chat before bedtime.

'I hear that Mecklenburg came to see you.'

'Yes. What a strange man he is.'

'A pompous fool, with nothing to boast of but his ancestry. And he himself is the whole argument against ancestry.'

She said, 'I found him . . .' She took a time to find the right adjective for him. 'I found him shocking.'

'All stupidity is shocking, to those who are not stupid.'

'No, really shocking. In the things he said.'

'Do you mean he was indecent? You surprise me. I didn't think he had it in him.'

'He asked me questions which were quite . . . no, not indecent, but improper. Improper for him to ask.'

Napoleon had almost been amused. Now he was curious.

'What sort of questions?'

She said, 'Oh, about you.'

He asked more sharply, 'What questions about me?'

She was pensive. 'As I say, he's strange. I didn't really understand him. He seemed to be trying to find out what you're like as a husband. As a lover.'

Napoleon stared at her, his face suddenly black as thunder. 'Mecklenburg dared to ask you . . . ?'

'Yes, I thought he was joking. Then I thought he wasn't joking, but the only way I could pass it off was by pretending he was joking. So I laughed.'

She looked at him appealingly, hoping that he would tell her she had done the right thing.

'And what did you say to him?' He was still thunderous.

'Darling, I said you were as marvellous at being a husband as you were at everything else. And I changed the conversation.'

337

The thunder-cloud lifted. She was pleased. She wanted to be sure that he was pleased.

'Should I have told him how shocked I was? Should I have been angry with him?'

'No.' He was still angry enough for two. 'I shall have Talleyrand send for Mecklenburg's *chargé d'affaires,* and inform him that the prince has no further business in Paris.'

She said, contentedly, 'Yes, I agree. Mecklenburg should go back to wherever he came from, as soon as possible.'

The next day, Talleyrand sent for Mecklenburg's *chargé d'affaires.* The day after that, Mecklenburg started his journey back to whoever sent him. As soon as he arrived in St Petersburg, he was received by the Tsar's mother. The same evening, the Tsar's mother dined with her son. A remarkably few weeks after that, the Tsar sent for the French Ambassador. The next day, General Caulaincourt set out for Paris. As soon as he arrived in Paris, he went to the Tuileries, to report to the Emperor.

'I thought I should come back myself, Sire. As quickly as possible. And not confide the news to anyone else, until I have told it to you.'

'What news?'

'The Tsar summoned me to a private audience at his palace, and informed me that he is about to announce the engagement of his sister the Grand Duchess Katarina—'

'What?'

Caulaincourt went on—bravely, considering: '—to the Duke of Oldenburg. The marriage is to take place very soon.'

Napoleon stood stock-still, his face frozen into a mask.

'The Tsar informed you.'

'Yes, Sire.'

'You. You alone.'

'Yes, Sire.'

'My ambassador.'

'Yes, Sire.'

'So that you could inform me. The Tsar does not speak to me. The Tsar does not ask for a meeting with me so that he can break the news to me. The Tsar does not write to me. The Tsar informs you.'

'Yes, Sire.'

'This is a masterpiece of treachery.'

'Sire, the Tsar asked me to assure you that his brotherly love for you is undiminished.'

Napoleon cried, *fortissimo,* 'Undiminished?'

'That was the word he used, Sire.'

'The Duke of Oldenburg is a fool! A petty princeling! A puppet! A nothing!'

'Yes, Sire.'

'His face is covered with spots! He stammers!'

'Yes, Sire.'

'And Catherine is going to marry *him!*'

'That is what the Tsar told me, Sire.'

Napoleon seized Caulaincourt by his shoulders and held him, looking closely into his face.

'Caulaincourt, there is a traitor. A traitor somewhere. Who is the traitor?'

'Sire, I do not know of any traitor.'

Napoleon stared into his eyes, unblinkingly. Caulaincourt stared back, also without blinking.

Talleyrand was delighted to hear the news.

Caulaincourt said ruefully, 'The Emperor is not delighted.'

'Ah, but he was in favour of a Russian alliance. I have always recommended him to be more moderate in his desires.'

'He spoke of treachery.'

'My dear Caulaincourt, whenever I speak of moderation, he reaches for the word "treachery". The Emperor does not wish to see that he was called on by destiny to make France strong again; but that no man is called on by destiny to rule the world. He is blinded by ambition and pride—and by the imbeciles he listens to: Murat and the marshals, who want more wars, in order to get more dukedoms and kingdoms for themselves. If he persists in this blindness, it will lead to his downfall; and he will destroy what he has created.'

Napoleon summoned an urgent and special meeting of his privy council—his grand dignitaries and chief ministers, those of them who were in Paris: Murat, Cambacérès, Lebrun, Admiral Decrès, Fouché, Maret, Berthier, Duroc and Talleyrand. Talleyrand was the last to arrive, limping in, bowing to the Emperor.

'A thousand apologies, Sire. Your messenger has only just found me.'

Napoleon stared at him with black malevolence. Talleyrand responded with an agreeable smile, sat down next to Berthier, and whispered, 'What is the subject to be?'

Berthier did not dare reply. He had read the signs on Napoleon's face: someone was about to feel the full power of the imperial wrath. The only question was, who?

Napoleon prowled about in front of them, staring at each in turn, demanding from each the tribute of uneasiness and fear, before he even began to speak.

At last—'I called you here today, to remind you of the obedience and the loyalty which you owe me. I took you all from obscurity, from nothing, and made you all what you are today: grand dignitaries and ministers of my Empire, with titles and lands and riches. Kings and princes and dukes: titles bestowed by me for your services to me, and for no other reason, as there can be no other. All glory springs from me, as a part of my glory which I can afford to bestow. All services must be rendered to me, since I am France, I am the French Empire. The Empire exists because of me, and in my person: the Empire contains your princedoms and dominions. But I hear—and you must know that I hear everything—I hear criticisms of my actions; I hear differences; I hear doubts. I tell you, you have no right to think for yourselves! If you do it, you have no right to give your thoughts expression! Doubt is the beginning of treason! And to differ from my policy is treason itself!'

He directed his stare at Murat, who reddened, then at Fouché, who avoided his eye.

'Some of you have dared to act as if the succession to my imperial throne were already vacant; as if it were to be had by the highest bidder; as if it were a matter for secret politicking and private intrigue. I make it clear to you now, none of you will be my successor; none of you will choose my successor; the choice will be made by me, and none of you will influence my choice!'

A heavy sweat broke out on Fouché's forehead. Napoleon suddenly turned and marched on Talleyrand, to stand in front of him, feet astride, hands clasped behind his back, eyes blazing with hatred.

'And you, Talleyrand, Prince of Benevento by my creation. Do not imagine that it will be otherwise. Oh, yes, you believe you're a great man, because you were a noble before the Revolution. Because I send you with messages to tsars and kings and emperors, and they flatter you in the hope of flattering me, in the hope of your influencing me—in the hope of your betraying me! But I know you for what you are. A coward. A thief. An apostate bishop who never believed in God. You have never in your life served anyone faithfully! You do not know what loyalty means! You would sell your own father for a piece of gold!'

His voice was hoarse, his face was dark with rage. His hands unclasped and came forward, in a sudden convulsive movement, his right arm half-raised as if he were about to strike Talleyrand in the face. Talleyrand sat motionless, expressionless, silent.

'You have been plotting to destroy my friendship with Russia. You have been plotting to drive me into the arms of the Emperor of Austria—I must suppose, because

Austria has the bigger purse and has dangled the bigger bribe in front of your nose. Well, Prince Talleyrand, you have failed! I am going to go to war with your friend the Emperor of Austria! And he will lick my boots or I will throw him off his throne!'

The hand was still poised for a blow.

'I know you, Talleyrand. You'd do anything to harm me. You hope to see me dead. You want to see France small again, weak again. Why do I let you live? Why don't I have you hanged from the railings outside this window? What are you? An infamous heap of corruption! A lump of dung in silk stockings!'

A single word from Talleyrand, and Napoleon's hand would have struck. But Talleyrand stayed silent, looking at Napoleon, not defiantly, nor scornfully, but as if he were not there.

Napoleon's arm jerked down to his side. He turned on his heel and marched out of the room.

The grand dignitaries sat in silence, looking at Talleyrand.

After a time Talleyrand rose to his feet and said, to no one in particular, 'What a pity that such a great man should be so ill-bred.'

The others were still silent: there was nothing they could safely say. Talleyrand limped away.

Josephine pleaded, 'Can't I come with you?'

'My dear, you are too beautiful for a battlefield.'

'Let me come with you as far as Munich.'

'No, my dear. It's not possible.'

'As far as Strasbourg, then.'

'It will be a short campaign. It's not worth your while. A few weeks only. One battle, perhaps two, and then I shall be back in Paris again.'

She said, 'I hate your going away without me.'

'I shall write to you every day. Or whenever I can.'

'I love your letters. But I'd rather be with you.'

'Ah, but I must have a court here, even while I'm away. With you at the head of it. My Empress.' He took her fondly in his arms. 'And you're a soldier's wife, a good wife for a soldier. I've gone off to war a hundred times, and you've been brave, and waited.'

She said in a tiny wheedling voice, 'Darling, please let me come as far as Strasbourg.'

He kissed her, and she clung to his lips, and he relented.

'As far as Strasbourg, then, if that will make you happy.'

She was radiant. 'Very happy.'

When he had gone from her room, she sent for Hortense.

'Hortense, I am going as far as Strasbourg. It's something. It's not enough. He has arranged for that woman to follow him to Austria.'

'Madame Walewska?'

'The Polish woman. Yes.' She caught Hortense's eye. 'Yes, Hortense, I have been spying again. And I shall continue to spy.'

In Vienna, after the Austrian defeat, Napoleon took a house for Marie, with a charming garden; and most evenings, in the calm splendour of that early autumn, they ate their supper on the terrace there, just the two of them, attended by Constant.

That evening she was sitting in the garden already when he arrived there.

'Marie . . .'

She smiled and rose and moved into his arms—not quickly: she did nothing quickly: everything she did was calm and graceful.

He kissed her cheeks. 'My angel, my loved one . . .' He looked into her face. 'No more kisses now. Constant is bringing our picnic.'

Constant came from the house with a tray of food and wine, and began to arrange the supper-table. He allowed himself only a discreet little bow towards Madame Walewska: he had come to worship her so devoutly, he was half-afraid that the Emperor might resent it.

Napoleon said to her, 'And what have you done today?'

'Walked about Vienna. Read a book. Walked again. Waited for you.'

'You walk too much. You're tired.'

'No.'

He took her chin in his hand, and gently turned her face towards him.

'You're pale. And you have dark rings under your eyes.'

'Whole rings?'

'No, not rings. But there is a darkness.'

'I'm growing old.'

He smiled and put an arm round her slender waist. 'All you grow is more beautiful. But you must see Corvisart. He must give you a tonic.'

She protested, 'Doctor Corvisart already comes to see me every day. Because you told him to.'

'But does he give you a tonic?'

'Oh, yes. Because you told him to.'

'And why does he say you're pale?'

'He says I walk too much. Because you told him to.'

'Corvisart is the best doctor in Europe.'

She made fun of him. 'Yes, I'm sure. But he is your doctor. So you are my doctor.'

He did not mind being made fun of. He was only anxious to take the paleness from her cheeks.

'Some wine. That'll do you good. Constant, give us some wine.'

'Yes, Sire.' Constant had had the same thought. There were two glasses ready poured.

Napoleon said to her, 'And something to eat.'

'Not yet. I'm not hungry yet.'

'What have you eaten today?' He was suddenly suspicious.

'Some things. Some fruit.'

'Only fruit?'

'Mostly fruit.'

'That's not enough. You must eat fish, meat, bread—'

'Yes, but not just yet. Later.'

'Drink your wine, at least.'

She smiled at him and sipped the wine. 'Yes, doctor.'

'Marie, I must prescribe for you.' He turned to Constant. 'Constant will choose the smallest, tenderest delicacies, which not even you can resist—'

'Yes, Sire!' Constant, prompt as ever and eager to please, was doing it as soon as Napoleon said it.

'And you will eat them to please me, if only to please me. I am always dying of love for you, but I can't have you die of starvation.'

Constant came to her with a plate of delicious tidbits. 'Madame . . .?'

She did not take the plate, but raised her eyes and looked at Constant, with her calm sweet smile.

'Constant, will you please go into the house, and not come back till we call you?'

'Yes, Madame.' He was desolated, but he obeyed. He put the plate back on the table, and went away.

Napoleon was seized by a dreadful anxiety, a growing anxiety. 'Marie. Are you not well? What does Corvisart say? Are you ill? What does he really say? Tell me!'

He sat by her and took her hands, and gazed into her face, trying to read her words even before she said them to him.

She said, 'I sent Constant away because I don't know if you'll be glad or sorry, happy or unhappy . . . I didn't tell you the truth just now. I didn't walk this afternoon. Doctor Corvisart came to see me. And since then I've simply stayed here, sitting here in the garden, wondering what you will feel when I tell you . . . Corvisart is quite certain. I've waited for him to be quite certain. I myself am very happy. I hope that you will be happy. I am pregnant.'

The shock of it was almost too much for him. His mind reeled. After the years of hope deferred, after the eternal disappointments, after the pretences and deceptions of Josephine; after the failures with other women— Pauline, Georgina; after the torturing uncertainty of Eléonore's child; now, the certainty that he was capable of being a father—this certainty given to him for the first time at the age of forty, when he was on the brink of believing himself forever infertile—this certainty given to him without a shadow of doubt, given to him not by a light-of-love but by the purest woman in the world . . . It was the most important moment of his life. His mind could not immediately comprehend the full importance of it. His heart could not straightaway accept the wonderful joy of it.

Marie said, 'Are you glad?'

'Oh, my dear darling, my darling, my darling . . .'

He covered her hands with a thousand kisses, weeping tears of utter happiness. He leapt up, a man illuminated, a man transfigured. He shouted at the top of his voice, 'Constant!'

'Yes, Sire?' Constant came running from nowhere.

'Champagne!'

'Yes, Sire!'

'Yes!' Napoleon cried, throwing his arms up to the sky. 'Sire! Sire! Sire!'

In the Tuileries, Josephine gave a terrible cry, and ran from her bedroom to where Hortense was sitting with Claire de Rémusat.

'Hortense! Claire!'

She stood in the doorway, haggard, in despair, an open letter in her hand.

She said, 'I am lost. The Polish woman is pregnant.'

23. THE ARCHDUCHESS MARIA-LUISA

Napoleon came back to Paris, cold, reserved, harsh, relentless. Josephine went to meet him at Fontainebleau. He had already sent orders from Austria that the door between his apartments and hers should be walled up. She wept, and he embraced her; but there was no warmth, no love, in his embrace.

After a fortnight, they moved to the Tuileries. They dined together, privately, in the Emperor's rooms. They ate in silence: she red-eyed with weeping, hardly able to swallow a mouthful; he indifferent to food as always, rapidly snatching at whatever was nearest to hand. The meal was over in ten minutes. They went into his drawing-room. The servants withdrew. They were alone, but apart, at the two ends of the room.

He said, 'You must by now be aware of the necessity. The necessity is now so absolute that there can no longer be any argument. I have decided, and nothing can change my decision.'

She said, 'We are married in the eyes of God. We were blessed by the Pope.'

'The Pope is my prisoner. The Church in France will do what I tell it to do.'

'You may order the Church to blaspheme against God. But I am your wife.'

'A wife who cannot give her husband children is herself a blasphemy—is not a wife.'

'I had children by Alexander. If I had none by you, it was not my fault.'

'I know for certain that it was. You have played a comedy with me, throughout our marriage. Corvisart tells me that some women go through the change of life in

347

their thirties, even in their early thirties.'

'Corvisart tells you what you want him to tell you.'

'No!' she cried. 'No! I could have had children! But you couldn't get them!'

He said, 'From the beginning, you have acted a comedy of pretences. You have concealed the truth.'

'A comedy?' she cried. 'I have given you my life!'

He said, with a terrible coldness, 'When we first met you were thirty-two, with a fourteen-year-old son, a twelve-year-old daughter, and a history which included more than one lover. I married you because I thought you were rich. You married me because you thought I would become rich. You have had thirteen rich years with me. Do you call that giving me your life?'

She said, 'I have loved you.'

She said it softly, but he heard her, even at a distance, and it softened him. He said, in a voice as low as hers, 'If I had not loved you—if I did not love you—I would have divorced you long ago.'

They came towards each other. She hoped, for a moment, that he would come close to her and take her hand or touch her face; but he stopped two yards short of her, and would move no nearer.

He said, 'Josephine, I am forty, and time is running out for me. I need a son. I need a belly that can give me a legitimate heir. Otherwise, my Empire will die on the day that I die. Don't you see that I must divorce you, for your sake as well as my own?'

She said in a whisper, 'No . . .'

'Then, at least, please come to understand that this has nothing to do with love. But that even I cannot fight against political necessity.'

He waited for a response from her. He got none. He went on, his voice growing sharper again: 'You can go on being rich. You can keep your title of Empress. You can have a kingdom of your own if you like. Rome. Would you like Rome? I'll give it to you . . . If you want to, you can live in Milan with Eugène and his wife, with your grandchildren . . . Or Malmaison. Then we could see each other sometimes. Would you prefer Malmaison? Malmaison with all its land; and you can keep everything you've had from me; and I'll pay you three million francs a year. Even you can't spend much more than that.'

She still made no response.

He said, 'Well? Choose.'

She said, 'I choose to stay married to you.'

'That choice is not open.'

She said, 'You told me you would not divorce me without my agreement.'

His voice had no tenderness left in it. 'All right, I'll give you a different choice. A divorce with your agreement—or without it.'

'Is it all over between us, then?'

'Yes.'

She gave a great heartrending cry. 'You can't say that! Do you want to kill me?'

She fell to the floor.

'Josephine—!'

Napoleon ran to her, panic-stricken. She gave one terrible sob, the sob of a dying woman, and collapsed, her eyes rolling upwards, unconscious.

Napoleon ran to the door and flung it open. Bausset, the Prefect of the Palace, was on duty, in attendance in the next room.

'Bausset! Come and help me! The Empress has fainted! 'Sire!'

Constant was there too.

'Constant, get Doctor Corvisart. Quickly. The Empress has fainted.'

'Yes, Sire!'

Napoleon ran back into the drawing-room with Bausset.

'Pick the Empress up. Put her on a couch. That couch there.'

'Yes, Sire.'

Napoleon ran back again, to catch Constant.

'Constant! And tell Queen Hortense to come here! And the Empress's ladies!'

'Yes, Sire!'

Bausset, a big man, with a barrel-chest and a great barrel-belly, put one arm under Josephine's shoulders and one under her knees, and lifted her off the floor. She was deathly pale. Bausset clutched her to his chest. There were pieces of furniture to be steered around. His sword clanked and caught in the legs of a low table. For fear of dropping the Empress, he held her closer. She, without opening her eyes, almost without moving her lips, murmured, 'Bausset, don't hold me so tight. You're hurting me.'

Bausset was so startled that he nearly pitched forward and fell to the floor. Napoleon, coming back into the room, cried, 'Be careful with her!'

He came quickly to help Bausset. They laid Josephine gently on a couch. She moaned feebly, without regaining consciousness.

Napoleon, with Bausset by his side, stood looking down at her. Tears started into his eyes.

Napoleon said in a low voice, 'Poor woman. I have broken her heart.'

Bausset was not so sure of that, but he kept his own counsel.

Eugène came hurrying from Milan, summoned by both the Emperor and the Empress, to propose his mother's divorce, and to support her through it. He found his mother pale and tearful, and over-anxious for her children. He tried to make her see reason.

'Mother, there is nothing more to be said.'

'He must promise to make you King of Italy.'

'Mother, I have told him that I want no promises.'

'Eugène, you must be a king. You must insist on it.'

'I will not make a bargain for myself out of your suffering.'

Hortense did her best to help. 'Mamma, the only thing that matters is your being properly treated.'

350

Eugène said, 'The Emperor is as concerned that this should be so as we are. He still loves you, Mother: you must realize that.'

Hortense said, 'He wants you to live at Malmaison. So that you'll still be near to him.'

'He doesn't want you to go abroad. He says your sacrifice must bring you honour, not banishment.'

'He says you'll always be his best-loved friend.'

Josephine said, 'Friend . . .', and the word was the tolling of a death-knell.

Eugène said, 'We'll go with you, and see you settled in Malmaison. And you'll be happy there.'

'But how shall I ever live through it, till then?'

Hortense said, 'We shall be with you, Mamma.'

'Hortense . . . Eugène . . . How shall I be able to face those Bonapartes, who hate me? This is their triumph!'

Eugène spoke strongly, to strengthen her. 'Mother, you are an Empress. You are still and always will be an Empress.'

Murat was in full court dress, even more fantastically gorgeous now that he was no longer a grand duke and not merely a prince, but beyond that, a king, the King of Naples and the Two Sicilies. Caroline, happy at being a queen, even if not finally satisfied, had made herself equally as gorgeous as her husband. They were so pleased at the prospect of what was going to happen at the family council that evening, that they had got themselves ready for it in plenty of time, and had gone to call on Napoleon while he was dressing, in case he needed their moral support.

They were sorry to find Napoleon silent and pensive. They themselves were in the best of spirits.

Murat said jovially, 'What news from St Petersburg? Has the Tsar agreed to the new marriage yet?'

Caroline said, 'The Grand Duchess Anna sounds charming. I'm told she's prettier than her sister.'

Murat said, 'How old is Anna now—fifteen?'

Caroline said, 'A good age.'

He gave his military laugh. 'The younger the better.'

'And certainly old enough to marry. Our own mother was married by that age.'

She looked to Napoleon for him to agree. But Napoleon was still silent. The king and queen had to continue.

Murat said, 'Of course, one sees why the Tsar was reluctant to give you his other sister. You weren't free then, you might still have changed your mind, you might have postponed the divorce for one reason or another, there was always the risk of its becoming an embarrassing situation. You couldn't really make a definite offer till now.'

Caroline said, 'But tonight you become a bachelor again.'

Murat waved his hand airily, to dismiss a ludicrous doubt. 'Oh, the Tsar's bound to agree to your marrying Anna. Why shouldn't he? You're the greatest man in the world, he's the second greatest. And after the marriage, you can divide the world between you. Let the Russians look to the east, to Asia. We'll have Europe.'

Napoleon said a word at last. He said, 'Yes.'

'This is a great day for France. And for you, Sire.'

Napoleon looked at him with bleak curiosity. 'Are all women the same to you, Murat?'

'I beg your pardon, Sire?'

Napoleon said, 'This is the saddest day in my life.'

At nine at night, in the Throne Room, the Imperial family assembled. A few of the Bonapartes had had to forgo the pleasure of being there: Joseph had his hands full in his new Kingdom of Spain, and, in any case, he and Napoleon were hardly speaking; Lucien was still the rebel of the Bonapartes, who still wouldn't do what his brother told him; and Elisa, less troublesomely, was expecting a child. But, of the brothers, Louis, King of Holland, was there, and Jerome, King of Westphalia; and of the sisters, Queen Caroline, with her King

Joachim, and Pauline, Princess Borghese. And Queen Julie Clary, Joseph's wife, was there; and Catherine of Württemberg, Jerome's queen; and the mother of the whole Corsican clan, Letizia, sitting stiffly in her stiff black dress, her face set in lines of rigidly watchful disapproval. Cambacérès was in attendance as Arch-Chancellor of the Empire, Talleyrand as Vice-Grand Elector, Regnault de Saint-Jean d'Angély as Secretary of State to the Imperial family.

The Emperor himself sat at a long table, in an armchair, facing his family but not looking at them. The other armchair at the table was empty: it awaited the Empress.

She came in, wearing a plain white gown, with no jewellery. Her hair was simply dressed, her face without rouge, seeming almost as pale as her gown. She was supported by her son and her daughter.

Eugène and Hortense took her to her chair. She and Napoleon did not look at each other. Their faces were sad, but composed. The family's faces ranged from grim satisfaction to ill-concealed glee.

Napoleon rose and took up the copy of his speech, but did not even glance at it: he knew what he had to say.

'Members of the Imperial family . . . You are all well aware of the decision that I have come to, and of the reason for that decision. My divorce from the Empress Josephine, which tonight we formally and finally agree, has been dictated solely by political necessity: by the necessity for me to provide a direct heir to my throne, and to found a dynasty which will rule over the French Empire for centuries to come . . . God knows what this decision has cost my heart! But there is no sacrifice which I will not make when it is necessary to the welfare of my country. It is indeed a sacrifice for me; but I must, above all, praise the goodness and tenderness, the affection and understanding, of my beloved wife. She has graced many years of my life, and the memory of those years will always be engraved in my heart. I crowned her Empress with my own hands: I desire that she shall keep

353

the rank and title of Empress, but before everything else
I desire that she shall never doubt my regard for her, and
that she shall always look on me as her best and dearest
friend.'

He sat. It was Josephine's turn to rise. Her hands were
trembling now. She had difficulty picking up her speech
from the table, and holding it in front of her eyes.

She read: 'With the permission of my great and dear
husband, I declare that since I no longer have any hope
of bearing children, and since this alone could satisfy the
demands of politics and the interests of France, it is therefore my pleasure . . .' She nearly broke down. She tried
again. '. . . It is therefore my pleasure to give the
greatest proof of love and devotion which has ever been
given on earth . . .'

She could not go on. The paper fell from her hands to
the table. She swayed, and felt for the arm of her chair,
and sat, or she might have fallen.

Napoleon looked quickly at her, with anxious concern.
She met his eyes and gave a little shake of her head, to
tell him she couldn't do it. He turned and made a
signal to Regnault. Regnault came forward and picked
up the speech, and read it aloud, from the point where
she had broken off.

'Everything I have comes from his goodness; his hands
crowned me; seated beside him on the throne, I have had
the happiness of being loved by the people of France.
I now wish to acknowledge these great gifts, by consent-
ing to the dissolution of a marriage which can no longer
serve France. Nothing can change the feelings of my
heart. I shall continue to love the Emperor, as I have
always done. I know what pain this act has caused his
heart, as well as mine. But we both glory in the sacrifice
we are making for our country.'

Regnault put the speech back on the table. He went
to Cambacérès and took from his hands the Act of
Separation. He brought it to Napoleon and put it in
front of him. Napoleon picked up a pen, dipped it in an
inkpot, and signed his name. Regnault carefully sanded

the signature, then took the Act to Josephine and put it in front of her. Josephine looked at it without moving. Regnault, politely, to help her, picked up the pen that lay by her hand on the table, dipped it in the ink, and offered it to her. She took the pen and signed her name beneath Napoleon's.

It was done, at last. They were divorced.

Nature was in sympathy with her. The next day, the day of her departure for Malmaison, it poured with rain.

There was no other reason to linger at the Tuileries. Her furniture, her belongings, her trunks and boxes and cases had been taken away earlier, while Eugène was asking the Senate to ratify the dissolution of the civil marriage of 1796. But still Josephine lingered.

Hortense said, 'Mamma, the carriage is waiting.' Then, more strongly, 'Mamma, we must go. However much it's raining.'

'Napoleon has not said good-bye.'

'But we're only going to Malmaison! He'll come and visit you there, you'll see him again very soon.'

'I must wait for him to say good-bye.'

'Mamma, the sooner you leave this place, the sooner your mind will be at peace.'

Josephine was impossibly obstinate. 'He must come to say good-bye.'

'It will only make you more unhappy.'

Josephine said, almost in a whisper, 'He might not be able to let me go.'

Hortense stared at her, incredulous. 'Mamma, you do understand you're no longer his wife? Mamma, you do understand that? He has divorced you! Nothing can change that now! You can't stay here! You have to go!'

Josephine stood, shaking her head uncomprehendingly, almost vacantly.

'I can't . . .'

Napoleon came in at the open door. Josephine saw him and ran to him and flung herself into his arms, sobbing. He held her and kissed her wet cheeks and her eyes and her forehead over and over again.

'My dear Josephine, my dear one . . .'

'I can't go. I can't leave you. Tell me I'm not to go. Tell me I don't have to leave you. I mustn't leave you . . .'

He said, 'Be brave, be brave . . .'

'Tell me you love me, tell me you still love me . . .'

He said, 'My dear, I shall always look after you, I shall always be your friend.'

The word was a knife in her heart.

'Friend . . .'

He slowly released her, and she let herself be released. She stood looking at him for a long time.

She said, 'Don't forget me.'

She took Hortense's arm and went, without looking back at him.

Talleyrand said, 'Sire, we should give some consideration to the fact that the Archduchess Maria-Luisa of Austria is, of course, a great niece of Queen Marie-Antoinette, so regrettably and unnecessarily guillotined by the foolish leaders of the Revolution.' His gaze travelled across Berthier and came to rest, ironically, on Fouché. 'Your marriage to her would, in a sense, absolve France from its complicity in that crime.'

Fouché said, 'It was not a crime at the time.'

Talleyrand was conscious of having used the line before once, but this second use was not to be resisted. 'It was worse than a crime: it was a mistake.'

Napoleon was not in a mood to appreciate epigrams. 'Who cares about Marie-Antoinette?'

'The other countries of Europe, Sire. You are still, to them, the inheritor of the Revolution.'

'An upstart Corsican?'

'They have yet to grasp, Sire, what we here have known for some time: that you have become the champion of law and order, of monarchy and dynasty and dictatorship.'

Napoleon looked at him sharply. Was Talleyrand being ironic at his expense, too?

Talleyrand continued imperturbably, 'It is also to be considered that, by marrying into the Habsburgs, you would also be marrying into the Bourbons. Since Marie-Antoinette was the wife of the last King of France, you would be able, if you wished, to refer to Louis the Sixteenth as your great-uncle. In a word, Sire, you would acquire not only heirs, but also ancestors.'

Napoleon said, 'I like your argument. I don't like your conclusion.'

'My conclusion, Sire, is a lasting peace in Europe.'

'Can I afford peace?'

'I must hope so, Sire.'

'Because the Emperor of Austria is your friend? Perhaps your patron? Perhaps your employer?'

Talleyrand put on his most innocent expression. 'Sire, would I wish to marry you to the daughter of my friend?'

Napoleon, uncertain whether to scowl or to laugh, ended by laughing, and turned to Fouché. 'What do you think?'

'Sire, I agree with Talleyrand.'

'That is a remarkable novelty.'

Fouché shrugged off the novelty. 'Given a choice between a Russian and an Austrian, I vote for the Austrian. For the reasons given.'

Napoleon turned again, to Berthier. 'You've heard the civilians. What do you say, as my Minister of War, which is something these two don't understand?'

Berthier shook his head in his military commonsensical way. 'Sire, you will either have to fight the Russians or to marry them. In the present state of our army—we have had losses, Sire—I should prefer you to marry them.'

Talleyrand said, 'May I speak with my usual frankness, Sire?'

'Preferably with more than your usual.'

'Your ministers, excellent men though they may be, are always seeking to base their plans on what you want done now. I myself seek to know something different,

357

which is what you will want done in the future. I read your stars, Sire.'

'And what does my horoscope tell you?'

'You will inevitably want to fight Russia, Sire. Because your ambition has no bounds, and there is not room for two great powers in your world. I advise you to start finding useful allies for your next war.'

Napoleon said, 'Austria is not an ally. Austria is a nation I have defeated.'

Méneval, the Emperor's secretary, came in.

'Forgive me, Sire. General Caulaincourt has arrived from St Petersburg. You wished to see him the moment he arrived.'

'Yes.'

Méneval went.

'Talleyrand, whatever you read or misread in my stars, I have offered to marry the Russian, because I have decided that it would suit me to marry the Russian. There is an advantage in making an alliance with one's next enemy.'

Talleyrand raised his shoulders. 'You think Russia can be deceived on this point, Sire?'

'Why not?' Napoleon looked at him keenly. 'Unless you are in secret correspondence with St Petersburg, as well as Vienna.'

Talleyrand was glad that Caulaincourt came in before Napoleon made any more guesses which struck quite so close to the truth. It was good to be ignored for a time. The Emperor had eyes only for Caulaincourt, and ears only for the latest report from St Petersburg.

'What has the Tsar to say to me?'

Honest Caulaincourt replied honestly. 'The Tsar will not give a clear answer, Sire.'

Napoleon shouted, 'I am the Emperor of France! I offer my hand in marriage! To the Tsar's sister Anna! Who is unattached, and is of marriageable age!'

'The Tsar's mother says the girl is too young, Sire.'

'The Tsar's mother?'

'Yes, Sire.'

'But what does the Tsar say?'

Caulaincourt stood stiffly to attention and said, 'Sire, may I have your permission to speak to you in private?'

'No. What does the Tsar say?'

'Sire, I beg your permission—'

'Tell me!'

'Do you wish me to tell you, Sire, here and now?'

'I command you to tell me here and now!'

Napoleon was livid with rage, shaking with fury, glaring at Caulaincourt as if Caulaincourt were the Tsar. Talleyrand thanked his own stars that he had become a man who never gave information, but only advice. Napoleon was becoming more and more like those ancient tribes which made a practice of killing the bearer of bad news.

Caulaincourt, commanded to give his news, gave it as a soldier should, bravely and plainly and directly.

'The Tsar's mother has—I do not know how or why—gained the impression, Sire, that you are incapable of fathering a child. She has told the Tsar this, as a certain truth. The Tsar can hardly believe it to be true, but he pretends to believe it. He says that it would be a great disgrace to his family if it were in fact true, and if he, believing it to be true, allowed you to marry his sister the Grand Duchess Anna.'

Napoleon grew black as thunder. 'Have you told him that Madame Walewska is pregnant?'

'Yes, Sire.'

'And what did he say to that?'

'His answer, in effect, Sire—'

'His words! Tell me his words! His exact words!'

Since Caulaincourt was ordered to tell them, he told them.

'He said to me, Sire: "But we all know that she's Polish. She may very well have had other men." '

He had said it. There was a silence. They did not dare speak. They knew the Tsar's words to be a terrible insult, to Napoleon and to his saint Marie. They knew that

Napoleon could choose to ignore the insult, or not to ignore it.

Napoleon strode to Talleyrand and stared him in the face.

'Inform your friend the Emperor of Austria that I will marry his daughter, the—whatever she is, whatever her name is . . .'

Talleyrand said, 'The Archduchess Maria-Luisa.'

Napoleon said, 'Marie-Louise.'

PART THREE

THE LAST
LOVE

24. THE EMPEROR'S BRIDE

The Emperor, in high good humour, stood drinking a cup of tea given him by Constant. He was still in his dressing-gown: now that he was growing older, he was taking to the habit of receiving early-morning visitors in his dressing-gown.

He stood with Duroc, surveying with a good deal of complacency a portrait of the Archduchess Maria-Luisa, newly received from Vienna, only just unpacked, and not yet hung.

'What do you think of her?'

'She is beautiful, Sire.'

'I hope so. I doubt it. Artists are liars.'

'When they need to be. He may not have needed.'

'She has the Habsburg lip.'

'Indeed, Sire.'

'What do I care? I'm not marrying a lip. I'm marrying a belly. She's eighteen, I'm reliably informed she's healthy. Her mother had thirteen children, her grandmother had sixteen, her greatgrandmother had dozens. So—!'

He turned abruptly towards the door as Constant showed in Murat, then Eugène, then Corvisart.

'Good morning, Murat, have you heard from your wife?'

'Not this last day or two, Sire.'

'I have a letter from her this morning, written from Strasbourg. Caroline tells me that Marie-Louise "very much wants to know what will make me happy". I am replying to Marie-Louise that all I need is a wife who is happy in our marriage.'

'A perfect answer, Sire.'

'I'm also writing to Caroline. She got rid of all the Austrian ladies-in-waiting, so Marie-Louise has been crying all the time, at the loss of her friends. Your wife is as high-handed as if she were . . . as if she were me. Eugène, I'm delighted to see you. How is your mother?'

'In excellent health, Sire.'

'Good, good.—Corvisart, you old quack. Have you killed anyone since yesterday?'

'Not to my knowledge, Sire.'

'Ah, your famous knowledge. Tell me, Corvisart. You're the most knowledgeable doctor in the world.'

'If you think so, Sire.'

'How long do men retain their fertility—on the average? For example, a man aged forty, like myself, with a young wife, can have children.'

'Normally, Sire.'

'A man aged fifty? With a young wife?'

'Very often, Sire.'

Napoleon persisted. 'A man aged sixty?'

'Sometimes, Sire.'

'Aged seventy?'

Corvisart raised his eyebrows. 'With a young wife?'

'Yes.'

'Always, Sire.'

Napoleon laughed. He was a happy man, he could even laugh at jokes about adultery. He turned to Eugène, still laughing.

'Well, Eugène? Is your mother settling in at her new château at Navarre?'

'Not yet, Sire.'

'What?' Napoleon was surprised.

Eugène was surprised too, at the Emperor's surprise. 'I dined with her last night at Malmaison, Sire.'

'Josephine is still at Malmaison?' Napoleon was suddenly black-browed.

'She spoke of going to Navarre, Sire. But I don't know when.'

Napoleon said, harshly, 'Duroc.'

'Sire?'

'I have an errand for you.'

* * *

363

Duroc rode out to Malmaison and saw Josephine.

'Your Majesty, the Emperor asked me to say, he gave you Navarre as yet another proof of his desire to make you happy.'

'I have already written to the Emperor, thanking him for his kindness.'

'The Emperor thought you would enjoy having a second home, further in the country than Malmaison.'

Josephine continued to take each statement at its face value. 'Yes, Navarre is certainly further from Paris.'

'And it will give you an additional income. The Navarre estate brings in two million francs a year.'

'The Emperor is most generous.'

Duroc was finding it difficult. The Empress was not helping him.

'The Emperor had hoped that you would have moved there by now.'

She was sweetly reasonable. 'Navarre is not ready for me yet.'

'The Emperor has ordered repairs, at his own expense—'

'Duroc, you know as well as I do, the repairs are not finished yet.'

He started to say, 'Your Majesty—'

'How can I live in a house which has not been heated for years? Where the panelling in the drawing-room is rotten with damp?'

'Forgive me, Your Majesty. We are doing our best.'

She gave him a radiant smile. 'Dear Duroc. Yes, I know you are.'

Duroc hardened himself to say it. 'But the Emperor did, in his last letter to you, ask you to go to Navarre on the twenty-fifth of March, even though the repairs were not completed, and to spend the month of April there.'

She was still smiling. 'So that I am further from Paris when Marie-Louise arrives?'

Duroc sought to put it more acceptably. 'The whole world knows of the Emperor's great love for you.'

'And of mine for him.'

'Yes, Your Majesty. It will be better for the new Empress not to be too constantly, or too closely, reminded.'

She said, gently, 'Since I sacrificed myself for her, and for him . . .'

He hastened to agree. 'Yes, Your Majesty.'

'Might it not have been better for me to have welcomed her to Paris? To the place where I used to live? To my rooms there? To my bed?'

'Your Majesty, you will be represented at the wedding celebrations by your son the Viceroy of Italy and your daughter the Queen of Holland.'

Tears were coming into her eyes. She said, 'Duroc. Please ask him . . .'

He was sympathetic, he was embarrassed, but he knew his duty. 'The new Empress will be arriving very shortly.'

'Duroc, ask Napoleon . . .' Her tears were flowing.

'The Emperor asks you, Your Majesty . . . The Emperor commands . . . that you leave Malmaison, and go to Navarre, today.'

She was brave and sweet and obedient. 'Tell the Emperor, I am always his most devoted servant.'

The Emperor had decided that the whole court would move to the Château at Compiègne, in order to greet the Archduchess on her arrival there, and entertain her for a day or two before the last stage of her journey to Paris.

Compiègne was chock-a-block with royalties and nobles and dignitaries who had come Pariswards to attend the marriage and the celebrations. It was true that the royalties were either Napoleon's kinsmen or Napoleon's vassals, and that the nobles and dignitaries were almost all either French or Austrian. Nevertheless, the uniforms and the gowns made a fine, brave show, and the food and wines were of the choicest, and the Emperor himself was the perfect host, and in brilliantly high spirits from morning to night. He seemed always to be surrounded by a circle of admiring young ladies, joking with them, as gay as they were, and almost as young.

He cried to them, 'I must learn to be less serious and more charming. I'm marrying a young wife, I must learn whatever pleases young women. I must do my best to adapt myself to suit her. Hortense, you should know: what must I do, to please my new Empress?'

'Your Majesty should learn to waltz.'

'Ah! Should. But must I?'

Hortense said, 'Of course! The Empress is German, and the Germans these days do nothing but waltz. It will be a great shame if you don't know how to partner her—since she cannot have any partner but you.'

He shook his head ruefully. 'I tried to waltz once, in private, by myself. It was not a great success.'

Hortense laughed. 'A remarkable admission, Sire. Have you ever failed to do what you wanted to do?'

Napoleon was laughing, too, at a memory. 'They taught us at my military school. I was top of the class in everything else, bottom of the class in dancing. We of the awkward squad were advised by our dancing-master to practise —not with a lady, that would have been far too dangerous—but with a chair.'

He picked up a light cane-bottomed chair, and held it in front of him. 'Alas, two or three turns and I was dizzy— I fell over, the chair broke—the chairs in my room, and in my friends' rooms, disappeared one after another.'

Merriment from the circle of young ladies. Napoleon was having a new success as a raconteur.

Hortense said demurely, 'Perhaps you should try again, Sire. You may be less subject to dizziness than you were.'

'Very well, Hortense. Teach me to waltz.'

She showed him. Since her mother had left the court she was the most admired dancer, marvellously light and graceful.

'One two three, one two three . . .'

'It seems remarkably simple.'

'It is.' She waltzed again. 'One two three, one two three . . .'

'I can count up to three as well as any man alive.'

366

She curtseyed to him. 'Will Your Majesty do me the honour of dancing with me?' He bowed and moved to her. 'Your right hand on my waist—'

'As I used to do with my chair.'

She said, 'When I say 'One', you start by putting your right foot forward . . . Are you ready to start?'

'Ready to advance.'

'Now. One two three, one two three, one two three, one two three . . .'

She did her best with him. He was awkward, he was impossibly awkward. He stopped, laughing. Everyone was laughing.

Hortense said, 'Sire, you are a very bad pupil.'

'I agree.'

'You were made to give lessons, not to take them.'

They looked at each other, and burst out laughing all over again.

'Poor Empress,' he said. 'I shall have to find some other way of pleasing her.'

A young aide-de-camp had come into the room and reported to Duroc. Duroc chose the moment to speak to the Emperor.

'Forgive me, Sire. Captain Lejeune has returned. You wished to have him report to you.'

Napoleon cried eagerly, 'Lejeune!'

'Sire!'

'What news? Where are they?'

'Sire, the Archduchess Marie-Louise and the Queen of Naples spent the night at Vitry. They are now on the road to Soissons.'

'Did you yourself see the archduchess?'

'Yes, Sire.'

'Tell me frankly. What does she look like? How did she impress you?'

Lejeune was young and pink-cheeked and not accustomed to commenting on the appearance of archduchesses. He found some words.

'Very favourably, Sire.'

' "Very favourably" does not give me any information. How tall is she?'

That was easier to answer. 'She is a good height, Sire.'

'What is a good height?'

'She is . . . ' Lejeune looked desperately around for help. His eye fell on smiling Hortense. 'She is much the same height as the Queen of Holland, Sire.'

'What colour is her hair?'

'Fair, Sire. Rather like the Queen of Holland.'

'And her complexion?'

Lejeune clung to the lifeline which was saving him from not being able to give a good answer. 'She has a fresh complexion, Sire. Rather like the Queen of Holland.'

'So she resembles the Queen of Holland?'

Lejeune's face went very red.

'Sire . . .'

'Well? Does she?'

'No, Sire. Not at all. But everything I've said to you is true.'

Napoleon punched him on the shoulder, not unkindly. 'Run away, you idiot.'

Lejeune gratefully did so as the Emperor turned to speak to Murat. 'Obviously she's plain. I can't get more than that out of anyone who's seen her. Oh, well. If she gives me big strong sons, I'll love her as if she were the most beautiful woman on earth.'

His eye lit up. He was struck by a sudden idea, of great, of blinding brilliance.

'Murat. Do you want to see your wife?'

'Naturally, Sire.'

'I am longing to see mine.'

'That is even more natural.'

'We'll order a carriage. No coat of arms, no livery, nothing to show it's us.'

'Yes, Sire. What for?'

'We'll meet them on the road!'

Napoleon marched towards the door, fast, shouting, 'Constant!'

'Sire?'

'My bath!'

They drove out on the road to Soissons in a light carriage, plain and un-Imperial, with Napoleon's driver in a plain coat and Napoleon in his plain green Chasseur uniform, and even Murat a good deal less flamboyant than usual.

Napoleon was as excited as a boy. He could hardly sit still. He could absolutely not stop talking.

'Better than a Russian. I was wrong to think of a Russian. The Romanovs are a new dynasty, like the Bonapartes. I'm a new dynasty, I must marry into an old one. The Habsburgs of Austria have been kings and emperors for over five hundred years. Seventeen generations. Think of that, Murat. My son by Marie-Louise will be the eighteenth generation. And there's no madness in the family. The Romanovs are impossible, a bad heredity, either they're geniuses or they're mad. No, it had to be a Habsburg. The Habsburgs may not have much brain, but what little they have is sound. What does it matter if the girl is stupid? I have brains enough for two.'

'Only two? Enough for a hundred.'

Napoleon laughed. 'Only a hundred? The Archduke Charles once said to me that my presence on the battlefield was worth ten thousand men.'

'So it is.' Murat flattered him. 'The Archduke Charles was not flattering you.'

'No, he was making excuses for himself. I'd just beaten him.'

Napoleon laughed again, positively gleeful. He was brimming over with glee. He leant across and slapped Murat on the knee.

'Well, Murat, we've not done badly, eh?'

'Not too badly, Sire.'

'You were an innkeeper's son, you married my sister and I made you King of Naples.'

Murat, who had a notion that he had made himself

369

king by his own efforts, answered a little drily, perhaps. 'Yes, Sire, so you did.'

In a larger and more sumptuous carriage, a 'berlin', Marie-Louise and Caroline approached Courcelles from the opposite direction.

Caroline was yawning. She had travelled with Marie-Louise all the way from the Austrian frontier, and the journey had been going on for too long: she had begun to find Marie-Louise inexpressibly boring. What had at first seemed to be charming innocence, fresh simplicity, amusing naïveté, had already, by the time they reached Strasbourg, ceased to charm and ceased to amuse. It had to be admitted that the archduchess was really quite good-looking, and not in the least unpleasant; but she was certainly not a person to share a carriage with on a long journey. She had no conversation, except for 'Where are we?' and 'When do we get there?' She was quite startlingly ignorant, and not at all anxious to learn. She lacked animation and expression: the cruel word for her was 'cow-like'. And to crown it all, these last few days she had developed a truly Germanic cold in the head, which made her sniff and sneeze with appalling regularity.

The archduchess pulled the curtain back an inch and looked out into darkness.

'Where are we now?'

Caroline yawned again. 'Oh, somewhere.'

'Isn't it time we stopped for the night?'

'I suppose we shall stop quite soon.'

'Where shall we stop? At what place?'

'I've forgotten. But it's all arranged. The same as every night. Napoleon has arranged it.'

Marie-Louise said dolefully, 'I hope it won't be the mayor meeting us, and the reception at the town hall.'

'It usually is.'

'And we have to listen to speeches before we can eat. I have this terrible cold.'

'Yes, you have.'

'When I have a cold, it makes me more hungry.'

370

There was a silence. Caroline longed for it to last till their arrival at wherever it was. No such luck.

'We are not far from Paris now?'

'I imagine, not very far.'

'I shall like to see Paris.'

'Paris can hardly wait to see you.'

Silence again.

Marie-Louise said, 'I wish I didn't have this awful cold.'

Silence again: though it was never a real silence. There were the wheels on the road, and the eight horses pulling the carriage, and the horses of the cavalry escort, and the wheels and horses of the carriages following with their loads of ladies-in-waiting and maids and officials and attendants. And among all these noises, there were cries of 'Stop!' and 'Whoa!', and the carriage came to a halt.

'Have we got there now? The place where we are to stop?'

'I suppose so.' Caroline pulled back her curtain and peered out through her window. 'I don't know. It just looks like a village. A dark wet village. With a church.'

The door was pulled open. A man leapt into the carriage.

Louise cried, 'Oh!'

Caroline said, 'Napoleon!'

Napoleon exclaimed, 'Caroline, you've spoilt it—I wanted to be a surprise!'

'You are!'

Napoleon plumped down on to the seat beside the astonished archduchess.

'I was going to say—I'm delighted to meet you! I am your husband!'

He threw his arms around her forthwith, and gave her a smacking kiss on both cheeks. Then he drew back his head, still holding her, and gazed at her full breasts, her full red mouth, her ruddy cheeks, her blue eyes—

'Thank God!' he cried.

She didn't understand him. 'Why?'

'My dear Louise, you are beautiful.'

He pressed her in his arms again, she supposed it was

371

to kiss her cheeks again; but he kissed her mouth instead, and went on kissing it for a long time. It was the first time anyone had ever kissed her mouth. She was startled by the sensation, but not in the least displeased.

When he had finished kissing her mouth, she said, 'Marie-Louise. My name is Marie-Louise.'

'I've decided to drop the "Marie".'

'Oh, why?'

'One name is enough. When we're alone together, like this.'

Caroline felt ignored and showed it, but he continued to ignore her.

'I suspected your portrait. I was right, it was a lie. You're a thousand times more beautiful than your portrait.'

He leant forward again. Another long kiss on the mouth. She was beginning to find it really enjoyable. She liked being kissed.

She said, 'And you are nicer-looking too.'

'Than my portrait? I thought it was good of me. Wasn't it?'

'No.'

'Ah, but you imagined me as a Corsican ogre.'

'No, I imagined that you would look like Marshal Berthier.'

He was vastly amused. 'Berthier?'

'Yes, someone told me you were like him.'

'But Berthier's ugly!' He was still laughing.

'Yes, you're not ugly.'

'And he's old!'

She said, 'Yes, you are not so old as him.'

'I'm young!' he cried, and quickly hugged her, and planted more kisses on her plump cheeks. 'Well, I'm certainly younger than Berthier! Dear Louise, I shall show you how young I am!'

He let go of her, and moved to the open door, and shouted through it, 'Murat!'

Murat hurried to the door of the carriage. 'Sire—Archduchess—Good evening, Caroline—'

Napoleon cried, 'Murat, we'll drive straight on!'

'Yes, Sire. Where to?'

'Where we came from!'

'Tonight, Sire?'

'Yes! Now! On! Now!'

He reached out for the door, and pulled it shut in King Joachim's face. He pulled the curtain across the window. He sat himself down next to Louise again, and put his arms round her again.

'You were to have stayed the night in the next town. It's the great thing about being Emperor—I can change my own plans without asking anyone's permission.'

He was ready to kiss her mouth again.

She said, 'I should have told you.'

'Told me what?'

'I've got a cold.'

'Dearest Louise, my love will cure you.'

He pulled her towards him again, into his arms, into an ardent kiss, as the whip cracked over the horses, and the carriage swayed forward.

Caroline decided to look out of her window, into the darkness, where there was nothing to be seen.

When they arrived at Compiègne, Napoleon hurried her through the great crowd of royalties and nobles and dignitaries, who had been waiting so many hours for the arrival. The archduchess had a bad cold in the head, the archduchess was tired, the archduchess was ravenously hungry. After the briefest possible presentations, she was escorted to her apartments.

There, a small dining-table had been placed in front of a good fire. Napoleon supped *tête-à-tête* with her. Perhaps not quite *tête-à-tête:* Caroline sat at the table with them; but Napoleon neither looked at nor spoke to Caroline. Constant was the only servant, bringing new dishes to the table from heaven knew where. Marie-Louise made a hearty meal. Caroline did not. Napoleon ate nothing at all. He simply sat there, not taking his eyes off his bride.

'Louise, what did they tell you to expect?'

'In Vienna?'

'Yes.'

'They told me that I would be taken to one of your palaces . . .'

'Yes . . .'

'And that I would go into the palace . . .'

'Yes . . .'

'With . . .' she took another mouthful, '. . . with the Queen of Naples, or whoever was taking me there . . .'

Caroline was not particularly grateful to be mentioned. Napoleon said, 'Yes . . . ?'

'And with my ladies-in-waiting following me, of course . . .'

'Of course. And where was I?'

'They told me that you would probably be standing in the great entrance hall of the palace. And I would kneel at your feet, and make a speech to you.'

'A speech?'

'Yes, I learnt it by heart.'

'Say it to me now.'

'But I don't have to say it now.'

'Say it.'

She said, 'It was . . .' She took another mouthful. 'It was very formal.'

'And we have gone past the stage of being formal.'

'Yes.' She almost blushed. The memory of those kisses almost made her blush.

He said, 'And they told you to expect that after your very formal speech . . . ? Forgive me, were you still kneeling?'

'They said that you would probably pick me up.'

'Probably.'

'Yes.'

'And if I didn't?'

'I was to stay kneeling until you did.'

'And when I did? Finally? Pick you up?'

A most charming, most enchanting blush was starting to show on her cheeks. She looked away from him.

She said, 'They said that you would probably kiss me on the forehead.'

'On the forehead.'

'Yes.' The blush was spreading.

'Louise, this is, for you, a day of surprises.'

'Yes.' The blush was covering her face and her neck.

'And after that? What did they tell you to do, in Vienna?'

She said, 'My father told me to do whatever you wanted me to do.'

Time passed. She ate, looking down at her plate. His eyes were on her. His eyes were eating her.

He said, 'Louise, they are expecting us, tonight . . .'

'They?'

'Kings, queens, princes, ambassadors . . . They are expecting us to go down to the salon, where they are waiting, and show ourselves to them, and say polite things to each of them . . .'

She said, 'Whatever you want.'

He smiled. 'I am full of surprises.'

He called Constant. Constant came hurrying to the table. 'Sire?'

Napoleon, without taking his eyes off Louise, said, 'I want . . . I want Marshal Duroc.'

In the salon, the great and famous stood waiting, as they had done for hours: it was their function to stand waiting, until someone even greater than themselves gave them instructions to sit or to move or to go. Talleyrand, bored to tears, decided that he might as well be bored to extinction, and listened to Berthier, who had gone to Vienna as Napoleon's representative, and had stood proxy for the Emperor at the ceremony there, and had come back from Vienna in Louise's cavalcade.

He was saying, 'A very charming girl. Well, perhaps "charming" isn't the best word for her. But very . . .'

He seemed at a loss for a word. Talleyrand tried to help him.

'Very young?'

375

'Very simple. Very natural.'

'The opposite of Josephine.'

Berthier welcomed the reference to Josephine. It did help to explain. 'Yes.'

Talleyrand asked, 'Will it work?'

'What?'

'Josephine, the soul of artificiality, was an excellent Empress.'

'Yes . . .'

'Will simplicity serve?'

Berthier might quite possibly have thought of a good reply to that; but they were near the door, and Duroc came to them first, to tell them the message from the Emperor.

'The Emperor and the archduchess will not be coming to join us. The Emperor gives permission for everyone to retire to bed.'

Duroc moved on. Berthier was surprised by the message. Talleyrand was unsurprisable, but he raised an eyebrow. He spoke, perhaps to Berthier, perhaps to no one in particular.

'The archduchess is all Europe, of course. Europa. And the Emperor is the great god Jove—disguised as a bull?'

Constant shaved him and eau-de-Cologned him and powdered him, and brought a long mirror into the best possible light so that he could study himself and admire himself.

Studying himself, he said, 'I am young.'

'As young as ever, Sire.'

'Will I do?'

'Sire, if you will permit me—'

'Won't I do?' He was anxious.

'—permit me one tiny . . .'

But there was a knock at the door. Napoleon said quickly, 'If it's Metternich, I want him. No one else.'

It was Metternich. Constant brought him in: Count Metternich, Austria's Foreign Minister, all ability and agreeableness and charm. He had done more than anyone

376

to arrange the royal match. Since Napoleon could not be beaten, it had seemed sensible to join him.

'Your Majesty . . .'

Napoleon did not waste time. 'Metternich, you're the Austrian Government. Tell me. Am I married to her?'

'You are bound by a contract, Your Majesty—'

'Yes. And a ceremony.'

'And indeed by a ceremony, a proxy wedding, at which Your Majesty was represented by Marshal Berthier—'

'In other words we are married?'

Metternich saw what the Emperor wanted to be told. 'Yes, Your Majesty.'

'Thank you, Metternich. I'm most grateful.'

Metternich bowed. 'A pleasure, Your Majesty.'

He went, happy to have played his small part in the history of that night at Compiègne, and hoping, without any real hope, that all future questions would be as simple to answer as that one.

Constant came back to Napoleon, to finish what he had begun: the putting of the best possible face on a forty-year-old with a receding hair-line.

'. . . one tiny stroke of the comb . . .'

He adjusted Napoleon's forelock.

Napoleon, no longer looking at himself, said, 'Constant. She is very beautiful, isn't she?'

'Very beautiful, Sire.'

'And a great princess.'

Constant, by now a diplomat second only to Talleyrand, said, 'For a great princess, she is quite remarkably beautiful, Sire.' He was satisfied with the forelock at last. 'Sire, you are perfect.'

Napoleon took one last proud look in the mirror. Even without benefit of uniform—even in dressing-gown and slippers, as he was—he looked every inch an Emperor. Constant had told the truth. He was perfect.

Head erect, full of youthful energy, he marched out of the room. Constant watched him go, with admiration, with sympathy, and with amusement.

*   *   *

In Louise's anteroom, then in Louise's boudoir, the ladies-in-waiting dropped startled curtseys as Napoleon marched through.

He was courteousness itself, though without stopping: 'Ladies, you may retire to bed.'

He marched into Louise's bedroom, where the principal ladies-in-waiting were helping the Archduchess into her extravagantly beautiful new nightdress. They, too, dropped startled curtseys.

'Ladies, you may retire to bed.'

They fled. He was alone with Louise.

She didn't know what to say to him. Instinct came to her aid. The ladies-in-waiting had curtseyed. Louise went to him and knelt at his feet.

He said, 'What is the speech that you learnt by heart?'

'The meaning of it was, that I will obey you in all things.'

'And then probably I pick you up?'

'Yes. Or I wait till you do.'

He looked down at her. He picked her up. He held her in his arms for a moment, and kissed her mouth, but only for a moment. He broke away, to speak to her, almost formally, from a distance.

'Louise, I am not a Habsburg. I am a self-made ruler, with self-made rules.'

'Yes . . . ?'

'However, there are forms—formalities—which even I accept, for the sake of—for the sake of what? The opinion of the world.'

'Yes . . .'

'We shall be legally married in three days' time, in Paris, by lawyers. I create the laws of this country, I must observe them.'

'Yes . . .'

'The following day we shall be married again in Notre-Dame. Religiously. I cannot totally ignore the power of religion.'

'No . . .'

'Even though the Pope is still my prisoner, and the

cardinals of France are in my pocket. I must be married to you in every binding way that God or man can devise.'

'Yes . . .'

'However, I am already in a sense married to you. I married you in Vienna, by proxy. Marshal Berthier was my representative. Old ugly Berthier, but my Chief of Staff, who worships me. Who better to stand proxy for me? And he made on my behalf a legally binding contract.'

'Yes . . .' She was nodding her head obediently, but she still did not understand why he was saying these things.

'We are married. Already. Do you believe we are married?'

'Yes, if you say so.'

'Louise, I want to go to bed with you. Tonight. What did your father that other Emperor tell you?'

She understood now. 'To obey you in all things.'

'Get into bed.'

She got into bed. He started to take his dressing-gown off. Then he stopped, and wrapped it around himself again.

'It's cold in here. I told them to make you a fire.'

'Yes. I told them to put it out.' She was sitting up in bed. She had a cold. Apart from that, she looked extraordinarily young and healthy and beautiful.

'You told them to put it out? Why?'

'I always sleep with no fire. And with my windows open.'

'Why?' Napoleon was becoming difficult, almost petulant.

'Why? Because it is healthy.'

'No.' He was determined and decisive. 'You have a cold. You'll make it worse. Pneumonia . . .'

She said, more firmly than him: 'It is not healthy to sleep with a fire in one's room, or with the windows shut. One must be cold at night, and have a draught. It is very much more healthy for me. My chest is not strong, therefore I need fresh air, cold air, at night.'

Napoleon, looking less young than he had done when

he entered the room, but still loving and patient, said, 'Louise, what did your father tell you?'

She knew the answer perfectly well. 'To obey you in all things.'

'Yes.' He was decisive again. 'I'll call your servants. They can make a new fire very quickly.'

'Oh, no.' She was quite clear on the point. 'I couldn't bear it.'

'Louise,' he said, with a bad attempt at a loving patient smile, 'I am accustomed to having a fire in my bedroom on cold nights.'

Her answers were all simplicity. 'But you mustn't. It's unhealthy.'

He went the other way about it. She was young, and to be reasoned with. He reasoned with her.

'Louise, a fire, a small fire, a moderate fire, is not unhealthy.'

'Oh, yes, it's terribly bad for you.'

He said, more firmly, 'I have had a fire in my bedroom all my life.' That he could be sure of, as a fact.

'That is why you have an unhealthy complexion.'

'Have I?' He was taken aback.

'Yes.'

He made a last feeble effort to hold on to what he knew to be good, and right, and French. 'A tiny fire . . . ?'

'No.' She was innocently absolutely firm. 'No, it's not possible.'

There was no point in arguing with her any longer: the argument was simply delaying the desired moment. He looked round at the several and various candelabra, each with its half-dozen candles burning. On that question, at least, there could be no quarrel.

He said, rather feebly for an Emperor, 'Well, I'll put the lights out.'

She said quickly, 'Oh, no, please. Not all.'

He was already snuffing the first of them. 'Why not? Is it healthy to have candles burning at night?'

'It's not a question of health.'

'Good. I'll put them out.'

'No. You mustn't.'

'Why not?'

She said, as if everyone knew it, 'I always have lights in my room at night.'

He had already decided to assert himself, if not as the Emperor, at least as the dominant male partner. 'Do you? I don't.'

She was very simple. 'I always do.'

'Why?'

'I am afraid.'

'Of the dark?'

She said, 'Of ghosts.'

He went on round the room, ruthlessly snuffing the candles, while he said, in the kindest, most loving voice, 'Dearest Louise. You have a husband now. You don't have to be afraid of ghosts. There's no reason to be afraid of anything.'

She said, 'Please.'

'Louise, what did your father tell you?'

'Please. I must have some light.'

He decided to be kind and loving and magnanimous. 'How many?'

'Five or six candles.'

There were five or six, or perhaps seven, still unsnuffed. He looked at them.

He said, 'One.'

She said, in a voice which he was to get to know better, a voice which was half a plea and half a command, 'No. Please, no. Five or six. I am used to five or six.'

He cried, 'One!'

He snuffed the last candles, leaving only one alight. He marched towards the bed, throwing off his dressing-gown. He was, after all, the Emperor, and not to be dictated to.

25. THE KING'S MOTHER

He was pleased, that first night, that she actually seemed to enjoy the loss of her virginity. He took it as a compliment when, only ten minutes later, she kissed him and whispered into his ear, 'Do it again.' He was enchanted when he found that he could, so soon afterwards, do it again.

In the morning, when he was back in his own bedroom, being shaved by Constant, Duroc came in to see him, and found him as lively as a cricket and as happy as a sandboy.

'Good morning, Duroc!'

'Good morning, Sire.'

'Well, did anyone remark on the change I made in the programme last night?'

Duroc was discreet as ever. 'It was assumed, Sire, that the archduchess was tired after her journey.'

Napoleon was much amused—so much so that Constant was obliged to stop shaving him, for fear of cutting his throat. Freed from the tyranny of the razor, Napoleon slapped Duroc on the back and roared with happy laughter.

'My dear fellow, let me tell you, you should have married a German girl! They make the best wives in the world! Fresh as roses, sweet, simple, docile, loving—!'

Napoleon spent the day in the Empress's rooms, much of the time alone with her.

They came down to the great dining-room in the evening, to eat their dinner in public. After dinner, there was music in the salon, Grassini singing, and Crescentini. The Emperor and the new Empress sat together, on chairs like thrones. The princes and nobles gave one ear to the music, and both eyes to Their Majesties. The Empress was in pink, and was pink-cheeked and bright-eyed, and looked marvellously healthy, positively blooming. The Emperor was very pale, not white, but a kind of pale yellow. He seemed to be having the greatest difficulty in keeping his eyes open. He managed to stay awake during the first group of songs by Crescentini; but then the orchestra played a saraband, and Napoleon's eyes closed, and he slept.

Marie-Louise saw Caroline smiling behind her hand, and looked at Napoleon, and discreetly jogged his elbow, and whispered, 'Wake up!'

Poor Napoleon, dragging himself back to waking. 'What . . . ? Ah . . . Yes . . . ?'

She whispered again. 'Don't go to sleep!'

'Ah . . . No . . .'

He blinked, pulled himself together, sat up straight in his chair. The saraband came to an end. He led the applause. Grassini came forward to sing, and he applauded her warmly. She sang, and Napoleon's eyes started closing again, and once again he sank into slumber.

Perhaps because he had slept, he was wakeful that night. At least, he woke up at three in the morning, and could not get to sleep again. He looked around: he could do so, there were five or six candles burning. He was shivering with cold: he could well shiver, there was no fire in the fireplace. He looked cautiously at Louise. She was sleeping, the very picture of a healthy young animal. He decided to slip away without waking her. But she woke.

'Napoleon . . . ?'

'Go to sleep again, darling.'

She snuggled up to him, before he could make his getaway from the bed. 'No . . .'

'Go to sleep . . .'

He tried gently to disengage himself from her, and to slide out from under the bedclothes. But she held him, murmuring, 'Darling, what are you doing?'

He had to say it. 'I'm going back to my own room.'

'No, you mustn't.'

'Darling, I'm cold.'

'No. I'll warm you.' She pressed herself against him with her full beautiful young breasts.

'Go to sleep, Louise. You must get some sleep. I'll see you at breakfast.'

'No. I've woken up now.'

'Please sleep.'

'No. Make love to me again.'

Her arms were round him, and her breasts and her loins rubbed against him. He had very little choice in the matter.

They were married legally, and then religiously, and she was an ardently loving wife, and he was, despite the difference in age, a really most attentive husband. He was hardly ever in his office, but always with her. He neglected his duties: that is to say, he neglected all his duties except the most important one of all, to get a child.

After two months there was a hope, then the hope was dashed to the ground. Corvisart, a prudent man, took the precaution of bringing Doctor Yvan with him when he came to break the bad news to the Emperor.

'I must confess, Sire, that Doctor Yvan and I were equally, and for excellent reasons, in error.'

The Emperor growled at him, 'There are no excellent reasons for error.'

'Sire, the Empress's periods are quite remarkably irregular. When I say "quite remarkably", I should add that this is not entirely unusual in a woman as young as she is: and I do not mean to imply that the irregularity indicates anything in the least abnormal in her general state of health. Her Majesty is as robustly healthy as one could possibly wish.'

Napoleon was not interested in Corvisart's additions and implications. Only one thing mattered.

'But she is not pregnant.'

'No, Sire.'

'Why not?'

Corvisart had expected the question, and had decided how to deal with it. 'Doctor Yvan and I have consulted together, Sire, and Yvan, perhaps more strongly than my-self, tends to believe—'

Napoleon had already turned abruptly to the other. 'Yvan? Well? What?'

Yvan, an excellent doctor but a poor politician, ac-cepted the risk, to Corvisart's delight. 'Her Majesty takes too many hot baths.'

'Too many? Or too hot?'

'Both, Sire.'

Napoleon swung round. 'Corvisart?'

Corvisart spoke as the good politician: 'It is a possible explanation.'

'She's fond of hot baths.'

Corvisart bowed. 'You might care to speak to her, Sire.'

'As I am myself. I take a hot bath every day. Very hot.'

Corvisart bowed again. 'You might care, Sire, to set her an example.'

Napoleon did indeed speak to his wife, only half an hour later, while she was sitting up in bed, shining and glowing with health, and making a late and very hearty breakfast.

She did not welcome his orders. He had to speak to her firmly.

'Louise, you are not to get up until two o'clock, so long as you have a trace of a sore throat. And you are certainly not to think of taking a bath.'

'I shall get dirty. I can't bear being dirty.'

'Louise, you can wash yourself all over, perfectly well, without taking a bath.'

'I like taking a bath.'

'Yes, I know.'

'It makes me warm at night.'

'If you want to be warm at night, you can have a fire here.'

'I can't have a fire at night. You know that.'

'Then you can have an extra blanket.'

'But that would be too heavy. I don't like the covers to be heavy.'

385

Napoleon was patience personified. 'Louise, my dearest one, my darling, do you know what you must give me?'

'A son.'

'Yes.'

'Yes, of course.'

He said, 'Please. Please. Anything else you want. But no baths.'

'Until I am pregnant.'

'Until you're pregnant. Then we can ask the doctors again.'

She thought about it, and said, 'Very well.'

He was greatly relieved. She was a good loyal docile wife. He kissed her hands, in gratitude. 'Darling, I must leave you for a moment.'

'Not for long.'

'No, of course not for long. I shall spend the whole afternoon with you. What shall we do? Shall we go for a drive?'

'Yes, let's.'

'Where shall we go?'

'I don't mind.'

'There are several places you must see, that I haven't shown you yet.'

'You can choose.'

What a truly good wife she was. More and more, every day, she was learning to leave all decisions to him, in all matters, great and small.

He said, 'Would you like to see Malmaison?'

She did not reply. He suddenly knew that he had made a mistake.

He said, 'It's a very pretty garden.'

She did not reply, but her eyes began to fill with tears.

He said, 'I only suggest it because it's a fine day, it's a very pleasant drive to Malmaison, it occurred to me that you might like to see the garden.'

Tears were rolling down her cheeks.

He said, 'If you don't want to go there, then there's nothing more to say. We'll go somewhere else. But it's nothing to cry about.'

But still she cried.

He said, 'Louise—dearest Louise—you don't have to meet Josephine. Ever. Unless you yourself decide that you want to meet her.'

Josephine had been allowed to come back to Malmaison, and had established herself there, in great style, though with a diminished entourage: only half as many ladies-in-waiting as she had had when she was a reigning monarch.

She had taken to playing patience, and to talking to Claire de Rèmusat while she did it. There was not much to do at Malmaison, most afternoons and most evenings: so she played patience, for several hours, from lunchtime onwards, four or five days of the week.

She said, 'Count Aldringen tells me, Marie-Louise received eighty or a hundred guests the other night, at the Tuileries. And to each one of them she said exactly the same words: "I am charmed to see you."'

'The Austrian Court is very stiff and formal. I suppose that's what they taught her to say.'

' "Stiff", that's the word Aldringen used. He gave an imitation of her. Like a great stiff clockwork doll.'

Claire said, 'She will learn, in time.'

'Will she? Aldringen's Austrian, too, but he's most amusing. He told me, Zamoyski came up to him afterwards, beaming with delight, and said that Marie-Louise had received him marvellously well. And Aldringen thought to himself, "Yes, Zamoyski is stupid enough to think that; and she is stupid enough to let him think it."'

'Aldringen is Austrian but not a Habsburg. The Habsburgs were never famous for their brains.'

'At the same reception, she said to Madame de Mortemart, "I have seen you somewhere before."'

'Really? That's incredible.'

'Of course, Madame de Mortemart said, "I have been one of Your Majesty's ladies-in-waiting for three months now" . . . I don't know how the Emperor puts up with such stupidity.'

Claire did not want to encourage her by agreeing with her too much; given encouragement, Josephine was likely to become hysterical. She said, peaceably, 'The Emperor has other things to occupy his mind.'

Josephine was not to be turned from her subject. 'Yes, he still has to decide what to do about the fifteen cardinals who refused to come to the wedding.'

'What can he do? He has imprisoned the Pope, but he can't give orders to the Pope. No one can, except God.'

Josephine was not to be turned from her progress towards hysteria. 'Count Lebzeltern heard the Emperor say, "They are trying to cast doubts on the legitimacy of this marriage." But the cardinals were doing more than that. They were denying that it was legitimate. And it was not. The Church in France had no power to annul my marriage. The Emperor and I were blessed by the Pope. Only the Pope has the power to undo that. He has not undone it. Napoleon is still married to me.'

Claire had heard this every day for a long time. She knew better than to say anything at this point.

'Napoleon will come to realize that I am still his wife, when he is bored out of his mind by her mindlessness—and by her childlessness. She won't have a child. He can't give her one. I know he can't. I don't believe in the Walewska child. That was just a trick, to try to persuade the world. The Tsar knew it was a trick; he wasn't deceived by it. And nor was I. Nor was anyone else with any sense.'

Claire had the sense to stay silent.

'Do you know what they call Marie-Louise, in the streets of Paris now? Claire, do you know what they call her?'

'Yes, Your Majesty, I do know.'

' "The Austrian woman." The same as they called Marie-Antoinette. They hated her, and they hate this one, too, in the same way. They want to get rid of her. They want me on the throne again. Because I was his good luck. They're superstitious about it. They're afraid that his luck has turned.'

Clair said, gently, 'Let us hope not, Your Majesty.'

Josephine felt the sense of the gentle reprimand. 'Yes, I hope not. I'm afraid it may have done. I am superstitious, too.'

She laid out new neat rows of patience cards.

She said, 'But Napoleon will come back to me.'

An hour later, a footman came in, with a letter on a salver, and brought it to Josephine.

She looked at it and knew it was from Napoleon.

'Thank you, Etienne.' She was always charming to servants. When he had gone, she tore the letter open and read it. She sat very still, but her other hand was mechanically disarranging the neat rows of cards.

She said at last, to Claire, 'The Emperor wishes me to be the first to know that she is pregnant.'

In the great salon of the Tuileries, Count Metternich bent over the new Empress's hand.

'Your Majesty, all Austria will be as delighted as all France, by the great news.'

'Thank you, Count.'

'Austria is, of course, already delighted by the evident happiness of your marriage.'

She was really a very simple and direct person, and she knew Metternich well enough not to be shy with him.

'Yes, we're very happy. He's not at all what I'd thought.'

'You have changed him, Your Majesty. You have tamed the terror of Europe.'

'Have I? I was frightened of him before I met him. But he really is kind and charming. He does whatever I want him to.'

'You're not frightened of him now.'

She laughed. 'I sometimes think he's frightened of me.'

It was almost time for Metternich to move on. He said, 'Your Majesty, with your permission, I shall later in the evening propose the health of the King of Rome.'

'Oh, yes, please do. I hope I shall have a boy.'

He said, 'We must not doubt it for an instant.'

Napoleon, vastly jovial, was at the centre of a circle of Bonapartes and admirers.

'He will be the King of Rome from the moment he is born: with the orders of the Legion of Honour and the Iron Cross of Italy pinned to his cradle. Napoleon Francis Charles Joseph: after his father, his Austrian grandfather, his Corsican grandfather, and his uncle the King of Spain.'

Caroline asked, 'What names if it's a girl?'

Napoleon laughed. 'Caroline, when did I ever fail to do what I set out to do?'

'Never, I agree.'

He spread his arms in a grand gesture. 'And after him, more sons. My parents had five sons, why shouldn't I? Every family should have five. One to succeed his father, two to be his chief lieutenants—'

'And the other two?'

'And the other two in case of accidents.' Napoleon led the general laughter.

Metternich smiled at his old friend Tallyrand. 'I'm glad to see that you are one of those called here to rejoice.'

'You and I made the marriage.'

'Yes. We are bound to rejoice.'

'At anything that makes another war between our two countries less probable.'

Metternich said lightly, 'For a moment I was afraid that you were going to say "less inevitable".'

Talleyrand shook his head, equally lightly. 'Nothing is inevitable, if only the world can convince Napoleon that he cannot conquer the world.'

'Is he open to conviction on that point?'

'He has had fourteen years as an irresistible conqueror. You do know, of course, who his two great heroes in history are? Alexander the Great, who had fourteen years of conquest and power, before he went mad. And Julius Caesar, who had fourteen years, before assassination forestalled his oncoming madness.'

Metternich looked at Talleyrand not quite with a sideways look, but almost.

'Prince, you are a man of peace, you would hardly wish . . . ?'

Talleyrand hastened to disclaim the thought. 'Good heavens, no. I detest all violence and all upheavals.'

'You and I must try to keep the world as it is.'

'My dear Metternich, I wish for no changes at all. It simply occurs to me that Austria, together with Russia, might be able to confine my Emperor's folly within its present limits.'

Metternich had mastered the art of looking as if he had not entirely seized the other person's meaning, and needed a clarification. 'Together with Russia—in a purely defensive alliance?'

Talleyrand had mastered the art of reassuring those who seemed to wish for reassurance, 'Purely defensive, that goes without saying.'

Metternich said, 'Yes, the thought has occurred to me too.'

'I'm sure.' They smiled at each other, each quite clear what the other had meant. Talleyrand said, 'I suppose this is a day for rejoicing. I am in favour of dynasties. I prefer founders to destroyers. But then, again, if the birth of a son reinforces my Emperor's belief that he is infallible and omnipotent, then there will be another upheaval; and his fourteen years will come to an end.'

They smiled at each other again. They were in perfect agreement.

Napoleon gazed at the baby in the cradle, and said, 'He is very like me.'

Marie Walewska said, 'He is the image of you.'

'Don't wake him. But I should like to see him when he is awake.'

'You shall see him whenever you please.'

They moved quietly away from the cradle, he holding her arm.

He said, 'Alexander.'

'Yes.'

'A good name.'

'A family name. My husband has accepted him as if he were his own son.'

'So he is Polish, and will be Count Walewska.'

'Yes.'

'I shall make him a French count too. I should like him to be at least half a Frenchman. He must serve in the French Army. All my sons must learn to lead Frenchmen in battle.' His eye gleamed at the thought. I'm delighted you've brought him to Paris. Are you proposing to stay here long?'

She said gently, 'As long as you wish me to.'

His voice was guarded, almost stern, though his words were carefully courteous. 'As long as you yourself wish, Marie. It is no longer a question of my wishes.'

'I always want to be near you.'

'As a friend,' he said warningly.

She had already decided to accept the word. 'Yes.'

She had accepted it. His voice softened. 'You must understand, my life has changed. It can only be as a friend.'

'I do already understand that.'

He said in a quick low voice, almost a murmur, 'Marie, if I could have married you, I would have: and he would have been named not Alexander but Napoleon; and he would have succeeded to the throne as Napoleon the Second.'

She refused to be sad at the thought. 'I never supposed there was any hope of our marrying.'

'I reached the point where nothing less than an Emperor's daughter would do.'

They looked at each other for a time without speaking. Then she said, 'People tell me you are happy with her.'

'Yes. Very happy.'

They were both realists, but kind to each other. She said, 'I'm glad.'

'She loves me. We suit each other. She will give me the one thing I need.'

'A Napoleon the Second.'

'Yes.' He decided to go further, and say what, out of kindness, he had not yet said. 'And I love her. She is simple, truthful, virtuous: everything that Josephine was not. She has made me into a faithful husband, at last.'

Marie smiled. 'A Corsican father of a family.'

He smiled in reply. 'It is what nature intended me to be.' He took out his watch. 'I must go back to her, or she'll ask me where I've been.'

'Is she jealous?'

'She wants me by her side twenty-four hours a day. As indeed I might be, if only she had a fire in her bedroom.' He went to Marie and kissed her hand. 'Good-bye, Marie. Thank you for not reproaching me.'

'I have nothing to reproach you with.'

He leant forward and gently kissed her forehead. She passively accepted the kiss, not offering her cheek or her mouth.

'You are the only woman who has ever loved me for myself alone.'

'Is that true of me? I think first I loved the hero, the liberator.'

He shook his head, in warning. 'Be careful of those words, Marie. A hero is a man who wins battles, that's all. A liberator is a man who wins battles against your own particular enemy.' He was ready to go. 'If there's anything you want, Duroc will arrange it. I shall see you —and our son, when he's awake.'

She said softly, 'I should like him to see you.'

At the door, on the point of leaving, he said, 'I may quite soon please you by fighting your particular enemy again.'

'Russia?'

'The Tsar is turning against me . . . Well, I am still a man who wins battles.'

He bowed again, and went.

As the nine months went past, and with each of them the Empress grew heavier and more fretful and more apprehensive of what might happen, the Emperor found himself progressively incapable of thinking of anything except the birth, and of organizing anything except the announcement of the birth and the subsequent celebrations.

Berthier had to be patient with him when Napoleon sought confirmation for the hundredth time.

'Berthier. The artillery—?'

'I shall be in charge of it myself, Sire.'

'The guns will fire—?'

'On my word of command, Sire.'

'How many—?'

'A salute of a hundred and one guns, Sire.'

'For a boy.'

'Yes, Sire.'

'And—?'

'And, Sire?' Berthier was puzzled. He did not understand Napoleon's meaning.

'And for a girl?'

'Ah. Twenty guns, Sire.'

Berthier was somewhat disturbed that the Emperor was seriously considering the possibility of having a daughter.

In fact, Napoleon was becoming obsessed by the impossibility of predetermining whether it would be son or daughter. He incessantly questioned Doctor Corvisart, and Doctor Yvan, and the Imperial accoucheur Doctor Dubois.

'Dubois. Is there any way of telling—at any time before the child comes out, and can be seen—any way of telling what sex it is?'

'None, Sire.'

'I have heard of old wives' tales.'

'They are nothing more than old wives' tales, Sire.'

'All the signs, the pains, the labour, the birth itself—all these are exactly the same for a boy as for a girl?'

'Exactly the same, Sire.'

Napoleon seized Dubois by his shoulders and stared into his face. 'Dubois. If my child is a boy—and you deliver him well—I shall make you a rich man.'

Dubois, poor fellow, with the possibility of riches and the possibility of disaster, became almost as apprehensive as the Empress.

Corvisart, suavely imperturbable, took on himself the responsibility of keeping the Emperor informed of events. The position of informant was a good one for him. If things went well, he could be the first to take the credit. If things went wrong, he could at once start to put the blame on Yvan or Dubois.

He came to the Emperor's room in the evening.

'Sire, the Empress's birth-pangs have begun.'

'Then why aren't you with her?'

'There is no cause for alarm, Sire. Nothing will happen for two or three hours yet. Perhaps longer. These are only the first pangs. Doctor Yvan and Doctor Dubois are with the Empress. Her Majesty is in the best of health.'

'I shall go to her.'

'I was about to tell you, Sire: Her Majesty asks to see you.'

Napoleon was out of the room before Corvisart had completed his reply. Corvisart sighed, and hurried after him: whatever happened, he had the task of calming and soothing the Emperor—not the easiest man in the world to soothe. And the Empress had already shown that she was going to be troublesome.

Napoleon marched through Louise's salon, where the court officials and their ladies were hastily assembling; through Louise's private rooms, where the Imperial family and the high dignitaries were coming together to witness the birth of the heir to the Empire; and into Louise's bedroom, where she was sitting in an armchair, vastly pregnant and vastly frightened by the whole business.

'My dearest. How are you?'

'Not well.' She clung to his arm.

'Be brave.'

'It hurts so much. In my front. But more in my back.'

Doctor Yvan said, 'If Her Majesty could walk about a little . . .'

'Louise, can you walk?'

'I'll try.'

Napoleon and Yvan helped her to her feet. Napoleon supported her while she walked a few steps, totteringly.

'Is that better? Does it help?'

She whispered, 'Napoleon, I think I'm going to die.'

'No. No, my darling. You are simply feeling what every woman feels at this time—'

She felt a sudden pang, and gave a great cry of pain. Napoleon panicked.

'Corvisart! Yvan! Dubois! Get her to bed!'

The doctors took charge of her. When she was in bed, Napoleon walked aside with Corvisart.

'Is she starting to give birth?'

'Not yet, Sire.'

'Why did she scream like that?'

'She is unaccustomed to pain.'

Napoleon went and looked down at her. She lay there groaning, her eyes shut, the Duchess of Montebello holding one of her hands, the Countess of Montesquiou holding the other.

He went back to Corvisart. 'When will the child be born?'

'As I told you, Sire. In two or three hours, perhaps longer.'

'What should I do?'

'Whatever you please, Sire.'

Louise moaned, 'Napoleon . . .'

He went quickly to the bed.

'My darling.'

'Napoleon, don't leave me.'

'Of course not, my dearest.'

'Napoleon, you won't let me die? Please don't let me die.'

'My darling, there is no question of your dying.'

Dubois was lying out on a table, in neat rows, his forceps and scalpels and other instruments of his trade. Napoleon went and looked down at them. Corvisart joined him. Napoleon picked up what looked like a giant pair of nutcrackers.

'These?'

Corvisart was as bland as ever. 'In case of problems, Sire.'

'What problems?'

'We expect no problems, Sire. But it is always possible that there may be problems.'

The hours of the night dragged by. Servants brought wine and food to refresh the waiting dignitaries and officials. The Empress whimpered and shuddered and groaned. Napoleon strode up and down her boudoir, unable to bear her groans but unable to leave her rooms. After midnight Corvisart came out to him.

'Her Majesty has fallen asleep for the moment, Sire.'

'Asleep? Why? How?'

'The pains have eased.'

'Is that normal?'

'Everything is normal. The child will not be born for a time yet—we think, not until four o'clock at the earliest. I advise you, Sire, to follow Her Majesty's example, and get some sleep.'

Napoleon went back to his own rooms. Constant prepared a hot bath for him, the way the Emperor liked it: hot almost beyond human endurance. Afterwards, Constant rubbed him with eau-de-Cologne. The Emperor was in his dressing-gown, still purple and sweaty, when Doctor Dubois burst into the room, ghastly-faced, distracted, frantic, babbling almost incoherently.

'Sire . . . Sire . . . Sire . . .'

Napoleon stared at him. 'Well? Is she dead?'

'Sire . . . She . . . Her Majesty . . . She . . .'

Napoleon said, in a hard high voice, not knowing what he was saying, 'If she is dead we must bury her.'

Dubois tried to put his words together. 'No, not dead, Sire . . . But the waters have broken too soon . . . It happens once in a thousand cases . . . And the child is being born askew . . .'

Napoleon cried, 'Well? Deliver the child!'

Dubois babbled, 'Sire, I shall have to use instruments— may I have your permission to use instruments?'

Napoleon shouted, 'Deliver it! Go on! What are you waiting for?'

'Sire . . . Sire . . .' He reeled like a drunken man. 'Sire, it may be a question of the mother or the child . . . It will be a question . . . Probably . . . Sire, which am I to save?'

Napoleon stared at him.

Dubois said, 'It is not for me to choose . . .'

In her bedroom, Louise screamed in terror.

Madame de Montesquiou said, 'Your Majesty, I have had two children born like this, there is nothing to be afraid of.'

Louise did not listen to her. She knew perfectly well why Napoleon had divorced Josephine, why Napoleon had married her. There was only one reason: to get an heir for the Empire.

She cried out, over and over again, 'I am an Empress! Must I die because I'm an Empress?'

Napoleon stared at Dubois.

Napoleon said in a dry whisper, 'Save the mother.'

He held Louise's hand throughout the operation. Corvisart and Yvan pinned the Empress down, one at her head, one at her feet. Madame de Montebello was like a madwoman. The ladies-in-waiting were in hysterics. The Empress sobbed and screamed without stopping.

Afterwards, Napoleon staggered out of the bedroom, his face ashen grey, panting and swallowing as if he had just vomited.

Hortense went quickly to him, but did not dare to ask. No one dared to ask.

He said, 'It is over. She is saved.'

She managed to say 'And the child?'

'Saved.'

She managed to say, 'Is it a boy?'

He said, 'Berthier?'

'Sire?'

Napoleon could hardly stand. He clutched at the arm of a chair.

'Berthier, give the command to fire a salute . . . of a hundred and one guns.'

26. 'DEAREST LOUISE'

Josephine wrote to him immediately, to congratulate him on the birth. He wrote back to her the next day:

My dear, I have received your letter, and I thank you. My son is big and is thriving. I hope that he will do well. He has my chest, my mouth and my eyes. I hope that he will fulfil his destiny.

That was Napoleon, flinging down on to a piece of paper the things that were uppermost in his mind, caring only for meaning, not for style. But the letter had a second paragraph that troubled her, because it might have more than one meaning:

I am always most happy with Eugène. He has never caused me any sorrow.

Taken at its face value, it was a compliment to Eugène's ability and amiability. But might there be a second meaning—that Eugène had never caused the Emperor any sorrow, though, of course, his mother had? Or, though his sister had? Hortense was divorced from Louis Bonaparte, at last. The Emperor had seemed to forgive her, and seemed as fond of her as ever: but perhaps—?)

Josephine decided that she was being foolish. Whenever Napoleon had wished to reprimand her or Hortense, he had spoken quite plainly enough to leave no doubt in the matter. It was not long since she had received yet another of his tirades, on the old familiar subject. The revenues of Malmaison and Navarre were eaten up—more than eaten up—by the expenses. She was finding it quite impossible to live on her allowance of three million francs a year. Napoleon did not understand why she should find it impossible.

She came back to Malmaison for the spring, and had half a hope that she might be invited to visit the Imperial baby: though she knew that when Napoleon himself had last consented to see her, the previous summer at Malmaison, Marie-Louise in her bedroom at the Tuileries had cried without stopping the whole day long.

In June she returned to Navarre. She had decided to celebrate her birthday there, where the sound of the festivities would hardly be heard in Paris. She was, of course, celebrating the day of her birth, but not the year of it. There were speeches and poems in her honour: none of them were so tactless as to mention her age.

She was forty-eight. Marie-Louise was nineteen.

Louise was pale and heavy-eyed and out of sorts. She thought she needed medicine: Corvisart prescribed pills for her. She decided that she would feel better in bed: Corvisart obligingly ordered her to bed.

Napoleon came hurrying to see her. She was of the opinion that the best thing for her would be for him to come to bed with her. He was not as eager to oblige her as Corvisart had been.

'My dearest Louise, I am simply thinking of your health.'

She pouted. 'My health is not so bad as that.'

'Your health is not as good as it was before the birth. You haven't recovered yet.'

'I have not completely recovered yet, but I have recovered enough.'

'You are less well than you used to be. I must look after you.'

She turned her head away and said, 'I think you don't want to make love to me any more.'

'What?' He was passionate with indignation. 'Darling I want to make love to you as much as ever I did!'

'As much?'

'Yes!'

'Then why don't you? As much?'

He had explained to her before. He had to explain to her again. 'Because of your health.'

She said, mutinously, 'I think my health would be better if you made love to me as much.'

'I do not want to take the risk of your becoming pregnant again. For a time.'

'How much time?'

'Say, for a year.'

'A year?'

'Well, perhaps something like a year.'

She said, plaintively, 'Don't you want more sons?'

'Yes, in time.'

'I would take the risk.'

At last he could say something that he felt strongly—violently—and also truthfully.

'Would you? I wouldn't. I am not so much in love with the human race that I would willingly live through another birth like that.'

The blood, and the screaming, and the great clumsy instruments like tongs, like nutcrackers, like sabres.

She was woebegone. 'I think you only wanted one son. And now you have him, you are tired of me.'

'Louise, my dearest, as soon as you are perfectly well again, I shall make love to you as often as you wish.' He kissed her cheek. 'Particularly if you come to my room.'

She snuggled up to him. 'No, your room is too hot. You must come here.'

'Gladly, if only you would have . . .'

He decided not to reopen the question of the fire. In any case, it was difficult to talk to her seriously. She had recently developed a habit of rubbing her breasts against him, to excite his senses. She was doing it again. He moved away from her.

'My dearest, you must see that my room would be more convenient. I'd be closer to my work. As you know, I often have to work at night. Sometimes for a great deal of the night.'

'You usen't to.'

'Exactly. I lost most of a year, getting married to you and having a child. Now I have to make up for it. I have things to do. I have a war in Spain. I have an Empire of ninety million people to organize—'

'You have ministers who can do it for you.'

'My dear, this is not Austria, where your father leaves everything to Metternich. In my Empire, I leave nothing to anyone.'

She would never understand. She wanted a husband who would be with her every hour of the day, every day of the year; and every hour of the night too, in a freezing cold bedroom.

He spoke to the Duchess of Montebello. He did not care for the duchess, nor she for him; but she was in Louise's confidence and seemed to have some influence over her.

'Madame de Montebello, would you be so good as to explain to the Empress that she should try to please me in small things—for example, by having a fire in her room at night?'

As always, she gave him a frosty answer. 'It is not for me to teach the Empress her duty, Sire.'

He could be as cold as her, and angrier with it. 'Madame, it is for you to advise the Empress on the customs of my court. The principal custom of my court is to do what will please me.'

Louise continued to be pale and tearful. Napoleon sent for Corvisart.

'What is wrong with the Empress?'

'Hypochondria, Sire. She imagines her ailments.'

'So what are those pills you're giving her?'

'Breadcrumbs and sugar, Sire.'

It was a consolation to talk to Berthier, who understood him better than a wife.

'I was not born for the petty problems of domesticity.'

'You have too great a mind, Sire.' From Berthier it was not flattery. Berthier was sincere.

'Well, I shall do one more great thing before I settle down to being a husband and a father. Berthier, you and I will go on one last expedition.'

'Where to, Sire?'

'Russia.'

Napoleon looked for the answering gleam in Berthier's eye. It was not there. Was Berthier too old, at last? He was fifty-eight. Was it time to think of choosing a new right-hand man?

Berthier said, 'Forgive me, Sire, but we are not at war with Russia.'

'The Tsar has played fast and loose with me. For a year now he has been talking eternal peace and brotherly love; but for a year, in secret, he has been building up an army to attack me.'

'Are you sure of that, Sire?'

'My incompetent agents were slow to find it out; but, yes, I am sure of it at last. Well, I can talk peace as plausibly as he can. And his army will be no match for mine.'

'I am not clear, Sire, why the Tsar should wish to attack you.'

'The Tsar's vanity is such that he cannot bear to be the second man in Europe. I must teach him that there is one first, and no second.'

Berthier coughed, and stared at the ground. Certainly, he was becoming slower at grasping the essentials of a situation.

'Sire, might it not be better to finish the war in Spain first?'

Other signs of ageing: caution, and desire for delay. Napoleon dismissed the thought of Spain.

'Spain is an island, cut off from Europe by the Pyrenees. The English army can do us no harm there, any more than it can in England. The only danger is if Russia joins with England and they attack us on two fronts. We must eliminate Russia before that can happen.'

Berthier listened with his invariable patient care to what the Emperor was saying. The Emperor's argument

made no good sense to him, but Berthier had been wrong
before, and the Emperor had been right, and Berthier's
strength was not in deciding on the masterstroke but in
organizing it. He kept his counsel, and said, 'Transport?
Supplies?'

'I want all the necessary transport for an army of half
a million men, starting from somewhere in Germany and
moving to Moscow. See to it, Berthier. Find it, com-
mandeer it, make it, build it. As quickly as possible and as
secretly as possible.'

'It will cost a lot of money.'

'Come to my strongroom at the Tuileries, I'll show you
four hundred million francs in gold.' He seized Berthier's
arm. The old warhorse must still be capable of enthusiasm: Napoleon had to make him feel it. 'The cost is not
important. We must strike this last great blow. Then we
shall have peace, and grow fat, with nothing to worry
about but our wives.'

(Berthier had married a German princess, and become
brother-in-law and cousin to the King of Bavaria. He was,
in any case, a prince twice over, marshal, Grand Chamberlain, Master of the Hounds, Vice-Constable of the
Empire. Napoleon had made him all those things.)

Berthier's eye showed what was perhaps not enthusiasm,
but was certainly love for the Emperor and willingness to
follow him to the ends of the earth. Very well: Napoleon had fire in his belly enough for two.

Napoleon said, 'Berthier, I want to bequeath to my son
a world without enemies. I can do that only if I have
made myself the master of the world.'

Louise was still keeping to her bed. After the reception,
Napoleon went to call on her.

'Hortense asked after your health.'

'That was nice of her. I like Hortense.'

He was encouraged by the response. 'She had a request
to make.'

'Oh, yes?'

'Which I must refer to you.'

'Whatever Hortense wants.'

'She asked that her mother should be allowed . . .' He was looking at Louise. Her face had suddenly shut down tight. He started again, and said the words more firmly. 'She asked that Josephine should be allowed to see the King of Rome.'

Louise said, 'No.'

'My dear, the request is a very natural one. Josephine agreed to my divorcing her, so that I could marry you and have a son. Well, we have a son. A fine healthy son. It's not strange that Josephine should want to see him.'

Louise sat tight-faced and silent.

'Josephine doesn't have to come here. You don't have to meet Josephine, nor do I. The baby doesn't have to go to Malmaison. A meeting-place could be arranged, where she could look at him for a moment.'

Louise's mouth opened for just long enough to say, 'No.'

'A moment. A moment only.'

'No. I don't want her to see him.'

'Darling, what harm could it possibly do?'

'No. I won't discuss it.'

It was useless to discuss it. He gave up. He would ask her again when she was in a better mood.

She said, 'Come to bed.'

'I must have another hour with Berthier yet, then an hour with Duroc—'

'They can wait till tomorrow. Come to bed. I am quite well enough.'

The room was distinctly chilly. He glanced at the fireplace. It was empty.

'Louise, did Madame de Montebello speak to you today?'

'Yes, we talked for a long time. Why?'

'But did she speak to you?'

'What about?'

'The question of a fire.'

'No, she didn't.' Louise stared at him blankly. 'Why?'

Again, it was useless to discuss it. Again, he gave up.

'Darling, I really must go and do some work. If I can finish it soon enough—'

'Please.'

'Then I shall come and wake you.'

'Please.'

'But, in case I can't—good night, my dearest . . .'

He kissed her fondly on the cheek, then stood up again, ready to go. Louise picked up a handkerchief and wiped her cheek, where he had kissed her.

'Louise, why do you always do that, these days, when I kiss your cheek?'

'You mean, wiping myself?'

'Yes.'

'It is a habit, I suppose.'

He said, 'Do I disgust you?'

'Oh, no. Not at all. I do the same with the King of Rome.'

'Do you?'

'Yes.'

'Always?'

'Yes. You should be here when I see him every morning. You would see me wiping my cheek just like that.'

He said, in a curiously flat voice, 'You see him every morning.'

'Yes, for ten minutes, while I am dressing. Madame de Montesquiou brings him to me here, then she takes him away.'

He said, in the same flat voice, 'Ten minutes.'

She said, 'Oh, and I see him in the evening, too, when I am dressing for dinner.'

'For ten minutes?'

'Five or ten. Why?'

It was the first time he had really felt the difference, and the distance, between a Corsican Bonaparte and an Austrian Habsburg.

Josephine was waiting in the garden of Bagatelle, the charming little house—it was hardly a house, one would call it a pavilion—that Napoleon had bought in the Bois de Boulogne.

Josephine looked eagerly, and looked every way, and saw Madame de Montesquiou in the distance, coming towards her along one of the paths, pushing a baby-carriage. Her heart was already beating strongly. Now it beat as if it would break. She did not know at all clearly what emotions she was feeling, or whether she was more happy than unhappy or the other way round. But, whatever she felt, it was a kind of love, it had a great deal of love in it, for her heart was full of love and overflowing.

'Your Majesty . . .'

'Madame de Montesquiou . . .' They knew one another of old.

'May I present the King of Rome?'

'How very kind of you to bring him.'

'I bring him here every day, when it's fine. The air is so much purer than in the city.'

Josephine looked into the carriage, at a handsome boy-child a few months old. It was extraordinary to her to see the child she should herself have had; the child that, if hers, would have kept her on the throne; the child for whose sake she had had to make her reluctant sacrifice.

The King of Rome was awake. He gazed at Josephine, and she at him, for a long time. She wanted him to smile. He did not smile, but looked at her steadily, seriously, holding her eyes with his own.

She said, 'Yes, he has his father's mouth and eyes. He's very like the Emperor.'

'Yes.'

'He's beautiful.'

'Yes. And strong.'

Josephine felt an irrational delight at finding that she could see a great deal of Napoleon in the child, but nothing of Marie-Louise (she had never seen Marie-Louise, but had heard her description a thousand times, from Hortense and from everyone). The child was not in the least like Marie-Louise, therefore the child might have been

Josephine's, could have been Josephine's, should have been Josephine's and would have looked exactly the same.

She said, almost humbly, 'May I perhaps, for a moment . . . hold him?'

Madame de Montesquiou gently picked the baby up, out of the carriage, and put him into Josephine's arms. She held him softly—she was good at holding babies, she had held so many in her time, her own, Eugène's children, Hortense's children, and nieces and great-nieces and cousins without end. She made little baby noises to reassure the King of Rome that she was an expert baby-holder and would not dream of dropping him.

She couldn't help it: her eyes started to fill with tears. She pressed the child more warmly to her soft bosom, then to her soft cheek. She kissed the child's face over and over again, with little gentle kisses. He was so beautiful, and he was Napoleon's son. She wanted to devour him with kisses.

Napoleon came from the house and saw her with the baby. She did not see him. He stood and watched her as she embraced his son, hugging him, kissing him and never wiping her cheek. Even at a distance, he knew from the look of her that she was crying. He himself was on the point of tears.

He waited, looking, until evidently Josephine was too overcome with emotion to hold the baby any longer, and gave him back to Madame de Montesquiou.

Then Napoleon went quietly to her. She did not see him until he spoke.

'Josephine.'

She turned and saw him and said, 'Thank you.'

He took her gently by the shoulders and kissed her wet cheek. She did not wipe off the kiss.

She said, 'And my warmest thanks also to your wife, for letting me see him.'

Madame de Montesquiou had put the King of Rome back in his carriage. Discreetly, she wheeled him away, out of earshot.

Napoleon said, 'Louise doesn't know.'

'Doesn't . . .'

'Please be silent about this visit.'

'If you say so, of course I shall.'

'I should prefer Louise not to find out.'

'Does she dislike me so much?'

'She is jealous of you.'

She said, 'Who am I, now, for anyone to be jealous of me?'

'Her emotions are simple and direct. She knows that I loved you for a number of years.'

Josephine turned away and plucked a leaf from a tree, and said, 'I should like to meet her. May I meet her?'

'No.'

'To show her that she needn't be jealous.'

'You must never meet her.'

'Never?'

He said—not reproaching her with lack of understanding, but simply trying to bring her to understand—'My dear Josephine, you are Hortense's mother, and Louise is eight years younger than Hortense. She imagines you as being old—an old woman, lined, grey-haired, sixty, eighty. She consoles herself with that thought. If she were to see you as you are, still beautiful, still desirable, she would want me to send you away, out of France, to Italy—no, to America, to the furthest corner of the earth. Do you want that? No. You are not too unhappy at Malmaison. Leave things as they are.'

They walked twenty steps together, along a tree-lined alley, in silence.

She said, 'He is a beautiful child.'

'I hope he will grow up to be a good Emperor.'

'I'm sure he will.'

They had stopped, and were looking at each other, into each other's faces.

He said, 'You have tear-marks on your cheek. May I wipe your cheek?'

'Yes, please.' She smiled. 'But please be careful. The rouge may come off. I use rouge these days.'

He smiled, too, at her vanity. 'You always did. Though you never needed to.'

'Ah, but now I am less of a liar. I have no reason to lie.'

Gently, with his handkerchief, he wiped off the tear-stain. She half-hoped that he would lean forward and kiss her cheek. He thought of kissing her, but decided against it. They were friends, they had arrived at friendship: that was good, that was proper.

She said, 'Shall I see the King of Rome again? I should like to.'

'I'll try to arrange it.'

'Shall I see you again?'

'I may be going away soon.'

'Another war? No, I won't ask, I shall read it in the newspapers. May I ask you something quite different?'

He was good-humoured. 'Anything, so long as it's not about war.'

'If I had had a son by you . . . a King of Rome . . . ?'

She left the question unfinished. She did not need to finish it.

He said, 'I would never have divorced you.'

'Do you say that to make me happier?'

'No. Does it make you happier?'

'Yes.'

They walked on again. He said, 'My dearest Josephine, make *me* happier, too.'

'Can I do that?'

'You are still living far beyond your means. Last month I had to pay your debts again—another million francs, for clothes, jewellery, furniture, works of art—'

He broke off, as she caught his eye, with a twinkle in hers.

She said, 'You do not change.'

'Nor you.'

'Dear Napoleon, you've always paid my debts.'

'Yes. I suppose I always shall.'

She touched his hand with hers for a moment.

'Thank you for not changing.'

She drove back to Malmaison with the curtains of her carriage drawn, so that no one would know that she had been at Bagatelle, and so that no one could see that she was very happy, and very proud, and very sad, and crying.

In council, Napoleon continued what seemed to the members to have become his never-ending quarrel with Talleyrand.

'Well, Prince? Are we to be favoured with your views?'

'I think everyone knows them, Sire, since I have never cared to conceal them.'

'Yes. You are my prophet of doom.'

'Your man of peace, Sire.'

'A poor boast. You have made my peace treaties, at my dictation, on my terms, after my victories. Any man could have done it.'

'I have in all those treaties sought the essential of peace: a balance of power.'

'Ah. You think yourself a realist.'

'Yes, Sire.'

'I am more of a realist than you. There will be no peace in Europe while I have enemies who can combine to destroy me.'

'I agree, Sire, that the most lasting peace is an uninhabited desert.'

'The only lasting peace is a single Europe with a single master. Read my career, Talleyrand. Everything points towards that, everything leads towards that; and that is the inevitable end.' He turned to the others, terrible in his contempt. 'Are there any more "men of peace" among you?'

King Joachim of Naples drawled, 'Delighted to lead the cavalry, Sire, as always.'

Silence.

Napoleon said, 'Gentlemen, I have an Empire, I have a son, I hold the future in my hands. All that is needed is one last great blow; and your sons will be dukes and princes and kings, after you.'

Louise went with him as far as Dresden. From Dresden, she was to return to Paris, and he was to ride onwards to Russia with the greatest army the world had ever seen, and finally make himself the undisputed master of the world.

He was to leave at half-past three in the morning. He was up and dressed an hour before that, in high spirits, humming a tune. Louise was loving and plaintive.

'Will you be gone long?'

She had asked him the question a hundred times. He was patient with her.

'No, my dear, not long.'

'How long?'

'Don't you know what my young officers call it? "A six months' shooting-party".'

'Six months is a long time.'

'It may not be half so long. If the Russians fight me on their frontier, it will be all over much sooner than that. In two months, perhaps.'

'But if they don't fight you on their frontier?'

'Then I shall march to Moscow, and install myself in the Kremlin, and send for you. And we shall have parties and dances, as if we were in Paris.'

'I shall be very sad and unhappy until I see you again.'

He kissed her, warmly, affectionately.

'You are a good wife.'

'Am I?'

'Dearest Louise, I am very glad that I married you.'

'I love you. So I don't ever want you to go away from me.' She embraced him and clung to him, kissing him. 'Two months. Not more than two months. Promise me.'

He said, between kisses, 'I promise. Not more than two months.'

She let him go at last, and he moved away from her, in a military mood, humming his tune again.

'Why do you hum that?'

'Was I?' He laughed. 'Constant tells me I always hum that when I'm off on a new campaign.'

'What is it? The tune?'

'It's called, "Marlborough is going to the wars".'

She looked at him doubtfully. 'I think you like going to the wars.'

'My darling, I'm a soldier, it's my trade.'

She said, 'I wish you weren't so happy.'

But he couldn't help it, he was undeniably, exuberantly happy. He caught Louise in his arms.

'Louise, do you know that I shall have been a great conqueror for more years than anyone else in the history of the world?'

He kissed her, triumphantly.

'And when I come back—'

She said, '—in two months—'

He agreed, '—in two months—all wars will be over, for always; and our son the King of Rome will only have to stretch out his arms, and the world will be his.'

27. THE EMPRESS REGENT

In June 1812, Napoleon issued a proclamation to his Grand Army:

> This second war against Russia will be as glorious for French arms as the first one was: but this time we shall make a peace which will be lasting: we shall put an end to the fatal influence which Russia has exercised in Europe.

He crossed the Russian frontier with four hundred and fifty thousand men. Another hundred and fifty thousand were in reserve.

In June 1813, Napoleon was in Dresden again, where he had started from, where he had parted from Louise.

The 'six months' shooting party' had lost him half a million men, some killed by the Russians, most killed by disease, famine, exhaustion, exposure: by a winter which the French had never imagined, and which they did not begin to believe until they died of it.

The Russian Army followed Napoleon into Germany. Prussia declared war on France. With an army of survivors and new recruits, Napoleon beat the Prussians at Lützen, pushed back the Russians at Bautzen.

He made a truce. The three armies all needed a time to tend their wounded and to count their dead.

Count Metternich, Foreign Minister of neutral Austria, chief adviser to Napoleon's father-in-law, came to Dresden, sent for by Napoleon.

He was escorted along the never-ending corridors of the Marcolini Palace by General Bertrand, Napoleon's new Grand Marshal: Duroc had been killed at Bautzen.

And how many others were dead now, of his most

trusted lieutenants? A few of the remaining few were gathered by the door of Napoleon's room. Berthier, Eugène, Caulaincourt and Marshal Ney, Prince of the Moskwa, bravest of the brave.

Berthier came forward to meet Metternich. 'My dear Count . . .'

Metternich bowed. 'My dear Prince . . .'

Berthier took him by the arm and led him away from the others, to say into his ear, 'Do not let him make you forget that Europe needs peace: especially France: France wishes for nothing but peace.'

Metternich inclined his head, to show that he thoroughly understood the message—indeed, that he was in complete agreement with it—and went on towards the door which Bertrand had opened.

Napoleon was standing: a tactic that Metternich knew well. Napoleon did not sit to receive visitors who were taller than himself, and whose advantage in height might give them notions of superiority. Metternich, however, did not immediately recognize why Napoleon wore a sword at his side, and held his hat in his hand. He supposed that it was to give him the impression that there was very little to be said—that Napoleon wished to leave (leave the room, leave the palace, leave Dresden, perhaps) as soon as the interview was ended—that the interview would, essentially, consist of Napoleon's making a statement, and Metternich's agreeing with it. Perhaps it was also to be deduced that Napoleon's being in full uniform, with hat and sword, was meant to signify that his martial ardour was undiminished, that he was ready for a battle at a moment's notice—at the drop, perhaps, of his hat, he would draw his sword?

Napoleon's face and figure were less well designed to impress. The complexion was pasty, with a yellowish tinge, almost as if he were sickening for jaundice. The eyes were dull, lacklustre, with muddied whites. The belly had grown to be a pot. Elegant Metternich, four years younger than Napoleon, felt fourteen years younger, and was pleased by the feeling.

The interview began, of course, with courtesies.

'Well, Metternich? How is your master, my father-in-law?'

'The Emperor Francis is in the best of health, Your Majesty.'

'Convey to him my most affectionate greetings.'

'I shall do so, Your Majesty.'

'And tell him that his daughter the Empress Marie-Louise and his grandson the King of Rome are equally in the best of health.'

'He will be glad to know that, Your Majesty.'

'They're in Paris, of course. But the Empress writes to me every day. I've appointed her my Regent while I'm away from France.'

'So I believe.'

'Yes, she's a good wife, and she's become a good Frenchwoman. She makes an excellent Regent. I have absolute trust in her.'

'I'm sure she deserves it.'

It was necessary to foresee the moment when the courtesies would suddenly come to an end. A diplomat must never feel, nor show, surprise.

Napoleon said, 'I only wish I could say the same of her father.'

The moment had come. Metternich was ready for it with a charming smile and the air of sharing a joke.

'Your Majesty—the Emperor of Austria is not a Frenchman.'

Napoleon, not to be outdone, went further than a smile. He laughed. He said, with the greatest joviality, 'Does he want to go to war with me, then? Does he?'

'No, Your Majesty.'

'Does he want to be beaten by me again?'

Still smiling, as if the joke was still a good one. 'My Emperor is not at war with you, Your Majesty.'

'Does he intend to be?'

'He has no intention of being at war with anyone.'

It was important to foresee the moment when Napoleon would suddenly stop smiling. The moment had come.

Napoleon said harshly, rudely, into Metternich's face, 'You mean, he has no intention, but it will happen. So be it. I've knocked him off his throne three times already, and put him back on it three times. I do not guarantee to put him back on it the fourth time.'

Metternich was imperturbable. 'That is understood.'

'We shall meet in Vienna. I shall be there with my army, as before. Is there any point in our talking now?'

Metternich saw that he had guessed right about the hat and the sword. They were for Napoleon to make what, on the stage, they call a false exit.

Metternich said, 'It is for you to say, Your Majesty. It was at your request that I came here from Vienna.'

'Well? If we are to talk. What would you care to discuss?'

It was time for Metternich to lead and not follow. 'May I put my Emperor's view more positively?'

'If you can.'

'He wishes to bring about a lasting peace in Europe. As he supposes you do.'

'I have always striven for a lasting peace.'

'Nevertheless, you are still at war with England, you are at war with Russia, with Prussia—'

Napoleon cried, in a voice that rose above Metternich's, 'I have smashed the Prussian army at Lützen. I have thrown the Russians back at Bautzen. Two great victories within eighteen days. Does Austria want to take its turn?'

Metternich said, with well-bred sorrow in his tones, 'While we speak of these victories, may I offer my regrets at the death of some of your best generals? In particular, Marshal Duroc and Marshal Bessières?'

'They were soldiers. Soldiers get killed.'

'And also my regrets at the death in these battles of so many more Frenchmen than of their enemies?'

Napoleon turned his eyes on to Metternich. The eyes were not bright, gleaming, as they once had been; but there was a massive hardness in them.

'You do not understand war, Metternich. We won. The only thing that matters is winning.'

They were cast in their parts for the play they were acting: the rough soldier, the smooth politician.

'My Emperor hopes for a peace achieved not by such costly victories: indeed, not by victories at all, but by mediation.'

'With Austria as mediator?'

'Austria, not being at war, is in a position to mediate.'

'Peace on terms dictated by Austria?'

'On terms suggested by Austria.'

'The same thing!'

'You know the terms, Your Majesty.'

'I give up the whole of Germany. I give up Poland. I give up my Illyrian provinces.'

'Yes.'

'And what do I get in return?'

'Peace.'

'Peace! I can secure peace for myself, whenever I want! Without the help of a mediator!'

'Your Majesty, I know the mind of your enemies. I do not think that you can.'

Napoleon changed his point of attack. His accusing finger pointed not at Metternich, but through him, towards perfidious Vienna.

'Your Emperor, my father-in-law, my ally until a few months ago—'

'Times change, Your Majesty.'

'—now, without striking a blow, seeks to rob me of what I have won with my sword?'

Metternich said, with great precision, 'No, Your Majesty. Of what you have lost, or must very soon lose.'

Napoleon was glaring.

'Your Emperor—with your help, Metternich—offered me his daughter, in order to gain my friendship. I married her, I gave your Emperor my friendship, my kinship, my alliance, my support. What have I gained by it? Another enemy?'

'Austria's position is one of armed neutrality.'

Napoleon shouted, 'Enemy! Against his own family!'

'Forgive me—my Emperor is not guided by family considerations—'

'Evidently not!'

'—but by his conscience. May I suggest, Your Majesty, that you should now consult yours?'

Napoleon had marched to his desk, so that he could bang it with his fist. 'My conscience will never let me sign a dishonourable peace. I am the guardian of the sacred interests of France. How could I accept terms which would be an outrage committed on my people? On my army? The greatest army that has ever existed!'

Metternich had come to the interview with one answer ready. He gave it now, softly.

'Your Majesty, your army was lost in Russia.'

'I lost soldiers. Killed not by the Russians but by the snow. But I did not lose my army.'

'I believe, five hundred thousand—'

Napoleon cried, 'The French have no reason to complain of me! I sacrificed the Germans and the Poles.'

'Your Majesty, you are speaking to a German.'

Napoleon did not hear him. 'I shall have the strongest fighting force in the world. I've more than made up my losses. Come and look at my army now. I'll hold a review for you.'

'I have seen your new soldiers. They are babies.'

'Young men who fight like men. Frenchmen.'

Metternich, with the slightest curl of the lip—'I believe that in France your recruits are called the Marie-Louises.'

Napoleon stared at him, at the aristocrat, the Austrian count, the drawing-room diplomat who knew nothing but drawing-rooms.

'Metternich, you do not understand what a soldier is, nor what I am. Your sovereigns, the seventeenth generation, can be defeated twenty times and still go home to their royal palaces. I am the first generation. An upstart. My reign will not outlast the day when I cease to be strong and therefore cease to be feared. An Emperor like me must fight to keep his throne, against all comers, whatever the cost. And here I have the advantage of your old monarchs. I was brought up on a battlefield, knowing that soldiers are killed in battle. So long as I win the victory: so long as I am still strong, and therefore still feared: I do not concern myself much about the death of a million men.'

He flung his hat into a corner of the room, as if his hat were a million men sent to their deaths.

Metternich waited until it was clear that the gesture had had no effect on him, and said, 'May I ask for the doors and windows to be opened? So that you can repeat those words to your army?'

'My army is ready to die for me.'

'Forgive me. Your army wants an end to this war.'

'My generals, perhaps. Not my soldiers. My generals want to be in their big houses in Paris, their big estates in the country—given to them by me. They've become cowards.'

Metternich raised his eyebrows. 'Do you think Ney a coward? Or Berthier? Or Eugène?'

'I've ruined them all with kindness. All my marshals. All my army commanders. They are monsters of ingratitude.'

'Many of them have paid the debt with their lives.'

Napoleon turned fiercely towards the non-soldier. 'They took the same risk as myself. They'll go on taking that risk. They must. If I lose what I have, they lose what they have. They're too fond of their dukedoms for that.'

Metternich let a moment go by, then spoke in his calm, lucid, reasonable way, without any anger, or prejudice, or emotion.

'Your Majesty, everything you have said to me proves to me once again that Europe and yourself cannot come to an understanding. With you, fortune and misfortune have the same result. When you are successful, you make war, to conquer yet another country. When you are unsuccessful, you make war, to try to win back what you have lost or to keep what you have conquered. The word "peace" means nothing to you but a truce to patch up your army and prepare for a new campaign.'

Metternich had looked deep into Napoleon's mind. In return, Napoleon looked deep into Metternich's.

'What does peace mean to you? A continent dominated by Austria—therefore by you, yourself?'

Metternich said, with an edge to his voire, 'I have proposed a basis for peace which would be acceptable to your enemies. I hope that it will also be acceptable to you—since my Emperor, and I myself, wish to see you remain on the throne of France, with my Emperor's daughter as your consort, and my Emperor's grandson as your successor. May I point out that you would still rule over a France far greater than the Bourbons ever knew—greater than France ever knew, until you became Emperor.'

Napoleon did not reply.

Metternich said, 'You can make this peace today. Tomorrow may be too late.'

Napoleon said, 'You, and your master, and your country, saved yourselves from me by giving me Marie-Louise. Was I a fool to marry her? Did I make a mistake? I wanted to join the new with the old. I wanted to unite the best of your Gothic traditions with the best of my modern ideas. I wanted to create a new Europe. A unified Europe. My marriage to Louise was to be a symbol of it.'

Metternich said coolly, 'Since you ask my opinion: yes, Napoleon the Conqueror made a mistake.'

'An inexcusable mistake. I repent of it now. I see the result of it now. For the first time in my life I am not offering terms, but being offered them.'

'Does Your Majesty accept the terms?'

Napoleon ground out his reply between his teeth.

'Sooner than accept, I will bury the world beneath my ruins!'

Metternich was almost taken aback, not by the reply but by the intensity of it, the violence in Napoleon's voice. He had diagnosed megalomania: he had not supposed that the disease was so far advanced.

He said, 'I am sorry to hear Your Majesty say that.'

Napoleon said, without intensity, but as a realist, 'In

421

this life there are only two alternatives: to command or to obey. I do not choose to obey.'

The interview was over. They had met, and spoken their minds, and their minds had failed to meet. Metternich had achieved his second-best solution. He would have preferred to have Napoleon accept his terms: but he was reasonably well-pleased to remain uncommitted, in a position of free choice—free to be neutral, or to join the enemies of Napoleon, or (the remote possibility had still to be borne in mind) to re-ally Austria with a newly victorious France.

Napoleon had achieved nothing. He knew it. He put his hand on the door-handle, to stop Metternich from going. He became roughly jovial again.

'We shall see one another soon.'

'As Your Majesty pleases.'

'You didn't expect me to accept your terms.'

'I had very little hope. I now have none.'

Napoleon said, gruffly, 'So. What's going to happen?'

'The inevitable.'

'My dear father-in-law won't declare war on me?'

'Your Majesty, it is the very heart of our policy to keep you on your throne, with your Empress by your side. We detest revolutions. We are in favour of order and calm.'

Napoleon said sharply, 'But?'

'But Your Majesty must be reasonable.'

His eyes were hard again. 'I am not yet reduced to being reasonable.'

'Then the future is not difficult to foresee. It is, quite simply, yourself against Europe. And Europe will not be defeated.'

'I am not yet so easy to defeat.'

They looked each other straight in the eyes: Napoleon iron-hard and defiant, Metternich indifferent, expressionless.

Metternich said, 'Your Majesty, you are a lost man.'

He made a bow, not the depth of the bow that he had made on entering the room. Napoleon said nothing.

Napoleon had released the door-handle. Metternich opened the door himself, and went.

The chief lieutenants were still waiting in the corridor. Berthier came to him, quickly, anxiously.

'What happened?'

'He explained everything to me. Very clearly.'

'And—?'

'He is done for.'

He turned away from Berthier, towards General Bertrand. Bertrand escorted him back along the corridors of the Marcolini Palace.

Talleyrand said, 'No, it is not the end. But it is the beginning of the end.'

Caulaincourt nodded his head, in understanding and agreement. 'What are you going to do?'

'I no longer play a part in the conduct of affairs.' Talleyrand's gesture disclaimed any intention even of forming an intention.

'The Emperor still asks your advice.'

'Don't talk to me about the Emperor.' There was an unusual impatience in Talleyrand's voice. 'We have to save France in spite of the Emperor.'

'But if he does ask your advice?'

'My best advice would be that he should gallantly die on the next convenient battlefield. His infant son would be proclaimed as Napoleon the Second, with a Regency Council to govern in his name: the Allies would accept the *fait accompli:* and peace would be signed within twenty-four hours.'

'The Emperor bears a charmed life on the battlefield.'

Talleyrand said, 'Then France is out of luck.'

Napoleon, preparing to leave Paris again, to rejoin his ever-diminishing army, conferred with his brother Joseph. Joseph, driven out of his Kingdom of Spain, was to make himself useful in Paris.

'Above all, beware of Talleyrand. He has only one principle: to be on the winning side.'

Joseph was surprised. 'Do you doubt that we shall be on the winning side?'

'Others may doubt it. I am surrounded by cowards and traitors. I trust almost no one now. Except you. I can trust you.'

'I'm glad you realize that.'

Joseph looked as if he were about to utter some pious words on the subject of brotherly love. Napoleon stopped him, with a quick contemptuous glance.

'I take a low view of human nature. You're a king because you're my brother. If I fall, you fall. So you will do your best for the Bonapartes.'

Joseph, still looking pious, said, 'You can safely leave everything here in my hands.'

'Louise will be Regent, of course.'

'Of course.' King Joseph had been deeply offended at not being appointed Regent. Napoleon had consoled him with the splendid title of Lieutenant-General, and the command of the National Guard.

'But you must protect her against my enemies. Most of all, against Talleyrand. Joseph, I tell you, I know what Talleyrand wants. To rule France, with my wife and my son as his puppets. I give you one categorical instruction now: you must not let Louise and the King of Rome fall into the hands of my enemies. So long as they are safe, the Bonaparte dynasty is safe. From Russia, from Austria, from England. And from Talleyrand.'

'I shall see to it.'

'In the meantime, try to keep any bad news from Louise. She's a child, she doesn't understand. I prefer her not to understand.'

Joseph had a bright thought. He was surprised that the notion had not already struck Napoleon.

'Shall I get rid of Talleyrand?'

'Get rid?'

'Put him in prison? Have him shot?'

Immediate and brusque. 'No.'

'Why not?'

424

'It would make him seem too important. I cannot allow anyone to be as important as that.'

He went down to the great salon, to show himself at the evening reception—to show, in front of the world, how cheerful and confident he was.

His eye fell on Talleyrand, talking to Berthier. He marched up to them, pushed Berthier aside, and stared Talleyrand straight in the face.

'Talleyrand. What are you doing here?'

Talleyrand bowed. 'Sire, I am still one of the Grand Dignitaries of your Empire.'

'I know what you're plotting. You think that if I disappeared you would be at the head of the government. Have a care. I have made my arrangements. If ever I am likely to die, you will die first.'

Talleyrand bowed to him a second time. 'Sire, I was anxious enough for your continued health, without needing this warning.'

Napoleon stared at him, but could never outstare him. He forced a laugh.

'Well, Berthier? What treason has he been talking?'

'None, Sire.' Berthier was puzzled. Why should the Emperor suppose treason?

'Has he no good advice for you, Berthier? Or for me?'

Talleyrand inquired politely, 'Are you consulting me, Sire?'

'I am always ready to hear your opinion.'

'My opinion was expressed in the Senate's loyal address, presented to Your Majesty very recently: "May your hand, so many times victorious, let fall its weapons, and assure the repose of the world." '

'Peace?' Napoleon cried. 'Who wants peace more than I do? But peace with honour!'

'Sire, you have told me so often, I do not understand the meaning of the word "honour".'

Napoleon said, harshly, 'You have never understood it.'

Talleyrand said, with his best smile, 'I agree that my own egotism has a different definition.'

Later that night, Louise came to find Napoleon in his study. He was burning papers in the fireplace.

'What are you burning?'

'Some of my secret papers.'

'Why?'

'Secret papers are meant to be burnt.'

'In case—?'

'No, simply because I have a moment now. It's a thing I do from time to time.'

'It's the first time I have seen you do it.'

He was cheerful, and confident, and affectionate. 'Darling, since I married you, I've been too busy—with you—or away, at a war—'

'Mostly away, at a war.'

'Protecting my wedding-gift to you,' he said cheerfully. 'My christening-gift to our son. I must keep it intact.'

'What gift?'

'The French Empire.' He had put the last of the papers on the fire. He rose. 'There, that's going well. Everything is going well. Have faith in me, that's all. Do you think I've forgotten my job?'

'Berthier says you have only fifty thousand men.'

'And me. I count as a hundred thousand. That makes a hundred and fifty thousand. With a hundred and fifty thousand I can beat any army in the world.'

She was still doubtful. 'Yesterday you said to the Senate—'

'Darling, one says to a Senate whatever will please them—or deceive them.'

'You said that within three months you would come back victorious to Paris, or be dead.'

'The truth, for once. I shall come back victorious. Of course.' He took her in his arms and kissed her. 'The truth. You must believe it.'

'I do.' She was convinced not by his words but by his kiss.

'Dearest Louise, you must not worry.'

'I love you so much, when you are away I worry about every little thing.'

'Not about whether I win or lose.'

He laughed. She laughed too.

'Oh no, not that. I know you always win.'

'Always.'

'But whether you are warm enough, or cool enough, if you have nice things to eat, if you have a nice bed to sleep in—'

'Darling, even on a battlefield an Emperor does reasonably well.'

'You see, I don't know what it's like on a battlefield.'

He kissed her fondly. 'It is no place for the youngest and most beautiful Empress in the world.'

She accepted the kiss, but then she drew away from him.

'Please don't treat me like a child.'

'Do I? Did I?'

'You are always saying "youngest".'

'Very well, I shall say something else. I shall say— what? Wife. Mother. Regent and ruler of France, while I'm away—'

'But you will still be in France.'

'Yes, till I drive the Russians, and the Prussians, and the Austrians, and the English, out of France again. Then I shall be in Berlin. In Vienna. Dictating terms to your dear father Francis. Meanwhile, my darling, you are in charge.' He led her to his desk. 'You'll sit here. Being me. Signing all the orders. All the State papers. All the new laws. As if you were Napoleon.'

He wanted her to sit down at the desk, but she would not.

'What will I really have to sign?'

'Everything.'

'How will I know if I should sign it?'

He was pleased that she had asked. It showed that she wanted to learn.

'Well, in the first place: the bulletin. I'll send you a

bulletin every day, giving the news from the battlefront. You have to sign it, and then it'll be published in the newspapers.'

'I see.'

'And every day my courier will bring you a letter from me, telling you how many cannons are to be fired—twenty, or thirty, or fifty—to celebrate my latest victory. And the secretaries here will write out a formal instruction to the Ministry of War, for the firing of the cannons. And you have to sign it.'

'But if it is not a victory?'

Fond and cheerful, he took her in his arms again. 'Darling, if it is not a victory, then I shall be all the closer to Paris, and my couriers will come here twice a day, or I shall come here myself. And, in any case, I'll be sending orders all the time to my brother Joseph. You can rely on Joseph. He will know exactly what is to be done.'

'Yes.' Her voice was remote.

'Don't you like Joseph?'

'Oh yes, he's very nice.'

'But——?'

'I like Murat better. I would have liked it better with Murat.'

Napoleon moved away from her, and looked into the fireplace, and poked the charred and half-burnt papers, so that they would be consumed by the flames.

He said, 'Murat is no longer with me.'

'Oh, yes, I know he's not here in Paris.'

He said, more strongly, 'Murat has sold himself to Austria, in the hope of keeping his throne. Metternich is a clever man: he tried to persuade me to sell myself, to sell France, with the same offer—that I could go on being a monarch. I was not such a fool as to accept. Metternich makes promises in order to break them when it suits him to break them. But Murat is a fool. He has swallowed the promises, and he has turned his coat.'

'I didn't know that.'

'I hadn't wanted to tell you.'

'And your sister Caroline?'

'Oh yes, and my sister Caroline. She was always the one who insisted on being a princess, who demanded to be a queen . . . Poor Caroline. Poor Murat. The worst that can happen to them is for their treason to succeed. They'll get less pity from Metternich than they would have got from me.'

'Murat is against you now?' She had still not quite got it into her head.

Napoleon laughed, to cheer her up. 'Murat has joined the Allies, with his ragamuffin organ-grinder army. Fortunately for us, the Neapolitans are the worst troops in the world; and Murat, without me at his back, is quite the world's worst general . . . But, you see why it must be Joseph: he's not such a fool, and he'll do what I tell him.'

She was starting to cry. 'I'm so sorry about Murat.'

He was tenderly consoling. 'Darling, Murat doesn't matter, there's no reason to be upset.'

'And Caroline . . .'

'Caroline doesn't matter.'

'They must be such a big disappointment to you.'

He said, still gently, 'I think nothing of people. How can I be disappointed?'

'It's only that . . . you really ought to be happy, you who are so kind and good. You don't deserve to have people behave badly to you. You deserve happiness, you deserve it so much, life can't possibly deny it to you. And you do know, if my prayers are answered, you will have everything your heart can desire.'

She was at her best: simple and truthful and warm and loving. His heart glowed.

He said, 'You do love me.'

'From the first day I met you. From the first night.'

He smiled. 'Ah, the first night.' She still blushed at the memory of it. She was blushing again.

She said, 'And you love me.'

'Yes.'

'I know you do. You must do. You saved my life.'

'Did I?'

'When my baby was being born. I thought I was going to die: that they were going to kill me, for the sake of the baby. But you said to Doctor Dubois, "Save the mother."'

'Darling, at a moment of crisis my mind works very quickly. I thought to myself, "It might be a girl, that's no good to me." And then I thought, "Even if it's a boy, better to save the mother—if she's had one boy, she can have another one."'

'I don't believe you. You are making fun of me.'

'Those thoughts went through my mind in the hundredth part of a second.'

'You saved me because you loved me.'

'Yes, I suppose so.'

They kissed again, a long kiss.

She said, 'I should like to have another one.'

'So should I.'

'Make me pregnant again before you go.'

'Darling, I am leaving in an hour from now.'

'An hour is enough.'

'And this is not a good moment for you to become pregnant.'

'Why not?'

'You have to rule France for me.'

'You told me what I have to do. I have to sign things, that's all. Sitting at your desk here.'

'You may have to move away from here. From Paris.'

'Why should I do that?'

He said lightly, 'I may want you somewhere else, as time goes by.' He quickly changed the subject. 'Oh, you must write to your father.'

'I do. But he doesn't reply.'

He had safely changed the subject. He said, 'Write to him, complaining that he has forgotten you. That he ought to love you better than that. He ought to help you, and help his grandson. He ought to have a mind of his own, and not just listen to Metternich.'

Louise said, sadly, 'He is much too kind-hearted to be against you like this. But he is weak.'

'Tell him how much you love me.'

She looked into his face. 'I love you more than all the world. I just wish that I could shut myself up in some remote little place and live unknown and see no one at all until the moment when you come back. Oh, darling, I pray for nothing but peace: if you come back soon and bring peace with you, I shall be filled with so much happiness, because then you will stay with me for always.'

Napoleon said, 'Tell him that. But don't tell him that you're praying for peace.'

'Shouldn't I?'

'He might think that I want peace.'

'Don't you?'

'My peace. Not his.'

She was sorry that she had said the wrong thing, or used the wrong words. 'I only meant, I want us to live happily ever after.'

He forgave her with a new fond kiss. 'We shall do that. I promise.'

The clock moved too fast. It was nearly time for him to go.

She said, 'I shall sign all my letters to you, "your true and loving wife, Louise".'

He said, 'I shall sign, sometimes "your loving husband", and sometimes "your faithful husband", and sometimes "yours as long as life shall last".'

'And while the weather is still cold, you must wrap up warmly and not let yourself get wet. And if there is anything wrong with you at all, you must go to bed immediately until you are quite well.'

He smiled. 'I shall obey your orders.'

'Napoleon. When shall I see you again?'

The smile went from his face. 'My darling, that is God's will.'

The fear was in his mind, but he could not know that he would never see her again.

431

28. 'YOUR TRUE AND LOVING WIFE'

Napoleon, letters from Paris in his hand, shouted, 'My troops, what do they mean, my troops? Do those fools in Paris think I've still got an army? Tell the Ministry of War I need two hundred thousand recruits! To be called up tomorrow!'

Berthier said drily, 'What age?'

'What do I care what age? So long as they have one eye to see where the enemy is, and one finger to pull the trigger!'

Louise wrote from Paris, every day and sometimes twice.

> My darling, we are having terrible weather, it must be awful for you and your poor troops. I have caught a bad cold, everyone seems to have one in Paris now. But it is you that I worry about all the time. I am so afraid that this weather may make you ill, and I love you so much that I could not bear the thought of it.
>
> Your son is very well, he sends you a big kiss, he has been very difficult all day long, but he has promised to be a very good boy this evening. It is such a pity that the bad weather has kept him indoors.
>
> People here in Paris are all very anxious wondering what was discussed at the Council today. They think it was about conscripting another two hundred thousand men, which has had a very bad effect in Paris, everyone here is longing for peace. I just want what you want, my darling, but I think that you, too, must be very tired and in need of a rest. All my fondest love.
>
> Your true and loving Louise

Napoleon wrote most days, whenever he could, from wherever he was.

My darling, I have been in the saddle all the last few days. On the 20th I took Arcis-sur-Aube. The enemy attacked me there at six in the evening, but I beat him. I have decided to make for the Marne and the enemy's line of communications, in order to push him back further from Paris. I shall be at Saint-Dizier this evening. A kiss to my son, and to you, my darling.

Nap

My darling, I am so worried at not having heard from you for two days, I am afraid that perhaps you are ill and they are hiding it from me. I hope that a letter from you will come soon with news of a great victory. We need a great victory to make people here less anxious, all the people in Paris are so alarmed. My fondest love.

Your true and loving Louise

Caulaincourt came back from Châtillon to Saint-Dizier, and reported to Napoleon.

'Well? What have the enemy to say to me?'

'Sire, they offer a peace treaty.'

'What sort of peace treaty?'

'The frontiers that France had twenty years ago: the Pyrenees, the Alps, and the Rhine.'

Napoleon took it in slowly. 'The frontiers that France had, before me.'

'Yes, Sire . . . The expression Count Metternich used was "restoring the natural boundaries of France".'

Napoleon said, 'My France had no boundaries.'

'They asked me to make one thing clear to you, Sire: that this is their final offer.'

He cried, in a passion of anger, 'You see what cheats they are! This is less than Metternich offered me at Dresden. Less than they offered me three months ago at Frankfurt.'

Since Berthier would not speak, Caulaincourt had to say it. 'Sire, three months ago they were not at the gates of Paris.'

'Can I be an Emperor with no Empire? Is it possible?'

Berthier spoke at last, in his heavy, bearish way.

'No Germans, no Italians, no Spaniards, no Poles, no Dutchmen. You would still be what your title calls you: Emperor of the French. Isn't that enough?'

'Is it?'

'It's more than most men have.'

Napoleon's voice grew harder. 'Then we'll make peace, when Metternich and the Tsar beg me for peace, to save their own skins! Then, and only then! On my terms, not on theirs!'

Time had been—and it lasted long—when Berthier and Caulaincourt, and so many others, would have sprung to attention at Napoleon's words and marched out cheerfully to die for him.

That time was past.

Berthier said, 'Sire, the French have come to believe that they have fought for you long enough.'

Berthier: the most loyal, the most devoted, the most worshipping.

Napoleon asked, 'Have you come to believe that, Berthier?'

'Yes. Take what they offer you.'

The Emperor was past helping and past saving.

'*No!*'

At the Tuileries, the meeting of the Regency Council had degenerated into an unruly squabble. Marie-Louise was not a chairman to dominate a dozen argumentative men. King Joseph, her helper and adviser, was himself the most violently contentious of all. The only one who did not raise his voice and shake his fist was Talleyrand.

'Your Majesty, if I may humbly offer my opinion—'

Joseph stared at him with black hatred. 'Do we want your opinion?'

'Her Majesty is entitled to hear it.'

'Her Majesty does not listen to enemy agents.'

Talleyrand raised a polite eyebrow at Joseph, and addressed himself to the chair again. 'Your Majesty, have I your permission to speak?'

Poor Louise, battered and bewildered, said, 'Yes . . .'

Talleyrand spoke deliberately. There was just a possibility that his slow coolness would calm them down.

'Your Majesty, we are told by the Minister of War that the invading armies will enter Paris within two or three days—'

'Do you dispute that?' It was Clarke, the Minister of War.

'I never argue with the Minister of War on a question of fact.'

'Thank you!'

Talleyrand gave him a little bow. 'But I shall always argue with him on a question of judgement. The armies will arrive here: therefore, the Minister says, Your Majesty and the King of Rome must immediately be conveyed to a place of safety away from Paris.'

'Yes, must!' Joseph shouted at him. '*Must!* So that she doesn't fall into the hands of your friends the Russians!'

Talleyrand looked briefly towards King Joseph, as if to decide whether he was really in the room or not, and turned to the Empress again.

'My opinion is briefly stated. If Your Majesty leaves Paris, it will appear to be not prudence but flight; the French will believe that all is lost; and the Allies will assume that the throne of France has been declared vacant. But if Your Majesty stays in Paris, as Empress and Regent of this realm, then the prestige of the throne will remain undiminished; you will meet the Allied sovereigns as their equal; and there will still be a reasonable hope of saving the dynasty and the Empire. To stay is to continue to reign. To go is, in effect, to abdicate.'

She was timid, but she knew her mind. She said, not very loudly but quite audibly, 'I think I agree with Monsieur Talleyrand.'

Savary said, 'I think the majority of the Council agrees with Monsieur Talleyrand.'

Talleyrand had never cared for Savary, but on this occasion he gave him a beaming smile. 'How splendid. Shall we put it to the vote?'

Marie-Louise, not quite sure of the procedure, turned nervously to her adviser Joseph. 'Shall we? Should we do that?'

'May I speak first?'

She said, faintly, 'Yes, of course . . .'

Talleyrand gave a private sigh. Joseph was rising to his feet with the air of a man who is about to make a totally humourless speech.

'All of us here are, or with whatever truth claim to be, loyal servants of the Emperor.'

Talleyrand whispered to Savary, 'And some of us have many years of service to prove it.'

Joseph stared blackly at his opponents. 'I am concerned not with opinions, but with instructions. The Emperor's own instructions, which must be obeyed by his loyal servants.'

Talleyrand sat up and opened his eyes wide. Instructions? Were there instructions? Joseph was bringing two letters out of his pocket, like a conjuror pulling rabbits out of a hat.

'From a letter written to me by the Emperor a month ago. "If Talleyrand has had anything to do with the suggestion of keeping the Empress in Paris in the event of a withdrawal of our troops, then you can be sure that he is practising treason."'

Joseph glared at Talleyrand with triumph in his eye as well as malice.

Talleyrand said quietly, to no one in particular, 'I was aware of the Emperor's hatred. But not of his blindness.'

Joseph brandished the other letter. 'From a letter written to me by the Emperor twelve days ago. "My brother.

As I have already instructed you verbally and also in writing, you must do your utmost to prevent the Empress and the King of Rome from falling into the hands of the enemy. If the Allies advance upon Paris in such strength as to make resistance out of the question, you must send my wife and son to the Loire, out of harm's way. The Allies' first act would be to make them prisoner, and I would rather see them with their throats cut than carried off as captives to Vienna." '

Talleyrand thought to himself: Poor Joseph: what a sad man, that the only moments of triumph in his life have been won for him by his younger brother.

Joseph, loudly, triumphant, said, 'There can be no vote. The Emperor has given his orders. It is impossible to disobey them.'

Louise spoke in a small sad voice: 'Yes.'

'The meeting is over. The Empress leaves Paris tomorrow.'

As the Empress was leaving, she came and spoke quietly to Talleyrand.

'I think you are quite right. But I must do what the Emperor says. Then he can't blame me.'

Talleyrand bowed to her. 'It is not Your Majesty who will be blamed.'

King Joseph came up to him, still with murder in his eyes.

'The Emperor has also ordered that the Grand Dignitaries—including yourself, Talleyrand—are to accompany the Empress to the Loire.'

Talleyrand bowed to the Empress a second time. 'Nothing could give me greater pleasure.'

Talleyrand walked away from the Council Room with Savary. He had always thought Savary a mediocre minister. He was now prepared to accept that there were good mediocrities and bad mediocrities, and that Savary was, on the whole, a good one.

He said to Savary, 'And that is how a game can be lost by throwing away the good cards. Tomorrow will see the end of the Empire: the Emperor himself has written

437

its death-warrant. What a failure he has been, from the point of view of history! An adventurer, who could have been the greatest man of his age.' He decided to risk the next line. Savary was not clever enough to know himself a mediocrity. 'Ah, the eternal pitfall for the omnipotent: they surround themselves with mediocrities and relatives.' He glanced at Savary, who was nodding agreement. 'Shall I allow myself one moment of vanity? If he had listened to me, he would be a great Emperor still. Oh, well. We are not involved in his ruin.'

Savary asked, 'Will you go to the Loire, with the Empress and Joseph?'

'I shall be unavoidably detained in Paris.'

'Till the Allies come?'

Talleyrand, a thoughtful man, had considered the future.

'My friend the Tsar of Russia will need suitable accommodation. I shall offer him my house.'

Napoleon sat in his office at Fontainebleau, with the few marshals who had not yet abandoned him, and with Caulaincourt, come from Paris.

The hopes and the delusions were over. He was quiet, and reasonable, and tired—so tired.

'A provisional government? Headed by whom?'

'Talleyrand, Sire.'

'Of course, Talleyrand. The only possible choice . . And my wife? And my son? Will my son have what is his by right? No, I imagine not. After me, all they can do is bring back the Bourbons.'

'Sire, the Tsar insists that your abdication must be definitive and absolute.'

'The Tsar. Prompted by Talleyrand.'

'Yes, Sire.'

'So they both have their revenges.'

Caulaincourt, his heart on Napoleon's side but his mind on Talleyrand's, said nothing. In any case, the Emperor's mind had turned elsewhere.

'A fortnight ago, in that battle at Arcis-sur-Aube, I di

my best to get myself killed. I rode my horse straight at a smouldering shell. It burst without touching me. I was condemned to live.'

In a sudden access of energy he took pen and paper and wrote, at his usual great speed:

The Allied Powers having proclaimed that the Emperor Napoleon is the sole obstacle to peace in Europe, the Emperor Napoleon declares that he renounces, for himself and for his heirs, the throne of France.

He put the pen down. He said, 'And the world will give a great sigh of relief.'

At Malmaison, Josephine read out to Hortense a letter from Napoleon.

' "At first I pitied myself, now I think myself fortunate. An enormous . . ." ' She peered at the letter. 'His hand-writing is as bad as ever. "Weight", perhaps? . . . "An enormous weight has been lifted from my mind and from my spirit. My fall is a great one, but they tell me it serves a useful purpose. Anyway, I have retired from the struggle. Good-bye, my dearest Josephine. Resign your-self to fate, as I am doing; but please keep the remem-brance of one who has never forgotten you, and will never forget you." Then, underneath his signature, it says: "They have given me the island of Elba. Write to me there with all your news. My health is not at its best." '

'Elba?'

'Yes. Is it a kingdom? I suppose he'll still be a king.' She folded the letter. 'Poor Napoleon. Should I go and join him there?'

Hortense said, 'Yes.'

Josephine looked at her almost reproachfully. Hortense was romantic, and made romantic decisions. But life was not romantic.

'I wondered if I should. But I must look after you and Eugène. I must make sure that you're properly treated.

439

And myself—the whole question of my title: shall I go on being an Empress? And my allowance from Napoleon, and from the Treasury: it's very important. I simply can't live here without it. I must stay near Paris, until these things are settled. So much depends on speaking to the right person at the right moment. I'm going to be very busy.' She walked about, nervously twisting her fingers. 'I think everything will be all right. I've had the nicest messages already, from Talleyrand, and all our friends in the new government, and from Metternich, and from the Tsar. The Tsar's letter was particularly charming. He says he's always wanted to meet me. He's coming to call this afternoon.'

Hortense was startled. 'Coming here?'

'Yes.'

'How dare he?'

'Darling, Napoleon was very fond of him once, not long ago, only a few years ago. And he was very fond of Napoleon.'

'Mamma, the Tsar is our enemy!'

Hortense was really too romantic. It was charming but it was childish. Josephine tried to explain.

'Hortense, there are no enemies now. Only people who can help us. Or it may be a difficult time for us. Darling, you must remember, I have lived through difficult times. I don't like them. I don't want them to happen again.'

She could see that Hortense still did not really understand. Hortense had forgotten the Revolution, and her father's death, and Josephine in prison and condemned to death and then penniless with two children to bring up. Hortense only remembered what it was like being rich, being a princess, being a queen. The rich are allowed to believe that it is love that makes the world go round. The poor know that what makes the world go round is money.

Hortense said, with that romantic intensity of hers, 'Mamma, do you love Napoleon?'

'Yes, of course, why?'

'You should write to him and offer to share his exile.'

Josephine's hand flew to her mouth, to prevent herself from crying out in agony. Her heart wanted to scream. She could not allow it.

At last she said, quietly, the words that she hated to say.

'He has a wife.'

Caulaincourt went to Paris again, and came back to Fontainebleau with the Allies' terms. Napoleon read the document through in silence, with knitted brows.

'Parma?'

'Sire, Metternich is insistent that the Empress should be given Parma.'

'They must do better for her than that. Parma is an insignificant little duchy, not fit for the wife of an Emperor, the daughter of an Emperor. Go back to Paris and tell them again: they must give her Tuscany.'

'Sire, at the conference table I am not in a position to use the word "must".'

'Tell them, if they give her Tuscany, I shall be content.'

'Sire, your contentment is not a bargaining counter.'

'They would prefer to have my agreement to their terms.'

'Yes, Sire. But they are prepared to do without it.'

'She must have Tuscany.'

Caulaincourt suppressed a sigh. Was there no way to make the Emperor understand that he had abdicated?

'Sire, the most I can do is ask them to be generous.'

'It's not a question of generosity, but of what is suitable for her rank. Metternich believes in suitability.'

'Sire, at my last meeting with him, Metternich said that the Empress can now only be considered as an archduchess of the ruling house of Austria: and her son as the son of an archduchess.'

Napoleon threw the document on to the desk. 'Metternich is not satisfied with my defeat. He seeks to humiliate me by denying that I ever existed. Tell him I have abased myself enough by accepting Elba.'

Caulaincourt shook his head. 'It would give him too much pleasure to hear me say that.'

'They must see that Tuscany would be the most convenient place for her.' Napoleon paced the room, irritated by the Allies' stupidity. 'Elba is off the coast of Tuscany.'

'Sire, that is the great unspoken argument against it.'

'Against it?'

Caulaincourt said gravely, 'I believe that it is Metternich's design to separate you from your wife and son.'

Napoleon considered this. 'Then we shall go over Metternich's head to his master.'

'The Emperor of Austria is ruled by Metternich.'

'The Emperor of Austria is a man who loves his daughter. He could not be so cruel.'

Caulaincourt told Napoleon what Napoleon had often told him. 'Sire, politics have no heart.'

'A man has a heart. A father has a heart. And he's a devout Catholic. He believes in the sacredness of the marriage vow.'

'Sire, forgive me. You, yourself, had no wish to divorce the Empress Josephine. You sacrificed your feelings for reasons of political necessity. The Emperor of Austria gave you his daughter, who did not love you then, who did not even know you then: may I say, at that moment he sacrificed his feelings and hers for reasons of political necessity. He will now try to take her away from you, for a new necessity—'

'What necessity can there be now?'

'To isolate you, Sire. So that your wife no longer seems to be your wife; and your son no longer your son.'

'They can't do it. Marie-Louise writes to me every day, telling me she will not be parted from me.'

Caulaincourt looked at him almost despairingly. Napoleon had been the harshest and most ruthless realist of his age. Why could he not bring himself to see that there were other realists in the world, almost as ruthless as himself?

He went closer to Napoleon, to look him in the face, to try to make him feel the full force of his earnestness.

He said, as strongly as he dared, 'I beg you, Sire, bring the Empress here before the Allies can stop her.'

'She is already on her way here from the Loire.'

'Then all may be well.'

'She'll arrive in four days from now.'

Caulaincourt stared at him. 'Four days?'

'Yes.'

'I implore you, Sire, make her arrive sooner. Make it tomorrow.'

'Her father is to meet her at Rambouillet, before she comes here.'

Caulaincourt was appalled by the sluggishness of Napoleon's responses. He cried, in a louder voice than he had ever before used to his master, 'Sire, it is of the utmost importance that she should join you as soon as humanly possible. Once you are together you can be separated only by force, and not even Metternich would dare do that.'

Napoleon said, with a dull heaviness, 'It is at my own request that she is to see her father. And I myself suggested Rambouillet.'

'Why Rambouillet? Why shouldn't her father meet her here?'

'I want her to meet him alone. I want him to know that I am not putting words into her mouth.'

'Will he be alone? Will no one be putting words into his mouth?'

Napoleon's face was set in unshakeable obstinacy. 'I will not have him here. I have no wish to see a victorious Emperor.'

There was nothing to be done. There was one thing still to be ascertained. Perhaps there was one thing that could be done.

'Sire, may I ask, with the greatest respect: have you ordered the Empress to come to Fontainebleau? Have you ordered her to accompany you to Elba?'

'She is a faithful and loving wife. She wishes to be with me. I have not ordered her. I do not need to.'

'Sire, the Empress's greatest virtue is obedience. I will

443

use the word docility. She obeyed her father in marrying you. After that, she obeyed her husband. She will always obey whichever voice will give her the clearest orders.'

Napoleon stared into nothingness. Caulaincourt had never seen him look so heavy, so lifeless, so old.

He said, 'Caulaincourt, I am at the end of my career. I can confine myself to an island sixteen miles by ten, because I have lived my life. Louise is young. I have no right to demand that a woman as young as her should accept the same confinement. At her age she still needs pleasures and playthings. That is why she must persuade her father to give her Tuscany. Italy is the most beautiful country in the world; Florence is the most charming city. She can have her court there, she can spend a great part of the year there. From time to time she can come and stay with me in Elba. She will see me with all the more pleasure if she does not see me every day: a husband less and less capable of being a husband every night, an old man growing older, writing his memoirs and bemoaning his fate.' He raised his head and looked at Caulaincourt with heavy eyes. 'She says she loves me. I should like her to continue to love me. I can see the best chance of it, and the best chance of her happiness. I cannot order her to be happy. I can only try to make it possible.'

Louise, at Rambouillet, rehearsed what she would say to her father when he arrived.

'I love Napoleon, I am going to join him now at Fontainebleau. Then I am going with him to Elba. Whatever anyone says, that is what I shall do. And I must have Tuscany, so that I can be close to Napoleon, and see him whenever I please. My father must agree to this, because it will make me happy, and my father does want me to be happy. That is what I must say.'

She looked at the Duchess of Montebello for approval. The Duchess knew that she had to say, 'Yes, Your Majesty.' She said it as indifferently as she could.

'Monsieur Corvisart, if my father asks you about my

health, you must not tell him any lies. But you must say that I am quite well enough to be able to do these things. And you must say that I shall be much better when I am with my husband again.'

Corvisart bowed. 'I shall not have to depart from the truth, Your Majesty.'

She went to the gates of the château to meet the Emperor Francis. He did not smile at her: it was not his habit. His face was unvarying: stiff, sad, lugubrious. He kissed her drily on the forehead.

'My dear. I am glad to see you.'

'I hope you had a good journey from Paris.'

'A fairly good journey.'

'I hope that my stepmother and my brothers and sisters are well.'

'They are very well. They send you their fondest love.'

'I send them mine.'

'Shall I say that you are well? You do not, in fact, look particularly well.' He was scrutinizing her.

They went into the great drawing-room: he followed by Metternich, she followed by the Duchess and Corvisart, in case she needed their support. They stood at a respectful distance.

'Papa, if I am not very well, it is because I am not happy.'

'I can understand that. It has been an unhappy time for all of us.'

'Papa, who won't you let me be happy?'

He said, with no warmth, 'My dear, I will do anything that will contribute to your happiness.'

'And give me anything?'

'Gladly.'

'Give me Tuscany, so that I can be close to Napoleon and see him whenever I please.'

'Tuscany is not mine to give.'

'Yes, it is.'

'Does your husband say that?'

'Yes.' She had not meant to say it. She automatically told the truth.

445

'Your husband has a curious notion of property.'

'I know it was French for a time. But it must be yours again now. Part of your Empire.'

Francis said, in his dry-as-dust way, 'The Grand-Duchy of Tuscany was given by my father, the Emperor Leopold, to my younger brother, your uncle Ferdinand. Ferdinand was driven out of Tuscany by a revolutionary army under a General Bonaparte. The French are now defeated. Ferdinand returns to his grand-duchy. Does your husband imagine that he can still dispose of Europe as he pleases? Do you yourself imagine that you can rob your uncle, and his son, and his descendants, of what is theirs by all the laws of hereditary right?'

'No . . .' She was starting to cry.

'No.' He turned away from her.

'Couldn't you give them something else instead?'

'My throne, perhaps?'

'I didn't mean that.'

'I have an Empire entrusted to me by God. I do not parcel it out to satisfy the whim of a defeated revolutionary general.'

'You mustn't call him that. Napoleon is an Emperor.'

'He called himself an Emperor, for a time.'

'Papa, you mustn't be cruel to him.'

He looked at her again. Since he never smiled, it was not a smile on his face, but there was something: a sardonic creasing of his cheeks.

'When I remember how he has treated the crowned heads of Europe, including myself, I must think that we are being remarkably kind.'

'By sending him to Elba?' she cried. 'A horrible little island where no one wants to go?'

'Shall I tell you how many hereditary rulers he turned out of their kingdoms, with nowhere to go?'

She would not be browbeaten. 'I don't care. I love him. I shall always love him. Whatever you say.'

He inclined his head, to show that there was no disagreement. 'It is a wife's duty to love her husband.'

'Yes.'

446

'I am only pointing out that we are merciful in allowing him to live.'

'How can you say such a thing? He is a great man! The greatest man in the world!'

Francis looked down his long nose and said, 'He has abdicated that position.'

She sniffed, and dabbed her eyes with a handkerchief. She would not cry. She would be brave and strong, as Napoleon would have wished her to be. And she would make her father see where he was wrong.

She said, reproachfully, 'Why did you turn against him? He would still be Emperor if you hadn't turned against him.'

'I did not turn. I was always against him.'

'Then why did you make me marry him?'

'At that moment, I could not afford to show that I was against him.'

'So you should be grateful to me.'

She had scored a point. But he refused to allow it.

'It is a daughter's duty to help her father protect his throne.'

'Napoleon would not have taken your throne.'

'For himself, or one of his family? He took a great number of thrones, and always wanted more. He wanted every throne in the world.' His eye had the pride of seventeen generations. 'The first virtue of hereditary rule: we are accustomed to the possession of power. It does not make us behave like insatiable madmen.'

Louise very much wanted to think of an answer to that, but nothing came into her mind at first. Then, for no reason, the King of Rome came into her mind, and she was pleased, because she could make him her answer.

'The madman's son is your grandson.'

Perhaps Francis became just a little less stiff? 'I look forward to seeing him shortly—and to seeing a great deal of him, from now on.'

Louise felt that she had found the way to her father's heart. He was not a man who showed his emotions, but he really did love his children. He loved her, she knew he did. He must love his first grandson.

She smiled. 'He is beautiful. He calls himself "The little king".'

His face did not change: she had not supposed that it would. 'I am aware of what is due to him as my grandchild.'

'I'm sure you are, Papa.'

'He will be an Austrian prince, with a suitable title; and he will succeed you as Duke of Parma.'

Her smile went. 'No, Papa. I am not going to Parma.'

'Whether you go there or not, I have given you Parma.'

It was time for her to make everything clear to him. 'I am going from here to join Napoleon at Fontainebleau, or wherever he tells me. And then I shall go with him to Elba.'

He raised an eyebrow. 'That "horrible little island where no one wants to go"?'

'Oh, I don't like the idea of it, I don't really want to go there. But it's my duty. You said so yourself, Papa. It is a wife's duty to love her husband, and be with him, and make him happy.'

He said gravely, 'I have my duty too, as a father. I am anxious for your happiness.'

'I can only be happy with Napoleon.'

'And anxious for your health.'

'I shall be well again when I'm with Napoleon.'

'In Elba?'

'I suppose so.' She said it not very strongly. 'Perhaps.' She did not sound at all certain. It was a nuisance, sometimes, that she could not say things unless she really meant them and believed them.

Francis was looking at her closely. 'The climate there is not good for your physical type.'

'Doctor Corvisart thinks I ought to take a cure first, at Aix or somewhere like that. To make quite sure I'm strong enough, before I actually go to Elba.'

'Corvisart? Your husband's doctor?'

'He has been with me these last few months, because I've been so unwell. He is the best doctor in Europe.'

'So I have heard.'

'He will tell you everything himself.'

She called to Corvisart, and he came forward and made a most courtier-like bow when she presented him to the Emperor of Austria.

'Now please tell my father what is wrong with my health.'

'Yes, Your Majesty.'

'And you must tell him the truth.'

'I shall, Your Majesty.'

Francis said, looking hard at Corvisart, 'It seems to me that my daughter's health has deteriorated grievously since I saw her last.' His tone did not suggest that he expected to be contradicted. But, then, Corvisart was not in the habit of contradicting Emperors.

'Indeed, it has deteriorated very markedly, Sire; and has given me cause for alarm.'

'You mean that she is seriously ill.' It was a statement rather than a question.

Corvisart said, 'She is suffering from frequent spasms affecting the chest, and causing a shortage of breath, at times approaching suffocation. This is accompanied by disturbing expectorations—'

Louise broke in. 'The other night I was spitting blood.'

'Additionally, there are feverish symptoms, with an abnormally high temperature of an undulating type—'

She said, 'And spots. When I have the fever I have red spots all over me.'

Francis had listened with enormous care. 'In her youth, my daughter was affected rather similarly by any deep nervous disturbance.'

Corvisart bowed to show his agreement with the Emperor's diagnosis. 'Indeed, Sire, I would say that Her Majesty's illness has been caused by—'

'By Napoleon's going away,' she said loudly. That was the important thing to prove to her father: with Napoleon, she would be well.

Corvisart said, '—and by the daily evolution of recent events.'

Louise said, 'Yes.'

'A general nervous debility has set in . . . .' Corvisart made a wide gesture. He had said enough.

Francis appeared to be considering his verdict. 'You will understand, Doctor, that my daughter's health is of paramount importance in deciding where she should go next and what she should do next.'

'I understand that, Sire.'

'What do you recommend for her?'

Corvisart gave the Emperor the benefit of his best bed-side manner. 'Absolute rest and tranquillity, Sire.'

Francis said, 'An absence of all nervous and emotional excitement.'

'Exactly, Sire.'

'Such as she would find with her family in Vienna.'

She cried, 'Papa!'

Corvisart said, 'Precisely, Sire.'

She cried, 'Corvisart!'

What had he done? He had betrayed her! Hadn't he?

Corvisart bowed deeply to her and said, 'Your Majesty, I am a doctor. I must tell the truth.' He turned back to the Emperor. 'Absolute tranquillity, of the kind that you suggest, Sire. Followed by a vigorous course of treatment at a suitable spa.'

Francis said, 'What would be the best climate for her? Temperate? Or the hot sun of, shall we say, Elba?'

Corvisart did not hesitate to give his professional opinion. 'Sire, the hot sun of Elba would kill her as surely as a bullet in the heart.'

Francis said, 'Thank you for your opinion, Doctor.'

Corvisart bowed himself into the distance again. Louise stood dumbfounded and confused. Corvisart had told the truth, like a good and honest man. She herself had told the truth. But the result of truth-telling had not been what it should have been. Her father had listened, and everything he had said had been perfectly kind and sensible

450

But his conclusion had not been what she had wanted it to be.

Francis said, 'I am your father. I have a duty towards you. I have your best interests at heart. I do not propose to let you die.'

She was crying again, big tears coming into her eyes. She wanted to protest, to explain somehow that it was all the truth but the truth was all wrong. But she felt a stronger impulse to throw herself into her father's arms, because there it would be safe, there she would have nothing more to worry about.

Napoleon wrote to her:

My dearest Louise, you must have met your father by this time. I wish you to come to Fontainebleau tomorrow, so that we may set out together for that land of sanctuary and rest, where I shall be happy, provided you can make up your mind to be so and to forget worldly greatness. Give a kiss to my son, and never doubt my love.

Nap

She replied from Rambouillet:

My darling, my father was most kind and affectionate towards me, but it was all cancelled out by the most dreadful blow he could possibly have dealt me; he forbids me to join you, or to see you. He says he wants me to spend two or three months in Vienna, and then go on to Parma. This will be the death of me, the only thing I can wish for is that you can contrive to be happy without me, for there can be no happiness for me apart from you.

I will write to you every day and shall be thinking about you all the time. I am hoping that I shall be able to join you in three or four months. I haven't told this to my father or Metternich, but I have set my heart on it.

My health is going from bad to worse. I am so wretched that I just don't know what to say to you. I beg you not to forget me and to believe that I shall always love you.

Your true and loving Louise

General Bertrand reported to the Emperor that the Old Guard was drawn up on parade.

Napoleon seemed not to hear him. He said, 'I wish Berthier had stayed till the end. All the others are gone. Dead, or traitors. But Berthier could have stayed here till today. And he could have come to Elba with me for the first few months. It would have been a sign of friendship.'

'Sire, Berthier is an old man and a sick man.'

Napoleon said, without rancour, 'Well enough to go to Paris and hand over my army and swear allegiance to the new regime.'

'He has a wife and children, Sire.'

'Yes, and a title, and a great estate. They impose a duty on him, too. He must try to keep what he has, for the sake of his children. I agree that I couldn't expect him to come to Elba. But I should have liked him at my side as I speak to the Old Guard for the last time.'

'The Guard is ready for you, Sire.'

Napoleon heard him this time, and stood more upright. His eye brightened.

'Well, you are coming to Elba. Thank you for that, Bertrand.'

'Sire, I shall be with you as long as you may have need of me.'

'You can help me write my history, to tell the world what I did. Well, we shall be contented enough on Elba. The Empress will join me there in three or four months.'

'That is good news, Sire.'

'Is it? Her father is taking her to Vienna, so that the Austrians can stare at the wife of a defeated conqueror.

452

Poor girl, she will have to live through it as best she can. In Elba I shall make her happy again.'

He was splendidly upright now. He had become a soldier and an Emperor again.

'Is my carriage ready by my position on the parade-ground?'

'Yes, Sire.'

'Tell my driver that, at the end of my speech, the ensign will march forward with the standard: I shall kiss it: I shall say, "Good-bye! Keep me in your memory!" I shall turn and step into the carriage: he must immediately drive off at a gallop. Towards Elba.'

29. JOSEPHINE AT MALMAISON

Everyone came to pay their respects to Josephine at Malmaison: the Tsar of Russia and his two brothers, the King of Prussia and his two sons, and a whole string of German and Austrian and Russian princes and grand dukes, a hundred diplomats and high officers and officials of every possible nationality: and, of course, so many old friends from Paris, so many who had served Napoleon well, and were now serving the government of Louis the Eighteenth.

Malmaison was a brilliant centre of society, and Josephine the brilliant hostess. And she was to keep Malmaison, for ever: Caulaincourt had arranged it.

'Dear Çaulaincourt, I am so very grateful.'

'My only remaining duty is to serve Your Majesty.'

'Now that poor Napoleon has gone to his island.'

'His last message to me was to ask me to protect your interests.'

'He was always the kindest of men.' She clapped her hands with joy. 'Oh, I'm so delighted that I shan't have to leave Malmaison. It's more than my home, it's my life.'

'Nothing will disturb your happiness here.'

'And a million francs a year, that's more than I expected. Oh, but I shall have to economize. How I wish Napoleon were here. He spent so much time teaching me how to economize. The one thing he ever tried to do and failed to do.'

Metternich came to one of her evening receptions, with Talleyrand. He found Josephine enchanting.

Talleyrand said, 'Ah, she and I are in our element re-creating the good old days before the Revolution.'

Metternich looked across the room at her, as she stood winning the hearts of a pair of grand dukes.

'What age would you say she is now?'

Talleyrand shrugged. 'Whatever age she cares to admit to. She has the great quality of all great ladies: she tells a lie with dazzling sincerity.'

Josephine came towards them, as well-shaped and as graceful as ever she was, as diaphanously dressed as ever she had been.

The soft but brilliant smile, with her mouth hardly open, so that her discoloured teeth should be concealed.

'Monsieur Metternich, Monsieur Talleyrand . . .'

Meternich bowed. 'Your Majesty.'

Talleyrand bowed. 'Your Majesty.'

'How very kind of you. Am I a Majesty still?'

Metternich said, 'There is no one who would dare to think otherwise.'

There was a special reason for her happiness—or rather, there were two special reasons. Eugène and Hortense were both at Malmaison: and Eugène had been well received by the Bourbons, and was to continue to be, at the very least, a Bavarian prince, by courtesy of his father-in-law, the King of Bavaria; and Hortense had been given a duchy, and was officially the Duchess of Saint-Leu, though out of habit and politeness everyone still called her 'queen'.

Eugène was with Berthier. Berthier was not happy, and Eugène could not cajole him out of his unhappiness. He did nothing but shake his head and say, 'I should have gone with him.'

'Berthier, we are released from our vows.'

'The new ones stick in my throat.'

Eugène said quietly, 'You are like my mother and myself. We shall always have Napoleon in our hearts.'

'He was a bully. A pig-headed slave-driver,' Berthier said. 'I'd give both my arms to have him bullying me again.'

Josephine came up, and Josephine charmed him into smiling.

Metternich said to Talleyrand, 'Yes, she was certainly the better of the two empresses.'

'It needed an Austrian to say that.'

'There is no great merit in saying it. It can hardly be disputed.'

Talleyrand said, 'I hear the second Empress is unwell.'

'The second Empress is suffering from hypochondria. She has a doctor who encourages her to do so, since he himself has not the slightest desire to go to Elba.'

Talleyrand looked in the air and wondered, rather than asked: "Will the second Empress's health ever be quite strong enough to allow her to join her husband on Elba?'

Metternich smiled. 'Never. It is arranged.'

'For her to be permanently not quite strong enough?'

'For her to find a new happiness, in Austria.'

Josephine's greatest friend was the Tsar. He delighted in her company. He was constantly at Malmaison. He was influential in ensuring suitable establishments for Eugène and for Hortense. He brought Josephine presents: it was not so much that they were magnificent as that they were thoughtfully chosen. He was tall, and marvellously handsome, and infinitely charming.

Josephine gave a great dinner for the Tsar and his two brothers. After the dinner there was a ball. She opened it, with the Tsar. Later, she walked in the garden with him.

He said, 'I dined at the Tuileries, with the new court, last night. What a difference! The dinner lasted four hours. The only pleasure they seemed to find was in their food. And I thought to myself, Once, not long ago, a great man lived here.'

She smiled. 'I could never make Napoleon sit at table for more than twenty minutes. He swallowed his food whatever was nearest to his hand, without even looking to see what is was. I'm sure it must have been bad for his digestion. But the only thing that mattered to him was that he had to get back to his work. Oh, sometimes we couldn't even get him away from his work. I had to be ready at six o'clock for dinner. Everyone had to be ready. And seven o'clock would come, and sometimes eight o'clock or nine. No Emperor. He'd forgotten about dinner, and no one had dared to remind him.'

They walked on.

The Tsar said, 'I thought, seven years ago, when we met at Tilsit, that he and I had become friends for life. We were together for days on end there, the two of us, talking, talking of everything under the sun. We rebuilt the world together. We planned a world so much better than this one, better than any that I can now foresee. A great pity that our friendship did not last.'

'You should have given him one of your sisters as his second wife.'

He shook his head. 'Napoleon should have stayed with his first wife, and made your son Eugène his successor.'

She shook her head, in turn. 'Ah, you don't know the Corsicans. It had to be a real Bonaparte.'

'Shall we theorize? If he had not divorced you—'

'He would still have wanted to conquer the world, and I could never have stopped him. So I would be in Elba with him now.'

He asked, 'Do you wish you were in Elba with him now?'

They walked on, as she considered her answer.

She said, 'For a time he loved me very much, above everything, and I loved him only a little. Then, after that time, I loved him very much, above everything. But I had come to be too old for what he wanted . . . Yes, I think I wish I were in Elba. We could have been old together. I'd have liked that.'

They walked on.

The Tsar said, 'We are only theorizing. The Allied sovereigns would never let you go there.'

'As they will never let Marie-Louise.'

'Has someone told you that, or is it intuition?'

'My dear Alexander, the Allied sovereigns, including yourself, will not allow Napoleon the tokens of his Imperial glory: an Empress, and a court, and a royal family.'

He smiled at her. 'I am selfish. I prefer you to be near Paris. It gives me someone I can talk to.'

'All we talk about is Napoleon.'

'He is worth talking about.'

She said, 'Do you know, I didn't really want to marry him? He was a pale-faced little soldier, and awkward, and shy, and his only subject of conversation was the proper handling of the artillery. Shall I theorize? If I had not married him—'

Suddenly she shivered, and coughed, and coughed again. The night was not warm, and her dress was impossibly diaphanous, and she had had a slight chill, the last few days.

The Tsar was instantly solicitous. 'My dear Josephine, I'm so sorry—it's my fault, I brought you out in the cold air with no cloak, no shawl—'

She said, 'It's the fault of my vanity. At my age I look best by moonlight.'

Two days later the cough was worse, and she had a high temperature, and her doctor ordered her to stay in bed. She said, 'I was silly not to wear a shawl. My vanity. People have always admired my shoulders. I think the Tsar admires them.' She looked at Eugène. 'I spoke to the Tsar about you, Eugène. It's still possible that he may be able to get Milan for you. He promised to do his best.' She looked at Hortense. 'Hortense, darling, what date is it? Is it the twenty-second?'

'Yes, Mamma.'

'I must get up. The King of Prussia is coming to dinner.'

'You must stay in bed, Mamma.'

'No. The King of Prussia can be very useful to us.'

Hortense said, 'Mamma, I will receive the King of Prussia for you.'

'No, I must talk to him. I must talk about you two. I must see if there's something more I can do for you. Oh, my darlings, I must, you don't remember what it's like to be poor. Hortense, will you tell my ladies-in-waiting I am going to get up now?'

'You are ill, Mamma.'

'No, it's only a chill, I shall put on a warm dress, I shall cover my shoulders. Hortense, please do what I tell you. I am an Empress, I still have my title. An Empress must be there to receive her guests.'

It was a fever. It grew worse. She was very hoarse.

'Eugène . . .'

'The Tsar has sent his chief physician to see you, Mamma.'

'How very very kind of the Tsar. The Tsar has behaved so well to us. Has the Tsar himself called?'

'He sends his excuses. He hopes to be able to call tomorrow.'

'He may have something to tell you about Milan.'

'You mustn't worry about me, Mamma.'

'Hortense. Is it the twenty-seventh?'

'Yes, Mamma.'

'Have I had a letter from Napoleon? He has been in Elba for three weeks now.'

'The post from Elba takes a long time, Mamma.'

'If I had been his wife still, I would have gone with him to Elba, and no one could have stopped me. She doesn't love him as I do.'

Hortense said, 'And he loves you best, Mamma.'

'We were married for . . .' She was thinking of the years together, and she thought of their first wedding, the civil wedding, and she thought of her age. She had been thirty-two then, and given her age as twenty-eight.

Now, she was almost fifty-one.

She said, 'Eugène . . .'

'Yes, Mamma?'

'If I die now, you must put on my tombstone . . . that I am forty-five . . .'

The next day, in a delirium, after the last sacraments, she murmured, 'Bonaparte . . .'

Hortense and Eugène strained their ears to hear.

She murmured, 'Bonaparte . . . Elba . . . Elba . . .'

Then no more words. Then she opened her eyes, and seemed to see her children, and stretched out her arms to them and said something to them, but nothing that was intelligible. Then she fell back dead.

30. THE END OF LOVE

Napoleon returned from Elba, and placed himself at the head of the French again, and was beaten at Waterloo.

He came back to Paris. Fouché, who had put himself in charge of the government, would not have him in Paris. He moved on to Malmaison, to be the guest of Hortense.

The armies of Wellington and Blücher followed southwards in his wake.

He asked Hortense, 'Well? What do people say of me now?'

'That you have met with misfortune, Sire.'

He said, 'I should have died at Waterloo.'

A moment later he said, 'No. I should have won. You have to win: I judge men only by the results of their actions. I judge myself by the same rule.'

He had been too sure of winning, at Waterloo. Once he felt a hundred thousand Frenchman under his hand again, he did not doubt that he could reconquer the world.

If he had had Murat at the head of the cavalry, it might have gone the other way. There was a moment when the cavalry should have charged at Blücher's flank: the same kind of charge that Murat had led a hundred times for Napoleon. Without Murat, the cavalry did not do it.

Murat: what a fool he continued to be! It was not enough to turn his coat, he had turned it a second time. When he heard that Napoleon had landed in France again, he led his raggle-taggle Neapolitans northwards through Italy, in a futile attempt to overthrow the whole might of Austria. Napoleon hadn't wanted Murat's army: whichever side they were on they ran away just the same. Napoleon had wanted one man, Murat, with him, under his orders.

Well, Murat would get the wages of his folly. The Austrians would catch him and would shoot him.

Napoleon thought, 'If I had had my old army, and my old generals. If I had had Berthier as my Chief of Staff.'

Berthier, hearing of Napoleon's return from Elba, had supposed himself too old and ill to join him; had imagined that, in any case, Napoleon would not want a man who had sworn a new allegiance to Louis the Eighteenth; and, in an agony of remorse and shame, had thrown himself from a high window and smashed himself to pieces in the street.

Napoleon said out loud, 'I must not make excuses. Success justifies everything. Nothing can justify defeat.'

Hortense said, 'You did a great and noble thing, coming back to lead the French in one last great battle.'

'Did I? I came back because I was not born to die of boredom on a tiny island.'

'You made France heroic again. It was sublime.'

'Yes, perhaps,' he said. 'From the sublime to the ridiculous there is only one step.'

They walked in the rose garden that Josephine had made.

He said, 'It seems strange to be here without her, among her roses.'

'She loved this garden so much.'

'It suited her. She was the most enchanting woman I have ever known. She was the most woman of all women.'

'Yes . . .'

Napoleon swept his eye around. 'Do you know the most foolish of all foolish ways of spending money? On houses and gardens. She spent millions here, and it is worth no more than when I first bought it for her.'

'It became her house and her garden, and it was all she had, at last.'

'Oh yes. I had never had any quarrel with her, except her debts. And I scolded her enough about those.'

462

'She was so generous.'

Napoleon smiled wryly. 'In the sense that she would have invited the whole world to lunch.'

'She gave money to so many people who needed help.'

'Yes. Putting her hand into my purse.' He touched Hortense's arm gently. 'It didn't matter. I loved her. I wish she were here now. Though she would be unhappy to see me at this moment.'

King Joseph Bonaparte, not at all like a king, came quicky from the house.

'Napoleon. We must get away from here immediately.'

'Must?' Napoleon did not care for the word.

'The Prussian advance guard has reached Saint-Germain.'

'Who told you that?'

'There was a report. Someone brought the news.'

'Do not believe it.'

'Why not?'

Napoleon said, with a fair amount of contempt in his voice, 'Because it's not true.'

'It could be true. Why shouldn't it be true?'

'It could be true but it isn't.'

Joseph was foolish enough to say, 'How do you know?'

'Joseph, I have taken my Master's degree in war. I know where the Prussian Army was four days ago. I know how fast an army moves. It may be that a pair of Prussian scouts have been seen near Saint-Germain. If so, they are a great way ahead of the main body. I have a battalion here that can very easily deal with them. Do you understand that I understand these things?'

Joseph wore the injured air of a man who was only trying to help. 'Blücher has sworn he will shoot you as soon as he catches you.'

"Whatever Blücher has sworn, I am perfectly safe here for twenty-four hours. Kindly tell Bertrand that I am ready for lunch.'

Joseph thought of saying something, and then thought better of it. He went to the house with an expressive back that said he was not accustomed to carrying messages about meals.

Napoleon said to Hortense, 'I once asked Corvisart, "How can two brothers be so different?" He replied, "A question of organisms. You are organized like that." . . . If I fell head-first from the top of Milan Cathedral, I would fall calmly, looking around to admire the view.'

Napoleon had sent for Corvisart. When the good doctor arrived, he was not greeted warmly.

'Corvisart. Why did you let Josephine die?'

Corvisart was too experienced to be taken aback by this gambit. 'Sire, I infinitely regret that it was not feasible for me to take care of Her Majesty. May I remind you that at the time I was, on your instructions, in constant attendance on the Empress Marie-Louise.'

'Did Louise need a doctor?'

'She needed constantly to be told that she was unwell.'

Napoleon looked at him steadily. 'Corvisart, you are a dog.'

'Sire, it is not for me to contradict an Emperor—or an Empress.'

'I chose you as my doctor because, of all that gang of quacks and ignoramuses, you were the only sensible man, the only realist. But you encouraged Louise in her delusions of ill-health, as a result of which she did not come to join me in Elba.'

Corvisart said, 'Sire, the mind has more effect on the body than human beings yet realize. You have reversed cause and effect. It was the thought of going to Elba that made her unwell.'

'She wished to be with me.'

'So she told me.'

'She is not a liar.'

Corvisart spread his hands. 'Indeed, Sire, the Empress Marie-Louise is all honesty and all innocence. But she has no understanding of her own mind and her own body. Certainly she wished to be with you: you were her husband. What she really wished for, without knowing it, was to have a man in bed with her, in her arms, at night, every night. It is her organism: she is organized like that.'

Napoleon, when he finally spoke, said, 'I gather that Metternich has arranged to provide her with a suitable man, from the ranks of the Austrian aristocracy.'

'I have heard that, Sire.'

'I should be obliged if you would not repeat it to anyone who has not heard it.'

Corvisart bowed obediently.

'Corvisart, I forgive you.'

'Thank you, Sire.'

'For everything except letting Josephine die.'

'Sire, I hurried here as soon as I was able. The Empress Josephine had had the best possible care. The Tsar's own physician, a wiser man than myself, was in attendance. But the case was hopeless. The lungs were suffused with blood. There are many things that medical science has not yet learned to cure.'

Napoleon looked at him with some respect for the doctor and much contempt for the man.

'I believe you. But I do not forgive you for letting Josephine die.'

Eléonore Dénuelle came to Malmaison, with little Léon, for Napoleon to see him. The boy bore a striking resemblance to the King of Rome. He was, undeniably, Napoleon's son.

Mother and son had been well provided for. Napoleon and Eléonore had never had anything to say to each other. They had nothing to say to each other now.

Marie Walewska came to Malmaison with her son. Hortense took charge of little Alexander. Napoleon walked in the garden with Marie.

'It is kind of you to come to say good-bye to me.'

'I am so glad to be in time. When are you leaving?'

'Tomorrow.'

'Where are you going?'

'America. At this moment, I think America. It may be that, tomorrow, I shall change my mind.'

She said, 'Wherever you go, may I go with you?'

He said quietly, 'No, Marie.'

'I love you.'

'Yes.'

'You need someone to be with you . . . if only your Polish wife.'

He said, 'Marie, I no longer need the love of a woman. I don't mean that I have ceased to be a man. But these last few days have changed me. I have become a solitary, a hermit. I no longer need the love of another human being.'

'At the least you will need someone to cook for you, to mend your clothes . . .'

He smiled. 'Oh, don't take me too literally. I shall be a hermit with servants.' He looked at her, his eyes full of laughter. 'Marie, tell me the truth.'

'Yes, of course.'

'I imagine that you might be able to sew a button. But have you ever learnt to cook?'

'I could learn.'

He kissed her fondly on the cheek.

'Marie, you are the only utterly faithful woman in the world.'

She said, very simply, 'Even if you do not want me or need me.'

'Will you obey me, Marie?'

'Yes, always.'

'You are young, you are beautiful, your old husband is dead at last. There is at least one man, and a good man, deeply in love with you.' She was about to speak, but he stopped her. 'Don't deny it. I know his name.' He took her face in his hands, so she could not avoid his eyes. 'Obey me. I command you. Marry again. Have more children. Be happy. I absolve you from your vow of faithfulness to me. And I shall think the worse of you if you reject your real future. Romantic longing is all very well in stories. I am a realist.'

His will was the stronger. She would have to obey.

The night before the day when he was to leave Malmaison for ever, he went to Josephine's bedroom and stood there for a long time, perfectly still, his chin sunk on his chest.

Hortense had kept the room as it had been when Josephine lived there, and died there. The whole room breathed her taste, her style, her charm, her incomparable gracefulness.

He felt her presence.

He had really loved her. In the first few years of their marriage he had loved her to the point of madness. No one else in his life, nothing else in his life, had made him suffer such agonies of torment and despair.

He had not respected her. She had always been selfish, and shallow, and a liar, and a cheat.

But he had loved her.

He had made her suffer the heart-wounds of jealousy as she had made him suffer them.

Her unfaithfulness had killed his heart. His neglect of her, and at last his divorce of her, had killed hers. But did she have a heart? Had wounded her, certainly. Had made her violently unhappy. Had made her love him, for fear of losing him, and love him more, when she had lost him.

If she could have given him a child he would never have divorced her.

Well, he had loved her, and she was dead, and he had done with love.

He said a silent good-bye to her, at that moment, there in her room. He was free to go.

The next morning, brisk and dynamic, he cried, 'Well? Do they want me or don't they?'

Caulaincourt, an envoy back from Paris for the last time, started to say, 'The Governing Commission—'

'You mean my old friend Fouché.'

467

'Yes, Sire.'

'Who has changed sides so often he looks like a weathercock.'

Caulaincourt did his best to make his statement. 'Fouché and his partners do not accept your offer to put yourself at the head of the army again—'

'I did not suppose they would.' He was quick, decisive, the old Napoleon, the not-old Napoleon. 'They are wrong. I could have kept Wellington and Blücher out of Paris, and given Fouché time to make better terms.' With a gesture he threw the thought away. 'However. I accept their non-acceptance. So?'

Caulaincourt looked at the carpet. 'I regret to say, Sire: nor are they willing to grant you passports and safe-conducts for a voyage to America.'

'So? Where do they want me to go?'

Caulaincourt had arrived at his difficult moment.

'Sire, the only clear statement I could get from Fouché was that if you did not leave Malmaison today, he would come and arrest you himself.'

Napoleon took it calmly. 'My old Minister of Police. Well, he has experience of arresting a great number of people.'

He marched to the other end of the room, at the fastest military step, and they wondered how he could still show such energy, and he cried in that vibrant voice of his, 'So much for the French! In fifty years they will erect a statue of me, whatever government is in power. In five hundred years they will dream of nothing but me, they will talk of nothing but my campaigns, and my victories, and my Europe. And every Frenchman will think himself brave, remembering me.'

He turned aside, and clapped Bertrand on the shoulder. 'Well? The carriages are ready?'

'Yes, Sire.'

'So. It's time to go.'

'To Rochefort, Sire?'

'Yes. Where two frigates are waiting for me. And we shall sail to America.'

468

Caulaincourt said, 'Sire, I must warn you—'

'Warn?' He did not care for being warned.

'I am told in Paris, Sire, that an English ship, the *Bellerophon,* is lying off Rochefort, in case you decide to embark from there.'

Napoleon was marvellously eupeptic and cheerful and dismissive of all fears. 'Thank you, Caulaincourt. My old problem. The English have their ships everywhere. Well, if we get to America, we shall make for New York, as Joseph has done. He has the notion of buying a farm, somewhere between Philadelphia and New York. I might do the same. Why not? . . . If that's not possible, if the English stop me—then, if I must, I'll go to England instead, and be a country squire and breed cattle and hunt foxes.'

Caulaincourt said, 'Sire, when you went to Elba, the English had proposed that you would be safer on an island further away. An island in the South Atlantic.'

But Napoleon was brimming over with confidence, under his lucky star again. He would not listen to warnings. 'The English have a tradition of hospitality for political refugees. The Bourbons spent their years of exile in England, while I was Consul and Emperor. Am not I entitled to take my turn? I shall go to England, and give myself up to the nearest magistrate, and put myself under the protection of English law. No one will dare to dispute my right to liberty—and a vote, if I have enough land or money. I shall become a Member of Parliament. I shall become Prime Minister.'

He turned to General Bertrand. 'It's time?'

'Yes, Sire.'

'Are you coming with me, Bertrand? To wherever it is?'

'To wherever, Sire.'

The moment before he left, Hortense came to him and offered a belt made of ribbon.

'A leaving present?'

'Yes.'

'Yes. Thank you. What is it?'

She said, 'You gave me so much. I am rich now, whatever happens. Some diamonds, from a necklace, I've sewn them into a belt. In case you need them.'

He took the belt, and held it in his hands, and looked at her.

'I shall send you a note for the value of the diamonds, payable in three months' time.'

'No.'

'Unlike your mother, I do not incur debts.'

He took a ring from his finger and gave it to her.

'Of no great intrinsic value, but a keepsake. The ring your mother gave me on our wedding day. I have worn it ever since. Take it. Keep it. Good-bye. I must leave, or the Prussians will shoot me.'

He kissed her on the forehead. She cried, 'But where will you be?'

He said with the utmost cheerfulness, 'I believe in my star. I shall go and discover what is my destiny.'

His first sweetheart, Désirée, was in Paris, but had not come to see him. She had married General Bernadotte seventeen years before, while General Bonaparte was in Egypt. Bernadotte had followed his own star, and accepted the succession to the throne of Sweden, and turned against Napoleon. Désirée went to Sweden one winter, and hated it, and fled back to France as soon as she could. She had come to care for her husband a good deal less than she cared for her sister Julie and for the pleasures of Paris and for the great couturiers of the rue de Richelieu.

Now, while Joseph Bonaparte, ex-King of Spain, fled to the coast and boarded a brig for America, Désirée took his ex-Queen, her sister Julie, and Julie's daughters into her Paris house. She could protect them from the Bourbons and the Allies and the Bonaparte-haters: even though she herself hated Sweden, it was an Allied power, and she was its Princess Royal, and was soon to become its Queen.

Now, the English general Wellington and the Austrian politician Metternich ruled over Europe. Wellington, the victor of Waterloo, had a taste for Napoleonic souvenirs, and had taken that great singer La Grassini as his mistress. She was forty-two, but still beautiful, for a middle-aged woman, and she still went to bed with only the most important men in Europe.

Napoleon's desiny was the port of Rochefort; the English ship, the *Bellerophon;* and the island of St Helena.

When the news reached Paris that the English were sending the Corsican, the ex-Emperor, to St Helena, Mademoiselle George wrote volunteering to go with him. He did not accept the offer. Georgina had not supposed that he would. She had simply wanted him to know that her heart was always faithful to him, even if her body was not. Like La Grassini, she had granted her favours to the Duke of Wellington, during the time that Napoleon was on Elba. She found Wellington stronger than Napoleon, but not so lovable. She was starting to grow conspicuously fat.

The one woman Napoleon wanted by his side on St Helena was the ex-Empress, the Duchess of Parma, Marie-Louise. But Louise, who needed a man in her bed, had already taken into it that dashing Austrian soldier and seducer Count Adam von Neipperg. She was madly in love with him. It would have been difficult and embarrassing for her to travel to St Helena: she was almost unceasingly pregnant.

In any case, she could have done nothing there but nurse a dying invalid; and he could have done little or nothing for her. He was burnt out. He made a half-hearted and unsuccessful pass at Madame Bertrand, the best-looking of the wives in his entourage. There was a moment, though not much of a moment, with Madame Montholon, who was more eager to please him. But, as Napoleon said to General Montholon, 'My dear fellow, when one is fifty and in my state of health, it is hardly worth the trouble of bothering about women any longer.'

When he finally died, on that infinitely boring island in the South Atlantic, the devoted General Bertrand, hovering over his lips to catch his last intelligible words, caught: 'France, army, head of the army.'

General Montholon, hovering over the Emperor from the other side, heard: 'France, army, head of the army,' and then, 'Josephine.'

Both men spoke the truth. Whether or not 'Josephine' was his last word before dying, undeniably she was his first great love, his greatest love, and in his memory, in the thought of her, his last love, his last attachment.